MW00829895

OF HEARTBREAK AND HARMONY

THE HOMETOWN HEARTLESS

BRIT BENSON

LOVE THAT GROWS

Copyright© 2024 by Brit Benson

All rights reserved.

No part of this book may be reproduced, distributed, or transmitted in any form or by any electronic or mechanical means, including information storage and retrieval systems, without written permission from the author, except for the use of brief quotations in a book review and certain other noncommercial use permitted by copyright law.

Any use of this publication to "train" generative artificial intelligence (AI) technologies to generate text is expressly prohibited. No generative AI was used in the writing of this work. The author expressly prohibits any entity from using this publication for purposes of training AI technologies to generate text, including without limitation technologies that are capable of generating works in the same style or genre as this publication.

This book is a work of fiction. Names, characters, places, and incidents are either the product of the author's imagination or are used fictitiously. Any resemblance to actual persons and things living or dead, locales, or events is entirely coincidental. Except for the original material written by the author, all mention of films, television shows and songs, song titles, and lyrics mentioned in the novel are the property of the songwriters and copyright holders.

Cover Design: Kate Decided to Design

Photographer: Katie Cadwallader at Cadwallader Photography

Cover Model: Daniel Hughes

Editing: Rebecca at Fairest Reviews Editing Services, Emily Lawrence at Lawrence Editing, Sarah Plotcher at All Encompassing Books

Original Music and Lyrics: Zachary Webber & Juno Cooper

❀ Created with Vellum

PLAYLIST

Where Do Broken Hearts Go - One Direction
Still - Niall Horan
Dancing in the Dark - LØLØ
Fools Gold - One Direction
High- Stephen Sanchez
Suburban Legends (Taylor's Version) - Taylor Swift
Slow It Down - Benson Boone
Put It on Me - Matt Maeson
Too Sweet - Hozier
Falling to Pieces - Two Feet
Imgonnagetyouback - Taylor Swift
Unlearn (with Gracie Abrams) - benny blanco
ceilings - Lizzy McAlpine

To listen to this playlist, visit my website at authorbritbenson.com

CONTENT WARNING

Please be aware, *Of Heartbreak and Harmony* contains some difficult topics that could be upsetting for some readers.

Topics that take place on page are: vulgar language, sexually explicit content, drug and alcohol use, traumatic car accident resulting in fatalities*, resulting injury from car accident, depression

Topics that are referenced but do not take place on page are: overdose, drug use, addiction relapse.

*If you require a content-specific chapter guide for these topics, you can find one on my website authorbritbenson.com.

A NOTE FROM THE AUTHOR

Of Heartbreak and Harmony can be read as a standalone.

However, full appreciation for the relationship dynamics and character backgrounds can only be achieved by reading *Between Never and Forever* first.

For reference, *Of Heartbreak and Harmony* takes place a few months after the epilogue of *Between Never and Forever*.

Of Heartbreak and Harmony **does** contain spoilers for the *Between Never and Forever*.

To my Emotional Support Pirates, Haley and Jessie, and to Becky.

Thank you for dragging me to the finish line.

PROLOGUE

Torren

"Where is she?"

Savannah glances up at me from her spot on the couch. She's got her legs thrown over Levi's lap with her lyric notebook on the coffee table, and her beat-up acoustic is resting on the cushion beside her. If it weren't for the fact that she's still in her on-stage outfit from the show, this would feel like any other night on the road.

"Where is who?"

I have to clench my fists to keep from shaking her. To make her answer me. To make her stop wasting time.

"Callie." I scan the room quickly. "She was just here. Where is she?"

Mabel is sitting on the floor next to Sav, staring at the ceiling with her headphones on, but when she sees me, her brow furrows and she slips them off. Mabes hasn't changed out of her outfit either. Jonah is probably still slumped over where I left him, bleeding all over his vintage Nirvana shirt from the jab I landed to his nose.

"She's not in the room?"

Sav's voice is laced with panic as she bolts up from the couch and crosses the floor of the hotel suite. My stomach twists with anxiety as I take out my phone and dial her number. I listen to it ring and ring before it goes to voice mail.

Sav swings the door wide to the connecting room and disappears inside. I know she won't find Callie in there. I already checked. Instead, I check the bathroom and the other two bedrooms while dialing Callie's number again.

"Fuck," Sav says, and I turn to find her staring into a small, sleek designer handbag. "My keys are gone. I think she took my keys." She drags her eyes to mine and chills race up my spine at the way her face goes ashen. "Why would she leave now? She was out there when—"

I push past Sav without an answer. I don't stick around to hear her say anything else. I know what happened out there. I don't want to recount it.

I storm back into my room and grab my own keys, grateful that I have my car here. Normally, I wouldn't, but nothing about this situation is normal.

Just before I reach the door, Red steps in front of me and puts his big hand on my shoulder. It doesn't matter that I'm almost thirty—Red makes me feel like a teenager trying to sneak out after curfew. He might be Sav's personal security, but he's become something like a surrogate father to me. To all of us, actually. Papa Red and the band of runaways. I'd laugh at the thought if I wasn't on the verge of succumbing to my panic.

"Let me go, Red."

He shakes his head. "Can't do that, kid."

"I have to get to Callie. She's alone. She's upset. I need to get to her."

His stern expression doesn't change, but I think I see a flicker of concern in his eyes.

"You don't know where she went."

He speaks slowly and with authority, studying my face as he does. He's going to shut me down again. He'll probably bind me to the chair with my own bootlaces in the name of safety. I've always appreciated that behavior when it was out of concern for Sav, but now, when I'm the focus, I hate it.

I narrow my eyes and open my mouth to argue, but Sav steps up behind me and cuts me off.

"She's in my Porsche," Sav says, her hand reaching past in my periphery, holding something toward Red. "The tracker says she's heading toward Santa Monica."

He takes Sav's phone and peels his eyes off me. My shoulders slump a little. I didn't even realize I'd squared off against him. I drop my attention to the phone screen. The security tracker Red put on all of Savannah's vehicles shows a little red dot heading west on the freeway.

"She's going home." My heart sinks, but I steel my resolve. "I'm going, Red. You'll have to beat me bloody to keep me here."

"Go with him if you're worried," Sav says, but Red shakes his head.

"I'm not leaving you."

"For Christ's sake, Red," Sav says, putting her hands on her hips. "This place is crawling with security. It's been swept twice already. I'm fine. *We're* fine. Go with Torren or you're fired."

A flicker of humor flashes in Red's eyes. He knows she's full of shit. She threatens to fire him at least once a week, and we all know she never would.

Finally, he nods, and I follow as he strides out the door.

In a matter of minutes that feel like hours, we're in the underground garage and he's tossing me a new set of keys. No explanation—Red's never been one to waste words—and I don't ask. Instead, I follow his lead and swing my leg over a black sport bike, taking a moment to shove the helmet on my head. Red starts his bike, so I start mine, and then I follow him out of the garage and toward the freeway.

Behind Red, I weave in and out of cars, moving onto the shoulder when traffic starts to thicken. It's late at night, way past rush hour, so it shouldn't be this congested right now. The coil of anxiety tightens in my stomach, and despite my rational mind screaming at me to stay calm, I can't. I have to get to her. I just have to make sure she's okay.

I speed up, blowing past Red and racing as fast as I can down the shoulder of the freeway. So fast that the cars on the road seem gridlocked and at a standstill. Faster than is safe, but all I can think about is getting to Callie. My heart speeds along with the bike. My need to get to her clouding my logic and taking over my instincts.

I can feel it, though.

In my stomach, in my chest, I know something is wrong.

The scene is revealed all at once, but my mind registers it in slow motion, one devastating detail at a time.

The cars are indeed at a standstill. No one on either side of the freeway is moving.

Flashing lights materialize into vehicles, and I slow the bike just enough so I can drop it to the pavement and take off at a run toward them.

A fire truck blares on its horn in the distance. A cop car parks on the shoulder thirty yards away. It's like scanning a junk yard. It's like a still from an apocalyptic movie, and I know. I *know* Callie is here somewhere.

The smell of burning rubber and gasoline stings my nose. My eyes start to water. More horns blare. Sirens wail. People cry out for help.

Among the wreckage, I hear shouts of first responders arriving, and I want to scream at them. Hurry. Find her. Run faster. How am I here first? Why aren't they helping? Why aren't they hurrying? A helicopter arrives overhead as my feet crunch over broken glass.

My eyes scan over the wreckage decorating every lane of the freeway. Skid marks and ashes. Car parts and broken glass. Papers blowing about, soaked with water and stuck to the pavement. A shoe. A child's car seat. I take note of four vehicles, all with varying degrees of damage, before I find the one I'm looking for.

And when I finally see it, all the air is sucked from my lungs.

1

CALLIE

It's close to two by the time I drag myself up the four flights of stairs to my apartment.

The elevator is finally working, but I no longer trust it. Not after last time. The last thing I want is to get stuck in that rickety metal box again. Especially not when I have to be up in five hours. Though, at this point, I'm so exhausted I'd probably just curl up on the dirty floor and fall fast asleep.

I unlock the deadbolt and slip in, kicking off my shoes at the door with a relieved sigh. My feet ache, I smell like bleach and Windex, and my hands are sporting a nice rash from my standard-issue rubber gloves, but I tell myself it's worth it as I drop my bag on the kitchen table next to our neatly stacked pile of bills.

At least the pile is getting smaller. I think.

In the fridge, I find a plate of food wrapped in plastic with a napkin note on top. In messy capital letters, my sister has scrawled EAT ME. I smile to myself. She loves me even when she acts like she doesn't. I pull the plate from the fridge along with the plastic containers containing the rest of the dinner leftovers and ignore the soft rumbling of my stomach as I scrape the contents of my plate back into the containers.

Broccoli with broccoli. Rice with rice. Chicken with chicken.

It's a much more balanced meal than we were eating a few months ago. It's actual *food* now that I've picked up another job, but there's still a paltry amount of it. Once I replace my portion, there's at least enough for both Mom and Glory to have lunch tomorrow. I'll grab a sandwich from the store after my morning shift.

I snag a pen off the counter and write *Yum!* on the napkin before sticking it to the fridge with a magnet, then I tiptoe into the bathroom to wash the stench of cleaning supplies off my body. By the time I throw myself onto the bed in the room I share with Glory, I'm so exhausted that I don't move an inch until my alarm goes off four hours later.

"Girl. You pick up another shift at the motel last night?"

I glance up at the other register where Quinton is scanning someone out and shrug. I opened today, and he got to come in at ten. Lucky dick.

"Yeah, I did."

He quirks a dark brow. "You look like death."

I narrow my eyes at him. I've known Quinton since high school, and five years later, he's still just as obnoxious as ever.

"Gee, thanks Quin. I love you too."

He winks and makes a kissy face at me. "At least I'm easy to look at."

I roll my eyes and flip him off before going back to my crossword puzzle. With any luck, we'll be slow today, and I'll be able to make it until the end of my shift without passing out.

I'm filling in a ten-letter word for "anything that unduly exhilarates or excites"—*intoxicant*—when the song on the radio switches to something familiar and wholly unwelcome.

"Nooo," I groan, tipping my head to the ceiling to glare at the speaker. "Turn it off, Dwayne!"

I shout the words, hoping my boss will hear me from his office. I know he does because instead of doing what I ask, he turns the song up louder.

The opening bass line creates a sinking feeling in my stomach and an ache in my chest. You'd think by now I'd have grown desensitized to The Hometown Heartless, but nope. They still make me sick.

I manage to avoid every fucking magazine cover, have even conditioned myself to ignore the giant poster Glory has pinned to our bedroom wall, but the music is another story. It hits harder, and it's nearly impossible to escape. Especially living so close to LA. Here, *everyone* has a strong opinion about The Hometown Heartless. You're either obsessed with them, or you loathe their very existence.

I'm of the latter camp.

Planted my flag here four years ago, and it's still standing tall, waving proudly in the wake of my simmering grudge.

I hate their sound. I hate their style. I hate the arrogant hold they have on the music industry, lording over everything like gods.

But what I hate most is their bassist, Torren Fucking King.

I cringe involuntarily when the first verse starts. His deep voice harmonizes with the lead singer, and before I can stop it, a carousel of pictures flashes through my mind. Full plush lips. Dark messy hair. Mysterious green eyes. Talented calloused fingers.

They just serve to stoke the embers of my irritation.

I step out from behind my register and march toward Dwayne's office. It's a small store—two registers and ten aisles of basic food and household items—so I make it to the cheap plastic door in a matter of seconds. I swing it wide and close the distance between myself and the stereo system.

Dwayne, because he's an asshole, laughs.

I swear, if I didn't get a 15 percent employee discount on everything in this place, I'd quit. This job is the only reason we have an almost-stocked pantry at home.

Jabbing my finger at the power button, the music cuts out immediately, leaving only Quinton's voice as he continues to sing the song.

"I haven't slept, Dwayne. I have a headache. I'm not in the mood for this uninspired, watered-down, poor excuse for rock and roll."

Dwayne grunts another laugh and shakes his head as I storm back out of his office, letting the door slam behind me.

"One of these days you're going to tell me the story behind your rage," Quinton says from beside me.

I don't acknowledge him. I'm not telling him shit. Instead, I grab my crossword and stare at it for the next hour. That's how long it takes to calm the vortex of memories swirling violently in my head.

2

CALLIE

THE BEST PART about public transportation is that it's cheap and relatively reliable.

The worst part is that it too often smells like sour milk, and I never know who is going to try to spark up a conversation with me. I don't know what it is, but strangers always want to talk to me. The women want to compliment my auburn hair. The men want to tell me to smile more. The elderly always feel the need to let me know I look tired or that I need more sun.

I suppose they mean well, and it's always easy enough to shrug them off with a thank you and a forced smile. But when I'm running on very little sleep and even less food, I'm not in the mood to fend off unsolicited social interactions.

My feet hurt. I'm tired. I want to be left alone.

My big headphones have been broken for almost a year, but I still put them on and shut my eyes. I might not be able to listen to music, but I can pretend, and it usually does a good job of keeping conversation at bay.

The bus takes thirty minutes to get from the store to the stop closest to my apartment. I nod a thank you to Esther as I step onto the curb.

"Have a good one, Calla Lily," she says in her rough voice, then she shuts the doors behind me and drives off.

Esther has been driving this bus route for as long as I can remember.

When I moved back home, she was the first familiar face I saw other than my family, and I've seen her almost every day since.

The muffled sound of music filters from the apartment when I reach it, telling me Glory has the day off from her new summer job. Our mother would never listen to music this loud on her own. Not anymore. I try the knob, but it's locked, so I take out my key and let myself in.

The living room and kitchen are empty, and I grab a glass of water from the fridge dispenser before heading to my bedroom. The bathroom door is shut, and the shower is running, so my mom is definitely awake. Hopefully, this means she's feeling well today.

The music is much louder as I stand outside my bedroom door. I don't know how we haven't gotten a call from the neighbors yet. They must be out for the day.

"Glory, I'm comin' in," I call out, announcing my arrival with a knock.

Except for the few years when I'd moved out, I've shared this room with Glory since she was a baby. Now that she's fifteen, though, she's asked that I respect her privacy and knock before entering. Because I'm a considerate big sister, I do, but she doesn't seem to think she should afford me the same courtesy. Not that it matters, I guess. The only thing I do in here is sleep.

When a minute passes with no answer—she probably can't hear me over the music—I repeat myself, louder this time, and push the door open.

"No! Wait!" Glory shouts, but it's too late.

I'm already stepping into the bedroom and watching her stuff something into our small closet. She slams the door shut and whirls around to face me, forcing a sweet smile onto her flushed face.

I arch a brow and look her over, then flick my eyes to the closet door.

"What are you hiding?"

"I said *wait*! You never listen. *Ugh*, I want my own room again!"

My sister stomps her foot and hits me with a glare, the sweet smile wiped away in half a blink. It's the look I'm used to getting from her these days. My fifteen-year-old sister thinks I moved back home just to ruin her life.

"Glory, what are you hiding in that closet?"

"Nothing."

I walk to her cheap Bluetooth speaker and turn it off, finally silencing her pop-punk racket, then cross the distance and stand in front of her with my hands on my hips.

"Is it Aleck? You know you're not allowed to have boys in here."

Glory rolls her eyes. "I'm not hiding Aleck in my closet."

She talks like the accusation is outlandish when I literally found him hiding under the bed two weeks ago.

"Open the door, Glory."

"No."

I raise my voice and direct it at the closet door. "Aleck, come out here right now or I'm calling your dad."

Glory snorts. "I told you it's not Aleck—"

A dog barks, cutting off her statement, and Glory's eyes go as wide as dinner plates.

"What was that?" I ask, even though I'm not an idiot.

"Nothing."

"Was that a dog?"

She shakes her head rapidly. "No. Nope."

I push past her and yank the door open myself, and sure as shit, there's a dog in my closet. A medium-sized black dog with long, shaggy fur hanging in his eyes. He's sitting and wagging his tail happily, looking as innocent as can be, but there's a chewed-up sneaker at his feet that gives him away. *My* sneaker.

"What the fuck, Glory Bell. Why the hell is there a dog in our closet?"

I flick my eyes from Glory to the dog and back. She folds her arms over her chest.

"He's my dog. I'm keeping him."

"You can't have a dog."

"Yes, I can!"

"No, you can't! I can barely afford to feed the three of us. I can't take care of a dog, too."

"You won't have to. I have a job now. I can take care of him."

"And what about when you go back to school in the fall, huh? What about then?"

"My boss already told me I can work nights, weekends, and breaks once school is back."

I shake my head, frustration tightening all my tired muscles until my fingers start to tremble, and I have to ball them into fists.

"No. Absolutely not. You're not working during school, Glor. We've been over this. You focus on your grades and basketball. You're not working. I'm working."

"I'm going to be sixteen soon, and you can't tell me what to do."

"Yes, I can, Glory. You're not wor—"

"You're not my mom!"

She shouts the words in my face, and I have to bite my tongue to keep from shouting back. It's not the first time she's said them to me. In fact, on the list of cruel shit she's said to me, this doesn't even register in the top ten.

It still sucks, though.

Not so much the statement—it's true, I'm not her mom—but the vitriol she hurls behind it. Being on the receiving end of her hatred hurts. I've thrown my entire life away to come back here and take care of her, and she still acts as if she hates me ninety percent of the time. I guess I'd rather it be directed at me than Mom, though.

I straighten my spine and take a few calming breaths. Glory's nostrils flare and she pants with rage. I look behind her at the dog. He hasn't barked again, but his head is tilted to the side and he's staring at me with eyes so green they could be emeralds.

He's judging me.

He's definitely *not* on my side.

I turn back to my pissed-off sister.

"Look, I'm sorry, Glor, but you just can't have a—"

"Mom already said I could keep him."

My jaw drops and she smirks at me. I had to have heard her wrong. She's got to be lying.

"Excuse me?"

Glory shrugs, then turns and kneels next to the dog, wrapping her arms around his neck. He licks her face, and she giggles.

"He's already been here for a week, and you didn't even notice."

I blink and run through the last week in my head. I worked doubles. I was home long enough to shower and sleep. And she's right. I can't think of a single thing that suggests there was a dog here.

"Why didn't you just lead with that?" I ask after a minute, and Glory shrugs again.

"Didn't think of it."

Little brat. She just wanted to argue with me. All she does these days is pick fights. I feel like I need to put on metaphorical boxing gloves the moment I wake up.

"Did I hear yelling?"

I glance over my shoulder and find my mom leaning on the doorframe. Her hair is wet from her shower, and she's wearing a big, fluffy robe despite the heat.

"Why didn't you tell me you told Glory she could have a dog?" I ask, and my mom smiles slightly, the left side of her mouth tilting up higher than the right.

"I haven't seen you."

It takes longer for my mom to say the sentence than it would most other people. "Healthy" people. Her speech isn't as slurred as it was, but she still speaks with long pauses. Her words come out clipped, yet soft around the edges, like her mouth is still relearning how to form them.

"Who is going to watch the dog while Glory is at school and work?"

"I will," Mom says with a small nod. I purse my lips, swallowing back the need to argue, and my mom laughs. "I can do it. I'm moving much better now."

I glance back at the dog.

"And what about the lease? We're not supposed to have pets."

"Rosa said it's fine," Glory chimes in, and my eyes widen.

"You got Rosa on board, too?"

Glory grins and bats her eyelashes. "Rosa loves me. Unlike you."

I glower at her. Rosa is our landlord. She's also our father's cousin and the reason our rent hasn't gone up in the last ten years. I'm not surprised Rosa caved. She does love Glory, and she loves my mom. Jury is still out on how she feels about me. While she was the one who called me to let me know my mom was in the hospital, I know she hasn't forgiven me for dropping out of high school my senior year and skipping town.

Rosa thinks I'm just like my dad, and it makes me want to throw up because I think she might be right.

I fold my arms over my chest and glance at the dog again.

"He ate my sneaker."

"Your sneaker is ugly. He did you a favor."

My jaw drops again, and Glory snorts out a laugh.

"I'm kidding! Sort of. I'm going to take him out to go potty. C'mon, King."

"King?" I ask, and she grins at me.

"His name. Torren King."

"You can't name your dog Torren King."

She rolls her eyes. "Too late. It's already on his collar. Besides, doesn't he look like him?"

I stare at the dog, and fuck me, he actually does kind of look like him. Shaggy black curls obstructing emerald eyes. The more I stare, the more I can see it.

Fuck. Me.

Glory is completely oblivious to my turmoil, as usual, but this time I'm grateful for it. She runs out of the bedroom without another word, and the adoring dog follows at her heels. A few seconds later, the front door opens and shuts. I look at my mom.

"A dog is a bad idea."

Mom shrugs. "She needs this."

I see the pleading in her eyes. The sorrow. The *guilt*, even though the last thing she should feel is guilty. And despite the fact that I still think letting Glory have a damn dog is a terrible idea, I concede. Because Mom is right. Glory *does* need this. A little spark of joy, of hope, when we've spent a year fumbling about in near darkness.

We *all* deserve that, but I think mine will be on hold for a while longer.

3

CALLIE

My sister and her dumb dog are waiting outside the store when I get off work.

I wish I could say I was happy to see them, but I'm not. I'm tired, and that dog ate the handle of my only hairbrush, so I'm pissed at him.

"What do you want, Glory Bell?"

"Gee, happy to see you too, Sis."

I arch a brow. I know she wants something. When I fold my arms and stare her down, she sighs and rolls her eyes.

"Ugh, fine. Mom said you'd take us to the pier."

I raise both brows and tilt my head, and she sighs louder.

"*Ugh*, you're the worst. Mom said to ask you if you'd take us to the pier, and, Callie, Mom said I can't go unless you agree to go so please take us to the pier."

I release a sigh of my own. There it is.

"I'm tired, Glor. This is like my fifth day of doubles, and I haven't had a break. I don't want to go to the pier with you and your dumb dog."

"Don't call Torren King dumb. He's not. It's your fault for leaving your hairbrush where he could reach it."

"It was on my dresser, and please don't start calling your dog by a full name. That's psychotic."

She shrugs. "Whatever. He answers better to Torren King, so I'm calling him Torren King."

"Glory..."

"Callie, *please*. Aleck broke up with me, and now he's at the pier with Lulu Stone-Meyers, and I hate that girl. Remember her? She's the one who told everyone when I got my period and stuck pads to my locker. She's horrible, and he's doing this to make me jealous, so I want to show up and flirt with one of his guy friends. Please, Callie. Please. I'll never be able to show my face at school if I don't do this. I need to assert dominance. I need to remind him he's a beta."

I choke out a laugh and open my mouth to tell her what a dumb plan that is, but then my phone buzzes in my back pocket, and my shoulders fall. I already know what it will say before I look at it, and from the way Glory's smile perks up, so does she.

MOM

Please take her to the pier love mom

I put my phone away and pinch the bridge of my nose. "I don't have a change of clothes."

I don't want to go to the pier in khaki shorts and my red, store button-down. I look ridiculous. It's got CLERK stitched into the front pocket, for Christ's sake. Glory snorts.

"Literally no one will be looking at you, Calla Lily."

"Gee, thanks."

She giggles and starts to walk toward the pier. Reluctantly, I follow.

The whole walk, she chatters about Aleck and this Lulu chick. The more she talks, the more I get on board with this plan of hers. Because fuck Aleck, and I'm not just saying that because he called me a bitch when I made him get out from under Glory's bed and go home. He really is a little asshole. By the time we get to the pier, I'm scanning bodies for him like a hitman looking for the kill shot. I can't wait to watch Glory Bell humiliate him.

"There they are," Glor says, pointing to a bench next to an ice cream cart.

Sure enough, there he is, sucking face with Lulu, a group of his friends standing about in a cluster around them. I glance at Glory, worried I'll see hurt in her eyes, but all I see is rage.

"Pretty sure he was talking to her before he dumped me," she whispers, and then my rage matches hers. "Will you take Torren King? I'm going in. Oh, can I borrow five dollars?"

I sigh, but I don't argue. I give her five dollars and exchange it for the mutt's leash. I give him a side-eye as Glory walks away.

"You better behave, dog." He blinks up at me innocently. "Don't pretend you're an angel. You ate my hairbrush *and* my sneaker."

When he looks away, I scoff. Fake contrition from a dog.

Laughter draws my gaze back up, and I find my sister licking an ice cream cone in the middle of the cluster of Aleck's friends. She's peering up at one of them, batting her eyelashes and giggling, and the boy is entranced. I smirk when I realize just who she's flirting with. Aleck's cousin and best friend, Parker.

Damn, Glory Bell is vicious. I'm proud. She's way more daring than I am. One flick of my gaze toward Aleck and I can tell her plan is working. He is *fuming*. I have to bite my lip to keep from laughing outright.

I'm so focused on the masterfully executed revenge plan in front of me that I'm momentarily shocked when the dog barks and takes off running, ripping the leash from my hands.

"King!" Glory yells and takes off running after him, so I follow. "King! Torren King, get back here!"

I'm wearing sneakers, not ridiculous platform flip-flops like Glory has on, so it doesn't take long for me to catch up to her.

"I'll get him," I pant out. "Stay here before you break your ankle."

Then I hustle after the damn dog. I weave in and out of bodies, once almost taking out a clown juggling bowling pins, but I don't take my eyes off the dog. My only saving grace is that the crowd is slowing him down, too.

"King," I shout after him breathlessly. "Someone stop that dog! King, come back!"

Goddamn this stupid fucking dog. I haven't run in years. I haven't run this far this fast since gym class in high school. I am very, *very* out of shape. I feel like I might die. Death by cardio will be in my obituary.

"Torren King," I screech, my words coming out in spurts. "Goddamn it, come back here!"

His fluffy black butt rounds a corner, so I barrel forward after him.

"Torren Kin—"

My words cut off when I crash into something hard, like a thin mattress on a brick wall, and my breath is sucked from my chest on impact. My vision blacks out, and I fall backward, barely recognizing the sound of clattering glass and splashing before I'm landing roughly against something warm and firm. My hands clutch fabric and muscle, and I gasp for air, getting a lungful of tobacco and leather.

It doesn't register right away.

Not until the hint of ginger follows, and then my eyes are springing open, and I find my shocked reflection mirrored back at me in a pair of aviator sunglasses shaded under a black baseball cap. In the reflection, I watch as tattooed fingers brush my hair off my face and tuck strands behind my ears. The silver rings glint in the sunlight.

My breath is gone again.

"You alright?"

I blink. My chest burns, needing more oxygen, but I can't...I can't...

"Breathe," he says, and I obey immediately.

I gasp, pulling in more of his familiar scent, hating it but needing it to survive. Sweat drips from my hairline and down my temples. It stings my eyes. I'm hot, but cold, and sticky with sweat.

"That's it. There you go. Just breathe. You're okay."

I close my eyes again and gulp back more air, wincing around the sound of my frantic heart pounding inside my head. The whole time, I will myself to disappear.

This is a dream. I wiped out and was knocked unconscious, and this is a dream. This is not real. This is absolutely, completely, a dream.

"You're okay. Just relax. Just breathe."

Damn it.

That voice is very, very real.

When the sounds of chatter get louder, then laughter, then someone says, *you need to step back*, I force myself to open my eyes. Confirmation that my most mortifying nightmare has come to reality.

"Shit." It slips from my mouth in a whisper, but he smiles, letting me know he heard it.

"Can you stand?"

I try, but nausea hits me hard, and my legs give out. God, I'm so freaking tired. I think my shock has used up the last of my energy stores. My body will shut down now. Not death by cardio. Death by Torren King. How poetic.

I close my eyes once more.

"It's cool. We can stay here for a minute." His voice switches from low and close, to louder and more distant. Like he's looking away from me, talking to someone else. "Hey, can you get some water and ibuprofen? Maybe some ice? I don't think she hit her head, but she's pretty rattled."

I groan and slowly bring my hand to my temple. "I feel like I was hit by a bus."

"Not quite, but close. Damon's not far off."

I furrow my brow and pop one eye open, allowing myself to look at his ear so I don't have to see how pathetic I look in his sunglasses.

"Damon?"

"Yeah... He, um, well, he kind of stepped in your path...on purpose."

I pop open my other eye. "What? Why?"

His lips curl into a smirk. "I mean, you were screaming my name and chasing after me. He's my security. It was either lay you out or taze you."

I groan again and push myself up slowly to a sitting position, so I'm no longer lying sprawled out in Torren King's—the rock star, not the dog—lap. What the actual fuck is my life.

"I wasn't screaming your name," I explain. "I was screaming the dog's name." I drop my head into my hands. "I feel like I might throw up."

A hand rests on my back and rubs up and down.

"Here. Drink this." A cool glass of water is offered to me, and I take it and gulp it down. "The dog?"

I nod. "Yeah. My sister's dog. He's black and shaggy and has green eyes. She named him Torren King. I told her not to—it's a horrible name for a dog—but he answers to it now."

"Huh. That's a first."

I snort a laugh and don't even care how unattractive it sounds. I attempt to stand, but I'm wobbly.

"You should wait another few minutes," he says, but I jerk my head no.

"I gotta get the dog."

"We got him. Just relax for a bit more."

I sit back down. I glance around and find Torren King the dog lounging on the ground next to some giant man in black pants and a black T-shirt. I scowl at the dog. He's definitely on my shit list now. Then I look beyond the dog, past the man, and find a crowd—a large crowd—staring at me. Phones are out, recording and taking pictures. People are whispering and giggling.

Then I notice everything else.

There's someone sweeping up what looks like broken glass. There are french fries all over the ground. What I thought was sweat on my skin and shirt is actually some sort of soft drink.

"What happened?" I gasp out, and Torren chuckles.

"Well, you bounced right off Damon, then took out a server's tray before hurtling to the ground. I caught you, but you really decided to do the most damage on your way down."

A quick glance behind me reveals a café and some dining tables filled with more people.

They are staring, too.

I start to stand again, but Torren places his hands on my shoulders, stopping me.

"Just hang out, yeah? We've got a medic coming."

"No. Thanks, but I'm fine. I have to get back to my sister."

When I move to stand this time, he doesn't try to stop me, but he does stand with me. It's not until he's towering over me that I remember just how overwhelming his presence is. He's so tall. He's so imposing. His head is tilted toward me like he's studying me, and I can't handle it. It makes me even more eager to leave.

"You look..."

He trails off, his brow knitting, and I narrow my eyes. I look sweaty? I look angry? I look like I might have a concussion? Or worse...I look *familiar*? When he doesn't finish his thought and the silence starts to feel awkward, I shake my head.

"Look, I really have to go."

He takes a step back, shoving his hands in his pockets. "Right. Of course. I'm sorry my security mistook you for a crazed fan."

I wince at his comment, but there's no recognition in it. I take a deep breath and let myself look at him head-on, grateful for once that he's wearing the sunglasses, so his green eyes don't steal my nerve.

I'm not sure at first if I want him to remember me, but when there's not a single sign on his face that he knows who I am, my stupid heart sinks and my anger flares.

He doesn't.

He has absolutely no idea who I am.

And damn it if it doesn't hurt even four years later.

4

CALLIE

PAST, ArtFusion Day One

Becket slides open the back door of the van, and I take deep gulps of the dry, hot air into my lungs.

It's fucking hot outside, but it's hotter in the van. Our AC cut out three states ago.

"Everyone out," Becket says. "We got one hour to make camp before it gets really nasty."

It's already stifling. I can't even imagine what noon will bring. I shield my eyes from the harsh sun and step out of the van, peering at the people around us. Tents are being erected everywhere, and I've already spotted license plates from thirty different states just from vehicle check-in to our assigned campsite. The nervous energy I've been harboring for a month starts to bubble up inside me, prickling my skin and forcing a smile to my lips.

"Fucking cool." Rocky's deep voice interrupts my visual exploration of our surroundings, and he throws his lanky, tattooed arm over my shoulders. "Does this mean we've made it?"

I grin up at him. "I think it means we're one step closer."

He laughs and gives me a squeeze before loping off to help Pike and Becket with the tents. I turn and look back into the van where Ezra is still sleeping. I punch his leg, jolting him awake, and laugh at his shocked expression.

"C'mon. We're here. Can't sleep the day away."

He groans and stretches, but I skip off before he can hurl groggy verbal abuse at me. Ezra is an asshole when he wakes up. He'd probably cuss out Jesus Christ himself if the poor guy disturbed one of his naps. Messiah or not, no one is safe from the wrath of a sleepy Ezra.

I help Pike, Becket, and Rocky set up the tents. Ezra, conveniently, doesn't show up until we're almost finished.

"I'm bunking with Rock?" Ezra grins at Rocky. "We get to be snuggle buddies."

Rocky rolls his eyes. "I swear to god, if you snore like you did in the van on the way here, I *will* smother you with your pillow."

"Then who will you get to play drums?"

"Drummers are everywhere, man. We could get a fucking chimp to play drums, and he'd probably be better than your sorry ass."

Ezra fakes a punch but gets pissed when Rocky doesn't flinch, so then he launches himself at him. Rocky barks out a loud laugh and takes off running with Ezra chasing him, and I watch until they disappear behind rows of tents and cars.

Pike shakes his head. "Those two are idiots."

"Yep," I say in agreement, popping the P.

Becket chuckles and grabs my belt loop, tugging me toward him. My stomach flips as he lowers his mouth to mine. He tastes like coffee and watermelon bubble gum, and I sink into him, humming as he kisses me.

"I told you I'd get you here." He slips his hands into the band of my shorts and holds me against him. "Didn't I promise you?"

I smile and nod. "You did."

I rise on my tiptoes and kiss him again, this time reveling in the way his hands move to my backside and squeeze.

This thing with Becket is only a couple of weeks old, but it makes my toes curl and my chest ache in the most exciting way. I like him, and I know he likes me. He's been trying to stoke the spark between us for a few months now, but I've been hesitant. I don't want it to go sideways and blow up in my face. The last thing I want is to get us into a Sav Loveless/Torren King kind of situation.

The lead singer and bassist of The Hometown Heartless are infamous for their toxic off-again, on-again love affair. It hasn't stopped the band from rocketing to the top of the music charts, but I don't want that kind of press—not that we're popular enough to warrant any press at all. But still, it looks miserable, and that's not just my jealousy speaking.

"Jesus, get a room."

At Rocky's exaggerated groan, Becket and I break apart, and I spin around to face my bandmates.

"Or get a *tent*," Ezra adds with a wink.

My cheeks pinken, and I drop my eyes to the ground.

Becket and I are sharing one tent, while Pike, Rocky, and Ezra are in the other. It's not out of the ordinary. We've slept in closer quarters before—motel rooms, living rooms, the van—but this feels different.

I think he's expecting something to happen. Something *more* than a hot make-out session and groping. Truth be told, I'm expecting it, too. If I weren't so damn shy about this shit, I'd probably haul him into the tent now and go at it, but I can't. I'll wait until tonight when the festival is in full swing, and I've acquired some liquid courage.

Becket laughs, and I feel it vibrate in his chest. He tips my chin up so I'm looking back into his eyes.

"Want to go explore?"

I nod. "Yes."

He laces his fingers through mine and tugs me toward the festival grounds.

The opportunity for people-watching is unmatched. The festival is estimated to have sold out at 125,000 tickets. One hundred and twenty-five *thousand* attendees. That's not even including security, volunteers, and festival staff. That's more than the whole population of Santa Monica, where I grew up. The numbers will fluctuate from day to day, but most people are here for the long haul. Five days and five nights of music, art, and culture. Probably a lot of drugs, too. The schedule boasts things like body painting, goat yoga, meditation, silent dance parties, fire spinning, candle making, yodeling, and my favorite part, more than 200 bands performing on six separate stages.

I've wanted to come to ArtFusion since its conception four years ago, and not only am I finally here, but my band is showcasing.

We're on the fucking poster.

Our text is the tiniest and we're at the bottom of the list, but I don't care. I'd take playing on the smallest stage in the afternoon of the fifth day over not being here at all. I still can't believe it's real. I keep wanting to pinch myself, but I don't want to be weird.

I'll do it tonight when no one can see me.

"Oh shit."

Ezra's voice has me turning in his direction, and I find him staring at a large line-up poster taped to the side of an information tent.

"What?"

He turns to me with a grin. "Guess who's headlining the main stage on night five?"

I raise my eyebrows. "The Pantomimes."

We've known this. It's been announced for months.

Ezra shakes his head. "Nope. Try again."

I sigh and step up next to him so I can read the poster for myself. The moment my eyes land on the main stage line-up, my jaw drops and nerves stir in my stomach.

"No way."

I breathe the words more than speak them. My voice is gone. The Hometown Heartless—or Heartless, as their fans call them—are one of my musical idols. Their sound is iconic, and they started out just like us: driving up and down the coast playing dive bars and house parties until a label rep discovered them. They're a pipe dream brought to life. Proof you can make it without connections and boatloads of money backing you.

"Do you think we'll get to meet them?" I'd die. I'd pee my pants first, and then I would die. But god, I'd die with a smile.

"Do you think I could bag Sav Loveless?" Ezra says, and I elbow him in the stomach with a laugh.

"She doesn't go for drummers," Rocky taunts, just dodging Ezra's foot as he swings a leg out at him.

"I wouldn't even attempt it," Becket adds. "You'll end up with the shit beat out of you like that roadie she screwed in Las Vegas a few months back."

"You don't actually believe that." I side-eye Becket and he shrugs.

"Dude did an interview for *The Star* and everything. Said Torren King caught them banging in Sav's dressing room and snapped. Beat the fuck out of him until security had to pull him off."

"And if that's true, why isn't there a lawsuit? Why wasn't Torren King arrested?"

"Because he's the bassist for the most famous band in the fucking world?" Ezra chimes in. "They probably paid that roadie off with album royalties and had it all swept under the rug."

I shake my head and push past them, throwing words over my shoulder as they follow.

"*The Star* is a trashy gossip magazine, and you're all idiots for believing anything you read in it."

I tune out their arguing as I weave in and out of the crowd. The diversity is astounding. People of all shapes and sizes and backgrounds. Some people in shorts and T-shirts and others in these elaborate costumes. And there are famous people here. I just walked past an actress who won an Oscar for a blockbuster movie last summer, and she was dressed like a monarch butterfly.

This is literally the most exciting experience of my life, and I once played a piano solo for a packed house at Barnum Hall when I was nine.

"The main is right over there," Pike says, pushing in front of me to take over the lead. I follow him, and soon we're standing in front of a giant stage already equipped with large speakers and massive lights. There are already people camping on the lawn for tonight's show.

The headliner is a really popular pop-punk band who blew up about a year ago. They went viral with the first video they ever posted on social media, and they got a record deal two weeks later. The real kicker is they'd only formed the band a month earlier. I can't help but be jealous of bands like this one. We've been trudging around the country playing dive bars and small venues for two years and our socials have never gotten more than a few hundred hits. This group is good, though. I can admit that. Begrudgingly.

"Dude, is that Heartless's tour bus?"

"No way they'd be here now. They don't play until the last night," I say, but I still crane my neck to scan the area. I can't see shit because Ezra is six-foot-six, and I'm more than a foot shorter.

"Right there. Behind the stage to the left."

I take a few more steps forward, pushing past the guys and standing on my tiptoes to look where Ezra is pointing, and sure enough, there's a bus parked behind the stage, and I can just see the edge of the The Hometown Heartless logo.

I speed walk closer until the massive bus is in full view. A giant image of the five bandmembers is plastered across the side of it with Sav Loveless front and center, but my eyes go directly to the dark-haired, green-eyed god standing at her right.

Torren King is gorgeous in a way that makes my throat feel parched, my tongue lolling about like a dehydrated sponge in my mouth.

I can't speak. I can barely breathe. I can only stare.

I choose to ignore the way his hand is gripping Sav Loveless's hip and instead focus on the rest of him. His stature is relaxed yet arrogant in a way that fits his surname perfectly. A surly, rebellious prince. Not quite a king, but soon enough. Slated for rock and roll royalty, no doubt.

Even in a posed photograph emblazoned on the side of a bus, his emerald irises burn right through me. He must be wearing some smudged liner because there's no way his lashes are that dark and thick in real life, but it makes his eyes sparkle brighter. My green eyes are pretty, but his are magnificent.

My knees feel weak, and I have the urge to fall to the ground before him as if being silently commanded. Forced by some power beyond my control. His sculpted chest is bare, his low-slung black jeans teasing just a hint of his taut stomach and the deep groove outlining his pelvis. I wish Sav weren't standing in front so I could see more than half of him.

I want to see all of him.

I don't even realize my feet are moving until I'm less than twenty feet from the door to the bus. I only stop when my eyes land on two security guards—one at the front of the bus and one at the back.

Is the band here for the festival? Will they be sweat-slicked and dancing just like the rest of us? Could *I* be in the same crowd as Torren King?

I laugh at myself. Surely not. Their mere presence would cause pandemonium. Sav Loveless has had multiple stalkers in the last few years. The bus is likely roadies and security prepping for their show. I doubt the band is here at all, probably sequestered in some well-guarded penthouse in Phoenix, waiting for their call time.

I know this, but I still have to wipe my trembling, sweaty palms on my shorts.

Just the idea of Torren King makes me nervous. Knowing he'll be breathing the same air as me in a matter of days makes my stomach tighten in a way that approaches uncomfortable.

Jesus, I'm such a fucking fangirl. Obsessing over a man I've only seen in magazines and social media posts. I need to get my shit toge—

The door to the bus swings open and Sav Loveless storms out, wearing short shorts that might actually be underwear and a large tank top, with her silver hair falling messily around her shoulders.

And behind her, hot on her heels, is Torren King.

He grabs her bicep and swings her around, slamming her into his chest. I can't see her face, but everything about her body language says she's pissed. They engage in some sort of angry, whispered argument. I can only make out a few words—mostly expletives—and then she shoves at his chest. He doesn't let go, so she shoves again, harder this time, causing his torso to jerk backward. I glance at the security guard, expecting him to interfere, but then a loud crack sounds through the air, and I look back just in time to see Sav stomping off and disappearing behind the bus.

Torren stands with his arms at his sides, his head still tilted downward from the slap she dealt him. Even from twenty feet away, I can see the bright red handprint blooming on his cheek.

Three deep breaths and he's reaching into his back pocket to pull out a small silver case. He places what resembles a cigarette between his plush lips, but when he lights it, a pungent smell wafts my way.

Weed.

He takes a long drag and tilts his head to the sky with his eyes closed, holding the smoke in his lungs before blowing it out slowly.

He exudes something I've never felt before. Something like sadness or sickness, but not quite. Different. Elevated. Pained, yet sexy in a way that makes no sense. I want to fix him. I want to worship him back to health.

I'm intruding on a personal moment. I know this. I feel ashamed, but I can't seem to tear my eyes away from him. The muscles in his neck strain, his Adam's apple bobbing as he swallows. The harsh sun seems to soften around him, blanketing his body in an otherworldly warmth. He glows, all golden skin and sculpted angles. The only shadows around him in this moment are the ones cast in the hollows of his face by his sharp cheekbones and messy black hair. He's *haloed*. A fallen angel being beckoned back to heaven.

Torren King is probably the most beautiful man I've ever seen, and I hate Sav Loveless a little more in this moment. Jealousy flares in my gut and mixes with a possessiveness that almost knocks me over. I want to reach out and touch him.

And then his head turns, his eyes landing right on me.

He doesn't smile. He doesn't speak. He just stares.

I *feel* his gaze. A tingling that makes my ears buzz. My heart pounds loudly in my head, my lungs burning from lack of oxygen. I don't think I even blink. I don't think he does either.

He drops his eyes down my body as he brings the pre-roll back to his lips, taking another long drag. When he meets my gaze once more, he blows the thick smoke out his nose, then turns and climbs back into the bus.

As soon as the door closes behind him, I gasp and suck in air. I didn't dare breathe for fear of disturbing the moment, and I nearly passed out because of it.

Now I understand swooning. I understand why fans collapse unconscious when they meet their idols. Because their essential organs cease to work due to shock—a near-death experience of the most exhilarating kind.

"Fuck, Cal." Rock's voice makes me jump, and I whirl around to find the boys staring at me. "I thought he was going to eat you."

"No shit. Was that an eye fuck or an eye murder?" Ezra adds.

I chuckle nervously, and then I look toward Becket. His jaw is tight, and his hands are clenched into fists. I smile sheepishly, and his nostrils flare.

"He was definitely pissed that we saw that," I say, trying to lighten his mood. "Such drama, right? Lethal amounts of toxicity."

I push through Rocky and Ezra and wrap my arm around Becket's waist, pulling him back in the direction we came. "Let's find drinks."

"You think I'd have a chance with Sav Loveless now?" Ezra says from behind me.

I laugh and roll my eyes as Rocky chimes in with a snarky remark.

"Dude, fuck no. If Torren King almost turned cannibal on Callie, you don't want to know what he'd do to you if you so much as breathe in Sav's direction."

Rocky grunts, and I don't have to turn around to know Ezra socked him in the gut. Before they can start brawling like siblings, I point out a food truck to distract them.

"Tacos."

"Tequila." Becket whispers the words suggestively into my hair. I guess his jealous anger is gone, replaced quickly with the promise of what's supposed to happen tonight.

But my stomach doesn't flip like it would have two hours ago.

Like it would have before my stare down with Torren King.

5

TORREN

PRESENT DAY

I HIT the button on Sav's gate, making sure to stare right into the camera, and wait for her security to buzz me in.

It used to be security would let any of us in based on our car license plates, but that's changed recently. I used to practically live here, and now I'm treated like a fan, and I have to pretend it doesn't sting.

I pull up the long cobblestone drive and park behind Mabel's car. From the looks of it, everyone else is already here. Even Jonah, which is proof he's still on the wagon. Jo's only on time when he's sober.

I climb out and nod a hello to the security she has stationed at the door, then let myself inside.

"Good. You're here. Let's begin," Hammond clips immediately.

No *hello*. No *how was traffic*. No *why are you late*.

Ham's all business, all the time. I suppose that's a good quality to have in a manager, even if it annoys the shit out of me.

"Hello to you, too, Hammond. I'm great, thanks for asking. How are you? How's your niece?"

He sighs. "I'm well, thanks. My niece is fine. Stop asking about her. You're not her type."

He goes back to ignoring me, so I throw myself onto the couch next to Jo. He hands me a bottle of electrolyte water from the coffee table without saying a word, and I fist-bump him in thanks. One thing about doing meetings at Sav's instead of the label boardroom is that she's got way better snacks. After a survey of the spread on the table, I grab a yogurt parfait and a spoon.

Hammond clears his throat. "Are you settled in now, Mr. King?"

I put a spoonful of parfait in my mouth and lick it clean before responding.

"Quite ready, Ham. Thanks for asking."

He starts to ramble, and I tune him out. It's all shit we've already been over. Album release, current charting single stats, what we'll submit to the Grammys when the time comes. We're still set to start the second leg of our US tour in a few days after our two-month break. We'll spend three months touring in America before heading to Canada, and then to the UK after three more weeks of downtime.

That was one of Hammond's stipulations for us staying with our label last year: more breaks interspersed throughout our tours and no legs longer than four months at a time. It was one of the things he wasn't willing to budge on—no breaks, no downtime, and we walk. For as much shit as I've given Hammond over the years, he's really come through for us, and I'm grateful. I won't tell him that because he'll lord it over me, but I am.

"Have you been writing?" Ham asks, and we all nod. We've probably got two albums worth of material right now. "Good. Great."

Hammond goes silent and picks up a folder from the side table that I didn't notice before. His expression is somber, and my spine straightens. I glance at Jonah, then Mabel, and then for the first time since I've arrived, Sav.

Everyone looks uncomfortable, and suddenly, I wish I weren't late for the meeting.

"Now, you've all noticed we've had to amp up Savannah's security recently. More so since the end of the first leg of the tour."

I furrow my brow and look at Sav again. This time for longer than I usually allow. This time, I let myself see her.

She has circles under her eyes that I haven't noticed before. Creases between her brows that almost look permanent. Her lips are chapped and dry. Even the way she's sitting is out of character. Usually, Sav sprawls and takes up space. Right now? I've never seen her look so

Of Heartbreak and Harmony

small. Even her dog, Ziggy, is lying protectively at her feet as if feeling her tension. Usually, that dog is an absolute menace.

Then I glance around the rest of the house, and my jaw tightens. There's no noise. No sign of her boyfriend or his daughter. No sign of her mother.

"What's going on?" I ask finally, and Hammond takes a deep breath.

"The stalker is back."

"The same stalker? I thought he was arrested."

Hammond shrugs. "Honestly, we don't know for sure if it's the same guy, but it would make sense. He made parole a few months ago, and since then, things have steadily gotten worse."

"Things have gotten worse over the last few months? Why the fuck am I just finding out?"

"I didn't want to worry you," Sav says, her voice weak.

It's like a punch to the chest. It just highlights how much we've changed in the last year. I used to be the first person she'd confide in. Now I'm on the fringes. Relegated to a footnote in her autobiography. I clench my teeth and shake my head.

"Did you guys know?"

I pose the question to the group, glancing around at my bandmates. Jonah shakes his head, but Mabel nods slowly.

"I knew."

I sit back on the couch and look back at Hammond. "Well?"

"*Well*, the tabloids over the last few months have started circulating more rumors that you and Savannah are back together."

I shrug. I don't pay attention to any of that shit anymore. Hammond rounds the corner of the couch and drops some papers in my lap. When I look at them, I feel the color leave my face.

They're pictures of letters.

As I flip through them, I feel sick.

The letters call Sav a whore. They say she's a cheating cunt. They call her out for getting back together with me. They say she deserves to die. Sav's gotten letters before from stalkers and crazy fans, but they usually profess undying love. Call her their soulmate. Threaten suicide if she doesn't respond. This is the first I'm learning of any death threats.

"The originals are with the police, but so far they have no leads."

I look back at Sav. "Where's Levi?"

She bites her lip. "I sent him, Brynn, and Sharon back to North Carolina. I don't want to put them in danger."

"He just agreed to leave? You're getting fucking death threats at your home, Savannah. He just *left you*?"

"He doesn't know. I didn't tell him." She drags her hand through her silver hair and sends me pleading eyes.

"You shouldn't have to protect your boyfriend. He should be protecting you. You should have fucking told him," I snap.

You should have fucking told me, I want to add, but I bite my tongue.

"Don't do this right now, Tor. Please."

The crack on the please guts me, and I flick my eyes back to Hammond. It hurts too much to see Sav in pain and not be able to hold her. That's not my place anymore, and the guy whose place it is...well, she's sent him off to *protect* him.

"We think since Levi and Sav's relationship is so low profile, it's not dramatic enough for the paps to cover, so it didn't piss off the stalker. But now that the *Torren King and Sav Loveless Toxic Love Affair* is back in the media...Well, death threats."

"Why didn't she get death threats before? You know, when we were *actually* together?"

Mabel snorts out a derisive laugh.

"She did, dumbass. She just didn't tell you because she wanted to *protect you*."

Jesus fuck.

I tear my gaze from Mabel and look right at Sav. She refuses to meet my eyes, but her jaw pops. Her nostrils flare. Her eyes go glassy. When I speak, there's no hiding the hurt—the *betrayal*—in my voice.

"You *never* should have hidden something like that from me."

She shrugs but she doesn't say anything. She doesn't snap back like she would have *before*. Sobriety has done wonders for her temper.

"Right. Well, if your emotional outburst is over, I'd like to get to the point."

Hammond's matter-of-fact tone pisses me off, and I whip a glare at him. He doesn't acknowledge me at all.

"We have two options right now. We postpone the tour—"

"No," Mabel, Jo, and Sav say collectively.

I'm the only one with fucking sense, apparently. Hammond arches a disapproving brow, like a teacher dealing with unruly school kids.

"*Or* we find a way to snuff out the Torren and Sav media fire. We can send cease and desists, but unfortunately the damage is done. I don't see a retraction working."

"Bring Levi out of hiding," Jo suggests, and Sav immediately shakes her head.

"Absolutely not. I'm not throwing him and Brynn to the wolves. They didn't sign up for tha—"

"Kinda did when he decided to get back with you," I interrupt, and she shoots me a glare so violent, it could kill.

"I will not do that," she says firmly, eyes still on me. "I *will not* subject them to this."

I open my mouth to tell her it comes with the territory, but she slices a hand through the air and raises her voice.

"Do not. Do not, Torren."

I clench my teeth.

"What makes you think that would even work?" Mabel asks. "Those assholes only care about what sells. They don't care about the truth."

Hammond pulls another magazine out of the folder and flashes the cover as he speaks.

"The only time the letters stopped was when this story was circulating. Now that it's fizzled out, they've started back up. Got the first yesterday, only days after a gossip blog reported that the woman is out of the picture, and Sav and Torren are on again. Seems the relationship with Torren is the problem."

I ignore the last sentence and focus on the magazine. It's from three weeks ago when I was at the pier, and we had the mishap with the redhead. In the cover photo, she's lying in my lap, and I seem to be caressing her face. I've never seen this picture. I meant it when I said I don't pay attention to any of that bullshit anymore, but I did have paps throwing out questions about her for weeks after the incident. I ignore them as best I can, too, always rushing past with my head down. They only ever get two words from me: no comment. I don't know why they still try.

The headline suggests it's the start of a new romance. I lean in and look closer. In a few smaller photos at the bottom, there are more pictures of her. One of her outside of a convenience store wearing the same shirt she had on at the pier. One of her leaving a hotel wearing some sort of gray uniform. One of her stepping off a city bus.

"Who is this girl?" I ask, opening the magazine and flipping to the article.

I didn't get her name at the pier, but I remember her eyes—green like moss. There's something about them that tickles my memory. And her hair—the most unique blend of colors. Reds, browns, blondes. I feel like I've dreamed about it in a drugged-out slumber. Like I know her outline but nothing else. At the pier, there was something strangely familiar about her. Some magnetic pull that made me want to step closer. To touch her. To see if the feel of her could pull the whisper of *something* from the recesses of my memory. The word *again* kept circling in my mind. It's doing it once more. *Again again again.*

I find the answer to my question in the article at the same time Hammond says it.

"Calla Lily Sunrise James. She's twenty-three. Santa Monica native. Works at Bruno's Market and the Oceanside Inn."

I flip back to the cover and study the small photographs again. Nothing else jogs my memory. The name *Calla Lily Sunrise James* doesn't ring any bells. A name like that stands out. She's young, too. The only time I interact with people younger than me is at meet and greets, and she didn't act as if she'd attend a meet and greet. But...there's just something about her...

The longer I study the photographs, an idea begins to take shape. My need to help mixes with my interest in the girl, and the words fall out of my mouth without care.

"I'll date her," I say, and the room goes still. I glance up and find everyone staring at me. "A PR relationship," I clarify. "Give the media something else to focus on."

"Yeah, because fake relationships have really worked out so great for us in the past," Mabel says sarcastically.

"Absolutely not," Sav argues, shaking her head and pursing her lips before continuing. "That's out of the question. We're not doing that."

"Why not?" I ask, my tone more biting than I intended.

"Because, Torren. Are you forgetting what happened last time?

You're not putting yourself through that again. Especially not for me. I won't allow it."

"It's not really your decision."

"It *is* my decision. It's *my* stalker. *My* problem—"

"It's *all* of our problem, Savannah. You think this shit isn't going to affect us, too?"

"He's right," Mabel cuts in. "It's fucking with all of us."

Savannah grits her teeth and shakes her head again, trying her best to put her foot down on the matter.

"No. We'll figure something else out. Red has brought on another security detail for me. We've added more cameras. We've got an investigative team combing over every letter and point of contact. We'll be fine. It will be fine soon. We don't need Torren to do this."

"Celebrities enter into fake relationships all the time," Hammond says slowly. "It could work."

"I said *no*, Ham. He's not subjecting himself to that kind of media scrutiny again."

"And *this* isn't media scrutiny?" I say, referring to the recent uptick in relationship rumors about Sav and me. If it's not this, it would be something else. And fuck, I'd much rather it be something else.

"We're *always* under media scrutiny," I continue. "At least this way, we'll be ahead of it."

"Torren, a fake relationship is a terrible idea. It was a terrible idea with you and me, and it's a terrible idea now. It will only make things messier."

I shrug her off like her words don't sting. At her suggestion that our relationship was anything other than real.

"This will be different," I say confidently.

"How?"

I make eye contact with Sav and keep my voice flat when I answer her.

"I won't be in love with this one."

6

TORREN

PAST, ArtFusion Day One

"WHAT THE FUCK did you do to her this time?"

Jonah's voice has me cracking an eye open and turning my head to glance in his direction. He's slumped in the chair, eyes closed, with a joint between his lips and a glass of clear liquid in his hand. It's probably vodka, but it might be tequila. He's not particularly loyal to either one.

"Nothing." I groan and close my eyes again. I have a pounding fucking headache. "You know how she gets."

It's not entirely true, but I don't elaborate. I don't want to talk about this shit with Sav. She's fucking volatile, and I shouldn't have to explain that to Jo. One day, she's obsessed with me, and we can't keep our hands off each other. The next, she can't stand the sound of my voice, and we're facing off like enemies in a death match. Usually, it's all connected to whatever she's on, and it's unpredictable. I was born with an abundance of patience, but fuck if this whole bullshit's not exhausting.

"Just fuck someone else."

I snort at his suggestion.

"I'm serious. It will make you feel better."

I shake my head with a sigh. "Savvy's not fucking anyone else. She's just pissy."

"You're in denial."

Jonah kicks the couch I'm sitting on, making my body jerk. I don't open my eyes. I just reach into my pocket for a joint and spark it up. I don't want to talk about Sav and her mood swings. I don't want to think about what she does when she's not with me. I don't want to admit to what I do when I'm not with her. It's not like we try to fucking hide it. We just pretend it doesn't happen.

"She's never going to love you the way you love her, you know. Stop tryin' to force it before you fuck it up for all of us."

Jo's voice is serious and somber, a tone I'm not used to hearing from him anymore. In the early days of the band, dolling out sage advice and profound opinions was a daily occurrence from our guitarist. Sav and Mabes used to call him *Papa Jo* because of the way he looked out for us. He was the responsible one. The thoughtful one. The *wise* one.

It's like that guy doesn't exist anymore, except in brief moments like this one. I just wish this glimpse of *Papa Jo* didn't cut like a fucking knife to the chest. I clench my teeth before taking another long pull from my joint. I let the toxins sit in my lungs as Jonah's words echo in my ears.

She's never going to love you the way you love her.

I don't respond. I don't want to fuck with any of it right now. I just need a break from all the bullshit.

Playing ArtFusion wasn't even supposed to be on the schedule. We're supposed to be enjoying some downtime between our North American and European tour legs. We're supposed to be *resting*, but the label doesn't care. They see dollar signs, so our downtime has been relegated to the fucking tour bus in middle-of-nowhere fucking Arizona.

We're on top of each other with no privacy and no space. It's uncomfortable. It's irritating. We piss each other off at least once a day. Sav's tried getting a second tour bus for her and Mabel to share, but so far, the label has turned her down. The rest of us haven't even bothered broaching the topic. If the bastards won't listen to Sav, they sure as shit don't care what we think. We just keep holding out for another Grammy, and then maybe our demands will be taken seriously.

"You gonna venture out tonight?" Jonah coughs out the last word, and I don't have to look at him to know it was accompanied by a cloud of smoke. I'm glad for the change of subject.

"Nah. You?"

I have no desire to go out there and push my way through crowds of people. Jo and Mabel fly under the radar better than Sav and I do, but I can still sneak by without causing too much of a fan frenzy. Sav, though? If she's not sequestered in the bus surrounded by security, then she has to have a security guard up her ass. It takes the fun out of it.

"Maybe." Jo kicks the couch again, so I roll my head toward him and crack open an eye. He gives me a rare, lopsided grin. "Might go score some molly from some Ivy League kids. They always have the best shit."

I choke out a laugh. "You're a literal rock star, fucker."

Jonah shrugs. "There's just something better about drugs bought on Mommy and Daddy's dime. The rich kids can share."

I raise an eyebrow, but he ignores me. Jonah doesn't like to admit it, but if he weren't lead guitarist in our band, he'd definitely be one of those Ivy League kids dropping trust fund money on drugs at a trendy music festival. He forgets that I know he dropped out of Yale. Asshole.

The door to the bus opens and Mabel appears, a frown marring the usually cheerful expression of our drummer. She sends a scowl my way, and I already know she's going to bitch about Sav.

"Don't look at me," I say before she can hurl accusations. "She woke up raging and hating the world. I was just the first one to set her off."

Like usual, Mabel implies with a quirk of her thin, dark brow, then she rolls her eyes and walks past me, disappearing into the back.

She's not wrong. I'm usually the first one to set Sav off. Admittedly, I say things that I know will irritate her. I do it intentionally these days. Like tossing rocks at a land mine. If she's feeling particularly vicious, I might as well trip the trigger early and get it over with. That way she can explode, we can move past it with an angry fuck, and then we can all go about the rest of our day.

When Mabel steps back in front of me a few minutes later with a duffle bag slung over her shoulder, I know the angry fuck is off the table.

"Savvy and I are going to a hotel in town. You are welcome to also come, but I think it's best for all of us if you stay here. We'll be back before the show."

I stare blankly at her.

Mabel is always taking Sav's side. They were a packaged deal when I met them, so it's fine. I get it. But the divide has been growing lately, and these days it almost seems like Mabel's defense of our frontwoman is done begrudgingly. Mabel definitely resents me for screwing up their friendship, but she resents Sav more, and she hates it. Jealousy is deteriorating Mabel's loyalty, and Savvy is too steeped in her own disaster to even notice.

I notice, though.

Finally, I concede with a nod. "I'll stay here."

Mabel turns on her heel and leaves without another word, and Jonah lets out a slow whistle. He's getting more fucked up the longer we sit here. I wouldn't be surprised if he passes out soon.

"Now you definitely can go out tonight."

His words are slow, groggy, and his head is starting to lull to the side, resting on his shoulder in a way that makes my own neck ache.

I push up from the couch and look out the window just in time to catch sight of Sav. She's standing with Mabel, surrounded by three security guards next to a black SUV. She's wearing sunglasses, but when she tilts her head in my direction, I know her eyes are on me. I don't duck away from her. I don't hide. Instead, I look her over.

The outfit she threw on to storm out on me—cotton pajama shorts and my tank—is gone, and she's wearing jeans and a plain black T-shirt. Her silver hair is still a mess, though. She probably hasn't done anything with it since I had my hands in it early this morning. Before everything went to shit.

Fuck, she pisses me off.

My attachment to her is deep in my veins, thrumming in my neck like my heartbeat. I have to keep myself from going after her. From provoking her. I want to fight with her. I want to hear her scream at me, to feel her lash out, because even her vitriol is better than being alone with my thoughts.

I take another drag from my joint, but I don't take my eyes off her.

It's unhealthy. I can admit that. Our relationship is built of the most unstable things—a house of matches over a lake of gasoline. Lately, our spark has felt dangerous. Lethal.

The only time we work is when we're high. The moment we sober up, the haze is lifted, revealing only a mess of live wires and hurt feelings. One wrong move, and we'll burn down everything and everyone around us.

But even knowing this, I still don't look away. I see her lips curve downward in a frown. Her eyebrows scrunch. Then, before she's shuffled into the back of the black SUV, she lifts her hand, brandishing her middle finger in my direction. On impulse, I do the same, making sure the expression on my face mirrors hers, and I don't lower my hand until she's in the SUV and driving out of sight.

I stare at it until my phone buzzes in my pocket. I take it out and read the text I was expecting. I read it and let loose a sinister laugh. I could have guessed, right down to the punctuation, what she sent.

SAV

I can't do this shit with you anymore. See you at the show.

ME

I'm sorry.

I hit send on the half-ass apology, but when the message doesn't show as delivered after a minute, I know she's blocked me. She certainly didn't waste time. She never does.

I close out of the text and block her number before deleting it as if it will do anything. Her phone number is one of the only three I have memorized, and now none of them will answer if I call. My mom's written me off, and my brother is in jail.

I shove the phone back in my pocket and close my eyes, breathing slowly through my nose. I wait for her dismissal to sting. I wait for my head to spiral into what-ifs and my heart to ache in that *unrequited love* way it always does when this shit happens. When I recognize the dull throb of pain, I open my eyes with a defeated sigh, then let them drift to the space where the redhead from earlier was standing. Was staring. *Eavesdropping.*

I wonder if she'll take what she saw to the media. I drag a hand down my face. That's the last thing I want, though I suppose there's nothing new they can run about Sav and me. They've already ripped us to shreds ten times over.

She was pretty, the redhead. Probably beautiful if I'd let myself look her over a little longer. And she didn't cower away from my stare. She wasn't panting after me. There was no phone out. She took no moves to approach me. It was like she'd accidentally stumbled upon us. She didn't seem interested in throwing herself at us for an autograph, either. Or throwing herself at me for *more* than an autograph.

There's a good chance she's not a fan, and that intrigues me more than anything else. More than her thick thighs and ample breasts. More than her unique hair color and full lips.

I'm tired of fans, and that stokes my interest in the girl.

I think about it for less than a minute before I make up my mind.

"Fine. Let's go check shit out."

All I get is Jo's deep breathing in response. When I turn in his direction, I find him passed out cold with a lit joint hanging precariously between two limp fingers. I shake my head, but I'm not surprised. I pull the joint from his hand, take a drag, then stub it out in the ashtray on the table. I push the little button on the side of his chair to recline the back so he's no longer hunched over and twisted.

"Gonna get into your stash, yeah?" He doesn't answer because he's passed out. I slap him on the shoulder. "Thanks."

I snag a hat and some sunglasses from my bunk, then dig through Jo's shit. I'll find something to make me forget about Savvy's bullshit, and then I'll slip into the crowd and pretend I'm someone else for the night.

7

CALLIE

"WAKE UP, slacker. If I can work three doubles in a row and stay awake, you can stay awake after two days off."

I throw a pack of gum at Quinton, and he grunts.

"Leave me alone. I'm hungover."

I groan and throw a candy bar at him. He lifts his hand like he's going to bat it away, but he's several seconds delayed. Dumbass. He is *hungover* hungover.

"It's boring here now that they stopped caring about you," he says, his voice muffled in his folded arms. "I thought you were going to be the next Sav Loveless and Torren King scandal."

"We agreed to never talk about that again."

"I didn't agree to anything." Quinton sits up and faces me with his dark sunglasses still on. "Having my photos taken by paparazzi is the coolest thing that's ever happened to me, even if I was blurred out and cropped in half in the background."

I shake my head and go back to organizing the candy.

"Those idiots got me fired from my job at the motel, so excuse me if I don't share in your mourning."

Over two weeks of being followed and photographed was a miserable experience. Longest eighteen days of my life, and that's

47

saying something. It almost makes me grateful that my band didn't work out. *Almost.*

Quinton picks up the candy bar I threw at him and unwraps it, then takes a bite.

"Yeah, that sucks," he says while chewing. "But now you get to see me more often."

He grins with his teeth covered in chocolate and I blink at him, unamused.

"Yes. Because doing twice the work while you sleep off your hangover and pore over tabloids is so enjoyable for me."

"I know, right?" Quinton sighs and shakes his head, reverting to his current favorite topic. "If only they hadn't realized how boring you are. It could have been my big break. I just need a less blurry picture. Maybe an interview—"

I close my eyes, take a deep breath, and ignore him. At least he's awake now.

Once I'm finished with the candy bars, I go to the back to grab things to restock the empties. I'm not in there two minutes when Quinton comes barreling through the door with his eyebrows raised comically high behind his sunglasses.

"Callie. You need to come out here."

The way he says it, almost like a whispered hiss, has my suspicions spiking, and I narrow my eyes at him. If he's fucking with me...

"Why?"

"There is someone here to see you." Again with the whispering, but this time he's spaced out each word with an unnatural pause, his eyebrows rising even higher than I thought possible. "Come out now."

"I swear to god, Quin, if this is another one of your stunts..."

I push past him and march out into the store, and then immediately skid to a halt. Pretty sure my eyebrows get higher than Quinton's did, and my jaw drops open before I can stop it. Torren smirks at me, though, and I snap it shut, bringing my eyebrows to slants.

"Hey. I don't know if you remember me," he starts, his voice making the skin on my neck prickle. "We met at the pier a couple of weeks ago."

"If that's what you want to call your hulking bodyguard almost killing me."

He shrugs, a weak gesture in place of an apology. "He thought you were a crazy fan."

I resist the urge to roll my eyes, then glance over his shoulder at the front door. There's a big, black, conspicuous SUV parked at the curb, and the aforementioned hulking bodyguard is standing by the door. Good lord.

"Can I help you? I'd like to get it over with quickly before anyone sees you here."

His brow furrows slightly, and he tilts his head to the side in a move so familiar, my own head spins. Motion sickness by déjà vu. Having those green eyes on me, assessing me like I'm something amusing. Like I'm something to be toyed with...

I have to look away before I snap.

When he finally speaks, his voice is soothing and sincere, but it has the opposite effect I think he wanted. I want to punch him.

"I'm sorry for the media circus you must have experienced after the pier. I know it can be a lot if you're not used to it."

I huff a sarcastic laugh.

"Yeah, you can say that. I'd like to avoid another one so I don't get fired from this job as well."

"You got fired?"

"Yep. So can you get to the point please?"

"When does your shift end?"

"IN AN HOUR!" Quinton shouts, cutting me off before I can tell Torren that it's none of his business. When I shoot Quin a glare, he's brazenly lying over the check-out counter so he can eavesdrop. I close my eyes and pinch the bridge of my nose.

"I'd like you to come with me to my studio in LA when you get off. I have something I'd like to discuss with you."

I shake my head. I don't open my eyes. I pinch the bridge of my nose harder.

"No."

"It will just be for a couple of hours."

"No."

He goes quiet. After a long pause, I finally open my eyes and meet his. I arch a brow, urging him to say whatever it is he's thinking so I can turn him down again and then kick him out. But when he finally does, I'm rendered speechless.

"I'll give you five grand to come hear me out. If you don't like what I have to say, I'll have Damon bring you home, and you'll never see me again."

"She'll go!" Quin shouts, and I glare at him again. He's eating potato chips like this whole exchange is some fucking blockbuster movie. "What? Five grand for a few hours? You're a dumbass if you say no."

Shit. He's right. Five thousand dollars would pay our rent for six months. I cave, and from that stupid infuriating twitch of a smirk on Torren's face, he knows it.

"Fine. I'll go. But you can't wait here. You have to go drive around the block for an hour or something."

"You don't really like me, do you?" he asks, catching me off guard, and my defenses become ironclad. A sword ready to swing if necessary.

"That obvious?" I snark, and he shrugs.

"Why?"

"I need a reason?"

There's a brief pause as his eyebrows slant, then he gives me a curt nod.

"Guess not. I'll see you in an hour."

"Forty-five minutes now," Quinton interjects again, and Torren releases a ghost of a laugh.

"See you in forty-five minutes," he amends, and then he's gone.

Quinton and I watch as he climbs into the back seat of the black SUV before it drives off down the street, and then Quin lets out a long, slow whistle.

"Girl. I don't care what it is he's offering. You better take it."

I pinch the bridge of my nose again. I'm too sleep deprived to deal with Torren fucking King.

I slide into the back seat of the SUV quickly, and the bodyguard shuts the door.

My movements are jerky as I pull on my seat belt. I don't look at Torren, but he's impossible to ignore. This whole car smells like him, and even though there's a good two feet of leather seat between us, I can feel him pressing against me.

It's probably his ego taking up space.

"Here."

I glance down at the check he's holding out to me. Five thousand dollars made out to Calla Lily James. I suppose it shouldn't surprise me that he knows my name—it was all over the tabloids—but the possibility that he knows *more* makes me uneasy.

Is that what this is about? Some kind of follow-up? Is he going to make me sign the NDA I refused four years ago? Belated bribery?

If my nerves weren't already sky high, they're in fucking space now. But I can't turn back at this point. Might as well just plow through for the 5k.

Six months of rent, I remind myself as I take the check and put it in my backpack, then pull out my big headphones.

"Thanks," I say.

Then I put on my headphones, turn my body away from him, and stare out the window until we're pulling into the private parking garage of a building of luxury apartments in Downtown LA.

I take off my headphones and sit up straight.

"I thought we were going to a music studio."

"Oh, sorry, no. My studio. My apartment." He must see the panic on my face because he responds quickly. "It's just a meeting. My manager will be there. My bandmates."

I blink at him and replay what he said over in my head. His *bandmates*. I'm about to walk into Torren King's apartment for a *meeting* with his *manager* and his *bandmates*.

Good lord, what have I gotten myself into?

I clamp my mouth shut and follow him stiffly to a private elevator, then I press myself into the corner with my hands folded in front of me while the elevator rockets up fifty-seven floors.

Every few seconds, I feel his eyes on me, assessing in that way that he does. That way I remember so vividly.

What does he see?

I'm a far cry from that girl at the music festival. I'm still in my stupid khakis and work shirt. My hair is dirty. I'm not wearing makeup. I haven't slept more than four hours for the last few nights, so I know I probably have purple circles under my eyes. I'm fucking exhausted, and it shows, and I hate that I remember everything while he seems blissfully ignorant. He made a lasting impression, and I didn't even make it past short-term memory.

The elevator doors pop open with a musical ding and then I'm following him into an expansive hallway. He punches in a code, unlocking a door, and swings it wide.

"After you," he says, gesturing for me to enter, so I do.

And then I stare.

Not only is this "studio apartment" four times the size of the apartment I share with my mom and sister, but it's got floor-to-ceiling windows and the most modern features I've ever seen. The most jarring thing, though, are the four people sprawled out on a large leather sectional that has to be custom-made for the space.

They're just *hanging out* as if they aren't three-time Grammy-winning rock icons.

Jonah Hendrix, the lead guitarist for The Hometown Heartless, has one of his legs thrown over the arm of the couch, while Sav Loveless, the band's guitarist and lead singer, sits with her feet propped up on a modern glass coffee table. The drummer, Mabel Rossi, is cross-legged, her socked feet tucked cozily under her knees on the couch cushion. Even Wade Hammond is here, the manager who made headlines last year for renegotiating the band's contract with their record label. The terms were kept confidential, but everyone knows they were groundbreakingly in favor of the band. It paved the way for a whole new set of possibilities for artists.

I hate how much I envy them despite my loathing. I remind myself how toxic they are. How they're rarely shown in a positive light in the media. And despite the good their recent contract did for the music industry, the iron hold they have on it is despicable.

Sure, they're talented as hell, and their rise to fame was mostly based on merit and hard work. Sure, they earned it, to an extent. But fame, as usual, has poisoned them, and now they'll step on anyone to maintain their place at the top of the industry hierarchy.

I can't stop the way my eyes narrow. I wish I had more control over my face, but I'm overwhelmed and running on no sleep. It cannot be helped.

"Hey." Torren steps beside me and addresses the group. Immediately, four sets of eyes settle on me. "This is Calla Lily. Calla Lily, this is Hammond, Jonah, Sav, and Mabel."

"Hi. And it's just Callie. No need to drop the government name."

The smirk that pops up on Sav Loveless's face fills me with a surge of pride before I beat it back into submission. I do not care about being liked by Sav Loveless.

I do not care about any of them.

As if hearing my thoughts, Sav studies me closer, her gray eyes narrowing slightly and her head tilting a bit to the side. I'm a bug under a microscope to her. Another person she might be able to use. My hatred surges up my throat like bile, but as much as I want to stare her down, I can't. I look away and focus on Jonah Hendrix and Mabel Rossi as they greet me, instead. Then Wade Hammond—or Hammond, as he seems to go by—claps his hands together once and gestures to a plush leather chair.

"Have a seat. We'll get started."

Like a robot, I walk to the chair and *have a seat*. Back ramrod straight. Hands folded in my lap. The picture of discomfort, and everyone can tell.

"Thank you for agreeing to meet with us, Miss James—"

"Just Callie. Please."

Hammond nods and plows forward. "I appreciate you taking the time out of your busy schedule."

"Sure."

"We have a proposition for you, but before we begin, I do need to ask that you sign a non-disclosure—"

My gut twists, and my mouth goes dry. Of course. The NDA. I almost want to laugh.

"—that states you won't talk about the topic of this meeting today. Even if you decline the offer, it is still imperative that this doesn't make it into the media. Should you take it to the media, we will take legal action—"

I open my mouth to protest, to say thanks but no thanks and leave, but Wade Hammond holds up a palm and silences me. Like witchcraft, the words turn to dust before even making it out of my throat.

"This NDA requires nothing of you but your agreement to keep what we discuss confidential, but there is a caveat that states you are free to share your story with anyone you wish should we suggest or engage in anything illegal. However, once you sign this, we will also ask that you sign a release allowing us to record this meeting. As a precaution."

My eyes widen. "I wouldn't lie," I protest.

"As I said. It's a precaution."

My nostrils flare, but the caveat has softened my resolve, and I take the tablet from Hammond's outstretched hands to look over the PDF document on the screen. Sure as shit, it's cut and dry. I understand every word. No sneaky legal jargon. No fine print. And no mention of the music festival four years ago.

Damn if my curiosity isn't thoroughly piqued.

"Fine."

Hammond offers me a stylus without my having to ask. Silently, I sign the NDA and then sign the video release form. Hammond takes it back, sets it on the couch beside him, then pushes a button on his phone, which I assume is starting a recording. I glance around the room for a camera, and Mabel laughs.

"You're very on it," she says with a grin, then she starts pointing. "There's one up in that corner, one on top of the television, and one in the kitchen. There's also one on the elevator, the emergency exit, and the front door. Nothing in the bathroom or bedrooms. And before you ask, yes, all of our places are like that."

My eyes flare at the need for such excessive security measures.

"A precaution?" I ask, and everyone nods.

"Now that that's done—Torren, you have the floor."

Hammond turns his attention to Torren, so I do too. Reluctantly. When Torren makes eye contact with me, my pulse starts to race. His face stays blank, his voice even when he speaks the words that completely knock me on my ass.

"I'd like you to enter into a PR relationship with me."

8

CALLIE

"No."

My answer is immediate as I shake my head and stand, ready to bolt.

Torren clears his throat and throws his palms up. "Just hear me out. Let me finish. Then if you still say no, you can leave, but I think you'll want to hear what I have to say."

I glare at him. I search his face. It doesn't look nefarious.

In fact, he almost looks desperate. *Almost.*

Mostly, though, he just looks detached. All business. That's why I sit down. I can handle detached.

"Thank you. I'd like for you to enter into a PR relationship with me. You've probably seen that rumors are once again circulating about a relationship between Sav and me. This is...not ideal...for several reasons. Our hope is that a relationship of my own will be enough to kill the rumors."

He pauses, but when I don't speak, he moves forward.

"It would be for the next three months while we're finishing up our American tour. We would engage in several public outings and some mild displays of affection. You would have to attend the concerts and travel on the tour bus—"

"I'd have to go on tour with you?" I interrupt, the shock evident in my tone. "I can't leave my job for three months. I can't just go gallivanting around the country to be your arm candy. I have responsibilities. I have—"

"We would compensate you, Miss James," Hammond says, and I sigh.

"It's Callie."

"We would compensate you. Sixty thousand dollars to be paid in six installments. Twice a month for the extent of the tour, but should you choose to leave early—and you are free to leave whenever you choose—you will forfeit the rest of the payments."

I blink. I blink again. My heart stops. I'm dead. No, I'm dying, and this is some weird fucking fever dream.

Sixty *thousand* dollars. It would take me years to save up that kind of money. That money could pay off Mom's medical bills. Pay for more physical therapy. It could help put Glory through community college.

"Breathe. Breathe, Callie."

Torren's voice breaks through the loud thumping in my ears, and I slowly raise my eyes to meet his. Then I gasp, sucking in mouthfuls of air. Why does this man always take my breath away? And not in a good way.

I close my eyes and focus on breathing until my brain is functioning, then I make eye contact again. I make eye contact and I do my best to pretend like it doesn't turn me inside out.

"What are the reasons?"

Torren doesn't answer. Instead, he flicks his eyes at Sav, which makes fire lick up my insides.

"You said there were several reasons why the stories aren't ideal. It must be something bad if you're willing to pay me to play pretend with you. I want to know the reasons."

"I have a stalker," Sav states, and I whip my head to her. She gives me a smile-like grimace. "I have a stalker, and they *really* don't seem to like the relationship rumors."

"And they *are* rumors?"

She nods sincerely. "Yes, they are."

I turn my head to Torren and try to read his face. It's blank. No heartbreak, but no confirmation, either. It leaves me feeling uneasy.

It's on the tip of my tongue to ask about the engagement debacle that took place last year—to dig into the details of that whole tabloid storm about a fire, a sex tape, and an affair—but something more pressing grabs my attention.

"Will I be in danger?"

Sav shakes her head.

"We don't think so. You'll have your own security, and the stalker pretty much disappears when someone else is in the picture." She laughs, but it's tired and makes me feel a twinge of sympathy for her. "And anyway, they usually only fuck with me."

I glance back at Hammond and Torren.

"So this whole thing will be to keep Sav safe? It's just for her benefit?"

It's Mabel Rossi who answers me.

"No. It will really help all of us. I'm sure you can imagine that having a stalker is really fucking annoying."

I quirk a brow. I've never once imagined having a stalker. She keeps speaking.

"It messes with group morale. It messes with Sav's performances, which messes with our performances. It stunts our creativity. It creates stress. Honestly, it's a huge fucking mess."

I glance at Jonah Hendrix. I could have forgotten he was here if I didn't constantly feel his stare. He hasn't said a word, but he nods in agreement.

I bring my eyes to my feet, my fingers once again coming up to pinch the bridge of my nose. I'm getting a tension headache, and what's worse is that my protective streak is forcing its way out of the box where I'm trying to shove it.

"I don't want you to feel obligated to do this," Sav says. I don't look at her, but I nod to signal I'm listening. "This isn't some minor thing. There will be press. Yeah, some of it will be arranged by Hammond, but a lot of it won't be. There will be a lack of privacy. Being on tour isn't always luxurious, especially when we're camping on the buses."

I want to laugh. I remember how their bus looks on the inside. It's a reminder of how different we are that they don't consider it luxury.

"And honestly, a PR relationship isn't much fun, either. Trust me on that. I would know."

I hear a scoff from behind me, and when I peek my eyes open to glance at Torren, it's obvious he took offense to what Sav said.

I sit up and sigh. "You're doing a shit job at selling it."

Sav shrugs. "I've learned honesty is the best policy."

"Consider it a favor for a favor," Torren says.

"And what favor are you doing for me?"

"You help us get through this PR disaster, and we make it so you don't have to work so much. We both get something out of this arrangement that we need."

When I don't answer right away, Hammond speaks up.

"Sixty thousand dollars isn't incentive enough?"

His question fills me with defeat. The truth is, sixty thousand dollars is all the incentive I need. I'd mentally agreed the moment the figure left his mouth. A disappointing fact is that I can, and now have, been bought.

Awesome. So much for integrity.

I nod slowly. "Okay. I'll do it. But I have stipulations."

"We'll consider them," Hammond says.

I swallow hard, channel all of Glory Bell's boldness, and begin.

"I want my own space on the bus."

"We've already arranged to give you the big room on our bus," Sav says, gesturing between her and Mabel. "Mabes and I will take the bunks, and you'll have your own room when we stay in hotels, too."

I furrow my brow, momentarily surprised. I'm getting the star's room? I almost tell her that's not necessary, but I choke it back. I'm going to need my own space if I'm going to make it through this emotionally unscathed.

"I also want the first two-week payment up front. I need to leave something with my mom and sister if I'm going to be gone."

"Done," Hammond says.

"And I, um..." I glance at Sav briefly, then back at Hammond. "I don't want to be around drugs. Especially anything with needles."

Sav groans immediately, and I flick my eyes back to her. Mabel is biting her lip to hide a smile, but Sav is staring at the ceiling.

"Why is that the one thing everyone seems to remember? One stupid magazine in the fucking UK prints the lie *one time*, and it's all anybody remembers. Why couldn't the *adrenaline junkie* or *sex fiend* articles be the ones that stuck in people's heads?"

Mabel laughs outright. "You thought it was hilarious at the time."

Sav shoots Mabel a glare. "That was before I knew it would follow me into sobriety."

My surprise once again spikes. "It was a lie?"

Sav rolls her eyes. "Yes, it was a lie. I hate needles. Can't stand the sight of them. They make me queasy. That's even why my tattoos are all on my back. Heroin was never my drug of choice."

"So...the alcohol and pills? The cocaine?"

She gives me a smirk. "That was true. Mostly whiskey and Xanax. Cocaine if I went too hard on those two."

"Bullshit. Cocaine before every show," Mabel says, and Sav laughs.

"That's because I always went too hard the night before every show."

"Touché."

"Anyway," Sav continues, looking back at me. "I'm sober. I don't even drink."

"And the rest of you?"

I don't miss the tension in Sav's shoulders when she gives me a flat smile.

"Mostly. But we'll make sure it doesn't affect you."

That was cryptic, but I suppose it's more than I can expect from a rock band. I nod.

"Anything else, Miss James?" Hammond asks, and I huff, frowning in his direction.

"Yes. Call me Callie."

"Noted. Anything else."

"I want eighty thousand."

The flash of surprise on Hammond's face matches the flood of shock I feel in my stomach. I can't believe I just said that, and the brief pause—the look he shoots at Torren—has me immediately wanting to walk it back. Sixty is fine. It's more than fine. I shouldn't spit in the face of this offer and risk losing it all. I open my mouth, but then Hammond nods, so I snap it shut again.

"Fine."

I try my damnedest not to look as stunned as I feel and clear my throat.

"And one more thing," I say.

I glance at Torren and find his eyes on me, then look back at

Hammond. He seems to be the safe landing. I feel nothing when I look at him except mild irritation.

But Torren? Sav? That's more complicated.

"No...um, sex stuff."

"Of course," Torren says, drawing my eyes back to him. "That's not expected of you."

"I'm not a groupie," I say firmly, and he flinches.

His brows fold in further and he nods. "I know. That's not what this is."

"Good." I take a deep breath. "Good. Where's the contract?"

Hammond hands me the tablet once again, and it takes me thirty minutes to read through the PDF. Hammond offers me a drink and I turn it down, determined to absorb every last detail. Once I'm sure I have, I sign the contract. Hammond sends me a digital copy, and then he reaches out his hand.

I take it, and he shakes firmly.

"Thank you, Callie. We'll have someone pick you up on Monday. That will be enough time to get your affairs in order?"

Three days. I have three days to quit my job, explain this to my mom and sister, and prepare myself mentally. No amount of time would be enough time for that last one.

"Sure." I turn to Sav, Mabel, and Jonah. "See you Monday, I guess."

Mabel smiles. "See you Monday."

"And thank you," Sav adds.

Jonah says nothing.

All I can do is nod, and then Torren is leading me out the door and to the elevator.

"I'm going to have Damon drive you home, but I'll be there to pick you up on Monday."

"Okay."

"Thank you for agreeing to do this."

I sigh. "Full disclosure, I'm not really in the position to turn down eighty grand, but something tells me you already know that."

He doesn't say anything, which is confirmation enough. He pushes the button on the elevator, and I turn to face him. One last time, I let myself peer into those mesmerizing green eyes, and he peers back. The eye contact stretches, making the skin on the back of my neck prickle with awareness, unearthing memories I'd much rather leave buried, but I can't look away.

Despite my better judgment, my eyes beg for some sort of recognition. Some sign that I was worth remembering. That I was *more*.

But I get nothing.

When the elevator door opens, the connection is broken, and I step into it without speaking. I breathe through my nose and keep my attention on the ground in front of me.

"See you Monday, Callie."

His voice draws my eyes up once more, and he gives me a small smile. I don't return it, but I don't look away either. Not until the elevator door closes, and I'm plummeting to the ground.

In more ways than one.

9

CALLIE

PAST, ArtFusion Day One

THE FIRST NIGHT of the festival, everyone dresses elaborately.

I know from the pictures and promo videos I see everywhere. Crowds full of faeries and Greek gods and goddesses. Butterflies. Angels. It's a whole thing, and people have already started emerging in their outfits before we even get back to our van.

I made my outfit from scratch. I've been working on it since we got our last-minute invite to play last month, transforming a red corset-type bra and lace-up red pleather skirt by hand-stitching feathers and sequins onto them. I even made a headpiece that resembles winged-flames and bought sparkling hair extensions. Putting the fucker on inside a tent is difficult, but I manage, and then I cover my chest, arms, and stomach in gold body glitter. To finish it off, I do a smokey eye with gold-glitter false eyelashes and dark red glittery lipstick. I'm stepping back to try to inspect my outfit in the side-mirror of the van when Ezra lets out a low whistle of approval, and Pike and Rocky do a slow clap.

"Damn, Cal. That shit is *fire*."

"*Literally*."

"Lookin' very good."

I smile at their compliments and do a little twirl, showing off the way my red and orange feathers flutter like dancing flames.

Rocky, Ezra, and Pike are dressed up, too, but not as elaborately as I am. No handmade accessories or makeup for them. Pike's got on leopard print bellbottom pants and a pink knitted crop top. Rocky has on low-slung black leather pants with a silver chain-mesh tank-top, which isn't much different from what he wears when we perform. Ezra is shirtless, wearing faded jeans, a giant silver belt-buckle, a cowboy hat, and black cowboy boots. He got the whole outfit at a thrift store for ten bucks, and he's very proud of that. He's sure to tell anyone who comments on it tonight. The equivalent of *this dress has pockets* for Ezra will be *this authentic rodeo belt buckle was only seventy-five cents.*

"Fucking hot, Cal." Becket wraps his arm around my waist and tugs me into his body as he speaks.

He did not dress up. He's wearing the same pair of shorts and Avenged Sevenfold T-shirt that he was wearing earlier. I open my mouth to tease him, but he leans in for a kiss, and I turn my face to give him my cheek.

"Lipstick," I explain feebly. "I don't want to mess up the glitter."

He nods, accepting my excuse. Only I know it was a half-truth.

I take a step back and smooth my hands over my skirt, then adjust my top. When I'm certain not a feather is out of place, I look back at my band.

"Alright, boys. Let's go."

I turn in my knee-high boots—I put feathers and sequins on them, too—and the guys follow.

As we get farther inside the venue, the crowd thickens, and lines have already started forming at various tents and food trucks. Music from the opening band grows louder, and the pop-punk headliner starts just after sunset, which is in about an hour. It's safe to assume there are already bodies camped out in the field in front of the stage.

"Let's split up," Becket suggests. "Grab whatever food or drinks you want and meet back at the guitar." He gestures toward a fifteen-foot sculpture of an electric guitar made completely out of recycled soda cans. "Then we can head to the stage."

Ezra salutes and heads off into the crowd without a word. He'll probably come back with something totally random, like a glow-in-the-dark lightsaber or someone's dog. We don't usually let Ezra out unsupervised, so this should be interesting.

Rocky tells us *exactly* what he's going to do—find a port-o-john, take a piss, then scarf some mozzarella sticks—before he's heading in the opposite direction as Ezra.

"Be back in a bit," Pike says with a grin, then he disappears into the crowd, leaving Becket and me to ourselves.

"What do you think? You get drinks, and I'll grab us food?"

I nod. "Sure. Any requests?"

"Nope. Just something to get me drunk." Becket punctuates his statement with a slap to my ass. "You?"

"I saw a truck with kabobs," I suggest, but Becket scrunches his nose. I laugh. "Fine. Just pick something that isn't pizza. I'm sick of pizza."

Becket slaps my ass again before he takes off to find food, so I turn to complete my mission as well.

I weave back through the crowd until I find a line for a beer tent, then I pull out my phone to scroll mindlessly through apps while I wait.

"Clever."

The voice over my shoulder, deep with a hint of humor, makes me jump, and when I turn toward it, my stomach falls to my feet.

Torren King stands in front of me with a lit cigarette hanging from his mouth. He's wearing a black baseball hat and mirrored aviator sunglasses, but I'd know those full lips anywhere. I've stared at them many, many times while watching clips of The Hometown Heartless perform. I'm surprised I didn't recognize his voice right away, because the few songs where he sings more than just backup harmonies are always my favorites.

I force myself to swallow, wetting my suddenly parched throat, before speaking.

"Excuse me?"

His lips curve up slightly at the corner. It's barely a smirk, but it's a *much* more welcoming expression than I saw on him earlier in the day.

"Your outfit," he clarifies. "A phoenix? It's clever."

"Oh. I made it."

"Nice."

"Thanks...What...Um, what are you supposed to be?"

He gives me a shrug. "A stoned musician."

Well. I guess he's not trying to hide who he is.

We fall back into silence as he takes a drag from his cigarette. I can't see his eyes, and it's unnerving. Every part of my body is buzzing because I don't know where he's looking. I don't even know if it's at me. I don't know if he wants to continue this conversation, or why he spoke to me in the first place.

He probably didn't expect me to turn around. Just a compliment thrown over my shoulder and a thanks back. I take a deep breath and give him a tight smile, then start to turn around, but his voice stops me once again.

"Will you talk?"

I look back at him and furrow my brow in question. His dark eyebrow quirks up from behind his sunglasses.

"About what you saw."

Ah. So that's what this is. I can't help the way my face falls.

"No, I won't talk."

"Because it would fucking suck if you did. And it wouldn't work out well for you. Probably not how you'd want it to."

I purse my lips. "I said I wouldn't talk. I had no intention of talking. I was in the wrong place at the wrong time, and it's nobody's business but yours."

"Then why stay and watch?"

He cocks his head to the side, assessing me as he takes a long drag from his cigarette. The end glows bright red, but all I can see is my nervous expression in his mirrored aviators.

I put a hand on my hip instead of wrapping it around my stomach like I want. I make my back ramrod straight and work to school my face into something less...*baffled fangirl.* I give what I hope looks like a nonchalant shrug.

"It's not every day you see one world-famous rock star slap another world-famous rock star across the face. I was curious. Sue me."

His lips twitch at the corners, and he slowly blows out a stream of smoke.

"I could. It'd make the pap payout look like chump change."

He's not smiling, but he's amused. I can hear it in his voice, and it gets my back up, squashing my nerves with anger. He's in this beer line trying to not-so-subtly intimidate me, and he finds it *amusing.*

I open my mouth to snap something snarky back at him, to tell him to stop with the back-alley shakedown because it's unnecessary and a waste of my time, but he cuts me off.

"Is that your natural hair color?"

My head jerks back in a flinch at the rapid change of topic. He bites his lip, stifling a laugh, and I scoff.

"Is this a *does the carpet match the drapes* kind of question? Are we in high school?"

His smile breaks free, full lips stretching over white teeth, and for some reason, my eyes zero in on his unusually sharp canines. Like understated fangs.

Jesus, Rock was right. This man would eat me alive.

"Does it?" he says with a low laugh.

I roll my eyes and turn around, giving him my back. I'm fuming. What an asshole. This is why they say to never meet your idols.

"Hey, I was just kidding," he says, and his voice is lower. Closer than before. So close that I'm afraid to turn around to see just how much distance is left between our bodies. "It's an unusual color, is all. Pretty, the way it's multicolored. Copper. Cinnamon. Blonde. Matches with your outfit perfectly."

I don't respond, but my lips curl into a tiny smile. A compliment from a hot rock star. It's probably shallow. It's probably just a line. A weak excuse to hopefully keep me from going to the media. But I smile anyway.

He doesn't speak to me again as the line inches forward. Not until we step up to the counter and I order my drinks.

"She's on mine," Torren says suddenly, flashing a badge of some sort to the bartender. The guy's eyes flare, and he glances quickly from the badge to Torren, then his head bobbles in a rapid nod.

"Yes, sir. Mr. King, sir."

I don't even have to show him my fake ID or flash my alcohol wristband. The guy just turns and gets to work grabbing our drinks. I flick my eyes toward Torren over my shoulder.

"You didn't have to do that."

His cigarette is gone, his face trained forward and not on me as he shrugs.

"Consider it an apology for insulting you. It's the *least* I can do."

I don't know if I imagine the veiled innuendo in that last sentence. Probably. But damn if my heart doesn't kick up anyway.

"Thank you," I force out, hoping he can't hear the breathlessness in my tone. "Consider yourself forgiven."

The bartender hands me my two drinks and Torren his one. I thank the bartender and turn to leave. To my surprise, Torren follows beside me.

"You *are* old enough to drink, right?"

I hold my breath for a moment, consider the question quickly in my head, then take note of the two beers already in my hands. I force a laugh.

"That matters *now*?" I deflect. "You already gave me the drinks."

I see him nod in my periphery. "It matters."

I force another laugh. I roll my eyes, then I raise the hand with the alcohol wristband...that I got with my fake ID. I wave it around as if it's proof enough, then add, "I can show you my ID if you don't believe me."

He hums and I feel his eyes on me. I wait for him to call me out. To catch me in the lie. But then I see him nod again, and I slowly release a sigh of relief.

"That second one for a...*friend*?"

The change of subject calms my nerves, and he draws out the word friend suggestively. Searching for a particular piece of information, I realize, and for a reason I don't want to admit, I nod.

"Yep. For a friend."

Not a pseudo-boyfriend. Not a guy I was planning on sleeping with tonight. Just a *friend*.

Torren hums and takes a sip from his drink. His head tilts downward slightly, and my nipples pebble as if I can feel his eyes caressing my skin. I would give anything to be able to see his eyes now.

Then he's leaning toward me, closer and closer, until I involuntarily hold my breath. His lips are inches from my ear when he finally speaks.

"I hope you and your *friend* enjoy the show. See you later, Firebird."

He leans back, and I suck in a harsh breath. He's grinning, obviously enjoying how he's unsettled me. Then he takes a few steps backward before finally turning around and giving me his back.

"Hey," I say loudly. He stops walking and glances over his shoulder. "It's my natural color."

He smirks, then disappears into the crowd, leaving me bereft and dazedly staring after him.

Someone bumps into me, jostling me and sloshing Becket's beer onto my hand. They apologize, but I don't acknowledge them. I'm grateful, actually. It's brought me back to reality.

Because...what the actual fuck was that?

The more I run the encounter with Torren through my head, the more I'm convinced it was a figment of my imagination. Far too bizarre to be reality.

I mentally berate myself as I head to the soda can guitar.

Did I really say *does the carpet match the drapes* to Torren fucking King? Way to make it awkward. He was probably just trying to compliment me, and I had to go and make it weird. My hair color *is* unusual. It's not uncommon for strangers to comment on it. Usually, old ladies at the supermarket or drunk girls in bar bathrooms. Definitely *not* hot rock stars I'm obsessed with. But still.

What the fuck.

By the time I make it back to the guitar statue, it takes Becket taking his beer from my hand before I finally pull myself out of my fanatical spiral.

"What took you so long?" Becket asks, and my cheeks heat with guilt I don't deserve to feel. I didn't do anything wrong. I didn't even flirt. It was just a casual conversation with a guy I've masturbated to. Nothing at all to feel guilty about.

"The drink line was long." I look away and take a sip of my own beer. "What food did you get?"

He holds out a triangular cardboard box, and I groan.

"I said no pizza, Beck. I'm sick of pizza."

He laughs. "We'll get you your kababs tomorrow. This pizza smelled too good to pass up."

I roll my eyes and take the slice, mumbling a half-hearted thanks as he throws his arm around my shoulder and steers me toward the main stage.

"Ezra," I say with a laugh as soon as my eyes land on him. "What in the hell are you wearing? It's ninety degrees!"

Ezra grins and spins with his arms spread wide to show off a shiny black fur coat that falls to mid-shin.

"Fire, right? It's *faux*."

"Fire as in you gotta be sweatin' your ass off," Rocky says with a laugh. "You're gonna reek, bro. Gonna smell like an old shag carpet soaked in beer and BO."

Ezra grabs Rocky in a headlock before wrapping them both in the ridiculous *faux* fur coat. Rocky gags, Ezra grunts and hunches over, then Rock falls to the ground, spitting profanities at Ezra before scrambling back toward him. I shake my head with a sigh. They're idiots. Pike, Becket, and I continue on our way to find a spot in front of the main stage and leave the other two to brawl in the dirt behind us.

"You look so hot, Cal." Becket puts his hands on my hips and tugs me into his body once we've found a suitable spot to watch the show.

I smile up at him and will myself to absorb the compliment in the way I would have yesterday, but my heart doesn't sputter, and my cheeks don't flush.

"Thanks, Beck."

I glance toward the stage while taking a subtle step out of his hold. I take a bite of my now cold pizza and sway my body to the music. The band is good. I'm familiar with them, but not well enough to know many of their lyrics. That doesn't stop me from enjoying the experience, though. I let the excitement of the crowd energize me. I jump when they jump, clap when they clap. At one point, Ezra grabs my hand and pulls me into a dance, spinning me quickly before dipping my body so low to the ground that I let out a shriek of laughter. He doesn't drop me, thankfully.

I'm able to sing along on a few choruses, and by the time the band's set is over, I'm determined to buy their album as soon as the festival is over and we're back to reality. That's the power of a good live show. A good live show can turn even the toughest critic into a fan.

I'm laughing along with the guys, sipping on my third drink, when something like ice licks up the base of my spine, causing the sticky sweat on the back of my neck to turn cold. I glance at the people on either side of me, all in various states of intoxication, but no one seems to be paying attention to me. I do a slow spin, careful not to irritate my own mild high, and just as I'm completing the circle, my eyes find him through the sea of bodies.

His are on me.

Torren is still wearing those aviator sunglasses even though it's dark now, but I know he's looking at me. When I furrow my brow in question, those full lips tip into an almost imperceptible smirk, and he nods. I nod back, and his smirk grows. He jerks his head to the side, giving me what I think is a *come here* gesture, and I purse my lips.

He reaches into his pocket and pulls out a silver cigarette case, then plucks out one and puts it between his lips. My eyes fixate on the silver rings adorning his long, tattooed fingers as he strikes a match and lights the cigarette. He takes a drag, puts the case back in his pocket, and raises his hand in my direction.

Then, in a gesture that I swear I can feel caressing my skin, he crooks his finger at me, and like I'm under a spell, my feet carry me toward him.

10

CALLIE

PAST, ArtFusion Day One

"WHERE YOU GOIN'?"

I don't take my eyes off Torren as I throw an answer at Becket over my shoulder.

"Getting another drink. Be right back."

One of them shouts a drink order at me, but I don't hear it. All my senses have zeroed in on Torren King as I push my way through the crowd of people. I don't want to lose the eye contact I know I have. I don't want him to disappear in a cloud of cigarette smoke.

When I'm ten feet from him, he turns on his heel and starts walking away. I follow. I follow him all the way to the edge of the park until we're in an empty pavilion of picnic tables. There's no one here. Everyone is either on the lawn for the headlining band or in one of the various arts and culture tents. When he turns back to face me, I stop in my tracks, leaving some space between us so I have room to breathe.

"Your friends?" he asks, and I nod.

"Yeah."

"Who was the drink for?"

"The blond in the shorts."

Torren lets out a low laugh, and it serves as a sever to the weird hold he'd had on me.

"Is that funny to you?"

He shrugs. "Didn't strike me as your type."

I prop a hand on my hip. "You don't know me. You don't know my type."

"Don't I?" he says with a grin, and I scoff.

"What do you want, Torren King?"

"Nothing. Just to talk."

"I'm not a Heartless groupie."

The grin doesn't leave his face as he shakes his head. "Didn't think you were."

"Do you always speak in fragments?"

My annoyance is clear as I look him over. My annoyance *and* my attraction. The fragments irritate me as much as they intrigue me. They fit the vibe he gives off. Like he's too cool to waste words. Like too many would inhibit the mystery surrounding him, lifting the veil to reveal the man beneath. My curiosity about seeing that man is too great to ignore.

"I can speak in full sentences, if you prefer," he says after a moment.

"I prefer."

"How are you enjoying the show?"

I roll my eyes. "I'm missing the band I wanted to see actually. Are you done?"

"You can go back if you want to. You don't have to stay here with me."

The last two words—*with me*—are like railroad spikes drilling my feet into the ground. I don't care about the band. I don't care about anything except staying right here with Torren King.

When I don't move, he does, closing the ten feet of space between us. He doesn't speak. He just keeps his face trained on mine. It's unnerving. Once again, I'm forced to look at my reflection in his mirrored sunglasses. My lipstick is dulled from the beers and greasy pizza. My eyeliner is smudged from the sweat. My hair is stuck to my neck. My red-feathered headpiece is still perfect, though, and my body glitter shimmers, drawing attention to my collarbone and cleavage, highlighting every inhale and exhale.

"Take off your sunglasses," I tell him, and he doesn't hesitate.

His long fingers remove the sunglasses slowly before hanging them on the collar of his shirt, and when he makes eye contact with me, my heart skips. Despite his dilated pupils, I can still see the glow of his irises. His eyes are so *green*. A different green than mine. Like emeralds instead of moss. Ethereal instead of earthy.

"Are you high?"

He tilts his head to the side. "Isn't everyone?"

I don't answer. I suppose everyone is. I've only had a few hits of a joint, but I'm definitely not sober.

"How are you here without swarms of adoring fans?"

He shrugs. "I don't usually draw much attention on my own."

I know what he's implying. Sav is the one who comes with the media frenzy and the fan mobs. Torren is popular, sure, but he's not the one people lose their minds over. Not most people, anyway. I might be a different story.

I should ask him about Sav. Ask where she is. Ask why he's not with her. I should, but I don't. I don't ask for the same reason I didn't correct him when he called Becket my *friend*, and the thrill of being in Torren's presence is enough to drown out any guilt I might feel from omitting the truth.

Sav and Torren are probably broken up...*again*. I saw the slap. I know the rumors about their relationship. As for Becket and me, we're not dating. Not really. We make out. We fool around. We're, in Becket's own words, *keeping it casual*. We *were* probably going to have sex for the first time tonight, but he's not my *boyfriend*. I'm drilling that fact into my head when Torren speaks.

"You want to go back to my bus?"

"No."

The answer comes out almost before he finishes the question, and he grins like he finds me entertaining. Almost like he expected my answer. He isn't disappointed at all. I scowl.

"I'm not going anywhere alone with you."

"You're alone with me now."

Any retort dies on my tongue, so I raise a challenging brow instead. He laughs, causing chills to skitter over my skin despite the heat, and then he shakes his head.

"I'm kidding. I just don't want to push my luck with the crowd. I want to get to know you without the threat of fanfare."

I open my mouth once more, to say I don't even know what, when my phone buzzes in my back pocket. I pull it out and look down at the screen.

BECK

Where you at? I'm in the beer line.

Nerves claw at my throat, suddenly protective of whatever weird bubble I've found myself in with Torren. I don't want it popped yet. I don't want to be the reason his cover is blown. I flick my eyes to the man in question to find him studying me intently.

"Your *friend*?"

I don't answer him. I type out a quick text to Becket, trying my best to ignore the way Torren's eyes make my heart quicken, mixing with my nerves and making me feel dizzy.

ME

Found a friend from high school. Be back later.

I've resolved to following Torren to his bus despite my earlier refusal. I shove down the niggling knowledge that it could be a very bad idea. Lust and curiosity suffocating every ounce of logical thought.

I put my phone away and look back at Torren. I'm about to tell him to lead the way when he shoves his hands in his pockets and straightens his back. I'm stunned a bit at how tall he is when he's not sporting his cool kid slouch.

"I'll let you get back to your friend. But if you care, I'll be in Picasso tomorrow night at ten."

Picasso is one of the activity tents dedicated to the arts. Every tent has a different name, and a different itinerary for the week.

"That's during tomorrow's headliner," I say, the statement coming out slowly, betraying the interest I've been trying to hide.

"It is."

"Are you going to tell me what you'll be doing there?"

He smirks. "Waiting for you."

He turns on his heel, and once again I stare at his retreating back, watching him leave and feeling like something I was gripping so tightly has slipped through my fingers.

"Why?" I call out, making him turn back around.

"Does it matter?"

"It matters to me."

The silence stretches between us, and the longer I wait, the further down my heart sinks in my chest. I didn't realize how much it mattered until I said the words. Am I just an opportunity? Was I simply in the right place at the right time to catch his eye? Or is it something more strategic—a ploy to make sure I don't go to the tabloids about Sav's slap?

Everyone wants to be special. No one wants to feel like just another warm body to be used. Even now, standing in front of this gorgeous rock star I've been obsessed with for years in a scenario most people would kill for, I want it to be more than it probably is.

If he says there's no particular reason, I won't go.

If I don't like what he says, I won't go.

I won't subject myself to any situation that will leave me feeling lesser. I have standards. I have self-respect. I won't let him turn me into just another Heartless groupie, no matter how beautiful or tempting or mysterious he is.

Resisting the urge to fidget with my feather skirt, I stand my ground instead. I don't take my eyes off him. I will him to tell me the truth. To tell me something compelling enough to make me meet him tomorrow night.

Then his lips curve slightly, slowly, into the kind of suggestive smirk I feel all the way to my toes.

"You intrigue me, Firebird," he says finally, his voice a sensual rasp. "And I think I might be a bit of a pyro."

I watch him turn to leave once more, and this time I don't stop him. I think about what he said the whole walk back to the tent.

You intrigue me, Firebird.

I might be a bit of a pyro.

It's corny, yes, but it's not *not* compelling. Having Torren King say that I intrigue him does more things to my insides than Becket calling me hot today, and I can't deny that.

And the nickname. Fuck. I'm a sucker for a good nickname.

I take out my phone and shoot a text to Becket. I tell him I'm going to bed because I have a headache and ask that he not wake me when he gets back to the tent. He sends back "K," and I can practically hear the disappointment emanating from the phone screen. Becket thought we were going to have sex tonight. Hell, I thought we were going to have sex tonight.

But now, instead of dwelling on the fact that my desire to sleep with Becket has dissipated like cigarette smoke into the hot night air, I'm pulling up the festival app and searching the schedule for tomorrow night in art tent Picasso.

When my eyes find it on the itinerary, my breath lodges in my throat and my nipples pebble. *Latex Body Painting.*

Fuck it.

Looks like I'll be meeting a rock star at 10:00 p.m. tomorrow night after all.

11

TORREN

CALLIE.

She goes by Callie.

Days later, and I still can't quite believe it.

I know her. I *know* I know her. That's one of the most frustrating things about getting sober. You realize just how much of your life was lost to the drugs. Whole chunks of time are black, and the memories that did manage to stick are distorted and hazy. I can't quite tell what's real and what's not.

But I know Callie James. I can feel it. I just don't know how.

The chances of her being a groupie are slim, given how much she fucking dislikes me. Was she at a party where I got into a fight? Did I fuck up her boyfriend?

A chill skates down my spine...

What if it was Sean? Could he have...?

No. It couldn't have been that. We kicked his ass out of the band before he could do any real damage, and while it's no secret that he's my brother, I'd have remembered something like that.

No. Sean can't be the connection.

It must be something else.

I turn down Callie's street at 8:00 a.m., revving the engine of my black sports car louder than necessary. My music is blaring as well, the bass turned up to obnoxious levels.

Anything to draw attention. The more nosy neighbors I intrigue, the better.

When I pull up to the curb of her apartment building, both Damon and I climb out. I stand beside the car for a moment and check my phone. I loiter. Three minutes. Then five minutes. Then I walk into the apartment building, leaving Damon to stand beside my car.

I consider the elevator, but it resembles a microwave from the 1960s, so I take the stairs. When I knock on the door, it swings open immediately, revealing a girl around fifteen. As soon as she sees me, her jaw drops, and she lets out a tiny squeak.

"Oh my god, she wasn't lying."

I smile. "She was not lying."

The girl's hair is a lighter shade of red than Callie's—closer to strawberry-blond—but her eyes are the same shade of green.

"You must be Callie's sister. I'm Torren."

"I'm Glory."

She stands in the doorway and blinks up at me, staring slack-jawed in shock.

"Can I come in?"

"Yes." She nods, but she doesn't move, so I gently step past her and into the living room.

When I do, I hear heated whispers coming from a room down a short hallway. I glance toward it and see Callie's back. She's standing half inside a room, and from the stiffness in her spine, I can tell this discussion isn't going the way she'd wanted it to go.

"Mom's pissed."

I bring my attention to Glory, and she shrugs.

"She doesn't want Callie to run off again. Thinks she's being irrational and stupid, which, *duh*."

"Again?"

"Yup."

I glance at her. "Care to elaborate?"

She pops her hand on her hip and arches a brow. "I don't know you. If she wants to tell you, she will."

"Okay," I say with a laugh. "Noted."

She huffs and walks away, apparently no longer dumbstruck by my presence, and leaves me standing awkwardly in her living room.

I can't help but look around at the small space. An older model television sits on a stand in the corner. A couch that has seen better days covers the wall to the left. There is a small dining table to my left full of papers, and my eyes scan it on impulse. I see what looks like bills. Electric. Sewer. Internet. Something that I'm pretty sure is an insurance company. I look away, not wanting to invade the family's privacy any more than I already have.

My eyes find a large dry-erase calendar stuck to the fridge in the kitchen. *Callie Work* is scribbled on nearly every day in red marker. *Glory Work* on a few other days in blue. I look away from that, too, but then my attention goes back to it. From the looks of the calendar, Callie works a lot. Two weeks in a row with no days off, with several days adding *DOUBLE* next to her name.

She really wasn't exaggerating when she said she wasn't in the position to turn down my offer. Part of me feels bad, but another more selfish part feels relieved.

When Callie steps out of the bedroom and starts walking to the living room, her face is twisted with disappointment, and she looks even more exhausted than she did when I saw her a few days ago. I didn't think that was possible. She stops in her tracks when she sees me and grimaces.

"You're early."

I check my watch. "By ten minutes," I say. "But I've been here for five, so fifteen minutes early, I guess."

She jerks out a nod and steps out of the hallway, toting a carry-on suitcase behind her.

"Let's go then." She turns back to the hallway. "Mom, I'm leaving. Just... Just call me, okay?"

Callie waits for a response, but when one doesn't come, she walks reluctantly to the door. Just before we step into the hallway, her sister comes running back into the living room with her dog trailing behind her. She throws her arms around Callie's neck in a hug, and Callie must be shocked because it takes her a moment to return the gesture.

They hug for a long time, and Glory whispers something into Callie's ear before they finally release one another.

"Be good," Callie says, and her sister nods.

"You, too. Call soon, okay?"

"I'll call every day."

After one last sad goodbye and a pat on the dog's head, Callie follows me out the door and down the stairs.

"That didn't seem to go well," I say to her, and she laughs.

"Yeah."

I glance over my shoulder at her. She has sunglasses on, so I can't see those light-green eyes of hers, but her body language is all I need to see to know she is less than thrilled to be leaving with me. I consider just asking her—just coming right out and saying it—but I decide against it. Now is not the time, and given just how blank my memory is surrounding her, it's a conversation that's probably best had in private after the tension between us has calmed a little. And it has to calm; otherwise, no one is going to believe this relationship is real.

Before stepping out of the stairwell, I stop and turn to face her.

"Okay, there will probably be some photographers outside," I warn her, and her eyes flare.

"Already?"

"Already. You think you can act a little more excited to be with me?"

She gives me an extremely unbelievable smile, and I can't help but laugh.

"Sure. They'll buy that," I say sarcastically. "Okay, new plan. Let me hold your hand and then y—"

"Hold your hand?" Her question is one of apprehension, and I nod slowly.

"Yeah, Callie. We're *dating*, remember? We'll be touching a lot more than that—"

"I said no sex," she whispers at me.

"Right, no sex. But touching. Hand-holding. Embracing."

When her face pales, I frown and step toward her. I lower my voice so only she can hear. "Are you sure you're up for this? We can stop it. We can call it off."

The silence stretches and my nerves stir in my chest before she finally speaks.

"I'm up for it." Then she's reaching for my hand and lacing her fingers with mine. The contact sends a flare of heat up my arm. "Let's just get it over with."

I nod and force a smile. "Right."

Because *Let's just get it over with* is exactly what I want to hear from my girlfriend, fake or not.

Callie's hand tightens around mine the moment we step out of the building and are met with the shouts of three paparazzi with cameras. I expected it—it's why I made such a scene when I got here—but Callie obviously hates the attention.

I lead her to the car where Damon already has the passenger door open, then I help her in and shut the door behind her. Damon takes her suitcase and puts it in the trunk, then he and I are both climbing into the car and driving away. Once we turn the corner, Callie lets out a slow breath.

"Will that ever get easier?"

"You kind of get used to it," I tell her honestly.

I don't tell her it will only get worse once we're on tour and word has spread that she's with me. Sure, the stalker will hopefully disappear, but the media will be relentless for a while.

"Your mom seemed angry," I say, changing the subject. "I could tell you were arguing when I arrived."

Callie rests her head on the seatback and sighs.

"Well, I'm not allowed to tell her the truth, so of course she's going to be pissed that I'm ditching my family to go on tour with some arrogant rock star with a bad reputation."

"Ouch," I say with a laugh. "Don't hold back. Let me know exactly how you feel about your *boyfriend*."

"Sorry, King. Her words, not mine."

"But you agree?"

She shrugs. "If it looks like a duck and quacks like a duck, it's probably an arrogant rock star with a bad reputation."

Well. These next three months should be easy. Assuming we make it that far.

I won't lie—I find the idea of a relationship with Callie kind of thrilling, even if it is fake. I need to unpuzzle my memory of her, and something about the fire in her, about the way she seems to absolutely despise me, has me intrigued beyond what's reasonable.

She's not falling at my feet. She's not throwing herself at me, which tells me she's also not trying to get on my good side or butter me up to use me. *I* approached *her* for this arrangement, and she agreed out of necessity, not some hero-worship obsession.

I like it. It's refreshing in a way I've never experienced. It's a nice change of pace from what I've come to expect from most people. With this level of fame and money, it's hard to find anyone who isn't clambering over themselves to kiss my ass. I loved it at first. Now I find it exhausting.

I can't help but smile, and I have to swallow back the urge to laugh at myself. I'm so over the fame that the idea of a fake relationship with a woman who seems to hate my guts has me more excited than I've been in a long time.

I should probably talk about this on Therapy Thursday, but I have a feeling I know what my therapist will say.

I like Callie's dislike of me because if she can't stand me, that means we're not at risk of fooling ourselves into thinking this arrangement is something it's not. We won't pretend it's more than it is. She won't take advantage of me. I won't fall in love with someone who's unavailable, and the only thing that matters in my life will be protected: the band.

If Calla Lily James hates me, I'm safe, as long as she can pretend like she likes me in front of the cameras. If she hates me, I won't be in danger of repeating recent history.

"What did you tell her?" I ask, breaking the silence we'd fallen into. Callie jumps slightly in the passenger seat. "Sorry if I startled you."

She shakes her head and stifles a yawn.

"It's fine. I told her I met you a couple weeks ago, and we've stayed in touch. That I like you, and I've decided to go on tour with you."

"She believed it?"

"Yeah, I guess. She was angry and hurt. I think maybe that clouded her ability to really question it."

I glance at her quickly before looking back at the road. Her eyes are shielded behind sunglasses, but I have a feeling they're closed.

"How did you explain the first check?"

"I didn't. I just deposited it into her account." She brings her hands to her head and presses on her temples. "I'll deal with that when she notices. If she talks to me again."

"I'm sorry this is causing you so much stress," I say quietly, and Callie scoffs.

"As long as it helps Sav Loveless, right?"

I'm surprised by the bite in her tone, but I don't respond. I focus on driving, and she says nothing else until we're pulling up to Sav's house where the tour buses are parked out front on the curb. We drive past the crowd of reporters and through Sav's wrought-iron gate. When I park in her circle driveway, Callie is alert and peering out the window.

"This is Sav's house. Everyone else is already here. We'll be getting on the road soon."

Callie nods and takes a deep breath. "Any more public appearances today?"

"Hammond wants us to pose for some pictures that he'll release to the media, and then we're going to have to walk past the crowd out front to get on the bus, but after that, you're free for a bit."

We fall back into silence as she continues to stare out the window at Sav's house. Damon hasn't said a word from the back seat the whole drive, but I can see him check his watch in my periphery. We need to get moving.

"Okay. I can do this," Callie says suddenly, then she opens the door and climbs out.

I follow, then round the car to stand next to her.

"Ready?"

She shakes her head. "No. But I have to be anyway. Might as well just rip the Band-Aid off."

"Get it over with, yeah?"

"Yep."

"Right. Well...this way."

I push past her and walk into the house. She sighs behind me. I can picture the way her brows are probably knitted in a frown right now, but she follows. Her footsteps sound heavy, tired. She makes no attempt to hide her reluctance, but I don't mind.

The more she dislikes me, the better. It's safer that way.

12

CALLIE

THE INSIDE of Sav Loveless's house is surprisingly understated.

Not at all what I expected for a spoiled rock star. Nothing looks overly lavish or dramatic. Nothing screams opulence or wealth. It's homey. Comfortable. It makes me dislike her more because it's exactly the way I'd want my own home to feel if I could ever afford to own a house.

The inside is a hive of activity. There are security guards moving about, lugging suitcases out a side door. Wade Hammond, the manager, is barking into a phone and scrolling on a tablet, and Sav and Mabel are nowhere to be found. Jonah, however, is digging through a refrigerator on the far side of the open-concept floor plan and my eyes lock on him. Something about seeing a rock star bent over with his head in a kitchen appliance helps to calm my nerves a little.

I didn't pay much attention to Jonah when I was at Torren's apartment, but if he knew who I was, he didn't let it show. He was never on my radar before. It makes sense that I also wouldn't be on his. For some reason, the threat of Jonah remembering me seems less daunting than Torren. Maybe it's because it feels less likely. Or maybe it's because, if Jonah remembers, the worst thing I'd be is embarrassed. Not humiliated and heartbroken.

Oddly enough, Jonah feels like safe, neutral territory, and my feet lead me to him without prompting. He's closing the fridge when I step up beside him, and he turns to look at me. He nods but says nothing, then hands me a bottle of water before opening the fridge again and pulling out a new one.

"Thanks," I say, then I uncap the bottle and take a drink without taking my eyes off him. He does the same.

He swallows, and my eyes fall to his Adam's apple. The anatomical heart tattooed on his throat bobs with the motion, almost like it's beating. I flick my eyes back to his to find him watching me. Without taking his eyes off mine, he brings the bottle back to his lips as if he knows what I was thinking. I drop my eyes back to his throat and he proceeds to take several more swallows of water. My eyebrows rise in appreciation. The heart definitely looks like it's beating.

"Cool," I say.

He doesn't respond.

I find Jonah easier to look at than Torren, so I do it openly. I run my eyes over his face. I study his hair—long and bleached blond—and his build—toned and lean. I drop my gaze down his body, then back up, noting the faded jeans and vintage-looking band T-shirt.

He doesn't move. He keeps his face blank but lets me look.

Briefly, I wonder if I'm being rude, but something tells me he doesn't mind. I'm about to spend three months in very close quarters with Torren. I can only assume Jonah will be around constantly, and I need to know who he is to feel comfortable.

I'm ashamed to say I never paid much attention to Jonah before now. I don't have his tattoos memorized the way I do Torren's. I didn't even know his eyes were such a striking blue until right now.

He's got a small hoop in his eyebrow, a small hoop in his nose, and a watch on his wrist with a faded leather band, but the rest of his accessories are inked onto his skin. He's similar to Torren in that way. No added frills because they're basically walking canvases.

"Verdict?" he asks, raising his eyebrow. I purse my lips.

"Jury is still out."

He nods. "Welcome to the band, Callie."

I don't know what to say to that, so I say nothing. Then Hammond steps up next to me and breaks whatever silent stare off Jonah and I have fallen into.

"Miss James—"

"Callie."

"Callie. If you wouldn't mind, we'd like to get some shots of you and Torren outside."

I narrow my eyes at Hammond. "Are these to leak to the press?"

"They are."

I take a deep breath and glance at Jonah. He's not looking at me anymore, suddenly engrossed in something on his phone. I don't know why I thought he might save me from this task—it is my new job, after all, and I'm nothing if not a model employee.

"Okay," I say with a nod. "Lead the way."

I follow Hammond as he leads me back out the front door and into the circle driveway. Torren's leaning on the rear of his car, his hands in his pockets and his focus on the ground. When he hears us coming, though, he looks up. He's wearing his sunglasses, but I feel his attention on me, and my stomach flips. I can't stop the scowl that follows. Goddamn stomach. Stupid nervous flips. Then Torren arches a brow, and I narrow my eyes.

"What?"

"You're going to have to work on that expression every time you see me. No one's going to believe we're dating if you always look like you want to stab me in the throat."

I roll my eyes, then force a smile. From the look on his face, he's not impressed, so I try again. I bat my eyelashes and saunter up to him, smiling sweetly. He doesn't move from where he's leaning on the car, and he doesn't take his hands out of his pockets. When I've reached him, I place my hands on his chest and look at my reflection in his mirrored sunglasses.

"How's this, boss?"

He cocks his head slightly to the side. "Boss?"

"I'm employed by you, am I not? This is a professional relationship; therefore, you are my boss."

"Hmm."

He takes his hands out of his pockets and pushes his sunglasses to the top of his head, then pins me in place with his gaze. I was doing so well until he had to go and bust out those green eyes. They're lethal.

I force a swallow as he bounces his eyes between mine. When he drops his attention to my lips, I wet them on impulse, and the small smirk he gives me makes my breath hitch. I can't look away. I find myself curling my fingers into his shirt, pressing my palms more firmly into the fabric so I can soak up the warmth from his skin underneath. My heart is beating fast in my chest, but his feels so steady. So calm.

He brings his hand to my face, brushing my hair behind my ear, and then his lips follow.

"That's better." My eyes fall shut as his breath tickles the shell of my ear. "That's so much better, Calla Lily."

I release a shuddering breath as he drags his knuckles over my jaw and then tilts my chin up so he can press a soft kiss to my neck. I stifle a whimper, but I can't hide the way my body shivers. Suddenly, I find myself imagining glitter and music. I smell smoke and paint. I feel four years younger and just as naïve. When he presses another kiss below my ear, the whimper I swallowed moments earlier returns with bolstered determination, and I can't fight it.

"That's it. You do it just like that, and we'll have everyone fooled."

I snap my eyes open, reality crashing over me like a tidal wave. It was a show. It was all a show, and fuck me, but my heart sinks. I stiffen, and then I hear a sigh. When I look toward the sound, I find Hammond staring at his phone.

"We got a few good ones, until you lost it," he grumbles. "Let's get one with a kiss, and then we'll be done."

My eyes widen and jump back to Torren. He must be just as against the idea as I am because he shakes his head and addresses Hammond without looking away from me.

"No kiss."

"An almost kiss, then."

Torren raises his eyebrows, nonverbally asking for my consent, so I shrug. He nods. "We can do an almost kiss."

"Make it believable, please," Hammond says, and I shoot him a glare.

"I'm not an actress, and I'm not an escort. If how I'm doing it isn't good enough for you, go find one of those."

Hammond blinks at me like he's waiting out a tantrum. I realize that's probably how I look when Glory is in one of her moods, and that pisses me off. Hammond says nothing—he just blinks and waits—so I roll my eyes and turn back to Torren.

"Fine. Let's just get it over with."

He nods curtly. "Close your eyes. It might be easier for you."

I obey immediately. It is easier, and I'm grateful he suggested it. Anything to not have to look into those green orbs of sorcery again.

"I'm going to put my hand around your neck, okay?"

I nod, and soon his warm hand is cupped lightly on the side of my neck, his calloused fingers teasing the hairline at my nape.

"Can you put your hands on my chest like you had them before?"

I do as he asks, but I don't curl my fingers into his shirt again. My hands hover more than anything else, but he doesn't say anything to correct me. I take a deep breath through my nose and immediately regret it. Leather and tobacco and ginger. Why does he have to smell so good?

"Can you tilt your head to the left for me?" I do as he asks, and I feel his thumb lightly caress my jaw. "Good. Can you part your lips for me just a little? Yeah, just like that. Now I'm going to lean in really close, okay?"

"Okay," I whisper, and then he's invading my space.

He closes the distance, shading me from the sun and grazing his nose against mine. I feel his mouth centimeters from my mouth. His breath tickles my lips as he inhales and exhales. His thumb once again rubs over my jaw, and chill bumps rise on my arms.

His proximity is unnerving. I don't know if I want to close the small distance between us and press my lips to his, or if I want to take three giant steps backward and then bolt away, but luckily, he makes the decision for me.

Too soon, he leans back, exposing my face to the sun and giving me space to breathe once more. I open my eyes and blink a few times, avoiding Torren's face, and then the person watching us from the front stoop grabs my attention. Sav Loveless.

She's standing with her arms crossed and her head tilted slightly to the side as she surveys me. She doesn't have to take off her sunglasses for me to know she's sizing me up. It makes me feel small. It makes me jealous, too. I can't help but feel like she's pissed that I've had this moment with Torren. She knows it's fake. She knows it's for her benefit. But still...

The way she's staring at me...

Were the rumors about their relationship *just* rumors?

I narrow my eyes at her, a silent, subtle warning, and then I look back at Hammond. I bypass Torren entirely.

"How was that?" I ask Hammond, my voice cracking a little.

Hammond is quiet for a moment as he studies his phone, and then he nods once.

"It will work. Time to go."

Hammond turns on his heel and disappears down the driveway. When I glance back at the front porch, Sav is gone, so I face Torren once more.

"Now what?"

"Now we go on tour. We'll hold hands. I'll walk you to Sav and Mabel's bus. We'll do a lovey goodbye for the cameras—don't worry, no kissing—and then we'll part ways."

I nod twice, repeating over and over in my head that this is a job. This band employed me. I agreed to do this for my family, and I need to succeed. I stick my hand out toward him and wiggle my fingers.

"C'mon. Let's—"

"Just get this over with?"

I give him a ghost of a smile. "Yep."

Torren laces his fingers through mine and leads me down the driveway.

"Your suitcase has already been brought to the bus, along with some other things. The big bedroom is set up for you, too. You should be all set until we get to Glendale, where we move into our hotel suites. We're in Glendale for four nights, and then—"

"You're in Vegas for four nights. Then Arlington, Texas, then Houston."

"You memorized the tour schedule?"

"Of course. I'm here for three months. You expected me to go into this totally blind?"

He huffs out a small laugh, and I see him shake his head in my periphery. "I don't know what I expected, honestly."

"I do. Someone who can fake it well enough for the cameras."

I feel him shrug. "Yeah. I guess that was part of it."

I roll my eyes. That was *all* of it, but he won't say it out loud and offend me. To him, I'm a means to an end. This is a business agreement. This is a job. Nothing more.

I'm basically an independent contractor.

I frown to myself.

I'm basically a high-end escort but without the sex.

I want to groan, but I bite my tongue. I signed up for this. It might be a gigantic hit to my self-respect, but it's for a good cause. Eighty thousand good causes, technically.

The bout of self-loathing doesn't last, thankfully. When I see the mob of paparazzi across the street from Sav's gate, all thoughts of everything else are forgotten. I squeeze Torren's hand on instinct, and he squeezes back, then releases my hand and moves his to the small of my back.

"I got you, Callie. Just keep your head down and I'll guide you. You don't have to look at them or talk to them, okay?"

"Kay."

"Put your arm around my waist. It looks more natural."

I do as he says. I wrap my arm around his waist and keep my eyes on the ground. I trust him to lead me to the tour bus, and he does. Once we're there, he spins me slowly and backs me up against the side of the bus, then props his forearm above my head. He leans into my space once more, the closeness no easier to handle than earlier. God, I hope this gets easier.

"I'm going to make it look like I'm saying goodbye to my girlfriend," he whispers, reaching up to trail his knuckle over my jaw. "Loosen up. Put your hands on me. You need to look like you're in love with me."

"I'm not a miracle worker," I grumble, but reluctantly, I place my hands on his waist and try not to think about the abs I know he's hiding under his shirt. He smiles.

"Good." He hooks his index finger under my chin and lifts my face up so I'm looking into his eyes. "Tilt your head to the left, and I'm going to move in to kiss your cheek. Don't flinch."

I frown in his direction but once more do as he says. This time, I hold my breath when he closes in on me. His soft, full lips land on my cheekbone softly, and then they linger. He nuzzles me, then kisses me again. When my heart starts to race and I can't hold my breath any longer, I clear my throat.

"That's enough," I say, and I feel his lips stretch across my skin into a small smile. When he finally releases me, though, the smile is gone.

"I'll see you in a few hours, Calla Lily."

I sigh. "It's Callie."

He takes two steps backward, then gives me a sexy wink that once again initiates vertigo-inducing déjà vu. *It's for the cameras*, I remind myself. It's all for show.

"See you in a few hours, *Callie*. I'll be waiting for you."

13

TORREN

"How was the ride?"

Callie whips her head in my direction, shock covering her features as if she's surprised to see me. The expression is wiped away within seconds, though, and she takes the last few steps off the bus and lands on the pavement beside me.

I take her suitcase with one hand and sling my other arm around her shoulder. She stiffens briefly before reluctantly relaxing into my hold. Once she does, I can't help but notice how perfectly she fits into my side, like our bodies are compatible puzzle pieces. Her curves fit my edges, and for a second, I want to hold her against me more tightly.

The thought makes me put more distance between us.

"Fine. I slept the whole way."

"Did you get on good with the girls?"

She shrugs. "Sure. They pointed me to the bedroom, and I didn't see them again until Mabel woke me up to tell me we were here."

"I'm glad you got some rest."

She nods, but she doesn't say anything else as I guide her from the bus and into the five-star hotel with Damon following behind us. The band has stayed at the hotel several times while touring, and we always return because they have top-notch security, and they take the privacy of their guests seriously.

"The whole top floor is ours," I tell Callie. "You have your own room, but it's in a suite with Sav and Mabes. I hope that's okay."

"And if it's not?"

"Then we get you your own suite," I say pointedly, and I mean it. We're prepared to rent out another whole floor for her if we need to. "Did you happen to go through anything in your room on the bus?"

"The only thing I paid attention to was the bed."

I huff a laugh and lead her through the hotel lobby. A bellhop greets us, then the attendant at the front desk, but no one else pays us any mind. I can almost pretend I'm invisible. It's how I prefer it these days.

"Did you meet your security detail?"

"I did. Craig. He seems...*large*."

I smile to myself. Craig Walton is six-foot-seven and solid muscle. Large is putting it mildly.

"He's great at his job. He'll keep you safe."

Callie nods, but she doesn't respond. I'm sure this whole thing is overwhelming, so I don't attempt further conversation.

We round the corner and run into Jonah waiting for the elevator with his security. He greets us with a nod, and I don't miss the way his eyes linger a little longer on Callie. He waits for her to return his nod before he glances back at me.

"They went up. I stopped to smoke."

"Okay..."

Jonah's never felt the need to explain himself to me, so I get the feeling it was for Callie's benefit. Why, I don't know. I arch a questioning brow, but his face stays blank. He's always a goddamn statue—impossible to read unless he allows it.

When the elevator opens, we step inside and ride it silently to the top floor. Jonah heads to our shared suite without a word, and I walk Callie to hers.

"I'll be back in two hours to take you out," I tell her, and she glances up at me nervously.

"Take me where? Your show isn't until tomorrow night."

"A date, obviously. We have to make public appearances, remember?"

She chews on that plump bottom lip of hers, straight white teeth denting the pillowy surface, and stares at something over my shoulder. "How much PDA are we talking?"

"Nothing big. We're going to dinner. I have reservations at eight."

Her eyes go wide, and she whips them back at me. "I don't have an outfit for somewhere that requires *reservations*. You saw my apartment. You know about my jobs. Hell, I've even allowed myself to be pimped out to you, for god's sake. What makes you think I go to places with *reservations*?"

My lips twitch with the need to smile, but I don't. She's cute when she's frazzled, and I don't want to think she's cute.

"If you check the closet in your room, you should be able to find something," I tell her, and she blinks rapidly at me. Before she can open her mouth to question it, I take two steps backward. "I'll be back at seven thirty."

I turn on my heel and head to my suite, running the day over in my head. Since our little photoshoot in Sav's driveway, I keep coming back to the light, fresh way Callie smelled. Every time I successfully direct my brain to something else, it somehow manages to revert back to her scent. Like a damn dog. It's all I thought about for the six-hour bus ride. Her scent, and the soft, sexy way she felt under my hands. The way her breath hitched. The way her lips parted. She acts like she can't stand me, but her body language when I touch her says something else entirely.

I find Callie James attractive and extremely intriguing, and that's not a good thing. Attraction is harmless. I've been attracted to a lot of women. But attraction paired with intrigue? That's dangerous.

I let myself into the suite I share with Jonah and find him already smoking another cigarette on the balcony. I take out my phone and text Sav.

ME

Jo's chain smoking again.

SAV

Watch him.

ME

No shit.

I wait a few seconds for a snarky retort, but when one doesn't come, I sigh and stick my phone back in my pocket, then walk to the balcony.

"You good?" I ask as I step through the door. He doesn't look at me when he shrugs.

"Been worse."

"Not what I want to hear, Jo."

"It's what I got for you."

I sit in one of the chairs and prop my feet up on the wrought-iron table. He flicks his eyes toward me and takes a drag from his cigarette. I wait him out.

"So, Callie..." he starts, then trails off.

He doesn't say anything else, but I know what he's asking, and my immediate answer surprises me.

"No."

"No?"

I shake my head. "This is too important. I don't want to do anything to blur the lines," I explain, but there's a whispering suspicion in my head that it's not the whole reason.

I should stop there, but I don't.

"You like her?" I ask, and Jo takes another drag from his cigarette before answering.

"I could."

"Don't."

His brows rise in surprise. It's more expression than we're used to getting from him. There's a hint of jealousy in my tone that he no doubt heard. It's completely out of character for me, and I see the curiosity in his eyes.

"Because it would *blur the lines*...?" he asks, distrust lacing every word. My nostrils flare at the challenge.

"Exactly."

I stare at him, daring him to question me further, but he doesn't. Not because he feels threatened, but because he just doesn't care enough to try. Jo doesn't care about much anymore, and right now, I'm torn between letting him drop it and wishing he'd show some emotion other than indifference.

I resist the impulse to poke at him. Even anger is better than this cold detachment. I'd rather him rage out and destroy another hotel room because at least it would mean he's allowing himself to feel something. But I'm selfish, and I don't want to be studied by Jonah's keen eye. His observational skills are better than most. Even when fucked up, his ability to read people is almost scarily astute. I'd rather keep my personal thoughts to myself right now.

We slip back into silence until we're interrupted by Hammond sliding the door to the patio wide open.

"We have a problem," he grunts, and then he turns and heads back inside.

I sigh, stand, and follow him with Jonah trailing behind me. The moment I'm through the door, my defenses go on high alert. Sav, Mabel, and Sav's dog Ziggy are already sitting on the couch in the suite, and they all look like they're about to attend a funeral. Even the dog.

"What happened?" I ask, eyes lingering on Sav's solemn face. "What's wrong?"

Hammond hands me his tablet, some sleezy gossip blog pulled up on the screen. When I scan the headline, my shoulders droop.

"They're not buying it? Why the fuck not?"

Hammond takes the tablet back and answers me in the matter-of-fact way that he does.

"Because they didn't see you together for three weeks until you picked her up this morning, and she looks stiff as a board when you're near her." He pulls up a photo and shows it to me. One of me walking her from her apartment door to my car. "Frankly, she looks like she'd rather be holding hands with a giant spider than with you."

"Spiders don't have hands," Jonah chimes in, and Hammond sends him an unimpressed side-eyed glance. I'd laugh if I wasn't so pissed.

"Of course she looks uncomfortable. She was bombarded with paparazzi at eight in the morning. It took us years to get used to it."

Hammond brushes me off. "The photos I sent out will help, but the seed of doubt is planted now. We'll have to do everything we can to counteract it."

I drag my hands over my face. "Fine. The dinner tonight should help."

"There's something else," Sav says, and when I look at her, her face is full of concern. "That article was texted to me from an unmarked number."

"The stalker?"

She lifts a shoulder in a half-hearted shrug. "Who else?"

My impulse to go to her, to hold her and protect her, makes my muscles ache. For years, I was the one comforting Sav. I used to be the one she confided in, but I can't be that guy anymore. She's chosen someone else to fill that role. But where the fuck is he? I grind my teeth as Mabel rests her head on Sav's shoulder, a gesture that lessens my anxiety by a fraction.

"Mother fuck. We have got to find this guy and have him arrested."

"We will," Hammond says. "We've got people on it. But in the meantime, you've got to step it up."

"Fine. I'll step it up. We'll be more convincing. By this time tomorrow, as far as everyone in America will know, Callie James and I will be totally obsessed with one another."

"I don't like this," Sav says. "I hate this, actually."

"It doesn't really matter what you think. I'm doing what needs to be done."

Sav shakes her head with a sigh. "Just...be fucking careful, okay? Make sure you both understand what this is about."

I arch a brow. "Are you worrying about my heart now or hers, Savannah?"

"Can't it be both?"

"No. It can't be. You didn't care about my feelings before. Don't start now."

"For fuck's sake, Torren. That's not fair, and you know it. I never wanted to hurt you. I've apologized a thousand times, but I can't help how—"

"You can't change how you feel. Yeah, I get it, okay? I understand. But you need to back the fuck off. I'm a big boy. I can fucking handle this."

"Can we...like...*not* do this again?" Mabel says. "Savannah, stop handling Tor with kid gloves. He can make his own decisions, and it's the best fucking option we've got right now. And, Torren, fucking lay off her. You're acting like a jealous, heartbroken asshole, and it's starting to get old. Your relationship was over way before Levi came into the picture, and you know it. Stop ripping open old wounds."

I clamp my eyes shut and breathe through my nose. I bite my tongue on the need to defend myself against Mabel's attack. I know all of this. I know everything she's said to be true. But how can I explain it to her? I don't feel like this because I want Sav back in that way. I just want back *in*. It's been over a year. I shouldn't feel so fucking lost around her anymore. She was my best fucking friend and now she barely speaks to me.

Things were supposed to go back to normal. To how they were before. With the band. With us. With *me*. I should be fucking fixed by now, and it sure as fuck shouldn't still hurt the way it does.

"I'm done with this conversation," I say finally. "I have it handled. So if you'll excuse me, I have work to do."

14

CALLIE

My jaw drops at the sight of the closet in my room. Not only is it a walk-in fucking closet in a hotel room, but it's full of clothing, shoes, and accessories.

They must have had it in here before we arrived, and I'm just...

I'm just *shocked*.

I run my fingers along the garments hanging in the closet. I check the tags and want to vomit. Just one of these dresses could buy groceries for a month for my family. I flip over one of the black booties on the shelf and slam it back down again when I see red.

Not metaphorical red. *Actual* red.

I feel so lightheaded that I have to sit myself down on the floor for fear of passing out.

For a brief moment, I feel those warm tingles at the thought of Torren doing all of this for me, but then I shake myself back to reality. This was likely all Hammond's doing. Torren doesn't even smile at me unless it's for show. He barely looks at me unless he has to. He wouldn't have done this himself.

I wipe the frown off my face and stand back up.

I am not upset. I do not care that this wasn't a kind gesture from Torren. This is a job, and I need to stop being a sensitive child. My mom hasn't returned my calls yet, but I'm doing this for her, and she'll understand. We need this. She needs it. Glory needs it. And damn it, as much as I hate it, *I* need it.

I go back to the rack of clothing and survey it with a critical eye. I pull out a sensible dress and a pair of heels. It looks like it would work for a simple dinner date. I'll curl my hair and do my makeup, and we'll go on a staged date for the press.

How fun.

I shake my head and scold myself in the full-length mirror on the way.

"This is eighty thousand dollars, bitch. Stop pouting and do your job."

Do. Your. Job.

I grab a towel and my toiletry set, then head into the bathroom, which happens to be larger than the bedroom I share with Glory back home. I've never taken a shower while not standing in a bathtub before. This bathroom has a large, glass-walled steam shower and a giant soaker tub. It's lavish and unnecessary, but I'm thrilled. I can't wait to take a bath in that tub.

I take a longer shower than usual, simply because the water doesn't run cold after seven minutes. I wash my hair twice, burying the concern of wasting shampoo, and then I shave my legs slowly, careful not to cause any nicks. I doubt the girlfriend of a rock star would have shaving cuts on their shins.

I turn off the water once I notice my fingers starting to wrinkle, then step out and reach for a towel. It is fluffy and white—nothing like the ones we have at home—and it's unbelievably soft on my skin. When I'm dry, I use some of the hotel lotion and cover my body with it. It smells like coconut and vanilla.

I'm more relaxed than I've been in a long time when I leave the bathroom, but it doesn't last. My breath catches at the sight of Torren sitting on my bed.

"What are you doing in here?" I snap, pulling the towel tighter around my body.

He looks up from his phone slowly, his eyes staying on my face and never once straying to my exposed skin. I don't know if I should be offended at his disinterest or grateful for his respect. I end up battling with a little of both.

"We've had a change of plans."

"It couldn't have waited until I was out of the shower?"

"You *are* out of the shower."

"You know what I mean."

He sighs. "We're not doing dinner anymore." I feel a sense of relief before he snatches it away with his next words. "We're going to a club, instead."

"What? Why?"

"The press isn't buying the relationship story. They say we have no chemistry."

I snort out a laugh before I can stop myself.

"Well, that's not surprising. I told you I'm not an actress. I can't just conjure up chemistry out of thin air."

"*Well*, it's unacceptable. So tonight, we're going to a club, and we are going to give them chemistry."

"How in the hell are we going to do that?"

Torren's lips turn up into a slow smile, and he stands from my bed. He takes a step in my direction, and I instinctively step back. Then, with predatory calm and a roguish smirk, he stalks toward me. My heart beats faster with each foot of distance he covers until he's standing before me, and I'm trapped with my back against the wall.

I bite my lower lip, and his gaze drops to my mouth. It lingers there for a moment before he looks back up. His eyes bounce between mine, those stupid fucking hypnotic green eyes, and then he's raising his hand to trace his knuckles over my jaw.

My nipples pebble. My thighs press together tightly. My eyes fall closed. Even my breathing quickens, making my towel rub against my chest with each shaky inhale and exhale.

He hums in appreciation, then drags his other hand up my arm, leaving goose bumps in its wake. He dances his fingers on my collarbone and along the edge of my towel, then slips them into my hair. He fists them, tugging my hair at the root, and I swallow down a moan.

My thighs have grown sticky. My core throbbing from his simple touch.

I tell myself I hate it, but goddamn, do I want it.

He leans closer. His chest brushes mine, and against my will, my body arches ever-so-slightly into him. His scent engulfs me, wrapping around me, permeating my towel and my skin. I might smell like him forever, and in this moment, I'd welcome it.

When his lips brush against the shell of my ear, mine part with a quiet gasp. His breath caresses my skin as he laughs softly.

"You might not like *me*, Callie, but you like *this*."

"Get over yourself, King. I can't stand you."

He smirks. My forced bravado is weak, and I can tell he sees right through me. My fingers tighten in my towel, and I'm suddenly grateful that I'm in *only* a towel. If my hands weren't occupied with keeping it up, they'd probably be all over Torren.

He laughs again, pressing his lips to my neck, then lays his palm on my chest, just above my racing heart.

"You can lie all you want, but your body gives you away. You like my hands on you. You like my lips on you. You like how I touch you. You like the tease of what my body could do with your body. We don't have to conjure up chemistry. We have it. You just have to give in to it a little."

I whimper, half-frustration, half-arousal. He's right, and I hate him for it.

"No sex," I say weakly. He drags his nose over the sensitive skin at my neck.

"No sex. I won't kiss you. But I'm going to touch you, and you have to allow yourself to like it."

I nod, and he leans back, narrowing his eyes slightly at me. His gaze bounces over my face, to my shoulders, to my ears, and then he frowns just a little.

"Is that your natural hair color?"

I freeze. My heart thuds in my head as I dart my eyes back to his face. I search for something—anything—to hint that he remembers, but once again, I see nothing. I'm the only one suffering from whispers of the past. To him, I'm just another woman in a long line of women that probably spans the globe.

I don't know what to say. My voice probably wouldn't work even I did, so I nod.

His hands drop away, cold air hitting me suddenly in the absence of his body heat, and in a blink, the sensual smirk from earlier is long gone. My eyebrows scrunch in confusion before I can stop them.

"If you can't sell it, then you can go home, and we'll find someone else. I'll be back at ten. Wear something to go clubbing."

The harsh statement, the way he delivered it without feeling, lingers in the room after he leaves. How he can turn it off and on so easily shouldn't shock me. After all, I've experienced it before.

This time, though, I have to shield myself. He won't burn me again.

15

CALLIE

PAST, ArtFusion Night Two

THE GUYS THINK I'm meeting my "friend from high school."

Never mind I didn't have any friends in high school, and they know that. It still wasn't hard to get them to buy the lie. Becket is giving me the silent treatment because my "headache" derailed his plans of getting lucky. Pike is distracted by his own plans, and Rocky and Ezra are too busy bickering to question me.

Once they're gone for the evening, I rush to get ready. The body painting itinerary said to wear a swimsuit if you want to participate, but I don't have one with me, so I have to stick with a strapless bra and a pair of underwear. Aside from my Phoenix outfit, I only packed the bare necessities—nothing frilly or sexy—and I pull on a pair of cut-off jeans and a plain tank over the top. There will probably be people in bikinis; hell, there will probably be people half-naked, but I'm more comfortable clothed. Besides, I don't even know if Torren will want to participate. Maybe he just wants to observe. Maybe he wants to meet there and then go somewhere else. The fact that I really don't know what to expect makes my stomach flip with nerves.

It's okay. It's good. I'm just going to go along with whatever.

I debate makeup, then decide against it. It's hot as fuck outside, and I'll just sweat it off anyway. I don't even bother checking my reflection in the van's side mirror. If I do, it will just make me more anxious. As it is, I spend the entire walk to the art tent with my head in a spiral. I tell myself it's not a big deal, just a casual meetup with a guy I met, but my pounding heart isn't buying my lie.

This is Torren King. *The* Torren King.

I'm sneaking off to meet *the* Torren King at ArtFusion to possibly do latex body painting, and there isn't a single thing I can tell myself that will make this feel less surreal. It's not until I turn a corner and find him waiting for me, standing just out of the beam of one of the light posts, that my nerves threaten to consume me. I stop in my tracks and stare.

He doesn't see me right away. His head is tipped in shadow as he scrolls on his phone with a lit joint hanging from his pouty lips. He's got the baseball hat and sunglasses on again, and there's more scruff on his face than there was yesterday, but there's no hiding who he is. If the colorful tattoos on his arms don't give him away, the god-like aura he exudes should.

God, he's so effortlessly gorgeous that it's unfair. Tattered blue jeans and a plain black T-shirt shouldn't look this good on anyone. I fist my hands, take a deep breath, then force myself to walk toward him.

I'm just out of arm's reach when Torren looks up from his phone and finds me. His smile is immediate, and my cheeks and chest heat with a blush.

"You came."

I shrug. "I did."

He stubs out his joint, then takes his sunglasses off and hangs them on his shirt just like he did yesterday. He never breaks eye contact. It's so intense, the way he stares me down with those impossibly green eyes. I almost forget how to speak.

"Have you done this before?"

Torren tips his head toward the tent. There are already about twenty people inside. There's a woman walking around in a fully painted colorful latex bodysuit, chatting up participants and handing out foam paintbrushes. I scan my eyes over her perfect body—a canvas of blue and purple swirls that somehow hides and accentuates every dip and curve—and determine that she's almost entirely naked. She might have on some sort of thong, but it blends with the latex paint so well that I can't be sure.

I swallow past the lump in my throat and shake my head.

"No. You?"

"Yeah. A few times." He turns and walks into the tent, so I follow him. "Are you allergic to latex? Sorry. I probably should have asked you that already."

"I'm not."

"Good." He stops in front of some buckets of paint, every color of the rainbow on display, then turns a mischievous smirk on me. "You gonna let me paint you?"

The bluntness of his question catches me off guard, especially after seeing that gorgeous model of a woman all sexy and painted. I about choke on my spit. I have to clear my throat before I can force words out of my mouth.

"Why can't I paint you?"

The words come out stuttered, clumsy, but I don't miss the flash of heat in his eyes. He cocks his head to the side and sinks his white teeth into his bottom lip before speaking.

"What if we do it together? You do me, and I'll do you."

I nod, and then stand frozen as he takes off his hat, then pulls his shirt over his head. When he drops the shirt and hat to the ground, my eyes fall to his chest and my exhale lodges in my throat.

I could probably draw his tattoos from memory, but the pictures I have stored in my head are nothing compared to seeing the art up close. His biceps, shoulders, collarbones, and chest are covered in intricate, colorful designs, and I scan them like I'm completing a seek-and-find.

The skull on his right pec looks even more menacing in person, yet the red rose growing from it looks so real, I want to lean in and smell it. I find the antique record player on the side of his rib cage, and I know from an interview he did once that the music notes filtering from the horn make up the opening chords to The Hometown Heartless's first single.

My eyes drift lower, searching for the moth inked onto his pelvis, the one he told a night show host represents rebirth and new beginnings, and when I find it, I curl my hands into fists. He's fucking art. This body I've dreamed about, that I've seen only in photographs, is real and close enough for me to touch.

"I think I'd feel bad covering them up," I whisper, and when he laughs, I flick my eyes from his pelvis to his face and blush. "Sorry."

He steps closer. "Don't be. I like it when you look."

Our gazes lock and hold. My heart thuds louder in my head the longer we stare at each other. He's older. He's unattainable. He's experienced, tempting, and so very *dangerous* for me. I've exchanged only a handful of sentences with him—hell, some of them weren't even full sentences—yet here I am, reaching for the hem of my shirt so I can strip it off for him.

I've done some reckless fucking things in my nineteen years of life, but this has to be top of the list.

Part of me wants to look away, *knows* I should break eye contact and flee.

But the other part...

The other part simply *cannot*.

"Would you like me to help you?"

The words are whispered seductively as he covers my hand with his. The feel of his long, calloused fingers sends a rush of shivers up my arm and over my torso. I know I'm blushing. My breathing is shallow. I might pass out from lack of oxygen.

Torren King is touching me.

I shake my head, and he drops his hand, severing the skin-on-skin connection right before my vision fizzles at the corners. I suck in a lungful of night air, the scent of latex paint and weed and leather consuming me, and then I turn my back to him so I can pull my shirt over my head. He chuckles, and goose bumps cover my back, chest, and arms as I drop my shirt onto the ground beside his.

I turn to face the instructor and don't look at Torren again as we're given a rundown of the dos and don'ts of body painting. Someone stops by and asks if we need help, and Torren says no. He's done it before. The instructor does a double take, obviously recognizing him, but she says nothing and leaves us to begin without assistance.

"You want to go first?" he asks, and I shake my head again, my tongue still incapable of forming words. "I'm going to fix your hair."

I nod, and he smirks as he steps in front of me once more. I try my damnedest not to think about the fact that I'm currently standing in front of Torren King in nothing but cut-off shorts and a nude, strapless bra. I fail.

Gently, he removes the claw clip from my hair, and my long auburn tresses fall to my back. He puts the claw clip between his teeth, freeing both hands so he can gather my hair and twist it into a bun at the back of my head.

My eyes flutter shut the moment his fingers make contact with my scalp. His tattooed forearms frame my face, his hands sinking into my hair and caressing in a way that has me imagining bed sheets and no space between our bodies.

I'm inches from his chest. Just a hitch at the waist and I could kiss the guitar pick tattoo on his sternum.

I pray he can't see how hard my nipples have gotten. I'm so fucking grateful he doesn't know how wet he's made me just from the simplest of touches.

He takes the clip in his hand again, then tightens his grip on the hand still fisted in my hair. A small tug, just enough to sting at the root, and I have to swallow back a whimper.

"Your hair is so soft."

I say nothing. I breathe him in, eyes still closed as he makes sure every strand of my hair is safely in the bun, then he secures it with the claw clip.

"There. Now we can start."

I clear my throat. "Okay."

"First, we have to put this on you."

He holds up some aloe lotion before squirting some on his hands and rubbing them together. He doesn't ask if I want to do it myself, and I'm grateful for that. I want his hands on me so badly I might die, but I don't think I could say it out loud.

The moment his hands land on my shoulders, I suck in a quick breath.

"Cold?" he asks with a smirk.

"Yes."

"Sorry. I thought I warmed it enough."

He did. It's not cold. His touch is just more than I expected. The jolt of electricity I felt from the brief touch of our hands was nothing in comparison. He slides his palms over my chest and down my arms, then over my stomach and back. It takes all my strength not to tremble under his touch. I have to remind myself not to lock my knees.

"Do you want to keep your shorts on?" he asks, and my eyes widen.

He laughs. "You can keep them on. I didn't know if you wanted to do full body."

I bite my lip, warring over the decision for all of two seconds before shaking my head.

"You can, um...you can take them off."

God, his mischievous grin goes right to my fucking clit. It's not until his long fingers are undoing my button and pushing my shorts over the curve of my ass that I realize this could make the wetness pooling in my panties visible to him. I start to panic, but he never pulls his eyes away from mine. Not even when I'm stepping out of my shorts and kicking them to the side. Not even when he lowers himself to his knees and runs his hands up and down my calves and thighs, coating me with the aloe lotion. The eye contact almost makes it worse, my arousal heightening, my attraction to him increasing tenfold. When he finally stands and turns away, my body sags as if finally released from the force field created by his green eyes.

He grabs one of the sponge paintbrushes and smiles. "I'll try not to get paint on your bra."

I swallow roughly and decide before I can overthink it. "You can take that off, too."

He arches a brow, his nostrils flaring slightly as he inhales. "You don't have to."

"I know," I say, then I force a small laugh. It comes out a breathy blend of nerves and arousal. "But I don't want paint on my bra."

He nods slowly, then doesn't take his eyes off mine as he reaches behind my body and undoes my bra with one hand and drops it next to the rest of my clothes. Skilled and swift. It shouldn't be a turn on, but it is. My nipples pebble in the warm night air, my breasts heavy and aching.

"Do you want to do the lotion?"

I shake my head no and watch as he puts the handle of the paintbrush between his teeth and reaches for the aloe lotion. He rubs more lotion between his hands, warming it, then pauses briefly, seeking my consent again. I give him a small smile and a nod, and then he puts his hands on me once more.

I bite my lip, my body erupting in chills as his hands glide smoothly, almost respectfully, over my breasts coating my sensitive skin in the aloe lotion. He doesn't toy with me or fondle me, but I still have to swallow back a whimper when his palms pass over my peaked nipples, his calloused fingers circling them briefly before his thumbs run under the curve of my breast. I think I see his eyes fill with heat. I think his breath grows shaky. But he never takes his gaze away from mine.

When he's finished, he takes the paintbrush from his teeth and smirks.

"Ready?" His voice is a low rasp, making my heart skip and my own words come out in a strangled whisper.

"Yes."

He dips the paintbrush in a bucket of red, and I gasp when he drags the cold paint over my collarbone in long strokes. I can't suppress my shiver. My nipples ache, my core throbs, and he's barely touched me. His eyes bounce from my chest, to my eyes, and back, dividing his focus between the painting and how I'm reacting to it.

He must like what he sees, because his own naked chest begins to rise and fall more rapidly, and his white teeth sink into his bottom lip in a way that has me wondering what his bite feels like.

He alternates brushes, moving between reds, oranges, and yellows. Some white. Some black, until my arms and chest are a canvas of swirling flames, and I feel like I might overheat from the lust churning in my stomach. He lowers to his knees again and freezes. When I glance down at him, I find his eyes focused on the apex of my thighs, and suddenly, I'm blushing so hot I worry I'll melt the latex right off my body.

I clench my thighs together, and slowly, painfully slow, he tilts his face up to mine. The look on his face—sex and hunger and primal need—makes my head spin. And then his full lips curve into a smile so devious, my core throbs. When his sharp canines appear, I fist my hands and try not to sway at the mental image that floods my mind. His teeth sinking into my thigh, my hips, my ass. Leaving red bite marks and bruises. Marking me.

As if reading my thoughts, he presses a kiss to my hip bone before nipping at the sensitive skin there. I gasp and reach for him, gripping his shiny black curls on impulse. He laughs, then whispers against my skin in a tone that almost sounds like singing.

"A fire-colored flower...burning in bloom...."

His lips drag over me, his tongue dipping into the band of my underwear once before he finally leans back and gives me space to breathe. To think. I drop my hands from his hair, and he grins up at me.

"You can leave them there," he says ruefully, putting the paintbrush where his lips just were and continuing his artwork. "Pull a little harder next time. But not *too* hard, or we might end up giving these people a show they didn't ask for."

My jaw drops and my eyes widen. He barks out a laugh so loud that it elicits one of my own.

"You're..." I start to say, shaking my head. "You're..."

"I'm...?"

"You're not at all how I imagined you'd be."

He smiles, but he doesn't look up at me. He keeps his eyes on my stomach as his paintbrush glides over my skin. Thank god. It's so much easier to form words when I'm not held hostage by his eyes.

"You've imagined me, hmm?" The humor in his voice makes me bite my lip and look away. I don't answer, and he doesn't stop painting. "I like the thought of you imagining me. Someday you'll have to elaborate. I want to know how reality measures up to your fantasies."

I snort out an awkward laugh. "Who said they were fantasies?"

My voice is high-pitched and breathy. A dead giveaway. They were *totally* fantasies. He doesn't comment on my tone, though. He just shrugs.

"I'll fantasize about you fantasizing about me, then. It will keep me company when I'm alone on the bus."

Jesus, the thoughts that spur in my head. Alone—so not with Sav. Alone—not with me, either. Unless this is another subtle invitation?

The retraction of my previous rejection climbs up my throat, but it gets stuck on the tip of my tongue. If he asks me to go back to his bus again, I'll go without hesitation. I'd go right now if he asks. He doesn't.

It takes Torren over an hour to finish my body paint. It goes by in minutes. When I'm spinning in front of one of the full-length mirrors, I find myself speechless. He's transformed me into a living, dancing flame. Even though I'm topless in just a pair of underwear, I don't feel naked at all.

"Can you take a picture?" I ask him, pointing to my discarded jean shorts. "My phone is in the front pocket."

"You like it, then?" He bends down and retrieves the phone.

"I love it."

"Good." He points the phone at me. "Smile, Firebird."

He snaps a picture, then types on my phone for a few seconds. I hear the familiar sound of a text being sent, and then he hands my phone back to me.

"What did you just do?" I ask.

"Sent it to myself."

My lips twitch with excitement. There's now a thread in my text messages with Torren's phone number, and I have to resist the urge to pull it up and look at it. It takes all my restraint to click the screen off and not hunt down his number like the obsessed fan that I am.

When I look back at him, he's pulling his shirt and hat back on, and my brow furrows. I thought I was going to paint him next, and the disappointment that floods me is immediate.

"I'll walk you back. It's late."

He hands me my shirt and bra, then holds my shorts out for me to step into them. The paint has dried, feeling warm and tight on my skin. Like a wet suit, or a second skin made of rubber. I wonder if this is what it would feel like to be a Barbie.

Torren tugs the shorts over the curve of my butt, then drops his hands, leaving them unbuttoned. He nods a thank you to the instructor, and when he turns to leave, I follow.

"Camp or car?" he asks, and I tell him where the tent is, then we fall into silence.

His sunglasses are back on, a new joint is lit between his lips, and I trail him as he weaves through bodies. It's only a little after midnight. ArtFusion events go until three every night, but I don't protest. I feel myself crashing from the excitement, like I've crested the tippy-top of a rollercoaster, and all that's left is the plummet.

He leads me all the way back to the park exit corresponding with my camping section, then he stops walking.

"Get that shit off before you fall asleep." Despite the sunglasses, I know he's not looking at me. Everything about him has cooled. From raging fire to burning ice. "You can overheat. Don't leave it on too long."

"Okay," I say with a sharp nod. "Thanks."

He blows a stream of smoke from his nose, the pungent smell of weed growing stronger, then he starts to walk backward.

"Sleep tight, Firebird."

I don't watch him leave this time. I turn and walk through the exit, heading for our campsite. Once I'm by the van, I try to peel the paint off my body, but it's not as easy as I thought it would be. I drag myself to the shower structures set up for our camping section and wait in line. When it's my turn, I use my soap to wash Torren's artwork from my skin. After fifteen minutes, I'm scrubbed clean of any proof that Torren King ever touched me, a chill settling deep in my bones despite the hot night.

When I get back to my camp and crawl into my tent, I take out my phone and finally check my message threads. I know what I'll find even before it's opened.

Or rather, what I *won't* find.

There's no text with Torren's number. There's no text because he sent the photo and then deleted the thread. That realization makes my breath catch for a whole new reason.

Torren deleted the thread because he didn't want me to have his phone number.

Guess I'm not that special after all. I'm an idiot for even thinking I could be.

16

TORREN

PRESENT DAY

I KNOCK on the suite door at ten on the dot.

It's Mabel who lets me in. I glance around the main room, but I only find Red, Sav's personal security, sitting on the couch with Ziggy on his lap.

"You working late?"

Red looks up from his phone as if he's just noticed me, but I know he was probably watching the live stream of this floor's security camera. He knew I was on the way the moment I stepped into the hallway.

"I'm working always," he says gruffly, then goes back to his phone.

Red takes Sav's security seriously, and he has since she brought him on a few years ago. I didn't stop to think about how much this stalker bullshit must be stressing him out, too. He barely took days off as it was. Now? I bet Sav has to force him to sleep.

"Savvy is in her room video-chatting with Levi and Brynn. But Callie will be right out."

I open my mouth to tell Mabel thank you, but I snap it shut again when Callie's bedroom door opens, and she steps out into the main room. When she sees me, she stops in her tracks and eyes me warily. She worries that plump lower lip, making the dark red lipstick glisten, and I zero in on it before I let my eyes roam the rest of her body.

I tell myself I'm doing it to get into character. We've got to go out and put on a show. I might as well start now. That's what I tell myself. I choose to ignore the fact that I couldn't look away from her even if I wanted to.

Callie's wearing a green minidress with cut-outs on either side, exposing her soft, pale skin. It fits her like it was painted on. The neckline sinks low, showing off cleavage that makes my mouth water, and the hemline stops just below her ass cheeks. The way she looks in that dress makes me want to bend her over every flat surface just to make her scream my name.

She looks good. Better than good. She looks gorgeous. Sexy. The kind of sexy that could cause me serious problems if I'm not careful.

I fist my hands and breathe through the onslaught of lust until it ebbs, becoming more manageable. Easier to ignore.

"Damn, girl. You look hot," Mabel says, pulling me out of my thoughts.

"Yeah? I've never worn anything like this before."

"It looks great on you. Hot as fuck."

Callie laughs nervously. "Well, thanks."

I clear my throat, drawing her eyes back to me. I don't miss the sparkle of excitement there.

"Are you ready to go?" I ask, and she jerks out a nod.

"Yep."

Mabel sends me a glare that I read clearly—*stop being such a dick*—so I narrow my eyes at her and force a smile before looking back at Callie.

"This way."

I turn and walk out, and she follows.

Once in the hallway, I offer Callie my hand. She takes it without hesitation.

"Good," I whisper to her, and she glances up at me with a flirty smile.

"Of course. Got to sell it, right?"

Her words are said sweetly, but her eyes flash with anger, and I don't bother hiding my grin when I respond.

"Exactly."

I can let myself have fun with this for tonight. Like she said. We have to sell it.

We take the elevator in silence to the first floor, then I put my arm around her, tugging her into my side for the walk through the lobby to the valet who has my sports car. The hotel and its employees are discreet, but the lobby bar is full of people, and those people need to see the act.

I open my car door for her and help her in before sliding into the driver's side with our security details following in a car behind us, then I speed out of the drive and head to the club.

"You sure you're ready for this?" I ask Callie, and she rolls her eyes.

"If I wasn't?"

"We turn around, and you can go home."

She shakes her head with a frown. "No. I'm ready."

I pull my car into the club's valet line, and just before I put it in park to climb out and hand the keys to the valet, I turn to her.

"Showtime?"

She takes a deep breath, then smiles. "Showtime."

We walk past the line and go straight through the VIP entrance. The moment people see us, they start calling my name. Phones are suddenly pointed in my direction, so I pull Callie closer and rest my hand just above her ass as I lead her through the club and up the stairs into the lounge, telling our security to make themselves scarce. I can tell Damon wants to object, but I shake my head. I need Callie relaxed, and that won't happen if Damon and Craig are breathing down her neck. Besides, they may be giants, but they blend into dark corners well. One eye on us, one on the crowd, ever ready in case of trouble. We'll be fine.

The lounge is lofted above the general admission dance floor, but it's separated by a glass half wall with its own bar, dance floor, servers, and couches. If you don't want to be seen, there are more private rooms in the back, but I make sure Callie and I are posted front and center. Anyone in the club can look up and see us, and that's exactly how I want it.

"Drink?" I ask Callie, and she nods.

"Yes. A double shot of tequila. Please."

I arch a brow. "You want to party?"

She rolls her eyes. "If I have to pretend to like you in front of all of these people, I'm going to need tequila."

"Tequila coming up," I say with a grin and flag over a server. Within three minutes, they're back with our shots, and I'm taking mine and handing Callie hers. "Cheers."

We take our shots, then trade the shot glasses for the limes on the server's tray before finally sending him away.

"So what now, boss?" Callie wraps her arms around her midsection and flicks her eyes to the crowd below. There are people watching. There are *always* people watching.

"Now, you loosen up." I erase the distance between us and slip my hands around her waist. Her breath hitches in that tempting way I've come to anticipate the moment I touch her, and I find it thrilling. "Put your hands on me. I'm your boyfriend. Touch me how you would touch a boyfriend."

"In public?"

I laugh and amend my statement. "Touch me how you would touch a boyfriend in a dark club after a double shot of tequila."

She blinks. A look of determination flashes across her face, then her lips are curling into a sexy smile. She slides her hands up my chest and hooks them around my neck, and I'm suddenly very aware of how close our faces are. Her soft breaths fan my lips.

"How tall are those heels?"

"I'm not sure. Six inches, I think."

"I like them."

"Yeah? I'm worried I'm going to break my ankle."

I pull her body into mine, bringing us closer in a way that makes my heart quicken, and I lower my lips to her ear.

"Don't worry. I'll keep you upright."

She huffs out a shaky laugh, her breath tickling my skin, and her hold tightens around my neck. I close my eyes and breathe, drenching my senses in the scent and feel of her. Once again, I'm bowled over by how much I enjoy it, and it takes all my restraint not to let go and step away. I could drown in her if I'm not careful. If I don't work to keep my head above this tidal wave of attraction.

It's strange how powerful physical touch can be outside of sex. It's bewitching, taking hold of my mind and heart with only the simplest of intimate caresses.

I've always put more weight on that connection than there should be, attached myself to it too drastically, and it's done nothing but cause me fucking pain. I get drunk on the flood of emotions, and I've let it manipulate me into believing something is more than it is. I've let it trick me into falling in love, and that's exactly why I've not held a woman in years. I've not spent time with women for longer than it takes to get us both off. It might as well be another form of masturbation at this point for all the attention I pay to the women who end up at the end of my cock. I don't kiss them. I don't engage in conversation. I don't remember names or faces. I don't stay in contact, and I prefer it that way.

Hell, *they* prefer it that way because that way no one gets hurt. It's strictly sex under the protection of an iron-clad non-disclosure agreement, and it's worked for years. This is more contact than I've allowed myself in a long time. Warning sirens sound in my head as I register all the ways our bodies are touching, but I silence them.

This is different, I remind myself. It's not real, it never is, and as long as I remember that, I can let myself enjoy it. I can take sips of it in small doses, stay buzzed, and avoid intoxication.

"Just close your eyes and pretend I'm someone else," I tell her.

"Is that what you're going to do?"

Her voice is quiet against the shell of my ear, vulnerable in a way I wish it weren't. I want to tell her the truth, but I lie instead. I lie because it's safer for both of us.

"Yes."

"Okay."

I let myself slip my fingers into the cut-outs on the side of her dress, absorbing her heat and reveling in the softness of her skin. Goose bumps form under my palms, and when she moves her hands into my hair, I squeeze the flesh on her sides and pull her even tighter against me.

"Dance with me, Callie."

Slowly, I start to sway back and forth, using my hands to move her body in time with mine. It doesn't take much before she's moving on her own. She closes her eyes as she lets the music guide her, but I keep mine on her face. Her soft features are highlighted theatrically in the multicolored lights from the DJ, casting her in blue, purple, and red hues. She looks like a dream, and I'm captivated again by how attractive she is. Beautiful, especially when she's not scowling at me.

Song after song, I can't take my eyes off her. She doesn't stop moving as each track blends into the next. When she throws her head back, her lips parting slightly as she dances, a picture flashes quickly in my mind. It's her. What she'd look like when she comes. I can almost hear her moans. So real that it almost feels like a memory, not a fantasy, but when I try to pull it back, it fizzles into nothing.

The urge to kiss her full lips overtakes me, and on impulse, I flip her body around, tugging her back to my front. I drag my palms down her rib cage and over her hips, stopping on her pelvis. One of her hands rests atop mine while her other comes up to thread into my hair at the nape of my neck.

"Pull it," I say into her ear, and when she does, I groan.

I push lightly on her pelvis, urging her to back farther into me, and she does. Her ass presses against my dick, and there is no hiding how sexy I find her.

She freezes, but she doesn't move away, and I chuckle.

"Have I shocked you, Calla Lily?" I tease, eyeing the rapid rise and fall of her chest, the way her breasts heave against the neckline of her thin dress. When the lights flash in the brighter colors, I can just make out the outline of her hardened nipples. Fuck, just knowing I can turn her on so easily gets me high. "Are you afraid?"

She glances up at me with a frown, then arches a brow as she tightens her fist in my hair.

"I'm not." The words are clipped, defensive, and she grinds her soft ass on my hard cock.

"Fuck," I choke out, and her lips turn up into a taunting smirk.

Her hips move to the music in a punishing rhythm. She makes no attempt to put distance between us, and it's torturous. I curl my fingers into the fabric of her dress, pressing into her abdomen. Keeping her close when I probably should be pushing her away. I lower my head, my lips dragging over her ear when I speak.

"Be careful," I warn.

Her breath hitches, and I take her earlobe between my teeth and bite lightly. At the sting of pain, her grip on my hair tightens and her ass grinds harder on my dick.

"Fuck, Callie."

The music of the club dulls, and the crowd of people fades away until all I can hear or see or feel is the woman in front of me. She's my only focus.

I press open-mouthed kisses to the sensitive skin at the slope of her neck, then slip my hand into the cut-out of her dress, needing my skin on hers. Wanting to erase the clothing barrier between us. I skate down her body, burning with heat, and tease the lacy band of her underwear. She shudders and moves her hand over her dress to cover mine under it.

"I want to touch you," I tell her. "I *need* to touch you. Let me."

Her grip on my hand loosens, granting silent permission, and I slip my fingers into her underwear. The moment the pad of my middle finger presses onto her clit, she gasps and jerks backward, her ass pushing even harder against my dick.

I groan and bite her neck, pulsing my hips, reveling in the friction of my erection between her ass cheeks. Seeing my hand moving under her dress, knowing what I'm doing to her...

Fuck, if only we were naked right now.

Skin on skin.

Sweat slicked and frenzied.

The thought makes me impossibly harder, and I have to grit my teeth against the need to pull her dress up and push my aching cock into her from behind. It wouldn't even take much. The heels make her the perfect height. A few adjustments, and I could fuck her right here.

"You're killing me, Callie," I say against her.

I dip my hand lower into her panties and feel her back vibrate with a groan as I swipe my fingers through her pussy lips, coating them in her wetness before moving back to her clit. I rub again, faster.

"God, what I wouldn't give to sink into your pussy and make you come."

She says nothing. Her head tips back and rests on my shoulder as I fold my body over her, one arm hooked around her rib cage, holding her to me, and the other snaked through her dress and into her underwear. I kiss and suck her neck, rubbing her clit and thrusting my cock against her ass. Her mouth falls open before she sinks her teeth into her lower lip, and then she starts to move on my hand.

"Torren."

Her cry is little more than a gasp of air, but I hear it. It echoes in my head. Louder and louder, drowning out everything else as I rub her clit, needing more. I push my hand lower and slip two fingers into her, crooking them until I'm cupping her pussy. The low groan she lets out is fucking musical, and I grind the heel of my palm against her clit as I pulse my fingers in and out of her pussy.

"I would give anything for you to come right now," I say into her ear. "I need to feel you squeeze my fingers, baby."

She turns her head toward me, pressing her forehead against me, her lips searching for mine, but I don't close the distance. I don't give her what she wants. What *I* want, too.

"Open your eyes," I command. "Look at me."

When she does, I stare into her eyes, pupils dilated so only a thin ring of color remains, and then it hits me.

An impact of memories so strong, it makes me flinch.

ArtFusion. A phoenix. Body paint. My tour bus.

Firebird.

All of it, a jigsaw puzzle dumped from a box, colorful scenes scattered about in disarray inside my mind. I grasp, sorting and organizing, piecing it all out, bringing the details into focus.

And then I'm startled by a bright white light.

Callie freezes, and my eyes whip toward the flash. A server has his phone pointed at us, a look of shock on his face as he realizes the flash was on.

"Stay here," I say to Callie, removing my hands from her body and stepping away before stalking toward the server.

The guy tries to run, but I catch him in three strides and grab the collar of his white button-down before putting my arm around his throat.

"Give it," I growl, but he tries to fight against me.

"Get off me, man. I'll sue you—"

I tighten my hold. He sputters and coughs, his next threat lost on a gag.

"Give me the phone," I repeat.

We've garnered the attention of a small crowd, but not a single person steps up to help this asshole. Everyone in the VIP lounge is here because they require privacy and discretion. The disgust radiating off them and toward this server is enough to make him cower, and he holds up his phone in surrender. I snatch it and shove him away, noting him stumble and fall to the ground in my periphery.

In a matter of minutes, I have the series of photos and videos he's taken deleted from both the phone and the cloud. Then I drop the phone onto the ground and stomp on it. Once, twice, three times, until it's smashed beyond repair.

"What the actual fuck, man! That's fucking illegal. That's my fucking property."

"It's illegal to take unauthorized photos and videos in the VIP lounge. You work here. You know that. It's in your employment contract." I shove past him and head toward the manager's office. "Congratulations, asshole. You just got yourself fired and blacklisted from every exclusive club in the country."

Before I even speak to the manager, they fire the guy and order security to remove him from the premises. I'm apologized to profusely and reassured that nothing will be leaked to the press because all employees have to sign a non-disclosure to work the VIP lounge. I'm also offered free bottle service, but I turn it down. My only concern now is to get Callie back to the hotel and finish what we started.

I stalk back into the lounge, sweeping my gaze through the crowd. No Callie. I swallow back the panic that starts to creep up my throat and turn to Damon. He's already checking something on his phone.

"Where is she?"

"She left. Walton took her back to the hotel."

Fuck. I close my eyes and take a deep breath. At least Craig is with her, but I can't seem to tamp down the anger swirling in my chest. When I open my eyes and glance back at Damon, his brow is knitted, irritation mixed with a hint of guilt.

"Don't," I say firmly. "This isn't on you. The only reason I got to him before you is because he was closer to me."

It's the truth, and I don't want to see Damon feeling apologetic for something that wasn't his fault. Shit like this happens. It's a risk we take when we go out in public, but our details have been more on edge since word of Sav's stalker was shared with the whole team.

There's not a chance in hell now that I'll convince Damon to give me space again. It's probably for the best. Finger-fucking your fake girlfriend is decidedly less sexy when two gorilla-like men who could kill you in less than thirty seconds are watching you.

I stalk out of the club with Damon on my heels and get the car from the valet. I crank the music and gun it toward the hotel, trying like hell to cleanse my brain of tonight's events.

But I can't. Fuck, I can't.

She was so close. So hot under my palms. She felt like she belonged there, pressed against me, panting for me. She felt like mine.

I clench my hands into fists, beating back the need expanding in my chest. I haven't wanted someone like that in a long time, like I would combust if I didn't touch her. I wanted to kiss her, and I don't kiss. I haven't in years. Not since Sav. Not since I fell in love with the wrong person and got my heart shattered. I don't fuck with intimacy. I don't blur lines. I don't kiss, but I wanted it with Callie, and that fucks me up more than anything else.

More than the server who took our photo. More than the ass-reaming I know I'm going to get from Hammond when I get back to the hotel. More than the memories.

More than all of it.

I *wanted* to kiss her, and fuck me, I still do.

My Firebird.

17

CALLIE

PAST, ArtFusion Night Three

THE NEXT NIGHT, I pretend I don't see him while waiting in line for lamb kabobs.

I'm alone because Becket decided he wanted pizza again and then to check out the hookah tent. I hate hookah, and I'm sick of pizza. I have no idea where the other three went off to. Usually, I'd make it a point to tag along with one of them, but I wasn't in the mood today, and they aren't like girl friends would be. My safety isn't even on their radar, so I have a little more freedom. Sometimes being the only woman in a group of idiots has its perks.

I thought I'd spend the evening wandering and wallflowering, but now it seems I have a shadow. It shouldn't thrill me, but it does.

"You got the paint off," he observes, finally announcing himself, and I let out an irritated sigh.

"What do you want?"

"Ouch. Tent life not suiting you?"

I fling around, folding my arms and raising a brow.

"What do you *want*, Torren?"

He grins. He fucking grins at me, and my nostrils flare. When he doesn't answer, I turn back around. Within seconds, I feel him step closer, his chest brushing my back and his scent surrounding me.

Tobacco and leather, first. Ginger and bergamot follow. I could get drunk on this smell.

"Don't be mad, Firebird. I just want to hang out."

Fuck me, I'm such an idiot, because the ice already starts to thaw.

"We had fun last night, right? Just wanted to see if we could do it again."

I release another sigh. This one, much to my chagrin, is less annoyed than the last.

"Are you a vampire?" I ask, immaturely snapping the words like talking to him irritates me when really it makes me feel alive. "You only come out at night."

"It's easier to go unnoticed at night."

"Are you high again?"

Another chuckle but no answer. I assume it's yes. Instead of letting it fester, I just word vomit the thing I really care about, then hold my breath for his response.

"Why did you leave so quickly last night?"

I also want to ask why he deleted the text thread from my phone, but I bite my tongue on that one. My boldness has limits.

"That's why you're angry."

I don't dispute it. I *am* angry. I'm not going to lie or placate him. I don't care if he thinks it's dumb. I'm angry, and my feelings fucking matter. It's quiet for so long that I think he won't answer, but when he finally speaks, it's like wind returning to my stupid, delusional sails.

"I left because the headlining band was ending, and I didn't want to fuck with the crowd surge in the main areas. It was safer to head back to the bus."

I nod slowly. It works. The anger bleeds from my muscles, and once again, I'm just nerves and obsession and fangirl putty in his tattoo-and-ring-adorned fingers. When his lips brush my ear, I freeze.

"Come back to my bus with me."

I turn to face him, then fold my arms over my chest and narrow my eyes. "Why me?"

"You intrigue me."

"Not good enough. Try again."

"Because you're not obsessed with me."

His answer comes so easily that I can't stop the way my eyes widen with surprise. I also have to bite the inside of my cheek to keep from correcting him. Because, well, I kind of *am* obsessed with him. He must take my silence to mean I'm still not convinced, because he steps forward and speaks again.

"Come back to my bus with me, Firebird. I'll behave. I promise."

I don't even think it through this time. I just nod, then I follow him out of the park, my lamb kabobs completely forgotten.

"What's your real name?" he asks randomly, and for a moment I don't answer. I don't want to tell him my real name. I like that he calls me Firebird. "I promise not to stalk you."

He says it jokingly, cajolingly, and I roll my eyes.

"My name is Callie."

Calla Lily Sunrise, to be specific, but no way in hell am I telling him that. That's what happens when you have a hippie mom and a musician dad. Weird fucking names.

"I like Firebird, though," I tack on, and he shoots me a grin.

"Me too."

When we make it to his bus, Torren shakes hands with a hulking beast of a man I can only assume is security.

"Callie, this is Beau. Beau, this is Callie."

I wave awkwardly, and Beau nods. No smile, and he doesn't uncross his arms from his chest. Torren reaches into his pocket and pulls out a black leather wallet, takes a fifty-dollar bill from inside and hands it to the security guard.

"Could you send someone to grab us some lamb kabobs?" He looks at me. "Veggies?" I nod. "Hummus plate, too?" I nod again, and he glances back at Beau. "Need me to write it down for you?"

Beau raises a brow and Torren laughs before slapping him on the shoulder and telling him thank you. Then I'm following Torren up the stairs of his tour bus and trying my best not to die on the spot. The bus smells of weed and spicy cologne, a hint of leather and sandalwood. The blend sounds weird, but surprisingly, it's not a bad smell. I imagine it's some sort of band mixture. If The Hometown Heartless released a candle, it would smell like this.

The inside is much larger than I expected. To say I'm in awe would be an understatement. Two black leather couches line either side of the bus, and a large flat-screen T.V. is mounted above the one on the left.

After the couches, there's a kitchenette, two small bench seats and a table jutting out from the wall. There's a dark hall beyond that I assume leads to a bathroom and some beds, but I don't venture down there. I wouldn't be surprised if this bus cost over a million dollars. Something like this would be the dream. For our band to get big enough to move out of our shitty van and trailer? After a year of vagabonding it, though, it still seems so out of reach.

I fold my hands in front of my body and try not to look as out of place as I feel. I turn back to Torren as he pulls a stack of papers out of a cabinet and hands it to me.

It's an NDA.

My heart sinks once more. Fuck, hanging out with him is affecting my equilibrium more than that time we tried to go whale watching up the coast. I feel like I'm going to get seasick from the ups and downs.

"The label requires you to sign this," he says pointedly.

I shake my head. "I'm not signing that."

I might have come here of my own volition, but I'm not signing anything that could tie my hands if this whole encounter goes south. I might be an idiot fangirl, but I'm not a moron, and I'm not a freaking groupie.

"Fair enough." He takes the NDA from my hands and sticks it back in the cabinet. I cock my head and purse my lips.

"That's it?"

"You gonna talk to the press?"

"No."

"Then that's good enough for me."

"How do you know I'm not lying?"

He shrugs. "I guess I don't. Just going on the honor system."

I have to hide my smile. I don't know if this means he trusts me, but I'm choosing to believe it does. He gestures to a couch, so I sit, then he takes a seat beside me and messes with his phone for a minute. Music plays through some sort of surround sound system, and then he puts his phone down and grins at me. He's finally taken his baseball cap and sunglasses off, so his shiny black curls and green eyes are up close and personal for me to ogle. He's so pretty. It makes my chest hurt.

"What do you want to do, Firebird?"

He asks slowly, the suggestive tone making my stomach flip for the hundredth time since meeting him as reality sets in. God, am I really going to hook up with the bassist for The Hometown Heartless? I keep wanting to pinch myself because not even in my wildest fantasies did I ever think I'd get this close to him. I clear my throat nervously and ignore his smirk.

"You invited me here. You tell me."

His lips twitch and he scoots closer, putting his hand on my back and rubbing up and down gently.

"Relax. You're sitting so stiff. You can leave at any time, and we won't do anything you don't want to do, okay?"

"Okay," I whisper.

"Do you want a drink, or to smoke?"

"Um, probably no to both."

I do have some sense. And honestly, if this is going to happen, I want to remember it. He doesn't try to convince me, which I appreciate, but he pulls out that silver cigarette case again. He's lighting a joint when there's a knock on the door. Torren shouts *come in*, and Beau enters with the scent of kabobs wafting from a stack of takeout containers, causing my stomach to rumble so loudly that I blush.

"Alright, we'll feed you," Torren says with a laugh.

He takes the containers, tells Beau thanks, then sits back down. He pushes a button, and a small table pops up from the couch. He sets the food out, then hands me a packet of plastic silverware.

"Eat."

"Thanks," I say, and we eat in silence.

Well, more like *I* eat. Torren sits, smokes, and watches me. I try to ignore it at first, but after about ten minutes, the quiet grows suffocating, and his unrelenting eyes make me feel like prey being stalked by a predator.

In a way, I guess I kind of am.

"You're making me nervous."

"I am? Why's that?"

"You're staring."

He laughs. "Do you want me to stop? I can if you want, but I really don't want to."

"Why not?"

He takes a pull from his joint and blows the smoke out slowly before answering.

"I like the view."

I bite the inside of my cheek to tame my smile. I can't fight the flush of heat I feel kissing my skin, though. Downfall of having such a pale complexion. I'll blush as red as my hair, and there's nothing I can do about it.

"You've got sexy freckles."

I snort out an unattractive laugh that fills me with immediate embarrassment, deepening my blush, and his grin grows.

"What? What's funny?"

I roll my eyes. "*Sexy* freckles? Who says that?"

He shrugs. "I do. I think they're sexy. The freckles on your nose are sexy. The freckle on your left earlobe is sexy. The freckles on your shoulders and chest are sexy." He gives me a devious grin. "I'll confess to imagining where else you had them last night. I wanted to take all your clothes off and explore."

I shake my head and close my eyes, overwhelmed and unable to process everything I'm feeling, and the couch cushion dips as he scoots closer.

"I like making you blush, too." His knuckle runs over my chin, making goose bumps erupt all over my body. "I like affecting you."

Then his knuckle is replaced with his soft lips, and I gasp.

"Is this okay?" I feel him speak the words over my skin. He doesn't break contact as he asks. He just drags his lips up and down my jaw, pressing soft kisses.

I nod slowly, swallowing hard before whispering my answer.

"Yes."

For the briefest of moments, I worry about my breath. I just ate kabobs and hummus. I haven't brushed my teeth. Am I going to smell like garlic? But then his fingers slide under the hem of my shorts, squeezing my thigh lightly, and all concerns fizzle from my consciousness.

"This pain...won't go away easy...I'm still here to please you..."

He drags his lips over my jaw as he whispers, a faint melody I can't place carrying every word. I fist my hands into his shirt as he moves to my earlobe, taking it between his teeth and biting down lightly.

While he caresses my thigh with one hand, his other moves my hair off my shoulder, and he continues downward, kissing my neck. Licking me. Sucking softly. Biting. God, the biting. I didn't think I'd be into biting, but I am. I really am. I hold him tighter. Pull him closer. Breathe faster. I will myself to calm down before I pass out, but I can't. I can't.

"Relax, baby. Do you want me to stop?"

His breath skirts over my collarbone as he drags my tank top strap down my shoulder, then he's pressing hot, open-mouthed kisses to my chest. My collarbone.

"No," I rasp. "Don't stop."

He laughs quietly, deep and sensual. The sound goes right to my core, and I clench, pressing my thighs together against the throb.

"Open your eyes."

I do, and my gaze connects with his. His pupils are blown wide, haloed by glittering, glowing green. It only serves to make me hotter, needier. He keeps his eyes locked on mine as he slides his hand under the neck of my tank top. His fingers rest lightly on my breast, and he presses his palm onto my chest. My heartbeat, I realize after a breath. He's feeling my heartbeat.

"Your heart is racing. Is it fear, or are you turned on?"

I choke on a laugh, then answer honestly.

"A little of both, I think."

Torren slowly removes his hand from under my shirt before sliding my tank top strap back up my shoulder. I don't understand what's happening as he presses a soft kiss to my forehead and then stands, offering me his hand.

"I'll walk you back."

I squint, suddenly fighting the urge to cry. He's...kicking me out? I shoot to my feet and wrap my arms around myself.

"What? Why? Am I not...are you not...into me?"

He laughs and makes a waving gesture between us.

"Does this look like I'm not into you?"

I'm confused at first, and then I realize he was gesturing to his lower body. To his...erection.

"Oh."

Oh. There is a sizable bulge in Torren King's jeans at the moment, and he's suggesting that *I'm* the reason it's there. My shock must show on my face because he laughs again, then takes my hand in his. He rubs his thumb over my knuckles and speaks slowly.

"You're visibly uncomfortable. I'm not going to pressure you into doing anything you don't want to do."

"It's not that I don't want to..."

I trail off, lost for words. How do I explain that this would be a *literal* dream come true without sounding like an obsessed fanatic? How do I tell him he's everything and nothing like I've imagined, and I'm overwhelmed by the absolute *realness* of him?

Torren King might as well have been a mythical hero in bedtime fairy tales before this weekend. Always pixilated or out of focus. Veiled in mystery. Idolized and revered and blurred around the edges. I'm still getting used to the technicolored reality of his presence.

He smiles and nods, then gives my hand a tug.

"C'mon, Firebird. I'll walk with you."

18

CALLIE

MY PLAN TO avoid Torren today is easier than I thought it would be. Not just because he's prepping for The Hometown Heartless's opening show, but because I have a sneaking feeling he's trying to avoid me as well.

I didn't touch myself to thoughts of him last night despite how badly I wanted to.

I couldn't make eye contact with either Sav or Mabel this morning at breakfast, either. I could feel their attention on me. Sav's especially. Studying me. Sizing me up like I'm competition. I don't want to know if they know what happened last night. I'm mortified.

I can't believe I let it get so out of hand. How easily I let him consume me.

I can't even blame the tequila. I very much knew how stupid I was being, but in the moment, I *very much* didn't care. I was overconfident and reckless. It started as a game—a way for me to get the upper hand and wipe that arrogant smirk off his face—but damn, I was in way over my head. I forgot how skilled of a player he is, and my inexperience was glaringly obvious.

I've checked the internet probably twenty times between leaving the club last night and now, though, and so far, Craig was right. There's nothing in the tabloids about me being a hussy in the club with Torren

King. There is a video of us entering the club hand in hand. Some grainy pictures of us dancing, which were obviously taken from the general admission dance floor below the VIP lounge. One photo of me leaving with Craig, and one of Torren leaving with Damon, but nothing that even hints that Torren had his hands in my dress. His fingers inside me...

I clamp my eyes shut and give my head a shake, trying and failing to erase the memories of our clandestine dance party. No matter what I do, though, I can't stop thinking of the contrast between his hot, calloused fingers and his cold silver rings on my skin. I can't stop replaying how his tattooed hand and forearm looked as they disappeared into the cut-out of my dress. And when he pressed his erection against my backside, nestling it between...

"Damn it!" I groan into my empty bedroom, dropping my head in my hands. "Stop it. Stop it."

I'm wound so tightly I might explode. My core throbs, and no matter how roughly I rub my thighs together, the feeling won't abate.

"Fuck it."

Hastily, I shove my hand into the front of my shorts, hissing the moment my fingers make contact with my clit. I bite my lip and rub in circles. When my imagination pretends my fingers are longer and adorned with tattoos and silver rings, I don't fight it. I clamp my eyes shut and lean into the fantasy. I think of the way my dress looked with Torren's hand moving beneath it, and soon my hips start to pulse of their own accord.

My breathing kicks up, and when a whimper tries to escape my lips, I let it. Sav and Mabel are gone. Craig is in the hallway. I'm blissfully alone.

I do my best to mimic Torren's actions from last night, dipping low and inside myself before moving back to tend to my clit. I get myself so close, close enough to detonate, and then a knock on my bedroom door halts me.

"Callie. You in there?"

Jonah? I jolt up from the bed, fix my shirt and shorts, then rush to the door. I swing it open and blink rapidly. Yep. It's Jonah.

"You okay? You're a little flushed."

I flush harder and look away. "Yeah, I'm...um. Sorry. Why are you here?"

He leans his shoulder against my doorframe and slips one of his hands into the front pocket of his jeans.

"Escorting you to the stadium."

"Shouldn't my boyfriend be doing that?"

Jonah shrugs, but he doesn't offer up any explanation. That's all the explanation I need, though. Torren didn't want to come get me. It just confirms what I suspected—he *is* avoiding me.

"You gonna wear that?"

Jonah drops his eyes down my torso quickly, then back up.

"Oh. Shit. No. Just...um...give me one second."

I shut the door in his face, and I think I hear him laugh. I hurry into my closet and pull out the outfit I selected to wear to the concert tonight. Tight black jeans—purposely not a dress—and a black halter top. I shove my body into the clothes quickly, double-check my makeup in the mirror, and tousle my hair before grabbing my heels and rushing back to the door.

"Sorry," I say again as I step out of the bedroom. "I lost track of time."

Jonah hums, and when I glance at him, I see the hint of a smirk. It catches me off guard. I've never seen Jonah with a smile on his face. While Torren doesn't smile for me, he still hands them out freely to his fans and the media. Jonah, though? I can't think of a single video or photo of him where he's wearing a smile. Not even when I first met him four years ago. Indifferent stares and angry scowls, but never a smile.

I follow him silently into the hallway where Craig and some other guy are waiting for us.

"Callie, this is José. He's—"

"Your security?"

"Got the look, right?"

I shrug. "I mean, he's built like a brick building. No offense, José."

José smiles. "None taken, Miss James."

"Well, it's Callie, or I will take offense," I say in jest, and his smile grows.

"Apologies, Callie."

"Quit flirting with Torren's *girlfriend*, José," Jonah cuts in. "You know what a possessive dick he can be."

The statement piques my interest, but when I glance up at Jonah, that ghost of a smirk is still on his face. Then he stuns me further when he drops his arm over my shoulder. The gesture feels so familiar that I wait with bated breath for him to point it out. To say anything that alludes to our first encounter in the desert. When he doesn't, I let myself relax a little.

"Was that a joke?" I ask, forcing bravado into my tone as Jonah leads me out of the elevator and into the lobby.

Jonah shrugs. "Was it?"

I shrug back, glancing around at the people watching us in the lobby.

"Must have been. If *my boyfriend* was so possessive, you probably wouldn't have your arm around me in front of so many people."

His lips break into a full grin then. A smile that nearly knocks me on my ass. And when he looks down at me, there's mischief in his eyes that makes my stomach flip over itself. It makes sense now. A smile from Jonah Hendrix is intoxicating. No wonder he keeps it hidden from the world.

"I'm the only exception. Torren doesn't mind sharing with me."

My eyes widen and my breath stops as his words sink in. Thankfully, we stop at the valet because I'm suddenly too unstable to stay upright in these heels. Jonah opens the back door of the black SUV, then laughs when he sees the shocked look on my face. I wait for him to walk it back, to say he was just kidding, but he doesn't. Instead, he takes my hand and helps me into the car before shutting the door and rounding the front to climb in on the other side.

We ride to the stadium in silence, the replay of his last statement echoing in my ears.

Sharing.

Torren doesn't mind sharing *with me.*

Does he mean they pass girls between them, or does he mean...they...together...?

I close my eyes and rest my head on the window. I try to think of anything else, but images of Torren and Jonah tag-teaming some faceless groupie keep invading my mind, and I'm dizzy from the jumbled way it makes me feel.

Am I appalled? Am I turned on?

Or worse.

Am I *jealous*?

The thought makes me want to laugh out loud. Am I jealous of the faceless groupie in the imaginary scenario I've created? For fuck's sake, I think I might be.

Jonah's hand comes down on my knee in a gentle, comforting touch. He pats twice before removing his hand and speaking to me as if he didn't just disrupt my equilibrium by suggesting that he and Torren might share women.

"Enjoy the show."

Then he's climbing out of the car at the same time that my door is swinging open. I take Craig's offered hand and hop out, then he leads me past some shouting fans and through a pair of double doors into a long, empty hallway. There's no one in front of or behind us, and I turn a questioning glance toward my security detail.

"Where'd Jonah go?"

"Autographs."

"Oh."

"This way."

I follow him down a series of hallways, and with each turn, they become busier and busier. People in blue polo shirts with the stadium emblem on the back rush about, pushing carts and shouting into walkie-talkies. I recognize audio equipment. Lighting equipment. Amplifiers and microphones. Coils and coils of drop cords. Judging by the hive of activity, we must be close to the stage. I glance around for the band, but I see none of them. Just roadies and stadium workers.

Soon, we're turning down another hallway, and I notice two security guards standing on either side of a door. We stop in front of it and Craig nods in greeting to both guards before he knocks. At first, I assume I'm being deposited into Torren's dressing room, but then a different voice rings out from behind the door.

"Come in," Mabel shouts, and Craig opens the door and ushers me inside. "Hey, Callie. You look great. Want a drink or something?"

Mabel is sitting in a red leather recliner wearing a black sequined tutu and matching bra. The black patent leather platforms on her feet have to be more than six inches high.

"How can you play the kick in those?" I ask, zeroing in on her shoes.

Ezra used to insist on playing barefoot because he said the soles of his shoes fucked up his feel for the bass and hi-hat pedals. Mabel grins and wiggles her feet in my direction.

"Practice."

I nod. Of course.

Ziggy bounds over and starts sniffing at my feet, her tail wagging so hard that her whole body serpentines. Ziggy and I haven't had much time to get to know one another, but apparently, she's decided we're to be friends. I grin and drop to my knees so I can give her some head scratches, and then I let my eyes roam the room.

It's spacious. There's a large glass-doored fridge stocked with bottled mineral waters and a large table along one wall sporting a spread of pastries and fruit. Sav's intimidating security guard picks around a tray and pops a grape into his mouth, and I wave awkwardly at him. A large vanity table and a brightly lit mirror line the other side of the room. I spot a few makeup pallets, a curling iron, and two hairbrushes on the vanity.

"Do you guys do your own makeup and stuff?" I ask Mabel, standing back to my full height and leaving the dog with one last pat on the head.

"Nah. Glam squad's been here and left already. Can't you tell?"

I glance at Mabel and find her batting long, fluffy eyelashes at me while making a kissy face with her shiny pink lips. I laugh.

"You look great," I say genuinely.

Mabel is gorgeous. She could easily be a runway model if she wasn't the drummer in the world's most famous rock band.

"I know." Mabel winks at me, and I laugh again.

Then I hear a toilet flushing and water running. I look toward a door in the corner, determine it must be an attached bathroom, and then the door flies open and Sav Loveless stumbles out.

"Mother fuck it. Mabes, can you help me do these up? These fucking laces make it impossible to pee."

Mabel hops up from the chair and bounces toward Sav with a laugh.

"Well, we've got a two-hour show, so you better stop hydrating now," Mabel says as she works to lace up the sides of Sav's black leather pants. "Can't I just do 'em loose?"

Sav groans.

"No. I tried that. They just fall down. Damn things have to be suctioned to my ass; otherwise, I'll be giving everyone a show they didn't pay for."

Mabel quirks one suggestive eyebrow, and Sav groans again. Mabel barks out a loud laugh and glances my way as if I'm in on the joke. I suppose, in a way, I am. Along with the rest of the country. I mean, we did all see the same sex tape, and I assume that's what Mabel is laughing about.

"Thank you," Sav says as Mabel finishes doing up the laces. "I'm never wearing these damn things again."

"They are fuck hot, though," Mabel says, and reluctantly, I agree.

The black leather molds to Sav's legs and ass like a second skin, with a gap on either side running from ankle to waist where the laces are. Along the sides of her thighs and hips, about four inches of skin shows through the crisscrossing of the laces, and Mabel is right. The pants are *fuck hot* all on their own, but with the cropped white T-shirt and red bra, Sav Loveless is sex in combat boots. I envy her, and then I frown, because I don't want to envy her.

"Callie."

I blink out of my haze and bring my eyes up to meet Sav's, her irises like molten silver.

"What?"

Sav smirks. "I said hi. I love your outfit."

"Oh. Um. Thanks. Yours is great, too."

"Thanks." She saunters past me and pulls a mineral water from the fridge, then turns and hands it to me. I take it and force a smile. "How are you hanging in there? I know this assignment is probably difficult."

"It's fine," I lie, but my eyebrows slant and my nerves spike.

Does this mean she knows about last night? Is she jealous? Angry? I uncap my water and take a drink just so I have something to do. Having Sav's scrutinizing gaze on me has me feeling more unsettled than usual.

"Is there anything we can do to make it easier?" Mabel asks. "You got any hobbies or something? Books? Instruments? We can get you something to kind of help you take your head off the job."

"Some kind of creative escape could help ease the stress," Sav adds.

I open my mouth to turn them down, but then I change my mind.

"Actually..." I say slowly, considering the question once more before finally putting it into the air between us. "Could you get me a keyboard?"

"You play keyboard...?"

I glance at Sav as her question trails off, and I find her watching me more intently now, her head cocked to the side just slightly. Scrutinizing. The same way she was looking at me at her house the other day. The same way she was looking at me in Torren's studio too. Like I'm a puzzle, or a problem. Like she's working hard to figure something out.

I look away from her and back at Mabel as I answer.

"Piano. But I figure keyboard is easier to tote around on a bus."

"We can definitely get you a keyboard," Mabel starts to say but then Sav blurts out two words I wasn't expecting.

"Caveat Lover."

My eyes go wide as I whip them toward her. Sav grins triumphantly. She's solved the puzzle, it seems.

"I'm right, aren't I? You were lead singer and keyboardist for Caveat Lover."

My mouth drops open, then closes. I don't know what to say, but she keeps talking.

"I saw you guys a couple of years ago when you played in that little venue outside of Chicago. You did a cover of 'Dancing In The Dark' that I couldn't get out of my head for weeks. And you had that guitarist with the glittery pink Fender."

"Rocky," I supply absently. "That was Rocky."

Sav marches over to the vanity and snatches her phone from a charger, then starts scrolling. She stops scrolling and grins, then snaps her fingers and points at me.

"Calla Lily Sunrise James. I fucking knew you looked familiar." She glances back at her phone. "Keyboard and guitar. Mezzo-soprano. Rocky Hallstrom, lead guitar. Pike Hallstrom, rhythm guitar. Becket Walker, bass. Ezra Hawke, drums. Two EPs. Signed by Black Widow Records. Debut LP TBA."

I jerk my head back in alarm, bouncing my eyes between Mabel and Sav.

Mabel laughs. "Sav keeps a spreadsheet of up-and-coming bands in her phone."

Sav shrugs. "I like to pay attention to female-lead rock bands."

"Because they're competition?" I ask, narrowing my eyes in her direction.

Sav arches an eyebrow and sends Mabel an incredulous glance before looking back at me. "Because they interest me."

I scoff, but I don't argue. I'm not stupid. In fact, my band being on a list in her phone is another piece of evidence in my already over-flowing mental bucket of reasons why I can't trust Sav Loveless. She's the ringleader. The mastermind. She didn't know me, but she sure knew my band. My now *defunct* band.

"And what do you do with that list?" I ask.

I'm certain I already know the answer, and I doubt she'll tell me the truth, but I ask it anyway. She flattens her lips between her teeth before giving me a forced smile.

"It's for personal use."

I flare my eyes and nod slowly. "Right."

A dozen different statements circle around in my head, but I don't let a single one of them fall from my lips because I have even more reasons to stay quiet. Eighty thousand of them, to be exact. I'm not flying off the handle and rocking the boat. I'm not screwing up this opportunity by being hotheaded. And anyway, what's the point of dredging up the past? The damage is fucking done, and there's nothing I can do about it now even if I wanted to.

"Okay, so, anyway," Mabel says, awkwardly cutting into the tension brewing between me and Sav. "I hope you weren't planning to keep that a secret or anything, Callie. It's only a matter of days before it makes it to the press, especially now that word is out that you're on tour with us. I'm surprised it hasn't already."

I sigh. "I wasn't trying to keep it a secret. It just didn't come up, and it doesn't matter anymore."

And honestly, I just assumed my band wasn't big enough to garner any sort of attention. Black Widow barely signed us before they unceremoniously *unsigned* us. We never even released a full album. For all intents and purposes, my time with Caveat Lover might as well have been a fever dream. Or, as my mom likes to call it, *an impulsive, immature mistake to be blamed on my father's wild genes.*

That last thought makes me check my phone, but my mom still hasn't returned my calls or texts. I do, however, have three new texts from my sister.

GLORY BELL

> Torren King ate ur other sneaker. Sorry.

> Can I have ur RazzyRed lipstick?

> Miss u.

I smile to myself as I text her back.

ME

> Your dog is a menace. Yes, you can have my lipstick. I miss you too.

> Tell Mom I love her.

I slide my phone into my pocket and look back up at Mabel and Sav. Both are watching me curiously, and since I don't know what to say, I say nothing. The flare of indignation I'd felt moments earlier flickers out, leaving me feeling awkward and uncomfortable. I look away, uncap my mineral water, and take another sip. I glance toward the spread of pastries and fruit on the table on the wall and intentionally avoid Red's eye. I take a deep breath and then blow it out slowly.

Awesome. Now it's even more awkward.

I'm relieved when someone knocks on the door, but my relief is short-lived when Jonah and Torren come walking into the dressing room. Jonah meets my eye and nods, all traces of his earlier humor gone, and I nod back. Torren, on the other hand, barely even looks in my direction. It hurts just long enough for me to harness that pain and turn it into anger.

Dickhead.

My ass cheeks were good enough to cradle his erection last night, but now he can't even spare me a second glance. I let that thought fuel me, pouring more and more gasoline on it until I'm raging on the inside. It's necessary because he looks so fucking beautiful right now that anything other than pure fury is at risk of being forgotten in favor of blind lust.

His curls are perfectly messy and artfully falling into his eyes. His fitted jeans are low-slung enough to show the deep V of his pelvis, and I can tell he doesn't have underwear on. I have to look away quickly the moment I notice a very defined dick print in the denim, but his bare chest isn't much better for my nerves. His chiseled pecs and abs must have some sort of oil rubbed on them because his tattoos and muscles are glistening. When I start to involuntarily catalogue his tattoos, I force myself to look away, and my eyes run straight into Jonah's.

He takes a sip from a bottle of water without looking away from me, and then he takes a few steps toward me.

"You look beautiful."

His voice is low, the words spoken so only I can hear them. I try to fight my heated flush and lose.

"Thank you."

His lips turn up slightly at the corner. Another ghost of a smile. Considering how rare they are, it makes me feel rich. A poor miner stumbling upon gold dust.

"Are you going to watch the show from the floor?"

"Is it up to me?"

"Here's a secret." He leans in close, tilting his head to position his mouth at my ear. He smells like weed, and his body gives off heat like a furnace. It makes me shiver, and I feel him inhale and exhale twice into my hair before he finally speaks. "It's *all* up to you."

"Callie."

I jerk away from Jonah at the sound of Torren's voice, immediately filled with shame that I don't fully understand. Jonah, however, moves with a casual nonchalance that makes me think I'd perhaps read more into our encounter than was necessary. The glare Torren gives Jonah, though, has me questioning everything.

"Torren," I say quickly, fisting my hands in front of me. I glance at Jonah and find him smirking at me. I'm not impressed to be on the receiving end of this smile. I want to glower at him, but I don't.

"Would you like to watch the show from a private box or backstage?"

I flick my eyes to Jonah once more, then back to Torren. "Can I watch it from the floor?"

Torren's jaw ticks as he bounces his eyes between mine. "I don't know if that's a good idea."

I square my shoulders, my determination to win this argument increases tenfold.

"I want to watch from the floor. Craig can be with me. Hell, so can your brick wall. But I want to watch from the floor."

We fall back into silence, his brows knitting as he considers it. He's conflicted. If he's concerned about my safety, I'll admit, it makes me feel warm. Protected. It makes me soften toward him.

I hate it.

He probably just wants to control me.

I raise my eyebrows like I'm irritated. "Well?"

Finally, he jerks out a nod.

"I'll tell Craig and Damon." Torren turns his attention to Jonah, and the look he gives him is pure ice. "Come with me."

Torren turns and stalks out of the room, then Jonah follows. Neither of them say anything else to me, and even though it shouldn't, it bothers me.

Then, as if I need more things to stress out about, I get a text from a number I've only seen sporadically over the last year.

Ezra.

It's a picture of a magazine in a convenience store rack, me and Torren holding hands on the cover, followed by a single sentence.

EZ

Are you fucking serious right now?

I stare at it for almost ten minutes before responding, running through every possible excuse. Of all the things I worried about before jumping into this PR stunt, pissing off my former band wasn't one of them.

Finally, I bite the bullet and text him back. One word because I'm contractually gagged, but I still can't bring myself to lie to him.

ME

Yes.

EZ

Fuck you Calla Lily.

I cringe. I'm not surprised, given everything, but it still fucking stings. And honestly, he's right. This whole thing makes me a traitor. To my band. To myself. Doesn't matter that it's fake. Doesn't matter that it's for my family. I've compromised my integrity. I've been bought, and that is by far the most difficult thing to deal with.

I'm sick to my stomach as I'm led to the floor for the concert. I'm so lost in thought that I don't even pay much attention to the opening band. Some local band Sav's handpicked for the weekend. It's what they do now. Every weekend of shows is a new opener, and it's usually an up-and-coming band that not many people outside of their home state have heard of. Opening for Heartless puts them front-and-center and allows them to perform for a crowd larger than they'd ever played before.

It's done a lot to repair Heartless's reputation, but I'm not fooled.

Nothing Sav Loveless does is altruistic, and this is probably just another way to sus out competition. To keep another iron fist around the throat of the music industry, and it makes me want to warn these unsuspecting bands. I want to storm the stage and tell them to run far, far away from The Hometown Heartless, but I keep my feet planted firmly on the floor.

By the time Sav, Torren, Jonah, and Mabel take the stage, my earlier anxiety has transformed into anger, and I find myself glaring at them. I swap my eyes between Sav and Torren, fueling my fury with every glance they send each other's way. I hold on to that feeling. I force it to the forefront of my mind, and I fool myself into believing I'm prepared.

Then they start to play.

They start to play, and my heart starts to ache. God, I used to love them. They're so fucking good, and there's no denying they put on one hell of a show. They love to perform. It's evident in every crowd interaction. In every note and lyric.

I want to hate them. I want them to suck so badly. But in this moment, I can't, and they don't. Torren looks at me several times throughout the concert. He smiles and winks, and my heart starts to race. It's all for show. I know this. But that stupid fan is still inside me, and the energy palpitating from the crowd threatens to coax her out.

The songs that I used to love flow through me, igniting every emotion. I sing along in my head. I feel my body swaying to the music, and I have to choke back tears.

I miss my band. I miss performing. I miss the thrill and the excitement and the utter sense of fulfillment that comes with playing a show. I miss running my hands over the keys of my keyboard. I miss singing songs I wrote into a microphone. I miss the applause.

I miss it all.

And that makes me furious all over again.

This is the last night I'll be watching from the floor.

19

TORREN

WHEN THE VOICEMAIL PICKS UP, just like I knew it would, I disconnect the call and drop my head back on the couch.

"No answer?"

I shake my head. "Is there ever?"

"You didn't leave a message."

I turn my head to the side and look at Jonah. "What's the point? She knows it's me."

Jonah and I fall back into silence as the bus makes its way down the highway toward Las Vegas. We played four sold-out shows in Glendale, each one better than the last, and now we have three days off before we get to do it all again in Vegas.

With all the downtime Hammond has had built into the schedule, I'm enjoying this tour much more than our previous ones, but they're still taxing on the body and mind. They're still exhausting. And on days like today, I can't help but wonder how much easier things would be if I'd never joined a band.

My eyes drift back to my phone, now lying discarded on the couch cushion beside me. Briefly, I let myself imagine it ringing. Answering it to hear my mom's voice on the other end. She tells me happy birthday. I tell her the same. We catch each other up on things that have happened since we last spoke. I offer to fly her to the next show. We make plans for the next holiday. And then we exchange *I love yous* and hang up with the promise to speak again soon.

I feel like an idiot for wanting something so impossible.

For longing for something I've never actually seen in real life.

None of my bandmates have good relationships with their families. Well, maybe Sav, but even that's new. It wasn't always good. For years, it was toxic before becoming nonexistent. In the grand scheme of fucked-up family dynamics, mine could be so much worse.

But goddamn it. A call from my mother on our shared fucking birthday wouldn't suck.

"What's the last you heard about her?"

I tear my unfocused gaze from my phone and look back at Jonah. He's lying on the other couch with a paperback novel open on his chest. His eyes are closed, and I'm grateful for that. I don't think I could handle his scrutiny right now.

"Not much. Still working at the local diner. Still dating random-ass men. Still supporting my waste of space brother."

Every few months, I have an investigator do a wellness check on my mom. I don't know what I'm checking for, to be honest. There's never any wellness to be found.

"And how is Sean?"

I sigh. "The same."

Nothing ever changes. I harbor a lot of resentment regarding Sean. Resentment and guilt. It's something I've spent many Therapy Thursdays unpacking. But no matter how many sessions we've devoted to my older brother, I just can't seem to reach the end of it.

The longer we spend on this bus in silence, the more restless I start to feel. It's my fucking birthday and I'm wallowing in self-pity. Two years ago, I'd have been celebrating with booze, drugs, and lots of sex. Now, I avoid hard substances to help keep my best friend alive, and the woman I used to fuck is in a monogamous relationship with someone else.

The realization pisses me off almost as much as it depresses me, and that makes me want to be reckless.

"This is fucking pathetic," I groan, pushing myself to standing. "This is a fucking pathetic way to spend my birthday."

"Ham asked if you wanted the week off," Jonah reminds me. "You said no."

"Shut up, Jo."

He shrugs. "Take Callie out."

"No."

My response is clipped, urgent, and Jonah arches a patronizing eyebrow. Even with his eyes closed, he looked judgmental.

"She's your girlfriend. You should be seen spending time with her on your birthday." When I don't say anything, he turns his head toward me and opens his eyes. I see the flash of challenge in them right before he speaks again. "Fuck her."

"No."

"Then let me fuck her."

Anger flares hot in my stomach and I glare at him. This isn't the first time since she got here that he's suggested it. It's not the first time I've shot him down.

"The fuck is with you?" I growl, and he shrugs again.

"Have you seen her?"

He shakes his head and lets the question hang in the air like it needs no further explanation. And really it doesn't. Because yeah, I have seen her, and that's the fucking problem. I've seen her, and I've had my hands on her, and I've jerked my dick to the thought of her every night since we danced at the club.

If I fucked her? It'd be game over.

"No, you're not fucking her, and neither am I," I say again. "No one is fucking her."

"Then fuck someone else."

"For fuck's sake, Jo. I'm not going to fuck someone else when I'm supposed to be dating Callie—"

"It's fake."

"So? It's still disrespectful as hell. And if that gets out to the media? The whole story will fall apart."

"You suck at celibacy."

I huff a laugh. "No, *you* suck at celibacy. I'm just a good fucking friend."

Jonah's lips curl the slightest bit. The kind of smile that puts my senses on high alert. The kind of smile that has me reaching for my phone to double-check that the hotel staff will have removed all hard liquor from the minibar in our suite before we check in.

"You're right," he says cryptically. "I do suck at celibacy."

"Happy birthday!"

Sav and Mabel shout as I walk back into my suite from the hotel gym. I'm drenched in sweat from my attempt at running off the pent-up sexual frustration coursing through my veins. One look at Callie, and I confirm my attempt was unsuccessful.

There's a cake sitting on the table with candles blazing, and everyone—including Red and Ziggy—are wearing cheap birthday hats.

"My birthday was yesterday," I point out, but they all ignore me.

"Make a wish, old man." Mabel gestures to the cake.

I grin and walk toward her. "I'm not old."

"Older than all of us."

"Except Red," Sav chimes in. "But he doesn't count."

I shake my head, flicking my eyes back to Callie briefly. She looks gorgeous but uncomfortable as hell standing in the back of the room. I haven't seen her since we got to the hotel yesterday, and even then, it was just a brief staged check-in for the tabloids. My fingers curl into a fist at the memory of her hand in mine, and I have to force myself to look away and back at the cake.

HAPPY BIRTHDAY TOR is written in blue icing with little black music notes piped around the words and twenty-nine candles dripping blue wax along a white-iced border. It's a small, simple cake, and it's perfect. It's just the reminder I needed that this band is better than any family I could have been born into. My mom? My brother? I don't need them as long as I have Sav, Mabel, and Jo.

"Blow 'em out before we catch the hotel on fire," Sav teases, and I narrow my eyes playfully at her before letting them fall shut and blowing. The candles extinguish immediately, and everyone claps. "What did you wish for?"

I glance at Sav and shrug. "None of your business."

She rolls her eyes, and it feels good. It feels like how it could be. How it might be soon if things continue in the direction they've been. Healing and growth aren't usually linear, though, so I won't get my hopes up.

Mabel steps up and starts cutting the cake, and I once again let my eyes stray to Callie. This time, she looks far less uncomfortable than she did moments earlier. This time, she's talking with Jonah, and from the smile on her face, she's enjoying it. Without overthinking it, I snatch two plates of cake from the table and head toward her. When I'm within arm's reach, Callie's attention turns to me while Jo's stays on her.

I hand Callie a plate of cake and fix my eyes on my guitarist.

"You hitting on my girlfriend? On my birthday?"

I attempt to say it jokingly, but there's still an underlying bite that can't be missed. Jonah doesn't even look at me when he responds.

"*Fake* girlfriend."

Callie's eyebrows shoot up, and I force a smile.

"It's got to look real, *Jo.*"

Jonah glances sideways at me, eyes glassy but clear, and arches a brow. "I'd think it would make it *more* realistic."

I grit my teeth. "Jonah."

I can feel Callie's attention on me, but I keep mine on Jonah. Glaring at him. Warning him to keep his fucking mouth shut. He holds my eye contact for one breath, then two, and then he looks at Callie and fucking grins.

"Think about it," he says to her.

My fury spikes further as he takes his finger and swipes it through the icing on her cake, then sucks his finger clean before giving her another grin.

"You've got my number." When he looks back at me, the grin is still fixed on his face. "Happy birthday, Tor."

I don't bother watching him leave the suite. I don't ask where the fuck he's going like I normally would. Right now, I don't care.

"What did he mean?" Callie and I say at the same time.

I shake my head and plow forward. "What does he want you to think about?"

Her eyebrows slant downward while a pink flush tints her cheeks.

"He invited me to hang out tonight."

"To do what?"

"I don't know. *Hang out.*"

"Jonah doesn't *hang out* with women, Callie. He fucks them."

Her eyes flare wide and shoot over my shoulder. The room has gone quiet, and I know if I look behind me, I'll find everyone's attention on me.

"Thanks for the cake," I say into the air. "I have to talk to Callie." Then I grab her arm and pull her into my bedroom, kicking the door shut behind me.

"What the hell is wrong with you?" Callie's words are hissed as she shakes off my hold. "He's not going to try to sleep with me, Torren. Jesus. He's just being nice."

I scoff and shake my head. How do I explain this to her without sounding like a complete asshole?

"Jonah isn't nice—"

"Oh, that's a great thing to say about your supposed best friend."

I raise a frustrated brow at her interruption and try again. "He's good with the band. But he's not nice to—"

"Groupies?"

"Women he doesn't know."

She rolls her eyes and folds her arms over her chest. "Maybe he's trying to get to know me. Maybe he wants to be nice to me since I'm stuck here for three—"

"Do you want to fuck him?"

Her jaw drops with a gasp before she snaps it shut, nostrils flaring. "You're an asshole. It's none of your business who I want to sleep with."

"It is if you're supposed to be my girlfriend."

She forces a sweet smile and bats her eyelashes. "*Fake* girlfriend."

"You're not fucking my bandmate, Callie. That just—"

"Do you share women?" Now my jaw drops, and her eyebrows rise to her hairline. "Oh, my fuck, you do."

I am going to kill Jonah.

"Did you share Sav?"

"No," I answer honestly. "Never. That was different."

She laughs. "Oh, so you only share women who don't matter."

"It's not like that." I drag a hand down my face. I don't know how we got to this place so quickly. I don't know how to explain it in a way that she might understand. "It's not that they don't matter, it's just—"

"It's just only something you do with groupies, right? You only fuck groupies together."

When I don't answer, she laughs again, louder this time. "Oh my *god*. Did you guys tag-team any groupies in Glendale?"

"No."

"Bullshit."

"We didn't. It wouldn't look good. We have to—"

"Sell it. Sure. Right." I watch as she drags a hand down her face and takes a deep breath. "Jesus Christ, I'm in over my head. What the fuck have I gotten myself into?"

I huff out a laugh of my own because she's just said what I was thinking. My heart is thundering behind my rib cage, jealousy and frustration and arousal swirling around like a fucking cyclone in my chest.

What the fuck have I gotten myself into? I'm teetering along the edge of an open firepit, and with every day, I'm caring less and less if I fall in.

She's right—Jonah and I have shared women. Often ever since Sav and I officially ended things. And seeing him fuck someone I've fucked has never bothered me before. Seeing him fuck someone I'm also fucking sparks no jealousy at all. But Callie is different, and I can't fucking figure out why. She's been different from the beginning. Jo wanting to fuck her is one thing—he'll stick his dick in anyone with a pretty face and tits—but if Callie wanted him? Not just for sex, but *really* wanted him?

The thought makes me murderous.

I shouldn't care if she develops feelings for Jonah, but I do.

She's *my* Firebird. *Mine.*

It's on the tip of my tongue to tell her I know who she is. That I remember her from ArtFusion. I know she remembers. It's the only thing that can explain her scathing attitude toward me. She's holding a grudge when she doesn't have a right to. I want her. I want her so badly that it aches, but she's lied to me more than once. I don't trust her, and that's the only reason I keep my mouth shut.

"Just...watch yourself around him," I tell her finally, meeting her eye and hoping I sound more protective than possessive. "If he thinks he can fuck you, he will."

She glares at me. "That's a dickhead thing to say."

I shrug. "I'm being honest."

"And if you're wrong? If he just wants to be nice?"

"I'm not wrong, Callie. I've known him for over a decade. He thinks you're hot. He wants to fuck you. If you let him, he'll do it, and then it will fuck everything up."

She shuts her eyes and tilts her head to the ceiling. "Right. If word got out, it would tank the story."

I let her infer what she wants. It *would* fuck up the PR relationship story. It would start a whole new cyclone of media bullshit. But I meant more than that. It would fuck up Jonah's and my relationship because I wouldn't be able to forgive him, and I'm not even remotely ready to explore that fact.

"Is he sober?" Callie asks, catching me off guard enough that I answer honestly.

"Most of the time."

"Most of the time?"

I purse my lips and run back over his behavior from moments earlier. Could he have been drunk? High? Possibly. I wasn't around him long enough to tell for sure, and that makes me feel like a shit friend. My fingers itch to reach for my phone, but I resist. Jo's an adult, and he gets pissed when he thinks I'm checking up on him like some sort of helicopter parent.

"Jonah's a really good guy with some really nasty demons," I say slowly, trying like hell to be honest without betraying his confidence. "He worked his ass off to get sober. But sometimes...he'll...backslide."

"And you're all okay with that?"

"Honestly? If it's weed or booze, I think we're all just happy it's not something harder. And we watch him. If he starts to spiral..."

I shrug, but I don't say anything else. I worry I've already said too much, but I wasn't going to lie to her. I wait in silence until Callie looks at me again.

"Fine. No hanging out with Jonah."

Then she turns around and walks out.

Around eleven, low music starts to play in the suite outside my bedroom door, signaling Jonah's return from his tour of the Vegas Strip.

According to José, Jo went to six different nightclubs. Drank and smoked, but he's not shitfaced, and he never tried to get his hands on anything else. I'm standing from the bed and dropping the book I was reading on the comforter, readying myself to go out and speak to him about Callie, when I hear a woman's laughter. It's muffled with the music, but I hear it, and my spine goes rigid. I wouldn't put it past Callie to come here with him just to piss me off. I wouldn't put it past Jonah to fuck her just because he felt challenged by me. It's a game to him—to us—and he still doesn't realize I've changed the rules.

Without thinking twice, I storm into the suite. The fucker didn't even make it to his bedroom before putting the woman on her knees, and I fume at the sight of her. Jonah's facing me, a redhead kneeling before him with his hands fisted in her hair, and he's thrusting into her mouth.

Callie.

Rage clouds my vision as I stare, and then Jonah looks up. He makes eye contact and gives me a sloppy grin.

"I knew you'd cave," he says, moving his hand to the back of Callie's head. I hear her gag, and he groans, eyes falling shut briefly before speaking to me once more. "Just getting her ready for you. You ready for Torren, sweets?"

I snap, closing the distance in three strides.

"You motherfucker."

With both hands, I reach over Callie's body and shove his chest. He stumbles back with a laugh, hand flying to wrap around his erection.

"Fine, fine! You can cut in. All you had to do was as—"

"I told you to stay away from her," I growl, snarling at his hard, wet dick before whipping my glare onto Callie. "What the fu—"

My words die on my tongue.

It's not Callie.

Instead of angry green eyes, I see excited brown. She wipes her mouth with the back of her hand and then eagerly reaches for the band of my sweats.

"I'm ready for you, Torren. I already signed the papers."

I step back. Relief floods me as I shake my head. "Not interested," I tell her before returning my attention to Jo. "What are you on?"

His smile turns into a scowl immediately. "Nothing I can't handle."

"What is it?"

"Weed, asshole. Vodka. That okay with you, *Dad*? I'm not a fucking idiot."

I sigh, shaking my head again. "Handle your shit, Jonah. Sav will call off the whole tour and send your ass back to Tranquil Waters the moment you fuck up."

He grabs the woman's head and shoves himself so far down her throat that she gags, but he doesn't take his furious eyes off me.

"Tranquil Waters can get in line to suck my fucking dick, and so can Savannah."

I scoff. I don't argue with him. I send one last disinterested glance to the groupie on her knees, and then I leave the suite. I'm barefoot and shirtless in just a pair of sweats, but I don't let that stop me from going to the terrace. It's reserved just for the band while we're here, and right now, I need some fucking peace.

20

CALLIE

As MUCH AS I can't stand Sav Loveless, I can't deny that the gift she's given me has softened me up a bit.

The portable digital piano she got me is state of the art. Even after not having played for over a year, the keys are familiar and welcome under my fingertips. They remind me of the baby grand I played at Barnum Hall.

I was expecting my playing to be awkward. Rusty. But it's not. It's like breathing, and I realized that for over a year, I've been deprived of oxygen. Closing my eyes, I get lost in the notes. Beethoven's "Für Elise" pours out of me from muscle memory. Three minutes of pure therapy, removing stress and anxiety for the length of the piece from the first bar to the one-hundred and third.

I don't bother trying to hide my smile. I let it out, unbidden, for the first time in a long time, and I let myself play.

When "Für Elise" ends, I move right into "Moonlight Sonata." I don't even let the final notes fade. I can't see the stars due to the light pollution, but the breeze is soothing, and the cover of night makes the song choice feel perfect.

I play the first movement seamlessly—not a single missed note, not a single fumble—and then I attempt the second movement. Once again, it comes as naturally as breathing. The second movement is faster with large jumps and a subtlety in places that took me almost a year to learn, but I get through it without error.

I pause before starting the third movement. I take several breaths and mentally run over the music in my mind. My fingers itch to begin, but I keep them suspended two inches above the keys, building my confidence. Preparing.

Just before I lower my hands to the piano, a clapping rings out from the corner of the terrace near the door, and my eyes fly open, whipping in the direction of the sound. Every ounce of air I inhaled escapes me in a violent whoosh.

"Torren," I gasp, folding my hands in my lap.

Suddenly, all I can think about is the club and how he touched me. How I *let* him touch me. Heat floods my body, and I force a swallow to wet my now parched throat.

God, why is he here? And shirtless. And gorgeous.

I had Craig haul this up here for me specifically so I wouldn't have an audience. Of all the people I'd want to watch me play for the first time in over a year, Torren King is at the bottom of the list.

Thank fuck I didn't attempt the third movement in front of him.

"You're really good. Don't stop on my account. I'd love to hear you play some more."

I laugh awkwardly. "Thanks, but, um, no. I was just messing around."

"Liar. You looked like you were about to play a solo concert at Carnegie Hall."

I roll my eyes, but I don't say anything.

"How long have you played?" he asks, walking toward me with a confidence I don't think I've ever felt in my entire life. "You're obviously not a beginner."

"Since I was six," I tell him honestly. "My dad used to play. He taught me."

"He *used* to play?"

"I mean maybe he still does. Probably. Wherever he is."

I shrug and look out at the Strip. Now that I'm not playing, the noise filters in. Muted, because we're so high up, but still noticeable without the piano. The worries in my head start to grow louder, too. My bones heavier. It was a nice respite, though.

"Ah. I see. I'm sorry."

"Don't be. I was relieved when he finally left for good. He taught me how to play, so I'm grateful for that. But that was really the only good thing he did."

Torren nods in my periphery. "I can relate to that. I mean, my dad didn't teach me much of anything, but I was relieved when he was finally gone."

I fold my lips between my teeth. I know all about his dad. How he died of liver failure when Torren was sixteen. Cirrhosis. Torren said in an interview once that his dad was an alcoholic, but he didn't go into detail. I inferred, though. His father wasn't a great person, and Torren didn't mourn him.

"I'm sorry," I say quietly, and I mean it. "Let's just tell ourselves we're better off."

"We are."

The silence creeps back up between us. A warm breeze tousles my hair, tickling the back of my neck, and I move to put my hair in a ponytail using the elastic on my wrist. I feel Torren's eyes on me as I do, and I'm thankful he can't see the way I blush in the dim light.

The longer he stares at me, though, studying me, the more I think I see a flicker of a memory in his eyes. Like he's so close to grasping it, but it keeps slipping through his fingers. It's as frightening as it is thrilling.

It feels a bit like an invasion, how much I know about him when he doesn't remember me. I'm embarrassed of my former obsession, and I'll admit that I've been hiding like a coward behind his ignorance. As much as it hurts knowing he's discarded me, I can't deny that it makes me feel less exposed. I don't have to own up to my past hero worship. I don't have to be ashamed of my naiveté.

"Have you ever played in front of an audience?"

His question—the way it almost sounds leading, searching—makes my heart thunder in my head. I won't lie, so I give him the barest of truths.

"I was in a band."

He hums, brow furrowing slightly before he gives me a small smile. "That's cool."

"Sav and Mabel didn't tell you?"

"No, *they* didn't, but it doesn't surprise me that Sav knew. She likes to keep her finger on the music scene."

I roll my eyes. Of course she does.

"Yeah, so my dad was a jazz pianist," I continue, "but when I started to play better than he could teach me, my mom got me lessons. I was in a youth music program for years. Played some solo recitals at Barnum Hall in Santa Monica. I loved it, and I was good, but I wasn't amazing or anything like that. Not a child prodigy. So, when I realized I wasn't going to be a famous classical pianist, I joined a rock band and played keyboard. But classical...that's where my heart is."

Torren laughs, eyes alight with humor. "Sounds like a natural progression of events, honestly."

I feel such warmth from his laughter, from a hint of his approval, that I almost tell him. I almost unleash the whole fucking thing—the memory, the anger. I want to shake him and scream REMEMBER ME, but I don't. I punk out because I'm a coward and because I'm ashamed.

And because it fucking hurts still, his rejection.

"Well, I should go..."

I stand from the little patio chair where I was sitting, but Torren takes another step in my direction, halting me.

"You don't have to. I'm not in a hurry to get back to my room."

I blink at him, and he must mistake my shock for concern because he throws his palms up.

"No touching. No fake dating stuff. Just two people having a chat on a rooftop terrace."

An unwelcomed smirk turns up my lips on impulse, my thoughts forming into words before I can think better of it. "Because you have such a great track record with keeping your pants on while on rooftop terraces."

Torren barks out a laugh and shakes his head while taking a seat in one of the patio chairs. I'm grateful he's sitting now. I don't have to worry about accidentally staring at his naked chest or studying his thin sweatpants.

"That wasn't me. I know some tabloids held to the story that it was, but it wasn't."

My jaw drops. "Really?"

"Really. It was Levi. I was at the hotel with the rest of the band."

"Damn."

That rooftop sex tape scandal was everywhere. I tried my best to avoid it, and everything I learned about it was against my will. By that time, The Hometown Heartless was on the top of my shit list, and Torren was King Shit. I didn't know much about this Levi guy—still don't—but I was certain it was Torren on that rooftop with Sav.

"How often does that happen?" I ask him. "How often do they just print stories that aren't true."

"All the fucking time."

"That would drive me mad."

"You get used to it." He shrugs, then reaches into his back pocket and pulls out a familiar silver cigarette case. "Is it cool if I smoke?"

I arch a brow. Torren from four years ago didn't ask my permission to smoke, and he practically hotboxed his tour bus with me in it.

"*Now* you ask?"

"Now?"

"Never mind," I say with a sigh. "I don't mind. Just don't blow it at me."

He smirks and puts the joint between his lips, and I watch his long, tattooed fingers as he strikes a match and lights it, inhaling so the cherry glows red on the end.

"Why matches?" I ask randomly. "Why not a lighter?"

He blows a stream of smoke out of the side of his mouth and examines his matchbook as he puts it back in the silver case.

"I could make up some bullshit about how the butane taints the flavor of the joint or something, but really, I just think they're cool. You're basically holding a flame between your fingers." He pauses and grins at me. "Who doesn't want to be a fire master?"

I force a smile and break eye contact. The nickname Firebird echoes loudly in my head, and I almost want to laugh. *Who doesn't want to be a fire master?* I guess that explains a lot.

"So, besides your dad, it's just you, your mom, and your sister, right?"

Grateful for the change of subject, I nod. "Yep. Well, and the dog now. Happy little family of four."

"Your sister is a crack-up."

"Yeah, Glory is a treat," I say wryly. "She texted me this morning to ask if she can have my half of the closet. As if I'm never going to come back."

Torren laughs, his white teeth glinting. "Typical younger sibling."

"Do you have any? Siblings, I mean."

I ask the question even though I already know the answer. His smile falls briefly. His brow furrows for just a second, then his expression is light and carefree once more. If I'd blinked, I might have missed the change entirely.

"No younger siblings. I have an older brother, as you probably know. We don't have the best relationship."

"That sucks," I say because I don't know what else to say.

I don't know how Torren feels about it. Last I heard, his brother was in prison, so I really have no idea if the lack of a relationship with him stings. I know it's not the same thing, but for as much grief as Glory Bell gives me, it would still break my heart if we weren't on good terms. Even when I was with the band, I called every few days to talk to her. I sent her postcards from all the states we played in. And she might act like she can't stand me sometimes, but she still keeps those postcards in her jewelry box. She texts me multiple times a day. She loves me. She's just a teenager.

"It is what it is. I don't have a great relationship with any of my family, to be honest. I share my birthday with my mom, and she didn't even pick up when I called. She never does."

"Wow. And here I thought my mom only talking to me via text right now was bad." I say it lightly, attempting to add some levity, and the way he smiles makes me think it works. "Is your family still in Florida?"

I realize my mistake the moment the words leave my mouth—revealing my hand, my knowledge of him—but it's too late to shove them back in. He doesn't seem to mind that I know where he's from, though. I suppose he's used to people knowing these details about him.

"Yeah. Same town I grew up in. It's a black hole. No one ever leaves." He says the last part quietly, almost sadly, as he flicks some ash into a small ashtray on the patio table.

"You left," I say. "You got out."

He huffs out a laugh and widens his eyes at me.

"I did. And that's one of the reasons my family disowned me. They think I *put the band before them*. Before my brother." He purses his lips and gazes out at the Strip for a moment. "They aren't wrong, though. I did. I'd do it again. This band is all I've ever wanted. Heartless is my family."

The silence stretches once more, but this time, it's not awkward. I prop my elbow on the arm of my patio chair and rest my chin on my fist. I'm getting tired, but I don't want to leave him just yet.

I roll Torren's words over in my head.

This band is all I've ever wanted. Heartless is my family.

I felt like that once. With Rocky, Ezra, Pike, and Becket. They were like a family to me, and I'd only been with them for a short while. But The Hometown Heartless? They've been together for a decade. That's a long fucking time. I don't even know if I can begin to understand the depth of their connection. No wonder Torren and Sav had such a hard time letting go of one another.

"Hey, what happened with your band?"

My shoulders stiffen at Torren's question, and I turn my eyes on him. He's watching me intently, nothing but genuine interest on his face. I blink a few times before deciding what to say, and then I force a smile.

"Just didn't work out. And then my mom had a stroke, so I had to move back home to help out."

"Shit. I'm so sorry, Callie. She's okay now, though?"

He sits upright and leans toward me. Interest morphing to concern. Sympathy. Literally every emotion looks sexy on him. It almost ruins the moment.

"Yeah, mostly. She's doing better than she was. That's actually why I agreed to do this. We have medical bills, obviously, and she needs more physical therapy, but it's not covered by insurance. Eighty grand is going to make a huge difference."

Torren blows out a slow breath. "Well, I feel like a fucking dick now."

"No, don't," I say with a laugh. "I'm sorry for being such a pain in the ass. I hope you don't have buyer's remorse."

Torren smirks and gives me a little shrug, and I roll my eyes.

"No, I'm kidding. You've been great. No buyer's remorse here."

I laugh. "Well, good. Because I'm going to try my best to stick it out for the whole three months."

Torren's smile softens, those green eyes of his glittering as he holds my gaze. For a moment, his eyes drop to my lips, and my breath catches. When he locks his eyes with mine once more, there's an intensity in them I've never seen before. It's a look I'm going to dream about, and when he speaks, I know I'll be playing his words on a loop for the rest of the night.

"I really hope you do, Calla Lily. I really hope you do."

21

CALLIE

"Is he at least taking care of you?"

Finally hearing my mom's voice after two weeks of sporadic text messages is such a relief, even if disappointment and sadness are dripping from every word.

"Yeah, Mom. Torren is great. I promise. You'd like him."

"You know I just want you to be happy. But I worry. I don't want you to end up like me."

"Torren isn't like Dad, Mom. It's not going to be like that."

"I don't like that he's paying our bills."

I told her it's to make up for my being gone. A *gift*. She doesn't like feeling like we're indebted to him now. It's killing me to lie to her, but I'm doing my best to sell it. *It's for her*, I tell myself. *It's for the best.*

"I know."

My mom sighs, so I change the subject. "I had a lot of fun in Vegas. We stayed in this really fancy hotel on the top floor. Private balconies and a rooftop terrace and everything. You'd have loved it. And Torren says the hotel in Arlington has a private pool just for us."

"I'm glad you're having fun."

"I am. And I'll be back before you know it. How's Glory's dog? Has he eaten any more of my shoes?"

My mom takes the bait and moves on to a new topic, and luckily, she doesn't bring up Torren or my skipping off to tour the country with a boy I've just met again. It's a nice conversation, and by the time I hang up, I'm feeling slightly less slimy about being a big, fat, stinking liar.

According to the GPS on my phone, we're almost to Arlington, and I cannot wait to be off this bus. This has been the longest stretch of time I've been on here and admittedly I'm going a little stir-crazy. Since we left Vegas yesterday, I've slept. I've read. I've eaten dinner and breakfast. I've read some more. I've played video games with Mabel. I've listened to Sav write a song, and then was sworn to secrecy about the song. (It's good. Shocker.)

I don't even remember how I handled being carted around by the guys in Pike's beat-up old van. I even have my own room on this bus and I'm still ready to jump out of my skin. At least my shared bedroom in my tiny apartment doesn't have wheels underneath it. By the time we're pulling into the hotel parking lot, I'm ready to sprint down the stairs just to feel stable, unmoving ground under my feet.

My phone buzzes with a text before we're in a parking spot, and I'm surprised to see it's Jonah.

JONAH

Lunch?

I know a place.

My stomach grumbles. I've only had a breakfast sandwich since waking up this morning, and eating food on solid ground is definitely appealing. So appealing that the idea of lunch with Jonah and Torren makes me less nervous than it probably would if I weren't approaching hangry territory.

According to the recent bout of articles, Operation Fake Dating seems to be working, and I haven't heard anything more about Sav's stalker. Being seen with the guys can only help the story along. I text him back just before following Sav and Mabel off the bus.

ME

Sounds good.

The moment my feet hit the ground, a tattooed arm is slung around my shoulder, and it's no less surprising than it was the first time.

"Hey." I shove my phone in my pocket. "What's up?"

"Lunch."

"Now?"

"Now."

Jonah steers me out of the path toward the hotel doors as Sav and Mabel disappear through them.

"They're not coming?"

"Nah. Savvy is going to use the high-speed WiFi to have video chat sex with her boyfriend, and Mabel is going to sleep."

"Oh." He opens the door to a black SUV, and I climb in. He climbs in after me. When his security starts to drive, I turn toward Jonah. "Isn't Torren coming?"

Jonah shakes his head. "Invited him. He said no."

Oh. Okay then. I try my best to ignore the way my excitement deflates. I guess he's not up for pretending today.

Jonah doesn't speak for the whole fifteen-minute drive, but it's not an uncomfortable silence. It's actually refreshing, despite the fact that I'm in another vehicle when I was looking forward to being stationary for a few hours. He doesn't probe me with small talk, and his presence doesn't make me nervous like Torren's does. I'm almost grateful for my fake boyfriend's absence.

The SUV pulls up to a small sushi restaurant in a busy strip mall. We get out on the sidewalk, and I notice a sign on the door that says *Closed For Private Event*.

"Um, I think we need to find somewhere else," I say as Jonah opens the door and ushers me inside.

He laughs. "You're cute."

And then an older woman greets us and shows us to a table. I know immediately she's the owner. I see no waitstaff in the whole restaurant.

"Welcome back, Mr. Hendrix. It's good to see you again."

"Thank you for doing this on such short notice."

"Of course. Anything for you." The woman waits while we sit, then she and Jonah exchange a few more pleasantries. Jonah introduces us, then asks for a single menu. Just for me.

"Take your time," he tells me, sitting back in his seat and crossing his arms.

"You don't need to see it?" I ask, and Jonah shakes his head slowly.

"I know what I want."

The comment seems suggestive, summoning a chill across my skin, and Torren's words from before flash in bright neon. *He's not nice. He just wants to fuck you.*

And then I think of something else.

The sharing.

I blush crimson, my cheeks flaming with heat, and Jonah's responding Cheshire grin makes me nervous in the most confusing way. So much so that I tear my eyes away from him and don't look up from the menu again until we've ordered.

"So how are you liking being part of the band, Callie?"

I take a sip of my water before answering, flicking my eyes from his face, then to the paintings on the wall. "It's been an adjustment."

"It's fucking chaos."

I laugh. "Yes, it is."

"Sorry if Torren's been a dick."

"He's not been a dick," I say, and Jonah smirks. "Okay, fine. He's been a dick. But I don't know, he's coming around."

It's not a lie. Torren *was* a dick, but he's been kinder. Softer. And unfortunately, it's softening me, too.

"Sometimes he takes a bit of coaxing."

I arch a brow at Jonah's comment. "What do you mean?"

He shrugs. "To get out of his own head."

"I still don't understand," I say slowly, frowning at his smirking face.

He doesn't clarify. He checks his watch, then changes the subject, but it takes me a minute to catch up. I'm still puzzling out his meaning when the door to the restaurant opens and I glance up to see Torren heading in our direction.

And he is pissed.

He doesn't even look at me when he makes it to our table. He just glares down at Jonah like he's ready to bite his head off.

"The fuck is this, Jo?"

Jonah grins lazily up at him. "I invited you. You said no."

Torren seethes. "You didn't think it was important to tell me Callie was coming?"

"Slipped my mind."

My eyebrows rise as I look between the guys, then Torren turns his attention to me.

"Get up. We're going."

The command in his voice, the utter entitlement, has my muscles going rigid.

"No," I snap. "I'm having lunch."

"Callie, get the fuck up and come with me."

His nostrils flare as he stares me down, the words said slowly and tightly, like he's trying his best not to raise his voice. Not to make a scene.

"I will not. I came here for lunch, and I'm going to eat lunch. You can sit down and join us, but I'm not leaving."

Torren huffs out a humorless laugh, then glares back at Jonah. "I'd stay, but I'm allergic to shellfish."

Jonah shrugs. "Slipped my mind."

"Yeah, you're real fucking forgetful today, aren't you?"

"Drugs, man. Lasting damage."

"You're such a motherfucker, Hendrix."

Jonah smirks. "If she's willing."

My jaw drops. Jonah did this on purpose—fucked with Torren intentionally—and I don't know what to make of that. I do know that I don't like feeling like a pawn or some toy they can fight over. I throw my napkin on the table and stand.

"I'm not hungry anymore." I glance between them once more before settling my eyes back on Torren. "I'll go back, but I'm not riding with you."

His nostrils flare and his jaw ticks as he bounces his eyes between mine, and then finally, he gives me one nod. I brush past him and walk right out of the restaurant.

Damon has the back door of another SUV opened for me before I even set foot on the sidewalk, and I slide in without a word. After a few minutes, he pulls away without Torren.

Good. Let those idiots ride together.

I don't want to deal with either of them.

It's close to eleven when there's a knock on my door.

I open it expecting Torren, but I find Jonah instead.

"What do you want?" I whisper the words angrily, looking past him into the main room of the suite to find it empty. "How did you get in here? Sav and Mabel are already in bed."

He leans on the doorframe and stares down at me.

"I'm sorry for earlier."

My eyes go wide with surprise before I narrow them at him. "Good. You're not forgiven. Now go away."

He doesn't budge, and I clear my throat, gesturing to the door behind him.

"You can leave," I say, but he still doesn't move. His big blue eyes bore into mine in a way that has me pausing so I can stare back.

"You want to know why I did it?"

I start to say no but I stop myself. "Why did you do it?"

"Because I wanted to."

I roll my eyes and start to shut my bedroom door on him, but he puts out his hand, stopping the door from closing. The move puts him farther into my space, and his scent overwhelms me. Something darker than Torren. More moody. Even in the moment, when my head is swimming, I can appreciate how fitting it is.

"I did it because you're special, and he's got his head too far up his ass to see it."

I arch a brow. "What the hell does that mean?"

"If he's not going to take you to lunch, why can't I?"

"Maybe because you're not my boyfriend?"

"*Fake* boyfriend, and I don't see him doing anything more than the bare minimum."

I scoff. "Because, like you said, it's *fake*. He's not required to do more."

"But he should."

Jonah takes a step closer to me and leans in, his long blond hair creating what feels like a curtain around our faces. Something in my head shouts for me to step away, but I don't.

"He hasn't taken you out since Glendale. Didn't show you any of Vegas. Two weeks and nothing but pap walks from the bus to the hotel, and from the hotel to the stadium." His eyes drop to my lips, lingering there as he speaks. "Tell me you're not bored."

I bite the inside of my cheek and shake my head, but he smirks.

"Torren wants to keep you all to himself. Wants to keep you

hidden." He looks back into my eyes, then reaches up and tucks a strand of my hair behind my ear. "But I think you should be seen."

My brows furrow as he drops his hand and steps backward.

"It's all up to you, Calla Lily."

He doesn't say another word. He just winks at me, then turns and walks out, leaving me staring a hole through the door.

Jesus, this just keeps getting weirder and weirder.

———————

The crowd roars as The Hometown Heartless take the stage for their second encore, and there's something even more magical about watching the show from backstage.

Getting to see the faces of the fans in the pit. The way they sing along with all their hearts. The way they cry and laugh. It makes me miss my band. Makes me miss being front and center on the stage. Our crowds were never even a fraction of this size, but the energy is still just as enthralling. And even now, years after I decided to hate The Hometown Heartless forever, I can't help but want to sing along. I can't help but want to dance and laugh and even cry with the crowd. They're just...

Magic.

This band is magic. It makes me regret everything.

When the last song is over, I walk to the pre-determined spot for our photo op. I plaster on a happy smile, and in full view of the crowd, I wait. The only thing Torren and I have spoken about since the sushi restaurant yesterday afternoon was this little show Hammond had planned for the media. A quick photo op to keep the press happy. I keep thinking about what Jonah said yesterday.

Two weeks and nothing but pap walks.

This is certainly not a pap walk, but it's just another version of the same old song and dance. I just want to get it over with, but I force a smile anyway.

Gotta sell it, after all.

The moment I see Torren, my heart picks up pace. He's sweaty, his tattooed skin glistening and his curly hair falling in his eyes. He took off his vest halfway through the second set, so he's gloriously shirtless, wearing just a low-slung pair of tight black jeans, and I have only thirty seconds to prepare myself. Thirty seconds where he's strutting toward me with a sexy smirk on his full lips like some kind of famous rock star, and I have to remind myself to breathe.

When he's within a few feet of me, I put my arms out like we discussed and let him swoop me up, spinning me in a circle before putting me back on my feet and smoothing my hair out of my face.

"Hi." His voice is raspy from singing for two hours, and it sends a shiver down my spine.

"Hi."

We hold the pose, gazing into each other's eyes for long enough that spectators can get photographs, and I wait for him to take my hand and lead me back to the dressing rooms like we'd planned. He doesn't, though. Instead, he lowers his face into the crook of my neck and kisses me there, once, twice, before biting me lightly.

My eyes fall shut, and I whimper, pressing my thighs together and tightening my arms around his neck. He chuckles, and the sound shoots right to my core.

"That's right, baby."

He slides his hands to my backside, squeezing my ass cheeks before lifting me. I wrap my legs around his waist on instinct, then gasp when my body meets his hard dick.

He bites me again and my hips jolt into him.

"Fuck, you burn so hot, don't you?"

The words float through the haze in my head, alarm bells ringing, but they're drowned out by lust and need. I don't notice he's walking until my back is pressed against a cold cinderblock wall. He squeezes my ass again and then pats my thigh. I unwrap my legs, and he sets me down. For the first time since he scooped me up, I take a full breath and try to clear my head.

His pupils are dilated, and he's fighting a smirk as his eyes sweep over me.

"Be ready at ten a.m. I'm taking you somewhere." His gaze fixates on my neck, and his eyes flare with heat. "And wear your hair up."

Then he turns and struts away. I close my eyes and rest my body against the wall, allowing the cold of the cinderblock to seep through my The Hometown Heartless tank top, willing it to cool me down. As my heartbeat returns to normal, my neck starts to throb. I press my fingers against the spot he assaulted and shiver. I don't even have to look in the mirror. I know what he did.

Wear your hair up.

The bastard marked me—*again*—and he's proud of it.

Then I remember something else.

You burn so hot, don't you?

Shit.

First the comment about my hair, and then this.

You burn so hot.

Fear licks up my throat, my heart racing for a whole new reason.

Until now, I've been hiding in plain sight, but I think my time might be running out.

22

CALLIE

PAST, ArtFusion Day Four

"You gonna go hang with your *friend from high school* again?"

Rocky's question is posed sarcastically as if he doesn't believe that's who I've spent time with the last two nights. I flick my eyes to Becket, but he refuses to look at me. I take a bite of my breakfast sandwich and focus on Rocky. I chew and swallow slowly, trying not to give myself away. I'm not a great liar, but I can omit the truth like a pro.

"You're just jealous I haven't introduced you," I state, and Rock rolls his eyes.

Ezra lumbers up to the picnic table where we're sitting, wearing the same outfit he had on yesterday. I jump on the opportunity to direct attention away from me.

"You're up early." I make a show of checking the time on my phone. It's a little after six in the morning, and Ezra usually sleeps until noon. "Where have you been?"

He bounces his eyebrows playfully.

"You want the short answer or the long, dirty, detailed answer?"

"Ew. No. Never mind."

"I was naked in a camper with three—"

"I said no, Ezra! No, no, no."

"I got to hit it from—"

"No!"

I punctuate my shout by landing a punch to his upper arm, and he barks out a laugh, then steals my breakfast sandwich. He takes a bite and speaks with his mouth full.

"Still a virgin, then."

Ezra elbows Becket like he's trying to razz him, but Becket shoves him back and storms off. I watch him go, my brow furrowing and my tongue turning to cement in my mouth.

"The fuck is wrong with you?" Rocky juts out his foot, kicking Ezra in the thigh.

"It was a joke!"

"It's not funny." Rocky looks at me. "You think it's funny, Cal?"

Ezra turns remorseful eyes in my direction. He can tell from my face that not only am I unamused, I'm also angry. One drunken game of *Never Have I Ever* a few months ago in San Francisco, and the guys all know about my absolute lack of experience. I trusted them, and now Ezra is making fun of me.

"I don't find it funny at all, Ez."

Ezra's shoulders fall and he throws himself onto the bench beside me, pulling me into a hot, sticky hug. "Sorry, Calla Lily."

"Ugh, you're forgiven. Now get off."

I shove him, and he laughs. Then I laugh, but it's forced. My eyes keep drifting in the direction of Becket's exit. He's nowhere to be seen.

"Beck's mad at me," I say, taking a sip of my iced latte.

The guys don't say anything, and that doesn't help to ease my inner turmoil. I'm struggling with Becket's mood. He's pissed we haven't had any alone time, and I get that. We had all these implied plans, and I've basically ghosted him three nights in a row. I've put us on ice, too, and he can tell.

I feel guilty. I feel *really* guilty.

And the shittiest part about it all?

Despite my guilt, I still can't stop thinking about last night with Torren. More specifically, how to get a *do-over* of last night with Torren. He walked me to my tent in silence, then told me *sweet dreams* before disappearing back into the crowd.

No *see you later*. No *meet me tomorrow*. Just *sweet dreams* and a goodbye nod.

My sense of rejection battles violently with my logical reasoning.

I should be grateful for his actions last night because the truth is that I *was* uncomfortable. I was nervous and overwhelmed and anxious and, yes, uncomfortable. There's a good chance that anything *more* with Torren would have left me feeling regretful in the morning, simply because I wasn't in the mindset to enjoy it. It doesn't make the memory sting any less, though. I almost wish I'd have taken him up on his offer of a drink and a smoke. At least then the replay loop in my head would be hazy.

"Who wants to do goat yoga with me?" Ezra asks, studying something on his phone. "It's in thirty minutes."

"Probably trying to get it done early to beat the heat," Pike adds, and I huff a laugh.

"It's already eighty."

"C'mon, Cal," Ezra pleads. "Come. Let's go do sun salutations with some cute little goaties."

"I'm down," Rocky says, turning to me with a grin. "C'mon, Cal. Ignore Beck. He'll be fine once he beats off."

I groan, then push myself to standing.

"Fine, assholes. Let's go to goat yoga."

I'm drunk.

Well, kind of drunk. More like decently buzzed. But I'm also sporting a nice high from half an edible I got from Rocky, so my courage is up, and my inhibitions are down. Sober enough to know better, stoned enough not to give a fuck.

It's been a long-ass day. We've listened to two other bands play, took a shag dancing for beginners' class, and of course did goat yoga between eating food truck food and drinking all the drinks. The whole time, I've been stewing.

My head's been on a swivel even when I knew it was stupid. Looking for Torren when the sun is up is pointless—he only ventures out under the cover of darkness—but it didn't stop me from doing it. Now, though, with sunset fast approaching and my bravery reaching moronic levels of fearlessness, I tell the guys I'm going to pee and steal away to make a potentially bad decision.

I know the chances of Torren coming to find me tonight are nonexistent. I'm going to put myself in his path instead. It's dumb. I know this, but I do it anyway. If I don't, I'll always wonder *what if*, and my dad says it's better not to live with regrets. Or he used to, anyway.

Halfway to the bathrooms, I take out my phone and send a group text to the guys that I'm going to hang out with my friend from high school. Rock, Ezra, and Pike reply. Becket doesn't. I put my phone back in my pocket, then change direction, heading for The Hometown Heartless tour bus. I don't know what I'll do when I get there—maybe post up and hope I catch Torren before he leaves for the night—but I don't dwell on it. I'm going to be spontaneous. I'm going to be a little reckless. I can do this.

I think.

Despite having dropped out of high school to drive up and down the West Coast with my band, reckless and spontaneous are not words I would use to describe myself. In fact, I went back and forth over that decision for weeks before finally making the jump.

College wasn't in my future. My grades weren't high enough for scholarships, and the aid I'd be awarded wasn't going to be enough to pay for much of anything. And even then, the idea of higher education made me want to pluck my eyes out and stomp on them. I'd never liked school. I'd always dreamed of becoming a classical concert pianist, but by eighteen, I realized the closest I'd probably ever get was playing the keyboard in the band.

When I finally decided to leave with Becket, Rocky, Pike, and Ezra, I did it in the middle of the day while my mom was at work because I was afraid to face her. I was a coward, and I didn't want to see the disappointment on her face. I told myself it was a calculated risk, and if I'm honest, it's one that has yet to pay off.

We're playing ArtFusion, though. Our band has a steadily growing community of fans. Decent enough that we're starting to be recognized in some circles. The fact that my band is on the ArtFusion line-up poster is proof that taking risks can be a good thing. I repeat this over and over in my head as I walk to the tour bus, and when I get there, I creep as close to it as I can before I'm stopped by a security guard.

"You can't come back here," he says, his voice low and intimidating.

"Oh. Um. Beau, right? I'm Callie, remember? From last night?"

He doesn't smile. No recognition at all on his face.

"You can go back behind the barricade with the rest of the fans, or I'll have you escorted there."

I glance toward where he's gesturing. A low, black chain-link fence separates the bus lot from the park, and there are people standing alongside it. I didn't notice it because I came from the opposite direction.

"Were they there yesterday?" I ask. He doesn't answer.

I nod, then open my mouth to apologize when the group of fans behind the fence start screaming. Two seconds later, a tan arm is thrown around my shoulder, and I look up to find the lead guitarist of The Hometown Heartless towering over me. My eyes widen and my jaw drops.

With dirty-blond hair brushing just above his shoulders and dark two-day-old scruff covering his jaw, Jonah Hendrix looks like grunge rock incarnate. His faded gray T-shirt is sporting tiny tears at the collar and sleeve, and it's frayed on all the hemlines. It's distressed in the kind of way that didn't cost him hundreds of dollars, but is disheveled without being outright sloppy. His bright blue eyes are red-rimmed, and there's a cigarette hanging from his lips. When he speaks, I watch the cigarette bob along with the movement of his mouth.

"She's with me."

I squeak but I don't protest. When Beau looks at me, he's not amused. Jonah sighs, already seeming bored with this interaction.

"You're with me, right, sweets?"

I volley my attention between Jonah and Beau before giving a small shrug, and then the security guard just...steps to the side. Jonah says nothing else as he steers me toward the bus. The fans on the other side of the fence don't stop screaming or shouting Jonah's name until he's pulling open the door to the bus and leading me inside.

The weed smell is stronger than it was last night, and the music is louder. I'm half expecting some sort of party when I step foot into the main living area, but instead, I only see Torren. The sight of him makes my mouth dry. He's sprawled on the couch in a pair of black boxer briefs, beautiful body on full display, and his hair is wet like he's just gotten out of the shower.

I stop in my tracks and stare.

My eyes rove over him—all colorfully tattooed skin and toned muscles—as I work to keep my breathing even. His legs look longer now that they're bare and stretched out in front of him, the pirate ship inked onto his right thigh seeming small on his six-foot-two frame. I make it a point to avoid the expanse of his body covered by the black fabric of his underwear, skipping entirely over the area between upper thigh and pelvis. If I look, I'll pass out. As it is, the scene before me makes my heart race in a way that's bordering painful, but Torren doesn't look away from his phone until Jonah speaks.

"Tor. Got a friend." Torren glances up slowly, his eyelids heavy as he focuses on Jonah. Jonah gestures to me. "Tor, meet sweets. Sweets, meet Tor."

The introduction is weird, but what's weirder is the way Torren reacts when he finally sees me. Or better, the way he *doesn't* react. For seconds that feel like hours, he stares blankly at me, pupils all but swallowing up his green eyes. My chest tightens and the floor feels unstable under my feet as I count his slow blinks.

One...two...three...

And then, like a haze has lifted, his brows rise in recognition, and his lips curl up at the corner.

"Firebird."

Awkwardly, I raise my hand in a wave. "Hey."

"You named this one," Jonah says, and Torren nods, breaking eye contact with me to drag his eyes toward his bandmate. Every movement is delayed, like a half-step behind, and it makes me so nervous that it takes a moment for Jonah's words to sink in.

You named this one.

I glance at Jonah with a furrowed brow.

"What's that mean?"

He looks right through me, no longer interested, and his body turns away, dismissing me as he speaks.

"Don't worry about it. It's a compliment."

And then Jonah's disappearing into the back of the bus, leaving me alone with Torren. His eyes drag leisurely over my skin in a way that feels both sensual and disconnected. He's looking at me, but I can't be sure that he's really seeing me.

"What all are you on?" I ask, and he tilts his head to the side, observing me like he finds me amusing.

"You want some?"

I start to shake my head, but then I take a deep breath and straighten my shoulders.

"I'll...um...I'll smoke with you? If you want."

Torren smirks again, and I stay frozen to the spot as he pulls a joint from his silver cigarette case. Absently, I wonder just how many he's got stashed in that thing as his long, tattooed fingers strike a match and light it up. He takes a drag and blows the smoke through his plush lips in a steady stream, then raises a hand and crooks a finger at me.

In three steps, I close the distance between us.

23

TORREN

PRESENT DAY

MY DICK IS PAINFULLY hard as I make my way to the dressing room I share with Jonah.

The adrenaline of playing a sold-out show always amps me up, but the encounter with Callie backstage has sent me over the edge. I took it further than we'd planned, but I can't bring myself to regret it. Not yet.

She's so soft. She's so hot.

I let myself indulge, and now my dick aches for relief.

And then I walk into my dressing room and find Jonah on the couch with another redhead. He wasted no time. I bet he had security pull her from the pit before we did the first encore, and she was waiting here for him.

The fucker really does suck at celibacy.

I roll my eyes but I still fold my arms across my chest and watch. When he sees me, he pulls his dick out of her throat and slaps his thigh.

"Climb up here, sweets."

She does, and he grabs a condom from the strip on the couch before she slides down on him with a theatrical moan.

"It's a nice one." Jonah arches a brow, eyes on me, and then slaps her ass. "Already prepped."

Then she turns and smiles at me, lipstick smeared and eyeliner smudged as she bounces on his dick. Jo's already done a number on her, and from her blissed-out expression, she's loving it.

"Ready when you are," she says, dragging her eyes to my crotch.

I almost want to laugh because I feel nothing. My dick's deflated. Nothing about this scene bothers me—I have no problem with consensual sex between adults—but it's not getting me hard like it would have a few weeks ago. I have no desire to join in.

Not right away, anyway.

Not until Jonah wraps his hand around the woman's throat and looks up at me with a lopsided grin.

"You think she'd like this? Because I think she would."

He's not talking about the woman riding him right now. I know it. And then, just like Jonah wanted, I see it.

The redhead is Callie.

Mossy green eyes and perfect tits and that round, full ass that I had my hands on just minutes ago. In an instant, I'm hard as a rock again.

"You can see it," Jonah says, and then he groans and closes his eyes. "Fuck, I can see it."

Jealousy mixes with my lust, a possessiveness I've only felt with one other person, and it's dizzying. It's confusing, and it's fucking terrifying.

Without another word, I turn and storm out.

By the time I'm back in my bedroom in my hotel suite, though, I've managed to wrangle my jealousy into something more manageable. I strip and throw myself onto my bed, then take my hard cock in my hand. I squeeze and stroke and bring the image of Callie between Jonah and me back to the forefront of my mind. I force myself to enjoy it. I ignore the possessive feeling clawing its way up my throat and instead focus on the image of her face as I fuck her. As we *fuck* her. Her breasts. Her soft, hot, perfect body. Her sexy, breathy moans.

It only takes a few strokes before I'm coming all over my abdomen with a groan.

But it's not enough.

It might never be.

"Hey."

Mabel swings the door wide and lets me into the suite. She's still in her pajamas, her pink hair standing up in all directions.

"Rough night?"

She grins at my question. "Yeah. And she's still asleep, so keep it down."

"Tell Kat I said hey."

Kat's a runway model. She and Mabel have been seeing each other for a few months, but they've been keeping it quiet at the request of Kat's manager. He thinks that if she came out as a lesbian, it would hurt her marketability. We all think that's bullshit, especially for Mabel's sake, but there's not much we can do about it. Mabes likes her, so I stay quiet.

"Have fun today." Mabel turns and heads back toward her bedroom. "And be nice."

I chuckle. "I'm always nice."

She scoffs just before she disappears through the door, shutting it behind her. I contemplate knocking on Callie's door even though I'm a little early, but then Sav's door opens and she stumbles into the main room wearing a white T-shirt that's a few sizes too big on her. It's probably her boyfriend's, because it falls just past her ass and brushes the top of her thighs. She's definitely not wearing a bra, and knowing her, she probably doesn't have pants on, either.

I clear my throat to get her attention, and she whips her head in my direction. When she sees me, her eyes flare wide, and she folds her arms over her chest. I smirk.

"Nothing I haven't already seen."

She narrows her eyes. "What are you doing here this early?"

"It's almost ten, Savvy. Not everyone sleeps as late as you."

"Do you see anyone else awake?" She arches a brow and gestures to the empty, quiet suite.

I shrug. She's got me there. I don't hear anything coming from Callie's room, either. I should go knock, but I haven't gotten to talk to Sav in a while. I close the distance between us and make sure to keep my eyes firmly on her face.

"How are you?" I ask, and her expression softens.

"Fine. How are you?"

"Fine," I say with a laugh. "Anything new with your biggest fan?"

"No." She shakes her head, and her eyebrows slant downward. "But it kind of freaks me out. The investigative team doesn't think it's Fieldman anymore."

"What? Who the fuck else would it be?"

Sav's had trouble with Dennis Fieldman a few times in the past. He once broke into her hotel room, and he was caught masturbating in her shower. The label wouldn't let her press charges, and then two months later, he ended up going to prison for attempted armed robbery of a sex shop. The guy is a fucking creep.

Sav sighs. "There's no shortage of gross men out there, Tor. It could be anyone. Hell, it could even be a woman. We just don't know, and now that they've disappeared, our ways of finding out are limited."

Her hands tighten around her biceps and her lips purse as she stares at the carpet. I want to comfort her. I want to make this all go away. We're not together anymore, but I still love her. I still want her to be safe and happy. Sav is my fucking family. She used to be my best friend. Seeing her like this and being able to do nothing to fix it? I fucking hate it.

"We'll get him, Savvy. We will. It will be over soon."

She sniffles, her eyes glossing over with a shimmer of tears before she frowns and blinks them away.

"I'm just scared," she admits, her voice shaking slightly. "And I'm tired. And I miss Levi and Brynn. Everything feels so ominous. Like, sure, the stalking seems to have stopped for now, but what happens at the end of these three months? What happens when the PR relationship ends? Do I just wait around until it starts back up again? I fucking hate feeling like I'm in limbo. I just wish things could be fucking normal for once."

I reach out and rest a hand on her shoulder. I squeeze gently and then rub, resisting the urge to pull her body against me in a comforting embrace. I wait until she makes eye contact before I speak.

"Sorry to break it to you, Sav Loveless, but this *is* your normal. You're arguably one of the most famous celebrities in the world. You lost your opportunity for a boring life a long time ago."

She laughs and shakes her head. "Do you ever wish we could

rewind and undo it all? Sometimes I think boring sounds like it could be nice."

"Sometimes," I say honestly, then my lips turn up into a small smile. "But then we play a show and I'm reminded that there's no way I could do anything else. If I wasn't playing with the band—with you—I'd be worse than bored. I'd be purposeless. Chaos is a fair trade for purpose, Savannah. At least I think so, anyway."

"Yeah. Yeah, I think you're probably right."

Sav sighs, then catches me off guard by wrapping her arms around my waist in a tight hug. I don't hesitate to return it, but for a split second, I brace myself for a rush of *something*. Lust or longing or that deep, deep ache of unrequited love. I wait with bated breath, my muscles stiffening, my heart racing, prepping for any kind of unwelcomed emotional invasion. But when nothing happens, my shoulders relax, and I pull her tighter against me.

I feel no hunger or desire. I feel no loss or heartache. Nothing impure or unwanted.

I only feel comfort, the love you have for a close friend, and relief.

So much fucking relief that I almost sway on my feet from the rush of it.

"We're going to be okay," I say quietly, resting my chin gently atop her head, and I hear her laugh into my chest.

"Thank god. But fuck, man, it would be nice if someone stalked one of you for a change. I'd like to be left alone."

I open my mouth to say something smart-assed, but the sound of a door opening behind me has me releasing Sav and turning around instead.

Sav lets out a low whistle. "Wow, smokeshow. You're looking good. Very classy."

Callie forces a stiff smile. "Thanks. It was in the closet."

The simple green and white polka-dotted dress looks amazing on her. It has a sweetheart neckline, flares out at her waist, and reaches just below her knees. She looks gorgeous despite the uncomfortable rigidity of her spine.

"You look beautiful," I tell her, closing the distance between us. "Perfect for what I have planned."

"Well, you didn't tell me what you have planned, so I had to guess."

"You guessed well." I reach up and thread a strand of her hair through my fingers. "Except for this."

She arches a challenging brow. "I wanted to wear it down."

"Hmm." I hum and fight my smile as I push her red hair over her shoulder, finding the bruise I left on her neck last night. I brush my thumb over it, loving the way her breath hitches. "I don't know why not."

Callie flicks her eyes over my shoulder to Sav before glaring back at me, lowering her voice to a hiss.

"Maybe because I don't want pap photos looking like I was mauled by a vampire."

"You're the girlfriend of a rock star, Callie," I say teasingly. "A few bite marks won't shock anyone."

I don't bother lowering my voice, and Callie's nostrils flare as a red flush creeps up her chest and colors her cheeks. Her jaw ticks with irritation and embarrassment as she flicks her eyes back to Sav once more.

"Your *fake* girlfriend."

I smile wide and lean in closer, running her red hair through my fingers again.

"My fake girlfriend who enjoys having my mouth on her."

Fuck, the way she blushes. The way her chest starts to rise and fall more quickly. It thrills me. Affecting her is an endorphin rush, and right now, I want it mainlined into my veins.

I turn to Sav. "We're heading out. Let me know if you need anything."

"Thanks, but I'm good." She waves me off with a sleepy smile and heads back to her bedroom. "Have fun."

For the first time in a long time, I feel like the ground under my feet regarding Sav isn't quaking with uncertainty. It's such a fucking relief. Heartless is my family. I don't want to lose it again.

I turn back to Callie and offer my hand, smiling bigger when she takes it, then I lead her out of the room and through the lobby to the valet.

"Aren't you going to ask me what we're doing for our date?" I ask once we're buckled into our seats.

She shrugs. "Wasn't planning on it."

I glance at her again. She's still stiff, her hands fisted together tightly in her lap with her jaw clenched. It's the polar opposite of the woman I had in my arms last night. The woman who had her legs wrapped around my waist backstage. Lust swirls in my stomach at the memory, but ice forms in my veins as I take in her body language.

Ham confirmed this morning that the photos of our embrace after the show are already all over the internet. That could be why she's uncomfortable, but I thought we'd started moving past that.

Seems I thought wrong.

The whole silent, uncomfortable ride, I remind myself that the chilling attitude coming from her is preferred. Sure, I like her warm and pliant, I like her burning under my palms and eager, but this is better.

This is *safer*.

More images from ArtFusion have been clearing in my mind. Details of each encounter coming back into focus. I waver back and forth between being pissed and wanting to replay each memory over and over. One minute, I want to win her over, and the next I want to shut her out. I need to choose one and fucking stick with it, and it's not lost on me what the smarter choice would be.

I tamp down the excitement I'd let build for today. I tell myself I put thought into this date simply because it would look good. I didn't do this for her. I didn't do this for myself.

I did it for my fucking job. For my band.

That's all that has ever mattered.

24

CALLIE

THE IMAGE of him holding her is burned in my brain.

His eyes were closed. He was smiling into her hair.

And she was in nothing but a T-shirt. His? Probably.

What pisses me off the most, though, is that I'm jealous. I'm jealous, and I have no right to be.

I mentally scold myself. Torren King and Sav Loveless are a foregone conclusion. Even I know that. Sure, she might be in a relationship with someone else, but history is notorious for predicting the future. Torren and Sav will always end up back together. It just is what it is.

And anyway. I don't fucking care.

I have no idea where we're going, but I'm too stubborn to ask. I keep my mouth shut and my gaze fixed out the window until my phone rings in my handbag. I pull it out and find a video chat request from Glory Bell. I push accept, and then I'm face to face with my sister. She's in the bathroom of our small apartment applying makeup, and she's dressed in her uniform, getting ready for work.

"Hey, Glor."

"Hey! I missed your call last night."

I smile and turn my body away from Torren. "Yeah. I just wanted to check in. See how you and Mom are."

"We're good, Cal. I'm working. Mom's back in PT. Oh, but Mom told me about the money. That's some—"

"Glory," I cut her off, flicking my eyes to Torren and back to the phone. I don't know what she was going to say about the money Torren gave me, but I could tell from her tone that it's not good, so I change the subject. "How's your dumb dog?"

Glory smiles as she runs a blush brush over her cheeks. "Torren King is almost completely potty-trained."

She looks so proud, and while I manage to stifle my laugh, Torren (the human, not the dog) doesn't even try. At the sound of his deep chuckle, Glory's eyes go wide, and then they narrow.

"Are you with him?"

I nod. "Yeah. We're, um, we're going on a date."

Torren leans into my space then, and I see his face join mine on the phone screen. His charming expression is the opposite of my dreadful one.

"Hey, Glory Bell," Torren says with a grin. "I'm glad to hear the good news about your dog."

Glory's eyes stay narrowed for a moment before she finally speaks. And when she does, my jaw drops.

"What the heck kind of fifty shades crap are you pulling with my sister?"

"Glory." I gasp, but she doesn't even look at me. She stays staring at Torren.

"Giving her a check like that just so she can come on tour with you? That's sus as hell. I don't care if you are a famous rock star. If she ends up trapped in some red room of sex torture, then you—"

"Glory Bell! Stop."

Glory closes her mouth and turns her accusatory glare on me.

"What the fuck? And I said you couldn't watch that movie."

My sister rolls her eyes. "*Please*. I read the books." Then she moves her attention back to Torren. "I don't trust you, Torren King."

I glance at Torren and find him fighting a smile. He nods slowly, and when he speaks, his words sound sincere.

"This situation is unconventional, and I understand why you don't trust me. But I swear your sister is safe. No red rooms. I promise."

Glory arches a brow, and even though she's a fifteen-year-old with mascara on only one eye, she still looks intimidating.

"You better not hurt her, or you'll regret it," she threatens. "I know people. Remember that. *And* I'll rename the dog."

Then she hangs up.

I blink at the phone screen. I can't believe she just said that. I can't believe she just hung up.

"Wow," Torren says with a laugh. "She's something else."

I huff and nod. "Yeah, she really is."

A text from Glory buzzes through before I even finish my sentence.

GLORY BELL

Sorry. Had to hang up for the plot. I'll call after work.

Stay out of the red room.

I smile to myself as I type out a quick *okay, talk soon*, then put my phone back in my bag.

My sister really is something else. *I know people?* Who the hell does she think she knows? I have to swallow back a laugh at the whole thing. My sister just threatened Torren. *Torren*, whom she loved so much that she named her dog after him. She threatened him *for me*.

Proof that my sister loves me. I knew it.

I'm still riding the high of the humorous exchange when the SUV pulls into the parking garage of a large music hall. I sit up straight and look back at Torren.

"Where are we?"

He smiles. "Oh, *now* you want to know?"

I arch a brow, and he laughs before answering me. "We're at the Texas Grand Performance Center."

The SUV pulls up to an elevator and a man in a black suit opens Torren's door. Torren climbs out, then rounds the car and opens my door, offering me his hand. I take it and let him help me out of the vehicle, then he puts his hand on the small of my back and leads me into an elevator.

"Are you going to ask me what we're doing here?"

I purse my lips. My curiosity is overtaking my desire to remain aloof. Of all the places he could have brought me, this is the best one to spark my interest.

"Okay, fine," I relent. "What are we doing here?"

He chuckles. "Do you know who Constance Chen is?"

My feet stop in their tracks. My eyes widen to twice their size. When he looks at me, his smile grows.

"Does that mean you do know her, or you don't?"

I stare at him and force words out of my mouth. "Is she here?"

He nods, and my heart thrums with excitement.

Constance Chen was one of my idols. I used to want to be her. A child pianist prodigy, she was accepted to Julliard at just six years old, and she's grown up to become a world-renowned classical pianist. She's arguably the best classical pianist alive. *A once-in-a-generation kind of talent* is what music critics have called her. It's said she could read music before she could speak. She's been winning international piano competitions for literal decades, and her last solo performance sold out in two minutes. I'd long since given up ever seeing her play live, but when she announced her retirement last year, I was still devastated.

The thought that I'm in the same building as her...

"Are we going to see her play?"

My question is posed quietly, tentatively, as if I don't want to get my own hopes up. Torren just winks at me and leads me through the double doors of the concert hall, then up a set of stairs. My pulse speeds up.

We are.

We are going to see Constance Chen perform. I'm drowning in my own excitement as my eyes scan the empty venue. The rows and rows of red velvet seats are vacant. I glance down at the main floor of the concert hall and find that it is vacant as well. In fact, it's all been strangely empty. I didn't register it until just now. Aside from one usher and a few security guards, I've seen no one. The parking garage. The lobby. All of it's been empty.

"Where is everyone?"

"Oh, I rented it out. It's just us this morning."

I look up at him with wide eyes.

"You did what?"

"Ms. Chen is retired, so she's not performing for large audiences anymore."

I shake my head and my heart sinks. "I don't understand. She's not performing today?"

"She is. But it's just for us."

I stop walking once more, my mouth falling open silently. Torren laughs and gestures to the row of seats I stopped next to.

"Is this where you want to sit? We can go back down if you want? Or we can move closer?"

"How?"

"We don't have assigned seats, Callie. We're the only ones here."

"No, I mean, how did you get her to come out of retirement to play for just us?"

"Oh, that." He gives me another of those charming smiles. "Her granddaughter loves the band. I got her VIP tickets and a meet and greet tonight. Also, you know, I paid her, too."

I can't think of anything else to say, so I just nod. He laughs again.

"Let's move just a little closer. I was told the front of the balcony is the best place for sound."

I nod again and allow him to lead me to the front-most row of the balcony. Once I sit, he takes out his phone and sends a text.

"Just another few minutes. Are you excited?"

I scan his face. It's hopeful in the most confusing, stomach-twisting way. Like maybe this whole date isn't just for show. He put this together for me, he planned it out with care, and he wants me to enjoy it, so I give him an honest answer.

"I'm so excited that I'm trying not to cry."

Torren's smile softens as his green eyes bounce between mine. My skin prickles with awareness the longer he looks at me. When his gaze drops briefly to my lips, I resist the urge to lick them. Instead, I let the words on the tip of my tongue fall loose.

"Thank you, Torren."

The lights dim, and I dart my attention to the stage. I feel him lean closer, his breath in my hair as he speaks.

"You're welcome."

The curtain opens then, revealing the most gorgeous white grand piano. I hear the tap of footsteps, and I can't help but lean closer to the stage, pressing my hands to the balcony railing in front of me. When Constance Chen steps out from behind the curtain, tears well in my eyes. When she sits gracefully onto the piano bench seat and starts to play, the tears fall.

They don't stop for her entire performance.

A steady stream of happy tears trails down my cheeks as she plays one perfect, beautiful piece after another. She plays with a level of finesse I've only ever dreamed of achieving. She possesses a comfort I've never been after to master.

Constance Chen belongs behind a piano.

She was born to play.

She was born to be the best.

She's absolutely brilliant. A true artist. And as she plays, I let myself float along on the music, reveling in the realization that I am in the presence of greatness. This is a once-in-a-lifetime experience. My eyes fall shut, absorbing as much of the sound into my body as possible. Committing every single note to memory.

I will never, ever forget this.

When the opening notes of Chopin's "Nocturne in E-flat Major" fill the hall, goose bumps cover my body, and I don't stop myself from blindly reaching for Torren's hand. He takes my hand in both of his, cradling it on his knee as I sit with my eyes closed. As I completely lose myself in the music, it feels like the only thing keeping me anchored is his hold on me. I'm so happy in this moment that I could die and float away with no regrets.

When the last song is over, I stand and clap so loudly that my hands hurt. She stands and bows, and I don't stop clapping until she's disappeared once again behind the curtain and the lights in the hall slowly come back on.

When I turn to face Torren, his eyes are already on me, and they're filled with a mix of emotions I can't decipher. I smile up at him through my tears, speechless. There isn't a single word in the English language that could adequately express how happy, how *grateful*, I am in this moment.

I don't flinch away when his hands cup my face, warm, calloused fingers and cold silver rings resting on my skin. I don't stop him when he gently wipes away my tears with his thumbs.

"Do you want to meet her?"

All I can do is nod.

He smiles, then takes my hand. "Come on then. I'll introduce you."

· · ·

I'm on a cloud as we drive back to the hotel.

I close my eyes, rest my head on the seat, and relive the entire experience. Every song. Every note. It was surreal, and she was just as magical in person. They say don't meet your idols, but in this case, they were wrong. Constance Chen is even better than I could have imagined. From her soft, lilting accent to the elegant way she moved, she exuded music. When she hugged me, I could have passed out.

But her parting words...

Those are what echo the loudest in my head.

Hold on to that one, she'd said, nodding at Torren. *They don't go through this amount of trouble for just anyone.*

I try like hell to beat it back—to silence it—but for the next few days, I sift through the tabloids. Despite the burning desire in my chest for it to mean *more*, I search for something, anything, to douse the growing embers of affection. A sign that it was all for show. Proof that it was an act. That the date was just for the job.

I find photos of Torren and me after concerts everywhere. Pictures and videos of us coming and going from the hotels and the buses.

But not a single mention of the private concert with Constance Chen.

Not a headline. Not a photo. Not a statement. Nothing.

Jonah's words once again flit through my mind.

Bare minimum. Wants to keep you hidden.

I think you should be seen.

The date Torren planned? It was more than the bare minimum. It was the opposite of a pap walk. And while it was a secret moment, hidden from the world, it made me feel *seen*.

And that? Well, that messes with my head more than anything else could.

25

TORREN

I LOUNGE on the couch in the girls' suite, my feet propped on the coffee table as Hammond scrolls through his tablet in front of us.

We're set to leave for Houston this afternoon, but Ham wanted to have a meeting before we set off on the buses. I figure the first order of business is the stalker, so I cut to the chase and ask the question that's on all our minds.

"So what's the update on Savvy's biggest fan?"

"They've been silent. The relationship story seems to be working. No texts. No letters."

I glance at Sav. "That true?"

"Yeah. It's like they vanished into thin air." She frowns. "I still can't make sense of it, though. It just...it doesn't sit right with me."

Hammond sighs. "Well, we'll take what we can get for now." He glances at Callie. "You're doing a great job. With any luck, the investigators will have something by the end of the tour."

"Sure. Um, thanks."

Callie looks and sounds extremely uncomfortable, but she's sitting too far away for me to comfort her. I send her a smile that she ignores, then Jonah places his hand on her shoulder, giving it a squeeze that somehow transfers to my windpipe. I glare at him in warning, but he ignores me too. Fucker.

Hammond goes on to give us a debrief of shit we already know, and when he dismisses us for the buses, I grab Jonah's arm, so he hangs back with me. I wait for everyone to filter out before I speak.

"Back off, Jo."

He arches an eyebrow. "Fuck you, Tor."

"I'm serious. This isn't a joke. She's not some groupie for you to fuck with."

Jonah rolls his eyes. "I'm not treating her like a fucking groupie, Torren, but maybe you should ask yourself why me interacting with her pisses you off so much. And don't tell me *it's for the job*. You're only a possessive asshole when you *care*."

I grit my teeth, but I don't deny it, and he laughs.

"Fuck, man. I know you so well it's almost sad. Have you kissed this one yet?"

"She's not a *this one*," I spit out, and he smirks.

I bristle. I walked right into his trap.

Jonah's real good at using people like pawns in a one-sided game, and you'll never even realize you're playing until it's too late. The balance is tipped in his favor, and it's frustrating that he thinks he's got it all figured out when I'm still fucking scrambling to understand it myself. I hate how well he can read me. I hate how I *can't* read him—not anymore—and that makes me feel exposed.

I shake my head with a laugh, forcing myself to appear unbothered. Forcing myself not to give him the satisfaction of thinking he's got the upper hand. I know it's futile, but I do it anyway.

"You don't know what you're talking about," I say with a sigh, and Jonah scoffs.

"Sure."

"I just don't want to screw this up. It's too important."

"You tryin' to convince me or yourself?" He shakes his head. "Never mind. Doesn't fucking matter to me."

I stare at him, running my eyes over his blank face. He's sober. He's only observant when he's not fucked up, but I can't read him, and it pisses me off. I hate when he turns to stone like this. I hate even more when he's right. Right now, I'd almost prefer the antagonistic, asshole version of him, but we only get that when he's high.

I resist the urge to argue and walk toward the door.

"Let's go before they leave us."

I don't look behind me to make sure he follows.

I reach the parking lot and jog to catch up with the girls, making sure to position myself next to Callie. I take her hand even though there are no paps in sight. I feel her look at me, but I keep my eyes on the pavement in front of us. I keep them there until I hear squealing, then I whip my eyes up to see Sav sprinting across the parking lot with her dog barking and running beside her.

I don't realize what's happening until Sav launches herself at someone and wraps her arms and legs around them, letting loose a stream of laughing sobs as the dog circles around them with her tail wagging and her tongue lolling to the side.

"Who is that?"

I look down at Callie, but it's Mabel who answers her.

"That would be Levi." Mabel laughs. "Tor, I might have to bunk with you guys for a while."

I nod. I don't blame her. Sav and Levi have been apart for weeks. I wouldn't want to be trapped on a bus with them, either.

When we catch up to Levi and Sav, he's already put her back on her feet, but she's still got her arms thrown around his neck like a lifeline with tears rolling down her cheeks.

"I wanted to be here yesterday, but this was kind of a last-minute decision. I couldn't get a flight out until this morning."

Levi smooths Sav's hair back, and she beams up at him in a way that would have pissed me off a year ago. It doesn't now, though, and I don't stop the small smile that curves up my lips.

"I'm just glad you're here," Sav says, her voice muffled when she presses her face back into his chest.

Levi glances over her head and nods in greeting, eyes jumping between us all as he speaks.

"Hey. Good to see you guys."

"You too." Mabel skips up and wraps Sav and Levi in a hug. "Where's Boss?"

"STEM summer camp for a few weeks."

"Damn. I've missed her more than I missed you."

Levi laughs and gives Mabel a *you're stuck with me* kind of shrug. His daughter, Brynn, is absolutely hilarious. She's a really cool kid, and while she was on the first leg of the tour with us, we all came to think of her as an extension of the band. Even Jonah, who kind of took on the role of her unofficial English tutor as she was finishing up the school year.

Mabel releases them, her smile belying her previous statement. "How long are you here for?"

"I can stay through Nashville if that's cool with you guys."

"Fine with me," Mabel says, then sends a smirk my way. "I'll just take over the guys' bus."

Levi smiles, but he flicks his eyes to me in question.

I shrug. "Fine with me."

I say it and mean it. This shit has been hard on Sav. She deserves some time alone with Levi. He nods at me, a silent thank you, and I nod back.

We're not friends. Not yet. But we might be heading that way, eventually.

"Did Ham know you were coming?" Sav asks as she finally steps back, moving her grip from Levi's neck to his hand.

"I told him when I bought the ticket yesterday, but I asked him not to tell you. I wanted it to be a surprise." Levi gives Sav a wry grin, but then his brow furrows slightly at whatever he sees on her face. "What's up?"

Mabel and I exchange a nervous glance as tense silence fills the air.

"Savannah." Levi's voice is low and commanding. "Tell me what's going on."

Sav releases a dramatic sigh and tugs him toward the bus. "Fine. I've got some stuff to fill you in on."

"Shit." Mabel winces and turns to Callie. "Hurry up. We got maybe five minutes to grab our stuff before they start fighting."

"Fighting?" Callie's eyes go wide as she darts her attention between me and Mabel. "Why fighting?"

"She hasn't told him about the stalker." Mabel gives Callie a grimace and starts walking quickly toward the bus. "Levi is going to be so fucking p—"

Muffled, raised voices come from the bus, halting Mabel in her tracks. Her shoulders fall.

"Fuck." She changes course and heads toward my bus. "Too slow. C'mon, Callie. We can get our stuff when we get to Houston."

Callie looks at me with wide, nervous eyes as Mabel disappears up the stairs into the bus I share with Jonah.

"Looks like you're riding with us for a while," I say to her, and she nods slowly before marching with heavy feet toward the bus. She's nervous, but I can't help but be excited. I'm grinning until Jonah steps up next to me.

His posture is relaxed, almost too relaxed, and his lips curve into a lazy smirk.

"This should be fun," he says slowly, making my spine stiffen.

When Jonah glances at me, his eyes are shielded behind dark sunglasses, but I have a feeling I'd find them red-rimmed and dilated.

Fuck.

We've only got four hours to Houston, but we're taking two days to get to Miami, then another two to Nashville.

Fun indeed.

"Thank you so much, Houston. You've been fucking amazing."

Sav's voice booms through the stadium, the roaring crowd drowning out the end of her statement, and she laughs into the mic.

"We've had such a great time with you. And even though this might be goodnight..."

Sav pauses, and just like at every show, the crowd finishes the statement for her.

"It's not goodbye!"

Sav sends me a smile before leaning back into her mic.

"But just in case, so you don't forget us, we've got Mabel on drums, Jonah on guitar, Torren on bass, my name's Sav Loveless, and we are The Hometown Heartless. Thank you for always showing up to rock with us. We love you so much. Have a great night."

I wave at the cheering crowd as the stage lights dim. A roadie rushes up to me and I hand him my guitar, then I follow Sav off the stage just as the house lights come on. I'm sweaty and riding the high of another successful show, so when I see Callie, I don't stop myself from lifting her into my arms in what's become our post-show performance. My blood heats in my body with the need to put my lips on her, the desire to pull her tighter and consume her, but I resist.

"How would you feel about going out tonight?" I ask as I set her back on her feet. "I know a good club."

"Do we need another public appearance?"

Her question is tentative, almost leading, as if she's searching for a specific answer, and I'm hoping I know which one. I shrug and give her a sincere smile.

"I haven't been given any orders by Hammond, if that's what you're asking. I'd just like to take you out."

"Oh." Her eyebrows rise in surprise before she catches herself, then she clears her throat and nods. "Sure. Of course. When do you want to go?"

I check my watch. "An hour? I need to shower."

"Okay. I'll be ready."

"You want to head back with me?"

"No. I need to call my mom. I'll just meet you back at the hotel."

"I'll see you in an hour then?"

"An hour."

She turns and heads the opposite direction, walking toward the girls' dressing room. When she opens the door and steps inside, I turn and head back to mine. I brace myself to find Jonah banging another groupie, but the room's empty. The urge to text him nags at me, but I don't. Instead, I grab my things and head to the car.

I'm showered and outside the girls' suite in forty-five minutes. When I knock, Callie opens the door and steps into the hallway. I look her over and force myself to breathe slowly. She's fucking stunning in a pair of skin-tight black jeans, a green tank top, and a pair of green platform heels. I put a lot of green in her wardrobe, and I'm so fucking glad I did.

"You're ready."

"I knew you'd probably be early."

"You look gorgeous," I tell her honestly, letting my eyes drag down her body once more. "I'll admit, though, I was hoping for a dress."

Her face and chest flush pink, and I can't help the smirk that curls my lips. I know she's thinking about it now, just like me. The way I've touched her. In the club. After the concert. In my bus at ArtFusion.

The way she set me on fucking fire.

Then she narrows her eyes, her lips twitching almost as if she's fighting her own smile.

"I didn't want to risk getting into trouble."

I let my smirk spread into a grin and take her hand in mine. I don't say what I'm thinking—that I could still get into plenty of trouble with what she's got on right now—as I lead her to the parking garage.

Things have been notably different between us since I took her to see Constance Chen perform. She's been warmer. More relaxed. The more time I spend with her, the more time I want. Jonah's words have been sneaking into my consciousness, getting louder and louder.

You're only a possessive asshole when you care.

I know you so well it's almost sad.

He does.

He fucking does, and I can't deny it.

At first, his statement irritated me. It made me anxious because he noticed it before I did. But now that I've been slapped in the face with the truth, I'm accepting it.

Calla Lily James is my Firebird.

She was burned into my chest four years ago, and even when I couldn't grasp anything more than the smoky haze of a memory, she'd stuck with me. I never even considered the fact that we'd ever cross paths again. I wasn't searching for her. I wasn't holding out for her. But in more ways than she knows, our encounter in the desert affected me. It fucking branded me, and as much as it scares me to have her this close, it excites me as well.

I hold on to that excitement on the drive to the club. I keep Callie's hand clasped in mine, absently rubbing my thumb over her wrist until we pull up to the valet, then I slide out of the car first so I can help her climb out after me.

I place my hand on the small of her back as I escort her through the doors and to the back of the club toward the roped-off VIP section. This club isn't as exclusive as the last one I brought her to, but since the stalker has pretty much disappeared, I'm not worried.

"Want a drink?"

"Sure. A beer is fine."

I smirk at her. "No tequila to make it easier to pretend to like me? Does that mean you're warming up to me?"

Callie rolls her eyes. "Maybe it means I'm just becoming a better actress."

I take a step closer. "Or maybe you're finally giving in to the chemistry."

"Don't flatter yourself, King." She bats her eyelashes, then pats my cheek. "I'm just earning my paycheck."

If it weren't for the sparkle of humor in her green eyes, the statement might sting. It doesn't, though. Instead, it flames the embers of desire stirring in my stomach. Without breaking eye contact, I take my knuckle and drag it across her collarbone. Her breath hitches, and I chuckle. I lower my lips to her ear.

"I like when you call me King."

"That's not surprising." Her voice is slightly shaky, as if she's unsettled but hiding it well. She exhales slowly, breath fanning over my neck before she takes a step back. "It's because you have a big, fat ego."

I laugh outright and raise my hand, signaling for a server. Someone shows up within a second, and I order two beers. Callie arches an eyebrow.

"Is it always that easy?"

"What?"

"Getting what you want. You just wave a hand, and it falls in your lap?"

"No, Calla Lily." I shake my head slowly and run my gaze over her face, settling briefly on her pouty lips before looking back into her mossy green eyes. "It's not always that easy."

I don't look away until the server returns with our drinks, and then I lead Callie to a couch at the back of the VIP section where we can sit. It's far enough from the dance floor that we don't have to shout, and it feels a little more private than the bar tables.

"How's your mom?"

Callie takes a sip of her beer and shrugs.

"Good, I guess. She says therapy is going well. Glory says Mom seems to be moving better. She's healing. She's good."

"And what about you and her? Has that healed?"

She pauses and thinks over my question before answering, her brows furrowing just slightly.

"I mean, she's not actively mad anymore. I'm not getting the silent treatment. But I can tell she's not forgiven me yet. She still thinks what I'm doing is stupid. And she still doesn't like you. At all."

I laugh. "I guess I don't blame her. I did steal her daughter away."

"Nah, I don't think it's so much that as it is you remind her of my dad."

I wince and blow out a slow breath. "Ouch."

Callie gives me a rueful grin. "A musician who sweeps the poor girl off her feet and promises her the world? For all my mom knows, you're *exactly* like my dad. And according to her, you're going to knock me up and then leave me home alone while you screw women all over the country." She sighs dramatically. "Oh, such is the lot of a rock star's girlfriend."

I purse my lips and lean in closer. "I wouldn't do that, you know."

Callie arches a brow in disbelief.

"Honestly," I insist. "I don't cheat."

She scoffs, then narrows her eyes at me. "You're saying you never cheated on Sav? Not once?"

I hear the challenge in her voice, and I understand why it's there, but it's important to me that she believes me.

"Sav and I were a toxic mess, but I never cheated. Not when we were together. We'd break up every other week, and we'd both..." I trail off and look away, gathering my thoughts. I'm treading on dangerous ground. When I look back, she's glaring, but I give her the truth. "When we weren't broken up, I was faithful. Always."

"I don't know if that holds as much weight as you think it does," she says, her voice flat, and I nod.

"I know. But it's the truth, for what it's worth."

"Would Sav agree?"

"Yes. You can ask her if you want."

Her eyebrows slant harshly and then she shakes her head. She looks away and takes a sip of her beer before finally looking back at me.

She opens her mouth to speak, and I brace myself for more harsh truths, but she stops herself when her phone buzzes on the couch beside her. Whatever she sees on the screen has her snatching it up, then glancing around the bar.

"Everything okay?"

"Yeah. I just, um..." She puts her beer on the table in front of us and pushes to standing, then gives me a forced smile. "I'll be right back."

As she steps away, I glance at Craig, but he's already turning to follow her.

I tell myself to give her space, but the look on her face when she saw her text has my protective side surging to the surface. I only make it three minutes before I'm standing and heading in the direction Callie went.

I find her in the hallway of the club's bathrooms. Her back is to me, her spine rigid, and when my eyes rise from her to who she's talking to, jealousy rages in my chest. There are people everywhere, so this is a terrible location for this *whatever it is* to take place. The guy must have been the text that lured her out of the VIP lounge.

I stalk toward them, putting my arm around Callie's shoulder, and pull her to my side without taking my eyes off Becket Walker.

"There a problem here?"

I cock my head to the side, meeting Callie's former band member's scathing glare with one of my own. I don't bother acknowledging the other two guys with him, but it's not hard to guess they're also former band members.

"Torren," Callie says, looking up at me with a tight smile and a warning in her eyes. "This is Becket, Ezra, and Rocky. They, um, they were—"

"We were in Caveat Lover with her. I'm sure you know this," Becket sneers, his words sharp and full of barely restrained rage. He doesn't even bother with fake pleasantries. He hates me. It's all over his face.

Good. I don't like him, either.

I tear my eyes off the snarling ex and look at the other two. They're also pissed, but their anger is mild in comparison to the bassist. I give them a nod, then look back at Becket with a taunting smirk.

"You played bass, right?" He nods, and I plaster on my most cocky smile. "Me too. Were you at the show tonight? It was sold out."

Becket snorts. "We're not fans."

I let out a humorless laugh and nod slowly. "Of course not."

I don't break eye contact with Becket as I slide my arm from Callie's shoulders to her waist, resting my hand on her abdomen. His eye twitches.

"Well, it's great to meet you, but we really shouldn't be out of the VIP lounge. Safety, you know." I wave the hand not gripping Callie in the air, pointing out the growing crowd around us.

"We were talking to Callie." Becket takes a step toward us, so I take a step back, keeping Callie at my side.

"Sorry," I say, clearly not sorry. "But my girl and I really need to get back to our date, and they won't allow you into the lounge." My words are veiled arrogance with feigned sympathy, and I can tell how much it irritates him. I could easily get them into the lounge, but I won't, and he knows it.

"Look man, I know you think you've got some sort of claim on her now, but we've known her a long time, and we'd like to talk to her," Ezra says, then he looks at Callie. "You met this douche, what, a month ago? Use your head, Cal. We've been with you *for years*."

I hear the hidden meaning in his statement. *You can't trust him. He's going to hurt you. This relationship won't last. Come back to us.* It fuels the fire inside me, coaxing out my possessive side until my hold on it slips. I force a smirk, flicking my eyes from Ezra to Becket.

"Callie and I actually go further back than the media knows," I say suggestively, and I feel her stiffen slightly under my arm. "We only recently reconnected."

Adrenaline pumps through my veins as I toe the line of truth. The surprise on the guys's faces is rewarding, but it's the need to finally come clean that keeps me talking. Keeps me *confessing*. I turn my attention to Callie's surprised face, my smile softening as I trace my eyes over her features.

"When I first saw Callie, she was dressed like a phoenix, and I thought, *I have to know this woman.* She was gorgeous and intriguing, and I couldn't stop myself from approaching her, even in a crowd full of people."

Her eyes widen as she tips her face up to mine, and I put my knuckle under her chin gently, holding her there. My voice drops slightly, so her bandmates can still hear me, but the message is clearly for her.

"I couldn't stay away from her. She consumed my thoughts. I only got a few days with her then, but now that she's back in my life, I plan to make up for lost time."

Her eyelashes flutter, and her lips part on a small gasp. I watch her beguiling green eyes as they change from confused to shocked to downright murderous. Her nostrils flare and she flicks her eyes to Becket.

"Beck, I'll call you."

She turns and storms back toward the lounge, and I follow. She bypasses the couch where we had been sitting and heads down the hallway of the VIP bathrooms before whirling on me. Fury. Nothing but pure unadulterated fury. I plant my feet and square my shoulders, readying myself for anything she might throw at me. It's been a long time coming.

"How long? How long have you known? Because you sure didn't fucking act like you remembered me when I signed that contract."

The words are a furious hiss. She's so angry that her hands are fisted at her sides, and she only unclenches her teeth to speak. I respond calmly and honestly, hoping like hell to defuse the situation. This conversation needs to be had, and I knew it would likely be messy. She deserved answers, and after weeks of keeping this from her, I deserve her ire.

"Since Glendale."

Her jaw falls open and she scoffs as she puts it all together. "That was weeks ago."

"The memories came back in waves."

She narrows her eyes and cocks her head, taking a single step in my direction. "And how much do you remember?"

"I remember everything." I close the distance and hold her eye contact.

"*What?*"

"Everything. I remember all of it."

Her eyes bounce between mine, her expression softening in a way that fills me with hope. She sinks her teeth into her bottom lip, then lowers her gaze to my mouth. When she speaks again, it's a shaky whisper.

"Was it real? What you just said? About when you first saw me?"

I take another step toward her so there's only a few inches of space between us.

"It's real. It's all been real. Every fucking word," I confess, and when her breath hitches, I lose all restraint. "Goddamn it, Calla Lily."

I wrap my hand around her neck and bring my face to hers, taking her lips in a searing kiss. I groan at the contact. I've not felt this in so fucking long. I've not wanted to. But now? Now I won't be able to stop. Until now, I'd never missed kissing, but the feel of her soft, plush lips sliding over mine is something I didn't know I needed.

I will *never* get enough.

Callie opens for me immediately, her tongue tangling with mine, moaning into my mouth. Her hands fist into my shirt. Her knuckles press against my abs. I bite her lip lightly, putting my other hand on her hip so I can tug her closer. So I can feel her entire body on mine. The contact fills in the fuzzy details of my memories. How her body felt under my hands. How she sounded. How she tasted.

She keeps her mouth on mine for a few more blissful seconds, and then her hands shove hard at my chest. Callie tears herself away from me and steps back. I have just one moment of warning—just one look at her pink, swollen lips twisted into a furious frown—before she shoves me again, hard enough that my body jerks backward.

"I'm not some starry-eyed fan you can manipulate." She steps forward and shoves me backward for a third time. "You can't just kiss me and expect me to forget everything you've done." On her next shove, my back hits the wall, and she stops with only inches between us. She seethes up at me, pure fury in her green eyes as she hisses her final words. "Stay the hell away from me, you lying, arrogant son of a bitch."

Then she turns on her heel and storms away. I watch her with wide, shocked eyes and a gaping mouth, my chest rising and falling rapidly, until she rounds the corner and disappears. I want to rush after her, but I know nothing good will come of it. We don't need a public shouting match, and rage like hers requires space to cool down or it will incinerate us both.

"You good?" Damon asks, slight humor in his tone. When I glance at him, he's fucking smirking.

"Walton?" is all I say.

"He's already with her. He'll drive her back. We'll have someone come pick us up from the back entrance."

I nod and close my eyes, dropping my head back on the wall.

Fuck.

I'll give her this head start. I'll give her some time to cool down. But then I'm going after her, and we're going to have a fucking chat. We're clearing shit up once and for all.

26

CALLIE

PAST, ArtFusion Night Four

With one hand on the joint, he uses the other to grip my waist and guide me on top of him, so I'm straddling him with my knees on the couch.

The fabric of my sundress bunches where my hips and legs connect. The feel of his warm skin on mine—my inner thighs pressed to his outer thighs, his cock nudging my center—is enough to make my mouth fall open with a quiet gasp. He doesn't take his eyes off me.

He brings the joint to his lips and slides his free hand from my waist, up my body to my neck. I watch the cherry glow red as he takes a drag, and then he removes the joint and pulls my face closer to his. The hand on my neck moves to cup my jaw, his thumb pulling my chin down, opening my mouth in a gesture that has lust shooting straight to my core and excitement making my head swim.

He leans close, his nose brushing mine as he opens his own mouth and breathes the smoke past my lips. His lips don't touch mine, but his thumb doesn't leave my chin, his fingers holding me close until I've inhaled his exhale. He tilts his head up, gazing at me as I release the smoke back into the air around us, and the smile he gives me leaves me feeling like I've won a prize. Like he's praised me without words. Like a sold-out crowd full of adoring fans. Like a standing ovation at Barnum Hall. That's what this smile from Torren King feels like.

He puts his lips on my jaw again, kissing his way to my neck and whispering words that sound like poetry in that same mysterious melody from before. Like fragmented song lyrics just for me.

"*Firebird...make it all new...we're just ashes in the end...*"

His words sound like the beginning of something. Or the end, but god, I hope it's the beginning. Without overthinking it, I reach for the hem of my dress, and he leans his head back on the couch to watch as I slowly strip it off and drop it on the cushion beside us. I'm not wearing a bra, so I'm straddling his lap in just a pair of cotton underwear, and his eyes caress my bare skin first before his hands finally follow. He brings the joint back to his lips, taking another drag as he trails the fingers on his other hand up my stomach and along the underside of my naked breast. My inhale is shaky as he circles my nipple with his calloused thumb, and his cock grows harder between my legs. Tentatively, I move my hips, and he hisses, pinching my nipple as smoke streams out between his teeth.

"Is this what you want?"

His question is a lazy rasp as his chest rises and falls more slowly than my own. His head still rests on the back of the couch, one hand still holding the joint as the other plays with my body. I nod. He shakes his head.

"You have to say it." I move my body over him again, but his hand clamps on to my hip, stopping me. "Say it, and then I'll let you play."

"This is what I want," I say finally, *firmly*, so he knows how serious I am, and he gives me a slow, sinful grin.

"Good girl."

The hand clamped on my hip loosens but then guides my movements, so I'm grinding on him slowly, his hard cock pressing deliciously against my swollen clit. Then he surprises me by leaning forward and licking up my sternum before taking my nipple into his mouth. I gasp, and he bites, which makes me press down harder onto him. He lets out a low groan, and my core pulses with arousal in response.

"You burn so hot, don't you?"

He whispers against the sensitive flesh of my breast before biting me again, this time following it with a hard suck that pulls a pained, needy cry from my lungs. His hips buck up into me, his hardness invading my softness, and my fingers sink into his hair in an effort to pull him closer. Torren thrusts upward while using the hand on my hip to pull me downward, my core hot and my panties drenched with my desire for him. Every pulse of pressure from his hard cock against my throbbing clit is paired with a bite or a suck on my breasts. Every zap of pleasure coupled with a sting of pain, the sensations lingering and mixing to create something heady and overwhelmingly intoxicating.

His hand leaves my hip and tangles in my hair, clutching at the roots near my nape, and then he tugs. I cry out as my face tilts toward the ceiling and his mouth moves to my neck. He bites, sucks, kisses, bites, sucks, kisses. He doesn't release my hair, never halts the motion of his body connecting with mine. My arms wrap around him, and I move faster, harder, my throbbing clit meeting his erection with every thrust of our hips. My breasts press into his chest, my sensitive nipples dragging over his sweat-slicked skin, sending tingles through me. My neck, my chest, my core. Flames engulf my whole body, on fire for him. He hums against my neck, teeth grazing over my pulse point.

"Burn for me." He whispers it once, then repeats it with more volume. "Burn for me."

Torren's movements grow more aggressive, pressing into me in a way that erases everything else. The connection is constant, the friction unrelenting, and all I can do is hold on as desire unfurls in my stomach and explodes, rippling outward and making everything around me shake. Torren's name escapes my lips on a moan as my pleasure crests, and then his thrusts slow, allowing me to ride out the waves of my orgasm until it's finished.

I'm still panting, my head tipped to the ceiling when his mouth leaves my throat and his fingers release the hair at the nape of my neck. His cock is still hard beneath me, but he's no longer thrusting against me. When I open my eyes, he's once more relaxing against the back of the couch with the joint between his lips. He smirks, his eyes running over my face, neck, and chest.

"You come so prettily, Firebird." He raises his hand and drags a finger over my chest in a lazy swirling motion. "So fucking pretty."

My lips part, but I say nothing.

I don't know what to do now. A thin sheen of sweat covers us both, my thighs and underwear are hot and sticky, and I'm too nervous to glance down and see what sort of mess I might have made in his lap.

My eyes zero in on the joint as he takes another drag and blows the smoke out of his nose. I wonder briefly where the ashtray is. There must be one, or there would be ash everywhere. Did he ever put the joint down? Was he holding it the whole time that I... That we...

Jesus, I just dry-humped Torren King in his tour bus while he smoked a joint.

I'm sitting almost entirely naked in Torren King's lap, and I just orgasmed in front of him. My body heats for a new reason, embarrassment mixing with the thrill of my arousal. Shame starts to creep into my conscious mind, but I force it back. Not now. I'll deal with it later, but not now. Right now, I want more. I *need* more.

Torren runs his fingers along the band of my underwear, halting my spiraling train of thought, and my eyes flare.

"What's going on in that head, hm?" He dips his fingers into my underwear, pulls the band back, then lets it snap back against my skin. "What are you thinking?"

"I don't know," I reply, my vocal cords sounding like they have been dragged over gravel. I clear my throat and try again. "I don't know what I was thinking about."

He smirks as if my answer pleases him, and it bolsters my confidence once more. Without taking my gaze off his face, I move my hands to his waist, tracing the band of his boxer briefs the same way he traced my underwear seconds earlier. Heat smolders in his eyes as he watches. I dip my fingers underneath the fabric and rub the taut skin of his lower abdomen, sinking lower until I graze the hot head of his cock. He grunts, jerking his hips upward, making me gasp. He licks his lips and holds eye contact as I do it again.

His breaths quicken, and I grow bolder, scooting back on my heels so I can free his erection. I ignore the dampness I feel on his boxer briefs as I tug them down and instead focus on touching him, on stroking him. He's hot and soft and firm in my hands. When I tighten my grip around him, his eyes flutter shut, and his mouth falls open. He wraps his hand around mine and guides me, up and down, up and down, until I finally let my eyes drift toward the motion.

I have to sink my teeth into my bottom lip to stifle a whimper. Seeing my hand wrapped around Torren's hard cock is hot, but seeing Torren's tattooed hand wrapped around my hand to help me jerk him off is almost unbearable.

"Fuck." The word slips from my mouth on an exhale, and Torren chuckles.

"You like this?"

"Yes."

He speeds up, tightening his hold on my hand so that I squeeze his cock harder, which makes me jerk him faster. Pre-cum leaks from him and glistens on the tip of his cock. When I lick my lips, he groans, and I tear my eyes back to his.

His eyelids are heavy, heavier than before, and his chest rises and falls rapidly as he bounces his attention between my face and my hand. When his nostrils flare and his lips part, I go rogue, wrapping my other hand around his cock and taking over. I want to make him feel good, and I want to do it on my own.

"Fuck, baby. Just like that. Don't stop now."

His face twists up into an almost pained expression, his mouth drops open on a choked moan, and then he cups both of my breasts and squeezes as he shoots his release onto his torso. Ropes of glossy white coat his colorful tattoos in spurts, splattering on his abs and chest and leaking onto my hands. I don't stop jerking him until he stops coming, until he releases my breasts and wraps his hand around mine once more.

"I've fucking never come so hard from a hand job," he says on a rough laugh, eyes still closed.

"Really?"

I try to sound nonchalant, try to hide the jolt of pride I feel at his praise, but I think I fail given the way his lips curl into a playful grin. I open my mouth to confess that I've never actually given a hand job before now, but my words die on my tongue as he moves me off him and stands. I watch wordlessly as he steps out of his boxer briefs and walks gloriously naked to the sink. He rips a paper towel off a roll, wets it, then cleans off his abs.

And I just *watch* and try not to swallow my tongue.

When he turns those lazy, heavy-lidded eyes toward me, my breath stops.

"Take off your panties, Firebird."

I don't move, and he cocks his head.

"You can change your mind. Just tell me no, and we can stop."

I swallow and shake my head. "I don't want to stop."

He grins as he closes the distance between us, then slowly lowers to his knees before me.

"I want to tongue-fuck your pretty little pussy, and then I'm going to flip you over and sink my aching cock into you, so should I take off these sexy panties, or do you want to do it?"

I lift my hips, giving him permission, and he quickly strips my underwear down my thighs and drops them on the couch beside me, then he spreads my legs wide in front of him.

I turn bright red. I can feel the heat creeping up my neck and chest, setting my cheeks ablaze, but he doesn't seem to notice. I've never been naked with a man. I've never had a man between my legs with his eyes greedily staring at my sex.

Before I can say anything, he moves his hand from my thigh to my clit and rubs lightly. I suck in a breath with a hiss, and he grins before bending forward and licking right up my slit. I gasp and buck, and he clamps his hands tightly around my thighs. His mouth leaves my core only to bite my inner thigh, making me cry out, and then he goes back to licking.

Tongue-fucking me, as he called it.

His fingers enter me without warning. It stings, but his tongue doesn't relent, and the pain fades quickly.

"Oh god," I moan, feeling the vibrations of his chuckle against my skin.

My hips start to move of their own accord, rubbing on his face the way I was rubbing on his cock earlier. I'm too focused to feel embarrassed. I don't even think about it when my hands slip into his hair, pulling him closer and moving faster. I'm chasing another orgasm when he removes his mouth and flips me onto my stomach.

My knees hit the bus floor roughly, my bare stomach and chest flat on the cushion with my face pressed uncomfortably into the back of the couch. Just as I push myself onto my forearms, he enters me, and I'm hit with a wave of stinging pain. I gasp out a yelp and grit my teeth, but he doesn't pause. He moves quickly, in and out of me, hitting my body in places I've never explored.

I brace myself against the couch with one hand and glance over my shoulder at him. His hands are gripping my hips tightly, eyes clamped shut and head tilted to the ceiling as he fucks me.

The pain blends with the pleasure until the pleasure has diluted the pain to almost nothing. I moan and push back into him as I brace myself on the couch. He thrusts hard and fast before reaching around and putting his fingers on my clit. He rubs fast, and I whimper, tightening my hold on the couch until my fingers ache.

I can't even describe the way I'm feeling. Like I'm on fire. Like electric shocks of pure pleasure are jolting through my bloodstream. I want more, but I also can't handle it. I'm overwhelmed in the most blissful way, and I already know I'll want to do this again when it's all over. If I survive it.

"Are you close?"

Torren's voice is raspy and strangled when he asks, tending to my clit while still moving in and out of me. I can't form words. All I can do is moan and nod.

"Good."

When I orgasm, he growls and picks up his pace, fingers digging into my waist and hips thrusting roughly until he lets out a groan so deep that it sounds like a roar. His body stutters, his grip tightens, and I know he's come. I hear his heavy breathing. Feel him slip out of me and throw himself onto the floor. Then slowly I turn around and perch my ass on the edge of the couch. My thighs are sticky, and my heart is still racing. I have this weird longing to be touched or held, but Torren's eyes are still closed and he's paying no attention to me.

I don't know what to say.

I'm running it over in my mind when a slow clap startles me, and I whip my head to the back of the bus to find Jonah stepping toward us. Immediately, my arms go up to cover my chest, but from the predatory gleam in his eye, I have a feeling he's already seen everything. I had completely forgotten about him.

Torren lets out a small huff of laughter and smirks as he peers up at Jonah. He doesn't move to cover himself, either. His arms are just sprawled out, his dick exposed and still encased in a cum-filled condom.

I don't know when he put the condom on, but I cringe when I see the faint ring of blood around its base. I frantically look at Torren, then at Jonah, but it seems neither has noticed yet.

"Told ya," Jonah says to Torren cryptically, then turns his attention to me. "Bathroom's back there, sweets."

To Jonah's credit, his eyes never leave my face, but he doesn't look away until I start to stand. Torren doesn't make a move to stop me.

I snatch my sundress and underwear from the couch and scurry in the direction of the bathroom, practically hurling myself inside and slamming the door behind me. When I catch sight of my reflection in the full-length mirror on the back of the door, my hands cover my mouth to stifle my yelp.

"Oh my god," I whisper into my hands. "What the actual fuck."

My upper body is covered in bruises. Hickeys and bite marks decorate my breasts and collarbone, with one particularly brutal one on my neck just under my ear. When I look down, I find two more bite marks on my inner thigh. Honestly, I look like I've been attacked by a vampire, and I stare wide-eyed at my body for several moments, trying to process what I'm seeing. After the initial surge of shock fades, though, I have to fold my lips between my teeth to hide my giggle.

"Oh my *god*."

Torren fucking King has left hickeys on my body. I just gave my first ever hand job and my virginity to Torren fucking King, and I have a body covered in bruises to show for it. I wish I had a friend I could talk to about this. I feel like I need to squeal into a pillowcase or something. Instead, all I have are the guys.

My stomach falls. Shit. The guys.

How the fuck am I going to explain this to them?

How am I going to explain it to Becket?

I pull my sundress over my head and take inventory of the bruises, heaving a sigh of relief when I realize all but two could be hidden by a regular crew neck T-shirt. The others I can probably cover with makeup. Hopefully.

God. Come to ArtFusion a sexually-inexperienced virgin, leave thoroughly fucked and covered in hickeys by a rock star. I roll my eyes.

This is like some low-budget porn script. Never in my wildest freaking dreams.

I pee and feel relieved when there's only a little bit of blood on the toilet paper, then slip my underwear back on. I wash my hands and pull my hair over my shoulders, trying to hide the hickeys, then take a deep breath before stepping back into the bus. Jonah is sitting at the small table, scrolling on his phone, and he doesn't look up when he addresses me.

"He's outside."

"Thanks." I walk toward the exit, stopping briefly to glance back at the guitarist. "Um...see you later."

His jaw ticks as if he heard me, but he doesn't respond and doesn't look up, so I let myself out. I find Torren waiting for me at the bottom of the steps. He's wearing a pair of shorts and a tank top, but he doesn't have shoes on his feet. When he sees me, he gives me a small smile.

"I'm going to have Beau walk you back."

I furrow my brow. "Why?"

"Cover's blown."

Ah. The crowd of fans behind the fence makes sense now. Someone must have finally recognized one of them. He reaches up and brushes my hair off my shoulder, then rubs his fingers over the large hickey just below my ear.

"Sorry."

I arch a brow. "Are you really?" He smirks but he doesn't answer. "Will I see you tomorrow?"

"Do you want to see me tomorrow?"

Excitement swirls in my stomach, and I try my best to swallow back my nerves as I nod.

"There's a band playing tomorrow from four to five on the west stage. Think you can make it out to watch?"

"They any good?"

I smile and shrug. "I think so, yeah."

He smiles back. "I might be able to make that happen."

"Cool."

Torren leans down and presses a kiss to my forehead, then winks as he steps away from me. It takes all my restraint not to reach for him.

"Sweet dreams, Firebird," he says, then I watch as he disappears back into the bus.

27

CALLIE

PAST, ArtFusion Day Five

"ARE YOU READY, CAL?"

Rocky's excitement brings a smile to my face, despite the nerves swirling in my stomach. I get nervous before every live show. I always have. But this? This is next level, and paired with exhaustion and budding dehydration, I have a real fear that I might vomit on stage.

I don't tell Rock that, though. Instead, I nod and flash him a thumbs-up.

When I got back to the tent last night, I lay awake for hours replaying the evening over and over in my head. I pretended to be asleep when the guys got back, but I didn't actually fall asleep until much later. I'm regretting it now.

Just the thought of my night with Torren makes my pulse speed up and the soreness between my legs throb, and for the hundredth time since we got to the stage, I glance around the crowd for his familiar black baseball cap and mirrored aviator sunglasses. He's not out there. Not yet. But that's okay. He has to be more careful now that everyone knows he's here. He said he'd come, so he'll come.

"Dude, there's like, a lot of people here," Ezra says, and when I glance at him, he's standing with his arms folded, staring out at the crowd. "Like more than I think we've ever played for."

"Yeah, well, that's what happens when you jump from playing dive bars with a couple hundred capacity to music festivals with over a hundred thousand attendees," I say, my voice breathy, betraying my lack of cool. "You get a much, *much* larger crowd."

"What if they, like, hate us?"

I turn all my attention to Ezra. He's looking a little queasy, so I put my hand on his back and rub gently.

"Ez. Aren't you the one who's always telling me how fucking amazing we are? And how it's only a matter of time before we blow up and make it big?"

Ezra rolls his eyes and shrugs. "Yeah."

I smack his arm. "Then stop saying dumb shit."

Ezra barks out a laugh and gives me a light shove. "You're right. You're right."

"I know."

I catch Becket's eye, and he squints at me before stalking my way. His movements are stiff and angry. I don't want to go into this show with tension.

As soon as he's within arm's reach, he grabs my waist, pulls me toward him, and plants a kiss on my lips. I'm frozen in place, nervous to make a scene. Worried that I'll fuck up the show. I don't really kiss him back, but I don't push him away. I let him kiss me until he steps back with a frustrated huff, and I heave a sigh of relief.

I force a smile. "You nervous?"

He shrugs. "I've been playing bass since I was fourteen, Callie. Been playing these songs for a year now. I could do this in my sleep."

"Good. That's good. Ezra is worried they'll hate us."

"Ezra is a moron."

I force a laugh and try to ignore his clipped tone. How would I have handled this six months ago? Teased him and told him to stop being so moody, probably. Six days ago? I'd have wrapped my arms around him and kissed him back. But now? I'm just kind of...lost.

"Bro, stop being such a dick," Ezra's voice chimes in. "Torren King has the broody bassist market cornered, yeah? We don't need another one."

Becket snarls in Ezra's direction, and I wince.

Awesome. This is exactly the opposite of how we should be going into the biggest show we've ever played. But what do I say? Play nice?

Am I even allowed to say anything at all, given my activities the last few nights? My guilt battles with my excitement—I don't want to hurt Becket, but I cannot get Torren out of my head. His hands, his eyes, his mouth. Everything.

Absently, my fingers brush over the hickey under my ear. I've covered it with makeup and braided my hair to the side, so it's well hidden, but I can still feel it. I press my fingers against it slightly, just enough to feel the sting of pain, and I smile.

I'm so fucked.

I bite my tongue and go back to waiting quietly, pretending everything is fine.

When a festival worker tells us it's time, we line up and climb the stairs to the stage. Ezra first, then Becket, Pike, and Rocky, then me. I'm not exactly the frontwoman—I kind of share the role of lead with Rocky —but the guys like having me come out last. Pike says I'm the *interesting one*.

I step up behind my keyboard and wave to the crowd, surprised by the number of cheers and applause we get. I flash a smile to Rocky as he slips his guitar strap over his head and winks at me.

"Hey ArtFusion, how are you all doing this evening?" I say into my mic, then I laugh as a roar erupts from the crowd in response. I scan the fringes of the crowd briefly, but there's no sign of Torren. I shove away the pang of disappointment and plow forward. "We're Caveat Lover, and we'd like to play some songs for you, if that's alright."

I get more cheers and applause, so with a grin and a nod at my bandmates, I place my fingers on the keys and launch us into our first song.

"Thanks for hanging out with us, ArtFusion! We had a great time playing for you. It's been an honor, and we hope to see you all in a bit for Heartless on the main stage!"

Rocky's words mix with the shouts of approval from the crowd. The guys throw out their final waves, I blow a few goodbye kisses, and Ezra takes a bow, then we exit the stage in a haze of euphoria. I'm buzzing with excitement. The show was amazing. I've never felt this charged after a performance. This is beyond anything we've done before, and now that I know how it feels—playing on a level like this—I want more of it. I'm disappointed that Torren never showed, but even that can't dampen my post-show high.

"Oh my god, I still can't believe it," I say, bouncing on my toes and whirling around to look at the guys. "That was fucking brilliant. I can't believe we just did that."

"Right? Low-key, I've been holding my breath for something to go wrong all week," Pike adds with a sheepish grin. "Didn't want to get my hopes up."

I open my mouth to tease him, but I'm lifted into Ezra's arms and spun in a circle, making me squeal with laughter.

"Put her down, Ez," Becket snaps, and Ezra gently places me back on my feet. Becket finally, after what feels like years, makes eye contact with me. "Callie, can I talk to you?"

I swallow and nod, sending the others a smile.

"We'll meet you guys for Heartless," Pike says, and then they disappear, leaving me and Becket behind the stage.

"What's up?"

"I should ask you that," he says, arms folded over his chest. "You've been completely MIA all week, and then I try to kiss you and you go stiff as a goddamn board. What the fuck was that, Callie?"

"I didn't...I wasn't..." I say slowly, shaking my head. "You startled me with that kiss. And I was with Pike and Rock and Ez all day yesterday. You were the one who—"

"And then where did you go?"

I blink at him, but I don't speak. His eyes scan my face, noting my scrunched eyebrows and my frown.

"Where did you go, Callie? To see your *friend from high school*? You didn't have friends in high school. You've told all of us that a thousand times. So where the *fuck* have you been going?"

My mouth drops open, and the confession falls out immediately. I don't even try to lie.

"I met someone. A guy."

Becket clenches his jaw and shakes his head, then he laughs. "A guy."

I squeeze my eyes shut and nod. "Yes. A guy. I've been hanging out with him."

"Have you hooked up with him?"

"Yes."

He scoffs, then silence stretches. When I finally open my eyes, I find him staring angrily at me, and my need to defend myself spikes.

"You said *casual*, Beck. Last week when I asked you what this was between us, you said *casual*. You said we *weren't anything serious. Just having fun*, remember? You can't get angry with me for spending time with someone else when you yourself said we weren't serious!"

"I wouldn't have said any of that shit if I'd thought you were going to turn around and hook up with some random douche at ArtFusion, Callie! Jesus. *It's not serious* isn't the same as saying *go fuck someone else*."

"I didn't—" I start to protest, but then I bite my tongue.

I don't even know what to say. I can't defend myself. I won't lie, but I can't bring myself to speak the truth. And fuck, I should be sorry, but I'm not. And damn it, even now, arguing with Becket about how I've fucked up our relationship, my pulse still races at the idea of being in Torren's arms again.

Flashes of being on his lap—of having his hands on me, him inside me—assault me, and the marks on my body sting in a way that makes me have to clench my thighs together.

I'm such a shitty person.

I drag my hands down my face and groan. I've never had anything even close to a boyfriend before Becket, and now I've gone and gotten myself into this weird love triangle mess.

"I'm sorry, Beck," I force out. "I didn't want to hurt you. It just kind of happened, and I thought since—"

"Who is he?"

My eyes flare and my mouth snaps shut. I won't tell him.

"Who the fuck is he?"

I shake my head and force a swallow.

"Um...he's just another attendee. I...um, I met him in the beer line."

He laughs again, but this time it's sinister. Cruel.

"Fuck it, Callie. I didn't think you'd be such a slut."

"That's not fair, Becket. That's so fucking not fair."

"What do you call hooking up with a dude within four days of meeting him? In a fucking beer line?"

My jaw drops, and I feel like I've been slapped. And what stings the most is that he's not wrong. Not at all. Teenage obsession or not, I still don't *know* Torren King, not really, and that fact makes everything that's transpired feel dirty. All I know is what I've read in the tabloids, and none of it is good. I feel fucking naive, and I hate Beck in this moment for ruining it.

"You're an asshole and a hypocrite," I seethe. "You've hooked up with girls after a single show. After meeting them for a matter of fucking hours."

"That's different. That's not you."

"Maybe you don't know what's me!"

"I've known you for over a year, Calla Lily. I know how you are. Why the fuck do you think I've been taking this slow? Why the fuck do you think I've been easing us into it? Because I know you don't do shit irrationally or without thinking it out, and I wanted to fucking respect that."

I bark out a laugh and let my biggest concern fly out of my mouth.

"Then tell me why you only pursued me after you found out I was a virgin, huh? Tell me why it wasn't until that fucking game in San Fran that you decided to try and start something with me?"

He clenches his jaw and I step forward, shoving his chest.

"Tell me that my being a virgin had nothing to do with it."

His nostrils flare, and angry tears sting my eyes. "I've liked you for a while, Cal."

I scoff. "Yeah, but not enough to stop playing up the rock star role and fucking pretend groupies, right? Not until there was an *incentive*."

He just glares at me, jaw twitching and brows slanted. God, I was right. I shake my head and roll my eyes. "That's what I fucking thought."

I brush past him and stomp my way to the main stage. I don't look to see if he's following me. I don't stop walking until I find the guys, and then I steal Ezra's drink and chug it. I don't let myself taste it.

"Cal, that was almost straight vodka," Ezra says with a laugh when I hand the empty cup back.

"Not anymore."

"Where's Beck?" Pike asks, and I shrug.

"Probably jerking off with his tears as lube after I told him he could give up trying to take my virginity."

Three pairs of eyes widen at me, and then Rocky reaches into his pocket and pulls out his little baggie of edibles. He bites one in half, then wordlessly hands the other half to me. I pop it into my mouth, chew quickly, and swallow.

"Thanks." I force a smile. "Now let's dance our fucking heads off, yeah?"

The opener is an alternative rock band I've been a fan of for a while, so it doesn't take long for me to get lost in the music. The half an edible and the vodka helps, too. By the time their set is finished, I've almost lost all the tension from my argument with Becket. I've almost embraced the feeling of numbness, and then the chant starts.

Heartless, Heartless, Heartless.

Immediately, my heart kicks up and my stomach flutters with butterflies.

Torren.

The stage lights have dimmed, and people have started pushing toward the stage, so the guys and I let ourselves be carried into a more cramped, bodies-on-bodies, type of pit. The energy and excitement are so palpable that I can't fight the way my grin takes over my whole face.

"I've wanted to see them live forever," Pike says over the roaring crowd, and I nod.

Me too. It feels different now. Like I've got a secret. I've got a connection to The Hometown Heartless that no one else does, and the thrill makes me almost lightheaded.

When the spotlight shines down on a familiar silver head of hair, the screams become nearly deafening, and then her low, raspy laugh booms through the speakers. As jealous as I am of Sav Loveless, her voice still gives me chills. She's an icon. She's one of a kind. And in this moment, I feel it more strongly than ever before.

The fan posts are right. You don't get it until you see them live. Not truly.

"That's what we like to hear," Sav says, punctuated by a drumbeat from the back of the stage. They haven't turned on the rest of the stage lights, but I can picture the drummer, Mabel Rossi's bright pink hair without them. "ArtFusion, how the fuck are you feeling tonight?"

More screams. So many screams. People are whooping and jumping and going crazy, and she's only said two sentences. I strain my eyes to focus on the shadowy figure just to the side of her. That's where Torren is. My pulse thrums rapidly in anticipation of finally seeing him.

"We're The Hometown Heartless. We're so happy to be here. Now let's fucking rock."

The stage lights come on with the opening chords of their first song, and I zero in on Torren. No one else on that stage exists the moment I see him.

God, he looks good.

Black, curly hair hanging in his eyes. Black ripped jeans hugging his long legs. Black vintage band T-shirt with the sleeves ripped off, showcasing his tattooed arms, and I can't help but focus on the way the muscles in his forearms flex as he plays his bass.

I had those hands on me last night.

I had that mouth on my neck. On my breasts. I have the bite marks to prove that it wasn't a dream.

My smile is borderline creepy, and I let out a giggle that sounds more twelve-year-old girl than nineteen-year-old woman. When Torren sings harmonies into his mic, it gives me chills.

"You think we'll ever be that good?" Ezra asks in my ear, and I shrug.

"I hope so."

I'm so enraptured by him that when he steps up to sing with Sav into her mic, my jealousy doesn't surge right away. They do it all the time. That doesn't mean they're back together.

But then the longer I watch, the sicker I start to feel.

The way he looks at her. The way he smiles at her. It's like she's some sort of goddess. Like she's the love of his life. And then that song ends, and it's like I imagined the whole thing. He goes back to his mic, and I feel like an idiot.

It was nothing. Nothing. They're broken up.

I repeat this over and over for the rest of the set, but something doesn't sit right with me. When the lights go down, just before they come back out for the encore, I slip out of the crowd and head to the back of the stage.

I listen to the encore song end, and when I attempt to make my way behind the stage, security stops me. This guy I don't know, and I sigh.

"I need to get back there," I say impatiently. I flash my musician badge. "I just played my set. I'm a musician."

"Sorry, ma'am. VIP performers only."

My nostrils flare.

"Look, I know Torren King, okay? I'm supposed to meet him."

It's a lie, and this guy doesn't buy it. He just folds his arms and stares at me. He thinks I'm a groupie. I can tell. Hell, I'd think that, too, if I were him.

"I'm not a groupie. I was supposed to meet him. Radio him or something and ask."

He still doesn't budge.

I flick my eyes behind him, then survey the surrounding area, looking for a different way in, and then just like last night, an arm drops over my shoulders.

"With me," Jonah clips out, and the security guy steps aside with one last judgmental glance at me. Jonah leads me behind the stage toward the Heartless bus, but this time there's a second one.

"That a new bus?" I ask, and Jonah hums.

"A win for Savvy."

He doesn't elaborate, and he doesn't remove his arm from my shoulder.

"Thanks," I say. He doesn't respond until we're almost to the buses.

"You sure you want this, sweets?"

His voice is dead. His words cryptic. When I don't answer, he stops and looks down at me. His blue eyes, once again, are red-rimmed. His face emotionless.

"Yes or no."

Slowly, I give him a single nod, and then he starts walking again. When we get closer to the buses, I notice the extra security surrounding them, but no one bats an eye at me. Jonah just slips past them, and within a few more breaths, we're stepping up between the two buses.

My feet stop immediately, and a ringing fills my ears. The noises don't break through until my brain fully processes what I'm seeing.

"Didn't even make it to the bus this time," Jonah says pointedly, but I can't tear my eyes away from Torren and Sav. He's got her pressed against the bus, his hands cupping her face as he kisses her ravenously. Opened-mouthed and sloppy, all tongue and teeth.

He never kissed me. Not once. It's such a devastating thing to realize in this moment. An eye-opening detail brought to light too late.

Then my eyes fall lower to his pumping hips.

To his jeans around his knees and Sav's legs wrapped around his waist.

He's fucking her. He's fucking her against this bus.

If the flexing muscles in his bare ass and the aggressive thrusting didn't give it away, the grunting and moaning does. Even the darkness can't disguise it.

Tears prickle my eyes as I watch, but I can't look away. Not until Torren moves his mouth to her neck and Sav turns her head in our direction. The way her face is twisted up in pleasure makes me want to vomit. I'm half a breath from turning on my heel and bolting when Torren opens his eyes, and they land right on me. They land, and they stick. They stay on me, freezing me to the spot, until his eyes clamp shut and his mouth falls open on a groan.

Of all the things I thought would happen when I came back here, watching Torren King come inside Sav Loveless wasn't even in the realm of possibility.

"Don't take it personally." Slowly, I tear my eyes from the horrific scene before me and look up at Jonah. He's lighting a joint. "He doesn't keep groupies around long."

It's the killing blow. The knife to the jugular. I turn and bolt.

I run the whole way across the park and back to the campsite, and when I find Becket, I grab his wrist and pull him into our tent.

"Fuck me," I command, and he blinks at me.

I strip off my tank top, then unbutton my shorts.

"I'm only giving you this chance once. You want to fuck me? Fine. But make me come first."

28

CALLIE

PRESENT DAY

BACK IN MY HOTEL ROOM, I fling open the closet door and tug out my duffle bag.

I throw the duffle on the bed, then head back to the closet with the intention of packing my shit, but when I glance at the hangers, I groan.

Nothing here is mine. None of it. Torren gave it all to me, and it feels like bribery now.

I take the duffle into the bathroom and start throwing my makeup and toiletries into it. I find the few articles of clothing I brought from home and shove those into the duffle as well.

The whole time I do, Torren's words bounce around in my skull like pinballs. They repeat over and over, giving me a headache and a twisting feeling in my stomach.

Since Glendale.

I remember everything.

All of it.

And then that kiss.

God, that messes with me more than anything else, and I angrily swipe a tear away when it escapes my lashes. Why did he have to go and kiss me now, after fucking everything? Not once in the desert did he kiss me. Not once. But now...

I remember everything.

All of it.

Firebird.

That's the problem. I remember all of it, too.

Fuck Torren King.

I feel so damn foolish. Cheated. Lied to. Vulnerable and exposed.

Worst of all, I feel embarrassed.

I knew this was coming. Part of me was longing for it. But now that I've been slapped in the face with it, a whole slew of formerly suppressed emotions has resurfaced, and I can't handle it all. I can't make sense of it. I need to get out of here.

Glory said Mom is doing better. She'll forgive me. I've already received the first two checks. We don't *need* the rest. We will be fine.

Fuck.

I sit back on the bed, setting the duffle beside me, then drop my head into my hands.

Why couldn't he have gone on pretending?

My phone buzzing interrupts my thoughts. A text message. I pick it up, expecting to see a text from Torren, but instead it's Ezra's name in the notification.

All the text says is *Sorry, Cal,* followed by a link from a gossip blog.

When I click the link, my stomach falls to my feet. Photos of me and Torren with the guys in the bathroom hallway at the club are already uploaded. They're dark, but they're in focus, and it's very obviously us. The blog post correctly identifies Becket, Ezra, and Rocky, then goes on to mention our band, Caveat Lover. The blogger says the band used to be signed but then was unsigned without explanation, and they promise to update later with more information about *that potentially juicy scandal.*

None of that bothers me, though. I had been waiting for news about the band to come out anyway. I'm surprised it took this long, to be honest. It's the rest of the blog article that has my heart thudding with anxiety in my chest.

The blogger claims Torren and I are in a PR relationship to help relaunch my music career. They go even further as to say how *curiously convenient* it is that the bad press surrounding Sav and Torren has died down, too. Luckily, there are no photos of me leaving the club without him or of our argument in the hallway...*yet*...but this is bad enough on its own.

Is our cover blown? Did I fuck it up?

"Goddamn it." I toss my phone on the bed and pinch the bridge of my nose. "Goddamn it!"

"Open the door, Callie."

Torren's muffled voice on the other side of my bedroom door has me groaning.

"Fuck you!"

"Callie, open this door before I open it myself."

"Fuck. You. I don't wa—"

The door swings wide open and Torren marches through it before slamming it behind him. I jump up from the bed, put my hands on my hips, and stare him down.

"You asshole."

"Get used to it."

When he's three feet in front of me, eyes locked on mine, he folds his arms over his chest.

"We need to talk."

"I have nothing to say to you."

"Fine, then you can listen." His attention falls to my duffle on the bed and his eyebrows furrow. "You think you're going somewhere? We don't get on the bus until after tomorrow's show."

"I'm not getting on the bus. I'm going home."

"You're not leaving."

"Yes, I fucking am. You said I could leave whenever I want, and I want to leave now."

"You're not fucking leaving over this." He takes another few steps toward me. "Not until we figure this out. I need you here."

I bark out a laugh. "*Figure this out*? Figure what out? You said you remember everything!"

"I do, Callie, and that's why I'm so fucking confused. You've been holding a grudge, and I want to know why, because I've been spending weeks trying to figure it out. I need to know what happened for you to hate me so much."

"What's there to be confused about? You fucked me like a groupie then went back to your ex-girlfriend."

"I didn't fuck you like a groupie."

"The hell you didn't! You think taking my virginity and then screwing Sav against your tour bus the next night is how you treat someone who isn't a groupie?"

His face pales. "You were a virgin?"

I roll my eyes. "Yeah, I was a virgin, you asshole. Though I suppose you were too high to notice. And my first time is unfortunately seared into my brain, yet it was just another groupie fuck for you."

"You weren't just a groupie."

"Oh, shut up. It doesn't even matter now."

"You had a boyfriend, Callie. A *boyfriend*."

I jerk my head back. "What?"

Torren takes another step toward me.

"I saw you with Becket before your set the next day. I saw you kiss him. You lied to me all week, came to me that night so we could hook up, and then turned around and kissed him before your fucking set. *That's* when I decided what happened between us was just a festival fling. You weren't just a groupie to me, but I was just a famous fuck to you."

My head spins for a moment at the revelation. First, that he came to the stage like I'd asked, and second, that he saw me kiss Beck. It did happen. I remember it clearly, but had Torren taken the time to fucking talk to me, he would have known that I also told Beck off after our set. If I was important enough to warrant a conversation...god, what a fucking mess.

"You weren't just a famous fuck," I defend. "I lost my virginity to you."

Torren lets out a sinister laugh. "Yeah. What a story, too, right? How many people did you dazzle with that story? Losing your virginity to *the* Torren King."

My blood boils. "Oh, get the fuck over yourself. That's not what it was for me, and you know it."

"Do I? Do I know it, Firebird?"

"Don't fucking call me that."

"Tell me he wasn't your boyfriend. Tell me you didn't lie."

"I didn't lie."

"Right." He laughs. "And you didn't lie about your age, either?"

My jaw drops. He's got me there, and he knows it. I shake my head. I'm speechless.

"You're twenty-three, Callie. I might only have a high school education, but I can do basic math. You were nineteen at ArtFusion, but you told me you were old enough to drink. You're going to hold a grudge and be pissed at me when *everything* you did was to get close to me. You lied about your age. Your boyfriend—"

"He wasn't my fucking boyfriend!"

"Whatever the fuck he was, then. It doesn't change the fact that you kissed him after we hooked up. He was more than just a friend to you. I liked you, but when I saw you kissing Becket Walker, I accepted it for what it was. For what *you* made it. You don't get to change the facts to make me the bad guy now."

For a moment, I start to spiral. I start to feel bad. I've never denied my part in our ArtFusion tryst, and I *almost* want to forgive and forget...but I can't. Not yet. I'm swept up in the argument. My anger is driving my actions, and my stubborn need to win is riding shotgun.

Torren King is a dick.

He's selfish, and I'm a solution to a problem. Nothing more. I won't let him shove my mistakes in my face while he refuses to acknowledge his own.

"You're not going to get me to feel sorry for you, Torren," I say, my anger still simmering at the surface despite all he's confessed. "I won't apologize. You act like you did nothing wrong here, but you looked right at me. Right at me! You fucked her against that tour bus one night after taking my virginity, and you were looking at me when you came inside her."

He shakes his head and closes his eyes. "Fuck..."

I scoff. "Don't tell me you don't remember that."

"I don't. I don't remember it. I swear. I'm sorry, Callie." He rakes his fingers through his hair and looks back at me with glittering green eyes full of sorrow. "I know you don't believe me, but I didn't do that on purpose. I didn't know you were there. Had I known you'd come to me, I never would have done it. I just...Fuck, Calla Lily I am so goddamn sorry."

I grit my teeth against the urge to fold.

"Bullshit," I force out. "Let's just cut our losses, King, and call it what it was. A big fucking mistake."

Torren's nostrils flare, and then he pulls out his phone. He breaks eye contact to scroll for a moment, then tosses the phone to me. I catch it, but before I can look at the screen, he's unbuckling his belt.

"What the actual fuck are you doing?"

"Look at the phone screen."

When he undoes his button, I spin around and give him my back. I close my eyes, and then he repeats himself.

"Look at the phone, Callie. Now."

I hear the sound of his zipper, followed by his pants being shoved down his legs. Because I need something to think about besides the fact that he's stripping behind me, I look at the phone, and then my jaw drops.

On the phone screen is the picture he took of me at ArtFusion.

The one he texted to himself after decorating my body with latex paint.

I deleted this photo the morning after I caught Torren with Sav. I'd all but forgotten about it. But seeing it now, the memory of it seems as clear and as crisp as if it were yesterday.

In the photo, I'm looking down and to the side, my face mostly in shadow due to the dim lighting in the tent that night. My hair looks more brown than red, and the features of my face are hidden, but the body paint is just as gorgeous as I remember it. Torren turned me into a living, breathing flame.

Emotions start to unfurl in my stomach. My heart starts to race. Then I clamp my eyes shut, severing the connection between myself and that naïve girl in the photo.

"So what? This doesn't mean anything."

"Turn around."

I don't know why I obey as quickly as I do, but I open my eyes and turn around without question. I make eye contact with him, slanting my eyebrows harshly as I glare, hoping my forced attitude hides my surging nerves. I hold the phone out to him, and he takes it, and I can tell from the edges of my vision that he's not wearing pants. My plan is to avoid looking down, but then he gestures to his left leg.

"Look."

I arch a brow.

"Look, Callie."

I blow out a harsh breath and look down, my eyes falling to his upper thigh. It takes a moment for what I'm seeing to register in my brain. At first, it's just a splotch of reds, oranges, and yellows, but then I blink, and like magic, it comes into focus. A viewfinder revealing an image that knocks the wind out of me. I gasp.

The splotch of colors on Torren's thigh is a tattoo of a faceless woman.

A woman standing among flames.

And the longer I look, the more I realize that the tattoo looks just like the ArtFusion photo. Instead of standing awkwardly, the faceless woman in the tattoo almost appears to be dancing, the flames resembling phoenix wings behind her.

As I stare at it, dragging my eyes over every detail, my heart starts to pound faster and faster, thudding loudly in my head.

The woman is *me*.

I shake my head. It doesn't make sense.

"When did you get that?" I ask, my voice almost a whisper. The ink is slightly faded. Hair lightly dusts his muscular thigh. I can tell it's not a new tattoo, but I need to know.

"Six months after the festival."

I finally tear my eyes away from the tattoo and look back at Torren. "Why?"

His lips twitch at the corners. I don't know if he's fighting a smile or a frown. Either option would piss me off.

"Because I couldn't get you out of my head."

I scoff. "Yeah, sure. Yet when I literally slammed into you at the pier, it took you weeks to remember who I was. I was playing your devoted fake girlfriend for an entire week before it clicked."

"I don't know how to explain it to you." He lets out a low, almost self-deprecating laugh. "It's hard to explain being an addict to someone who's never walked that path. When you're high—and I was almost always high—the specifics are hazy. Chunks of time are black holes. Not every memory is readily available. Not everything sticks. But you? You *stuck*. The idea of you. Abstract images of you. Fleeting fractions of memories. When I found the picture in my phone, I latched onto it. I'd stare at it for hours, trying to memorize your outline. Trying like hell to fill in the missing details. But then I'd get high and have to start all over again, and time tends to erode anything that remains."

He laughs again, this one louder. "I actually got that tattoo while fucked up, too. I don't regret it, though. Never have."

His words pierce through my armor. They make my chest ache and my eyes sting. My years-long desire for him bubbles up. My past hero worship. My envy.

"I'm sorry, Callie. I'm so fucking sorry. Please believe that you were more to me. I fucked up, but you were more. You *are* more. This is real. This is real, for me. It always has been."

I start to crumble. To give in, but then I stand taller.

I shake my head once more. I got swept up in the argument—in the emotions and insignificant details—and I remind myself of the *real* reason I've been hating him all these years. Not because I caught him screwing Sav the night after he fucked me. Yeah, that sucked, but it didn't derail me. Having sex with him at ArtFusion was a stupid decision, and I made peace with it a long time ago.

But he's right about one thing. I don't get to change the facts, and neither does he.

"None of this changes anything, Torren."

His face falls, brows slanting in a defeated, confused expression that makes my throat feel tight. I sigh and close my eyes so I don't have to look at him.

"You still fucked up my band. You can apologize all you want about what happened at the music festival, but you still took Caveat Lover away from me, and that hurts worse than everything else. Watching you fuck Sav the night after you fucked me was a punch to the gut, but losing my band was debilitating, and I can't forgive you for that."

I drag a hand down my face and tilt my head to the ceiling, my throat cracking more and more with each word.

"Jesus, you have no idea how hard it's been for me to be here knowing how you all operate. I just kept telling myself it was okay...that you owed me that money based on what you did to Caveat Lover alone. But fuck, I can't stay here anymore. I can't. That tattoo, your story—they don't change any of it."

When I look back at him, his face is twisted with confusion. It fans the flames of my grudge. When he speaks, I want to punch him again.

"I have no idea what you're talking about. I thought you left the band to take care of your mom."

"No. My mom was after."

When his confused expression doesn't lighten, I scoff in disbelief.

The lengths he'll go to use me...

My eyes start to sting with tears. I don't want to cry, but this hurts. Uncovering it all. Remembering it. Forcing myself to reckon with the fact that the man I've been spending time with for the last few weeks, the man who has been slowly charming away my pent-up anger, is still the man who fucked me over.

Tattoo or not, he's still Torren King.

"You have to be kidding me," I rasp, peering at him through watery eyes. "You can't possibly expect me to believe that any of it happened without your knowledge."

He takes a step closer to me, reaches for me, but I back away.

"Any of *what*? Explain. Please, Callie. Explain."

I suck in a slow, shaky breath through my teeth, then blow it out. I glare at him, searching his face for a lie, but there's nothing but genuine confusion.

"*Your* label threatened to sue *my* band and the label that signed us. You accused us of stealing music and branding. You claimed we were guilty of copyright infringement."

His face pales and his mouth gapes, but he says nothing.

"We didn't steal anything. Our manager said that we could probably fight you in court and win, but we didn't have the money to pay for all the legal fees, and our label didn't want to try to go up against yours. I found out after that you were rumored to do this to smaller bands to kill any kind of competition, but our label was small, and they just couldn't risk a fight with you... So they fucking dropped us. They dropped us, Torren, because of The Hometown Heartless, and then no one else would touch us. We tried. We kept trying, but we were pariahs. Then my mom got sick and..." I shrug. "And we just had to admit defeat. Heartless attacked and won. You all got what you wanted. One more band out of the way."

Silence envelops us as Torren stares at me with shock, and I watch as his expression morphs quickly into rage. He clenches his jaw, grinding his teeth as he dials someone on his phone. They must answer quickly, because he barks out an order.

"Band meeting in the girls' suite. Now." He hangs up and looks at me. "You too."

Then he turns and walks out.

I take ten deep inhales and exhales before I follow, and when I step into the suite, Mabel, Sav, and Levi are already there. When I glance around the room, I find the security details on the perimeter.

"You guys can leave," Torren says to the security, but Sav interrupts.

"Red stays."

Torren nods. As all the security guards except Sav's file into the hall, Hammond walks into the room with Jonah in tow.

"This better be fucking good," Jonah grumbles as he throws himself into a recliner. "I was busy."

I catch Sav as she rolls her eyes, and Mabel tosses a small throw pillow at Jonah's head. It hits him and falls to the floor, and he never even flinches. Then Torren cuts to the chase, his voice shaking with barely restrained anger.

"Ham. Did our label threaten to sue Callie's band?"

I flick my eyes from Torren's murderous expression to Hammond's blank one. He studies Torren before speaking.

"Probably."

Mabel and Sav both shout, shock evident in their tones.

"What the fuck? Why?"

"Are you fucking kidding me?"

Torren remains silent, nostrils flaring, glare still stuck on Hammond. "What the fuck does *probably* mean?"

"I don't know the specifics. I only discovered it when I renegotiated the contract last year, but they had done it more than once. If Callie claims her band was one of them, I believe her. I demanded they stop, and as far as I know, it hasn't happened since."

Sav shoots to her feet, fury emanating from her. Her body practically quakes with it.

"Why *the fuck* are we just now hearing about this?"

Hammond looks at Sav, face still placid. His tone never rises. He never sounds anything more than matter-of-fact. Not apologetic. Not defensive. Not even angry. A consummate, unshakable businessman. I both hate and respect him for it.

"Because you only had a couple of years left on your contract. We'd gotten the terms we'd wanted, and at the end of the contract, we'd walk. There was nothing I could do about the past. I ensured the foreseeable future would be ethical. I didn't want to add anything else to the band's already overflowing plate."

"Bullshit," Sav says. "This is something we should have known."

Hammond's eyebrow lifts just slightly. "We were dealing with Jonah's rehab visit. With the fallout from the engagement. From the mental and emotional impact of the fire. Of your mother's hospitalization. Of Levi's and your relationship going public. Savannah, I will not apologize for keeping this from you. I would do it again. I'd fixed the problem. It was no longer an issue. Everything else took precedence."

Sav stares him down, obviously warring with her feelings. Hell, even I understand where he's coming from, but I can tell she's not ready to forgive it.

"How many bands?" Her voice is still shaking with anger when she asks, and Hammond sighs.

"I don't know the exact number, but I'd wager it was close to twenty."

"Jesus Christ," Mabel mumbles, dropping her head to the back of the couch. "This is so fucked up."

"We're out, Ham," Sav says, and I see Torren nod in my peripheral. "I don't care what you have to do. I want us out of the contract."

"Done."

"And I want the names of every band our label fucked over."

"That will be harder."

"I don't fucking care."

"I know you don't."

"So you'll get them, then?"

"Yes."

In the silence that follows, I start to feel lightheaded. The tidal wave of information hits me hard, and I feel the color drain from my face. My extremities feel cold. My stomach roils. Slowly, I walk backward until my legs hit a couch, and then I sit.

As soon as I hit the cushion, familiar tattooed hands cup my face.

"Are you okay? Do you need anything?"

"No."

"No, you're not okay, or no, you don't need anything?"

I want to roll my eyes at Torren's question, but I don't want to risk overexerting myself.

"I'm fine."

His lips press to my forehead and his fingers slide to the back of my neck.

"I'm going to fix this," he whispers. "You'll see."

29

TORREN

"You're backstage tonight."

"What?"

"For the show. You're watching from backstage."

Callie blinks a few times, licking her lips nervously before responding. "Why?"

I give her a small smile. "I've got a surprise for you."

Her gaze flits away from mine, and she nods. "Sure. Whatever you want."

She brushes past me without another word, and I watch her back until she disappears into the girls' dressing room.

I haven't spoken to her since everything blew up last night. I tried once, and she asked me to give her space. She said she was tired and overwhelmed, so I backed off. I left her alone for the rest of the night. I didn't seek her out this morning. In all honesty, I needed the space, too.

My mind is still reeling from everything that was revealed last night.

On one hand, I'm glad everything is out in the open. But on the other hand, I just can't fucking believe our label pulled that shit right under our noses.

Though, I suppose a lot could have happened over the last few years without us knowing. We were a fucking mess. It was all Hammond could do to keep us from falling apart and self-sabotaging. It shouldn't surprise me as much as it does.

No wonder Callie fucking hated me. I'd hate me, too.

Truthfully, I kind of do now.

How many bands did we screw over? How many dreams did we crush? How many lives did we irreparably alter? It was all I could think about last night. That, and the look on Callie's face when she told me about my band's role in ruining hers. *Pain.* There's no other way to describe it. She was in pain. She'd been holding on to it for years, letting it fester, believing that I'd betrayed her in that way. She hated me. She blamed the band. And truly, she had every right to.

While I didn't have a direct hand in the label's actions, it still happened *because* of me. Because of The Hometown Heartless. We're all guilty by association, and I know it's going to take a while to repair the damage that was done in our name.

Tonight, though...

Tonight, I'm going to work on repairing the one thing only I can fix. The thing I care about the most. Tonight, I start winning back my Firebird.

"We've got a little surprise for you all tonight."

The crowd cheers loudly and Sav laughs into her mic.

"Oh, you like the sound of that? Good. Because you're going to hear something never before played in public." Sav pauses dramatically, letting the roar of the crowd climb higher and higher before she laughs once more. "But to play it, we've gotta switch some things up."

One of the roadies comes walking out to the stage with an acoustic guitar. Sav slips her electric off and trades it with the roadie for the acoustic as the venue practically shakes from the sounds of the crowd's excitement. Instead of putting the guitar on, though, Sav turns to me.

"Hey, Tor?"

I grin at her and speak into my mic. "Yeah, Savvy?"

"How would you feel about taking the lead on this one?"

Sav's such a fucking showman, and the crowd eats it up. I can't help but laugh at her theatrics. There are multiple reasons why she's our frontwoman, and one of them is how well she works a crowd. They start chanting my name as I set down my bass and walk up next to her. When she hands me the guitar, another surge of screams floods the stage.

"Thanks, Sav."

She winks. "It's all you now."

Sav saunters over to my mic stand, so I turn and look for Callie. I find her standing in the wings of the stage, right where I wanted her. I lean into the mic, speaking to her but broadcasting it out into the stadium.

"I don't suppose I can get you to come out here with me?" Her eyes widen comically as she shakes her head. I chuckle into the mic. "Didn't think so. Well, just stay right there then, because this one is for you."

When she nods once, I turn my attention back to the roaring crowd.

"This is a song I wrote a few years back after meeting someone at a music festival. We've never played it live until tonight. It's called, 'Firebird.'"

As I begin to play, the crowd's cheering grows softer, everyone eager to hear this never-before-heard song. I keep my eyes on the wings of the stage, never taking my gaze off Callie, and when I start to sing, the first verse flows out of me as smoothly as an exhale. It feels like I'm sharing a long-kept secret, finally revealing it to the one person for whom it was meant.

When I reach the chorus, the tears welling in Callie's eyes start to trickle down her cheeks, and I watch her laugh. I wish I could hear it over the music and the crowd.

A few months after ArtFusion, I'd discovered lyrics scribbled in a notebook. A song I'd been writing over the course of the five-night music festival, inspired by a gorgeous woman backlit by glittering flames. We never recorded it, partly because I didn't want to share it, but we will now. I already talked to the band. "Firebird" will be on the next album, and tonight is its hard launch.

By the second chorus, the crowd is singing along, and Callie is swaying lightly to the music. She's still crying, but she's also still smiling, and it makes me want to rush to her. When the last notes fade out, the venue erupts in cheers and whistles and praise, but instead of bowing, I slide the acoustic to my back and walk toward Callie.

With every step toward her, I brace myself for her retreat, but she stays put. She doesn't move, so when I'm finally within touching distance, I thread my fingers through her hair and bring her lips to mine.

Fuck, I haven't been able to stop thinking about this kiss. About her.

About how much I need to feel her mouth on mine. Our tongues tangle greedily, and she doesn't shove me away. She doesn't break our kiss. She pulls me closer. She threads her fingers in my hair and tugs, making me groan. My dick aches, and I press my growing erection into her body.

God, I want to fuck her right here. I'd do it on stage in front of everyone. I don't even fucking care.

"You have to get back out there," Callie says against my mouth. "The crowd is getting antsy."

"They can wait." I bite her lower lip and she laughs, pressing lightly on my chest.

"Go. You've got three songs left. I don't want the media to start saying the show ended early because of me."

I pull back and smile down at her, rubbing my thumb over her swollen lower lip. "Did you like the song?"

She smirks. "It was okay."

"It was for you. It was always for you."

"I know." Callie smiles softly and presses a kiss to the pad of my thumb. "I remember."

I kiss her once more, this one quick and chaste before finally stepping back toward the stage. "See you in three songs, Firebird."

"I'll be here."

I hand the acoustic off to a roadie, then leave Callie standing in the wings to walk back to my spot on the stage. We play the rest of our set. We do the whole *leave then return* game for the encores. Then, when the show is finally over, I rush off the stage to find Callie.

I avoid everyone else. I don't speak to anyone. I don't look at anyone. The only thing I care about is Callie, but when I find her backstage, my feet slow to a stop, and the high I'd been riding moments earlier rapidly declines.

"Thank you," she says, giving me a wry grin as she closes the distance between us. "But you know calla lilies are really popular wedding and funeral flowers, right? I never understood why my parents named me after a funeral flower, but I guess it could be worse. They could have named me Glory Bell."

I narrow my eyes at the bouquet of flowers in her arms, every warning bell in my body sounding loudly. "Where'd you get those?"

"Some roadie brought them to me." She studies the bouquet with a furrowed brow. "I thought they were from you."

I shake my head. "No. Is there a note?"

"Yeah..." She plucks a small white card from inside the bouquet and hands it to me. "It doesn't say who it's from."

I take the card from her and look it over. The outside has *CALLA LILY SUNRISE JAMES* typed on it, and the inside just says *FOR YOU*. No name. No company. Nothing.

My first thought is that it's Jonah trying to fuck with me, but the moment my furious eyes land on him, I change my mind. If he'd done this, he'd look smug, but I call out to him anyway.

"Jo. D'you send these to Callie?"

Jonah arches a disinterested brow. It's all the answer I need, and I quickly take the bouquet and gesture for Damon. When he's next to me, I hand him the bouquet.

"Someone gave Callie these flowers. I need you to find out who."

"He, um, he was dressed as a roadie, and he looked like he was about my age. If that helps."

Damon nods at Callie. "We're on it."

When Damon stalks away, Callie turns concerned green eyes on me. "What's going on?"

"I'm not sure yet." I put my arm around her shoulders and tug her into my side before leading her toward the dressing room. "Could that bouquet have been from your mom? Or maybe someone else?"

"No. I don't think so."

Jealousy swells in my chest and I breathe through it. "What about your ex?"

Callie huffs out a laugh. "Becket wouldn't have sent me flowers."

"You sure? He didn't seem too happy at the club."

"Yeah, because I'm allegedly dating the douche who torpedoed his music career, not because he wants me back or whatever other bullshit you're thinking."

I glance down at her and arch a brow. "Allegedly?"

"Don't think you're off the hook yet, King. It's going to take more than one secret song sung in front of an audience to win me over."

I stop walking. "Sung in front of a packed stadium," I correct. "There were nearly fifty-thousand people in that audience."

She shrugs. "And?"

"And..." I lower my hands to her waist and walk her backward slowly until her back is against the wall, then I rest my forearms above her head, caging her in. "I got you tattooed on my fucking leg. *And* I'm going to fix the mess our label caused you. *And* I like you, Calla Lily Sunrise James."

She tips her head up, her lips just inches from mine. "You like me, huh?"

"I do."

"Hmm. I might be starting to like you, too." She folds her lips between her teeth, bouncing her eyes between mine before giving me a small smile. Then she slides out from under my arm cage and turns to face me. "But I don't trust you."

I tilt my head, considering her words carefully. If I can understand anything, it's how difficult it can be to trust someone with your heart. Especially *after* that person has already caused you pain. It's taken me a long time to come around to the idea of actually allowing myself to fall for someone again. To trust them completely. I can't expect her to accept me overnight.

"Do you think you could, though?" I ask finally. "Do you think you could, *eventually*, trust me?"

She purses her lips, then gives me a one-shouldered shrug. "Maybe."

I grin. "I can work with that."

I take her hand in mine, give it a squeeze, then walk her back to the dressing rooms. I'm about to drop her off and head to my own dressing room when Hammond comes stomping up behind me.

"Inside. Band meeting." He brushes right past us, so we follow behind him. As soon as we're in the room with the others, Hammond speaks again. "We found the kid who gave Callie the flowers. He was paid one hundred dollars in cash and didn't get a name. Can't remember a face."

"Someone gave you flowers?" Sav asks Callie, alarm in her voice. "And you don't know who?"

"No." Callie shakes her head. "Honestly, I thought it was Torren."

Sav pulls her lower lip between her teeth, then she looks at Hammond. "You think it's him? The stalker?"

Hammond shrugs. "I don't know. We don't have any reason to

believe it would be. He's never made contact with anyone but you before, and sending flowers isn't in his bag of tricks as far as we've seen."

"Maybe Callie's got a fan," Mabel chimes in. "But, like, a nice, normal fan. Not the stalker kind that Sav has."

The suggestion is said lightheartedly, but it makes me frown. Fan or not, the whole situation is creepy, and it doesn't sit right with me. I glance at Levi, who has been standing with his arms crossed behind Sav like a third security detail.

"How long are you staying?"

"As long as I have to."

"And Brynn?"

"She's staying with Sharon."

"Good," I say with a nod. I was expecting that. Now that he knows about Sav's stalker, there's no way she's going to convince him to go back to North Carolina. Then I look at Callie. "You're moving in with me."

30

CALLIE

I FOLD my arms across my chest, watching as Torren opens the door to the back room on the bus and tosses my duffle on the floor. In Sav and Mabel's bus, this area is a room with a bed and a dresser. In this bus, though, it's just a couch and a television.

"The bed is in the wall," Torren says, answering my unspoken question. "Jo and I usually just sleep on the bunks and use this as a second lounge area, but I'm setting the bed up for you."

After Levi's surprise arrival, Mabel and I rode on Torren and Jonah's bus to Houston, but we never actually had to sleep here. After spending the weekend in the hotel suites, Mabel's decided to move back to the bus she shares with Sav.

"If Mabel's staying on the bus with Sav and Levi, why can't I?"

"You can if you want. I'm not forcing you to stay here."

Torren doesn't look at me as he gets to work on *setting up the bed*. Turns out it's pretty simple. A portion of the back wall just kind of pops out and hinges downward, revealing a plush-looking mattress and transforming the room into a replica of the one on the other bus. He pulls some silky sheets out of a cabinet and starts putting them on the bed, and without overthinking it, I step up to help him. In a few minutes, the bed is made, and Torren is pinning me with his emerald eyes once more.

"You can go back to the other bus if you want to. Walton will be in

257

an SUV following whichever bus you're on, but I'd rather you be here with me."

I arch a brow. "Why? You heard Hammond. There's no reason to believe those flowers were from Sav's stalker."

He shrugs. "I know."

"Do *you* think they were from Sav's stalker?"

"No. But I still want you here."

I let us fall into silence as our gazes stay locked together. There's no avoiding the effect that statement has on me. My stomach does flips of glee as I replay it.

I want you here. I want you here.

But it's been a long time since I've been on this bus, and admittedly, I don't know how I'm going to feel when my past memories start clashing with my present reality. As if reading my mind, Torren takes a step closer, putting himself only a few feet in front of me.

"You don't have to stay if you're uncomfortable. You can go back to the other bus."

His voice is lower, softer, this time. Letting me know that I have a choice. That it's up to me. Jonah's words flit through my mind. *It's all up to you, Calla Lily.*

I nod, but I don't speak.

I'm *not* uncomfortable, but I can't help but feel like I should be.

I haven't had much time to process everything that's come to light in the last few days, but the only thing I'm certain of at this point is that the pull to be closer to Torren is growing. It's getting stronger. But can I trust it? Can I trust *him*? I'm not sure. I'm not even sure if I can trust myself right now.

The problem is that even after four years of heartbreak and disappointment, I've still somehow found myself back in the same shoes of that naïve, starry-eyed nineteen-year-old girl. A girl who wants things she shouldn't want. Who dreams about things she'll never have. Who makes questionable decisions in the name of once-in-a-lifetime experiences.

I don't want to be that girl again, but I can't deny how tempting she is. I was my happiest when I was her. It's not lost on me that I was also my most carefree. My most care*less*.

I think back through the last couple of days. The meeting with his band. The song. The tattoo. All of it. It's overwhelming, the surge of emotions I feel. It's scary, too. Part of me wants to run, but the other part...

The other part wants to see what happens next.

I take a deep breath, then blow it out slowly.

"I'll stay here."

Torren's mouth stretches into a grin, white teeth peeking out just a little through plush pink lips. "Yeah?"

I try like hell to keep myself from smiling back, but I can't fight the way my lips curve up at the edges. When I speak, even my tone is giddy. "Yeah."

He reaches up and cups my neck, rubbing his thumb over my jaw, and I lean into his touch without thinking. His warm hands. His cold, silver rings. My eyes flutter shut, and I feel him lean in closer. He brushes his lips lightly over mine, but before the kiss can grow heated, I step back. Just one light touch and I'm at risk of combusting.

"I'm going to take a nap," I whisper, and Torren nods, a hint of disappointment flitting over his face before it's replaced with a soft smile.

"Okay. Sure. Let me know if you need anything."

When Torren pulls the door shut behind him, I lower myself to the bed. It's jarring how badly I want him. It's as if the revelations have opened the floodgates of my attraction and it's nearly impossible to keep it hidden. I'm more at risk than ever of falling in over my head. It's equal parts exhilarating and terrifying.

I just need to slow it down a bit. That's all. Keep this desire for him contained.

We're taking two days to get to the next stop. Miami, where The Hometown Heartless was created. Two days on a bus with Torren King, making only brief pit stops for meals and refueling. I inhale and exhale slowly.

Two days.

I can control myself for two days.

I wake after a few hours to my phone buzzing on the mattress beside me.

I don't remember when we started driving, but one look out the window tells me we're well on our way to Miami. I grab for my phone expecting to see Mom or Glory on the screen, but I shoot up to a sitting position when I see Ezra's name. For a moment, I contemplate denying the call, but then I decide against it. I have no reason not to talk to Ez, and given the recent news about Heartless's hand in our band's downfall, it's probably better that I speak to him. I straighten my shoulders, take a deep breath, and answer the call.

"Hey, Ez."

"Hey, Cal. Have you checked your texts? I've sent you, like, a shit-ton of messages."

"No. I've been asleep, actually. Why?"

"Our old social media accounts have blown up."

"What?"

"Yeah. Videos and pics of old shows and shit. We're talking millions of views. Thousands of friend requests. We're a fucking trending hashtag."

I put Ezra on speaker and go to my texts, scrolling quickly through the screenshots he's sent me.

"Oh my god," I gasp out.

Even during the brief period when we were signed to a label, our accounts didn't see this much engagement. Ezra isn't exaggerating. We haven't posted on these accounts in over a year; yet we still have probably twenty old videos with over a million views each, photographs with thousands of new comments, and our follower counts have grown substantially.

"How? Why?" I ask, and I hear Ez laugh.

"That article after the club. The one that identified us? It all started after that. It's just...it's completely fucking insane."

"Have you talked to the guys?"

"Yeah, I'm with them still, actually. Well, not Pike. He's back home, but Rock and Beck are inside the hotel room."

"Where are you?"

"Houston."

"Oh..." My brow furrows. "What the fuck were you guys doing at that club? Did you honestly follow me to Texas?"

Ezra snorts out a laugh. "Fuck no. We were already there when you showed up with that fuckhead. I can't believe you're fucking dating that prick. I can't believe *he* was who you were meeting at ArtFusion. Like, that's just fucking mind-blowing considering everything that happened after."

I wince at the note of disgust in his tone. I close my eyes.

"Actually, Ez...I kind of need to talk to you about him."

"Thanks, but no thanks. Don't care how you fell on his dick, Cal."

I roll my eyes, but I don't even bother commenting. I just trudge forward with the truth.

"Torren didn't know about the lawsuit. None of the band did."

"Bullshit." Ezra barks out a laugh. "Is that how he got you? Told you he didn't know? Wasn't his fault?"

"I'm serious, Ez. I was there. When I told him, he blew up. Called a band meeting. The only person who knew was Wade Hammond, and he only found out last year. Torren. Sav. Mabel. Fuck, I think even Jonah— they were all angry. They had no idea."

Ezra goes silent for a moment. I can picture him in my head, his brows furrowed, and his lips pursed. It's on the tip of my tongue to tell him about what Sav said—she wants the names of the bands their label screwed over and out of the label contract—but I bite it back. That information isn't mine to share.

"How could they not know?" Ezra asks finally, and I shrug even though he can't see me.

"I don't know. I really don't. But I believe it."

It goes quiet again, and then I hear Ezra sigh. "We're in Houston auditioning for a band."

Something about that information makes my stomach twist. "All three of you?"

"Yeah. It's like this talent agency. Open call for musicians. If they like you, they'll manage you. Fill in the holes of your group with other musicians they handpick. Pike didn't want to do it. He's got a job working at an autobody shop and a pretty steady girlfriend. But me, Rock, and Beck figured why the fuck not?" Ezra lets out an uncomfortable laugh. "Think this new internet interest will help us?"

My heart sinks at the idea of the guys making music without me. I knew it was possible when I left, but I didn't have much time to dwell on it. I was too busy working my ass off to keep my family afloat. Now, though...

Now it fucking stings, and my eyes burn with the need to cry.

"Oh." I force a soft laugh and make myself smile, blinking back tears. "Maybe. Probably. They, um, they'd be stupid not to pick you guys."

Ezra hums. "It's not the same without you, Cal. You and Pike. I know we said we'd wait until your mom was better, but when we saw all the press about you and that fuck—well...but you and Torren King..."

"No," I breathe out, sniffling. "No, I get it. You guys have to do what's best for you. You shouldn't have to wait for me."

"Right...Well, anyway...Think you can introduce me to Sav Loveless?"

I laugh. "She's not going to bang you, Ez."

"She could, though. She just needs to meet me. You're my *in* now."

I roll my eyes and wipe the tears off my cheeks. My heart hurts, but my smile is genuine. "I've missed you."

"I miss you too, Cal. Maybe respond to my texts once in a while, okay?"

"Yeah. Okay. Tell the guys I said hey?"

"Sure. Tell Sav Loveless I have a ten-inch cock."

"Goodbye, you idiot."

"Bye, Calla Lily."

I hang up with Ezra, then spend the next fifteen minutes sifting through the band's old socials. It's unbelievable. Of course, there are some really mean comments. Comments like *their music is trash*, and *no wonder they were dropped from their label*. One comment says I look like a *porno leprechaun*, and my personal favorite, posted by "bamaboy885" says *apparently to become relevant you only have to suck Torren King's dick*.

That one made me laugh out loud.

For the most part, though, the comments are really positive. They like our sound. They like our style. They like *us*, and it makes me miss the guys. It makes me want to make music as Caveat Lover. It makes me long to be back in the band playing in front of an audience. It boosts my spirits up until my happy balloon is popped with the sharp prick of reality.

Ez is right. This new social media attention probably will help the guys with this whole talent agency audition thing. Beck, Ezra, and Rocky are going to continue making music while I'm stuck here collecting a paycheck for pretending to be Torren's girlfriend for the rest of the American tour. By the time my job with Heartless is over, it will be too late. The guys will have already moved on without me.

Now, the more praise I see in our comments, the more my chest aches with loss. It's almost like watching my dreams be crushed all over again. The day we were dropped from our label, it felt like someone close to me had died. The potential for success had become nothing but smoke through my fingertips.

Abruptly, I push myself off the bed and drop my phone behind me. I'm hungry, and I need to be out of this room for a bit. I need to get this shit out of my head and to stop wallowing, but as I step out of my bedroom, I run smack into a firm, tattooed, shirtless chest.

Jonah. He must be readying to take a shower, judging from the towel in his hand.

"No road legs yet?"

I huff a confused laugh. "What?"

"You should be a little less wobbly at this point."

I arch a brow. "You've had a decade of riding on tour buses to get your *road legs*. I've had a few weeks. Cut me some slack."

"No can do. Rope's pulled tight. I'm fresh out of slack." His lips curve up slightly, just a hint of a taunting smirk. He's definitely flirting, and I have to fight my own smile. He leans in a little closer, blue eyes clearer than I've ever seen them. "Though I don't mind you bumping into me."

I roll my eyes and step away from him, my smile threatening to break free. He can tell. I know it.

"Cute," I say flatly. He shrugs.

"Take as long as you need, sweets." Then he brushes past me and heads into the bathroom.

I blink a few times and shake my head. *Sweets.* He called me sweets, and I'm instantly transported back to those two nights four years ago in the desert.

She's with me.

You sure you want this, sweets?

Honestly, any possibility of Jonah remembering me from ArtFusion has never crossed my mind. He was so obviously on something both nights, and given everything I've heard about him...Well, it just didn't seem like something to be concerned with. Plus, Torren might claim I wasn't just a groupie to him, but I *definitely* was to Jonah. Jonah doesn't strike me as the type to remember groupies.

But this...

This is so fucking *weird*. All of it.

I don't think I'll ever get used to being submerged in the Heartless universe. There's still so much I don't understand, and the band dynamics are at the top of the list.

The relationship between Sav and Mabel, I get. They're best friends. They act like best friends, talk like best friends, and willingly spend time together outside of band-related things. They're almost like sisters, actually. It feels like the strongest, most solid relationship among the four, and I've come to really like them, even if I didn't want to.

Sav and Torren are a little more complicated.

Their past is messy, and their present feels so...muddy. One day, I think I have it figured out, and the next, I'm clueless. Do they still have feelings for one another? Will they get back together? I know Sav is with Levi now, but how long will it last? How long will my...*thing*...with Torren last? Another months and a half, at least. That's what I'm contracted for. But after that?

My brow furrows at the thought. Everything he's said and done recently suggests this fake dating thing isn't so *fake* anymore, but fuck me...

I used to think Torren and Sav were a ticking bomb. That it was only a matter of time before they fell back into bed together and everything else imploded. But now...well, now, I just don't know what to think.

And then there's Jonah.

He's an anomaly. A complete and total mystery on how and where he fits into this band. Sure, he's the lead guitarist. Sure, he's been here from the beginning. But I rarely see him talk to Sav and Mabel. Other than wary glances or the occasional failed attempt to be playful, they don't interact with him, either. I can tell they care about him, but I get the feeling that he doesn't care about much of anything. The music, yeah. The lifestyle, definitely. But what else?

Jonah is obviously closest to Torren, but even that relationship seems off. Fractured and precarious. Not for the first time, thoughts of him and Torren with groupies flit into my mind, and my face and chest flush involuntarily. The way my stomach flips is different than how it reacts for Torren alone—for them together, it's more lust and curiosity than anything else—but the acrobatics are still shocking. I'm embarrassed by how quickly it turns me on. By how often I've thought about it.

When I hear the shower start to run, it jolts me out of my thoughts, and I walk into the main room of the bus. I need a cold drink and some food, and then I need a distraction.

Torren is sitting on the couch with a guitar on his lap and a notebook open beside him, but his eyes are on me. I can tell from the smirk that he knew I was coming, which makes me think he heard my conversation with Jonah in the hallway. *That* gives me pause. Every interaction with Jonah so far has been met with anger from Torren.

A smirk—which is *almost* a smile—is...confusing.

These guys are so fucking confusing.

"What?" I ask, narrowing my eyes at him quickly before switching my attention to the fridge.

"You *do* need to get your road legs."

I don't look at him as I grab a water and move to the opposite couch. "You heard that?"

"It's not that big of a bus."

I finally make eye contact, studying him carefully. I contemplate just coming out and asking. I almost change my mind to avoid yet another uncomfortable interaction, but I'm tired of feeling off-center. I'm tired of the *confusion*. And so far, nothing good has come from beating around the bush, anyway.

"Okay. So, you're not going to puff up your chest and tell me to stay away from him? To be careful? Where's the jealous, possessive act you've been throwing around recently? You're *far* too calm."

His smile stretches into a full-blown grin, and he sets his guitar on the floor.

"Does it bother you?"

"Yes."

"Do you want me to be jealous and possessive?"

"No. But I want to know what to expect. I don't like being caught off guard."

"Fair." He nods, pausing briefly before explaining. But when he does explain, it just makes me more confused. "That was *before*."

I sigh with irritation. "Before *what*?"

He shrugs. "Before I figured shit out."

I cock my head to the side. "What shit? Quit speaking in riddles. It's annoying."

Torren laughs, then braces his elbows on his knees, leaning forward. The move confirms what he said moments earlier. It's really *not* that big of a bus...

"You're mine, Firebird, and he knows it. I'm just waiting on you."

I force a scoff to try and hide the way my pulse picks up pace. I look away in hopes that he doesn't see the blush rushing to my cheeks.

"In your dreams, King."

He nods. "Yep. Every single one of them."

31

CALLIE

"Stopping for dinner in ten."

The driver's voice rumbles through the bus intercom around 9 p.m. I sigh and drop my e-reader on the bed beside me. I've been holed up in my room for the last few hours, avoiding the rest of the bus. There are too many pheromones floating around out there. It's making my head spin. Every time I think of Torren's confession, my pulse picks up speed.

You're mine, Firebird. I'm just waiting on you.

He's just *waiting on me.*

Goddamn it.

Slowly, I trudge out to the front of the bus, finding Torren and Jonah lounging on the couches. Torren's got his guitar on his lap again, and when he glances up at me with a smile, I gesture to the guitar.

"So, which came first, the acoustic guitar or the bass guitar?"

"Acoustic. Then electric. Then bass." His smile flickers as he sets his guitar on the floor. "My brother taught me. He actually plays piano, too. Tried to teach me that, but I wasn't interested."

I put a palm over my heart and gasp like I'm wounded. He laughs.

"Sorry. Not everyone is as skilled as you on the keys."

"You'll have to play for me," Jonah cuts in.

I turn my attention to him and find him smirking at me. When I flick my eyes back to Torren, I expect to see a scowl, but he's smirking as well. My stomach flips, and then I frown. These stupid attractive men and their beguiling smirks. I clear my throat and look back at Jonah.

267

"Sure. Sav got me a keyboard, so maybe I can play something when we get to the next hotel."

"We'll have to see how you measure up to Sean." Jonah's smirk falls with the words. "He's a prick, but he's a great musician."

I'm not sure what to say to that. I want to ask about Sean, but I don't want to pry, and judging from the uncomfortable silence, my instinct says changing the subject is the best course of action.

"So...we rented out a diner?" I say awkwardly. "Those more rock star perks?"

Torren smiles, apparently welcoming my conversational pivot.

"Hammond started doing it once we realized we can't go anywhere public without causing mayhem. On overnight drives, he'll pick a place in some smaller town. He tells the owners it's a private party and has them sign NDAs, but they never know it's us until we show up."

I laugh. "That must be quite a surprise for them."

"Sometimes. Once we had a server start sobbing because she was such a huge fan. We ended up taking a ton of pictures, and Sav signed a practice guitar and gave it to her."

"Remember that pizza place that was owned by the veteran?" Jonah cuts in. "Guy had absolutely no idea who we were. It was great."

Torren nods, laughing with Jonah. "He did spend the whole dinner telling us some great stories, though."

The bus starts to slow, the sounds of the road changing from smooth pavement to crunching gravel.

"So, what's this one?" I ask. "Where are we?"

"Should be a small town just on the Georgia/Florida border. Burger joint." Torren takes out his phone and checks something, then stands as the bus pulls to a stop. "It's called Frank and Anne's Diner."

I follow him and Jonah down the stairs and into a gravel parking lot. It's dark, only two lights illuminating the lot, and I watch as the tour buses pull out of the lot and drive away, leaving us with just the SUVs.

"They'll park at a gas station a few miles away or something while we eat," Torren explains. "Less conspicuous."

I nod and turn to assess the small mom-and-pop looking diner

"Well, this place is adorable."

"Bet they cook a mean burger," Jonah says, giving my shoulder a nudge.

"These kinds of places always do," Torren agrees, then he takes my hand and leads me toward Sav, Mabel, and Levi. Their bus was in front of ours, so they're already standing with their security details as Hammond speaks with the owners.

Torren nods in greeting to his bandmates, then stands next to Mabel as he addresses the group. "They know it's us, yet?"

Mabel laughs. "Yeah, I think so. I just saw two people peeking at us through that window."

Hammond opens the door and waves at us to come in, so I let Torren lead me by the hand into the diner. Several tables are pushed together, forming one large table capable of seating all of us, and there are already waters and several different appetizers on the table.

"Thanks, Ham," Mabel says, throwing herself into a chair and pulling a basket of mozzarella sticks in front of her. "And these are all for me."

Sav darts a hand over her shoulder and snatches one, taking a bite out of it and flashing Mabel a grin as Mabel scowls up at her. "I'd have given you one if you'd asked."

Sav shrugs and speaks while chewing. "S'more fun this way."

I bite the inside of my cheek to keep from laughing.

Torren pulls out a chair at the end for me, and I sit. He takes a seat next to me just as an overexcited server comes skipping out of the back. She looks to be about my age, maybe a little older, and she's grinning from ear to ear, so she must be a fan of The Hometown Heartless. When she greets us, her voice is high and quivering, belying her excitement.

"Hi there. Welcome to Frank and Anne's. We're so happy you chose to dine with us tonight. My name is Abigail. I'll be your server."

She takes our orders, then brings our food, and I notice the entire time that her eyes keep drifting back to Jonah. He ignores her all through dinner, but when she starts picking up the empty food plates, he finally makes eye contact.

"You were great tonight. Thanks for taking care of us."

Abigail turns bright red and bites her lip, obviously trying to keep from giggling. She nods. "Yes, of course, my pleasure Jo—I mean, Mr. Hen—I mean...uh...sir."

And then she curtseys. Now I have to bite my lip to keep from giggling. Poor Abigail. He's said two sentences to her, and she's about to swoon. I can empathize, though. Four years ago, I was the same bumbling mess of a fan.

Jonah flicks his eyes briefly to Torren, then looks back at Abigail. He gives her just a hint of an amused smirk, and she gasps.

Good god, the woman is going to expire.

"You can call me Jonah, sweets."

"Jonah." Abigail's voice is a giddy whisper as she replies, and then she turns and rushes back into the kitchen. As soon as she's gone, Mabel groans loudly and throws a napkin at Jonah.

"No," she hisses, keeping her voice low so only we can hear her. "No way. Tor's not playing, and you do not fuck where we eat, Jo."

I feel Torren stiffen beside me, and Jonah sighs, slouching into his chair, that signature disinterested expression back on his face. I furrow my brow. He wasn't even flirting. He just thanked the lady. *Playing? Do not fuck where we eat?* Mabel's reaction more than confuses me.

"What?" I look from Jonah to Mabel. "What are you talking about?"

Mabel sends another glare to Jonah, then rolls her eyes. "This dumb game they like to play. You nickname the girl first, you get dibs."

My jaw drops, and my heart starts to pound in my ears, but Mabel doesn't seem to notice.

She throws another napkin at Jonah. "But she's a *server*, not a *groupie*, dickhead."

The rest of what she says fades out. If Jonah responds, I don't hear it. All I hear is his voice from four years ago.

You named this one?

It's a compliment.

My head starts to swim with all the contradicting statements swirling around inside it. *You were more. A* game *they like to play. You were* more. *Nickname the girl, you get dibs.*

You. Were. More.

"Thanks for dinner," I say abruptly. "I'm tired. Night, everyone."

I shove up from the table and rush out the door, ignoring the questions and concerned looks. Thankfully, the buses have returned, and by the time I reach the door to the guys' bus, Torren is hustling in my direction.

"It's not what you think."

His voice carries across the parking lot, but I ignore him and climb the stairs into the bus. I'm just reaching the door to my bedroom when he's climbing in after me.

"God damn it, Callie, would you talk to me?"

I whirl on him. "Is it true? You guys play a game where you nickname groupies to see who gets a crack at them first?"

He winces. "Not anymore. Not exactly."

I raise my brows. "Okay. So, *what* exactly?"

"Now...it's more like...a *selection* thing."

My eyes widen and my jaw drops as I process what he just said.

A *selection* thing.

It ignites both excitement and jealousy, and because I'm a glutton for punishment, my questions spew from my mouth shamelessly.

"Selection for who you're going to *share*? We're you planning to share *me* at ArtFusion?"

"No." He shakes his head and steps toward me. "We weren't doing that yet."

I bark out a laugh. "So, at ArtFusion it was the dibs game, then?"

He nods slowly. "Yeah. It was."

"You fucker," I seethe. "You lying son of a bitch. I *was* a groupie, and you called dibs." I laugh again. "God, if you'd have just told me the fucking truth from the jump...It's been *years*. I'm a big girl. I could have handled it. I would have preferred it over being fed this *you were more* bullshit."

"That isn't bullshit, Callie." He steps toward me again. "You were more. You *are* more. I never, not even when I first saw you, thought of you as a groupie."

I fold my arms over my chest and glare at him. "How many women have you played this game with?"

His eyes plead with me as he lowers his voice in warning. "Don't do that."

"Tell me, Torren. I want to know. How many?"

"Callie. Stop it. That's not going to help anything."

I know he's right—this line of questioning solves nothing—but I press forward anyway. I'm rolling downhill and rapidly picking up speed. The thoughts that were already circling my head are finding reasons to finally jump out of my mouth and into the conversation.

"Okay, then how many have you tag-teamed? How many have you and Jonah *selected*?"

"Callie."

"I want to know."

"Why?"

"I want to know, Torren."

"Why?"

"Because I fucking do."

He grinds his teeth and his jaw pops as he takes a step toward me. His eyes run over my face, and I tilt my chin up. I stare him down.

"Okay. What do you want to know?"

I flinch with shock. For all my bravado, I never thought he would just...give in. It takes him arching an eyebrow expectantly for me to actually form words, and when I do, I stun even myself with the question I decide to toss at his feet.

"Why didn't you ever do it with Savannah?"

He narrows his eyes, no doubt weighing the pros and cons of giving me an answer. When I see the resignation flicker across his face, I hold my breath and wait.

"Because I didn't feel secure enough in my relationship with Savannah to invite another person into the bedroom with us."

I know he can see the surprise on my face. There's no way I can hide it. That wasn't at all the answer I was expecting. Because he was jealous. Because he was possessive. Because she was *his*. Any of those. But an admission like that? Never crossed my mind.

He takes another step in my direction.

"Anything else you want to know?"

I force a swallow and stand up straighter. I try to school my face into something more neutral. Business-like. I'm just seeking information. That's all.

"You didn't feel secure in your relationship with Savannah, but you felt secure with groupies? Was that the only selection criteria? Groupies?"

His head tilts slightly to the side, and I see something flash in his emerald eyes. I swear his pupils dilate, and when he speaks, his voice sounds rougher than it did seconds earlier.

"I...*selected*...women who were interested in being shared for the sexual experience—for the extreme pleasure we could bring each other —without threat of getting my heartbroken."

"So...it's not something you'd do with someone you have feelings for...?"

His lips quirk up a fraction at the corner, and he shakes his head once. "I didn't say that."

I furrow my brow. "But with Savannah—"

"With Savannah, there was no trust. I had no desire to be vulnerable with her in that way, and I wasn't confident that our connection could survive it."

I sink my teeth into my lower lip and hold his gaze as I contemplate his words. I keep coming back to one question. One follow-up that threatens to launch from my mouth with excessive force, so I bite harder. Torren's lips twitch again, and he closes the distance until he's less than a foot in front of me.

"Ask me."

My forehead creases with doubt, and he finally lets his smirk break free. It's small, yet infuriatingly taunting.

"Ask me the question."

I take several more breaths. "So, if you were in a relationship with someone you felt...secure with...?"

"If I was in a relationship with someone who I trusted—who I was confident would still be mine after—and she wanted to experience it, I would do it. Once."

"Oh."

His admission brings a visual to the forefront of my mind. A fantasy that makes my nipples pebble and a heated flush surge to my cheeks. I watch as his eyes grow hooded, and the small smile spreads, showing those white teeth and sharp canines. I can practically feel them biting into the soft flesh of my thighs, and my blush spreads to my neck and chest.

"You naughty girl. How long have you been thinking about it?" His fingertips trace my jaw, then ghost over my lips, pressing on the bottom one before wrapping lightly around my neck. The cold silver of his rings feels erotic against my burning skin, and my eyes flutter shut. "You want to be fucked by me and Jonah, Firebird?"

I don't let myself say yes, but I don't say no. I *can't* say no, because *fuck*, I *do* want it. I've wanted it ever since I learned about it. Just once. Just to know what it's like. Just to have the experience. They've done it before, so I'm sure they'd make it good for me, and it's been over a year since I've had sex. Goddamn Jonah for sparking these thoughts. Goddamn Torren for seeing right through me.

I press my thighs together, and Torren tightens his grip on my neck, coaxing a tiny whimper from my lips.

"Are you picturing it? Pressed between us. Both of us on you. *In* you."

I suck in a shuttering breath and force my eyes open. I'm met with dilatated pupils deep with hunger. This is not where I saw this conversation going when I stormed off at dinner, but now that we're here, I don't even try to get out of it.

"We'd worship you," he says, his voice low and husky. "But you already know that, don't you?"

He gazes into my eyes, and I just know he can read my thoughts. I just know he can see the nights and nights of my fantasies portraying exactly what he's just said. I can't hide any of it from him anymore, and I don't want to.

He leans in close, brushing his lips over mine before putting his mouth to the shell of my ear.

"If you want it, if you *really* want it, I'll give it to you. All you have to do is ask. But only once. Your heart belongs to me, Firebird, and once you're mine, I *won't* share."

When he steps away from me, dropping his hand from my throat, I turn and bolt for my room. I can hear his chuckle through the door. I give myself ten deep breaths to try and calm down, but when that doesn't work, I dig through my duffle for my pajamas, my toiletries, and my toothbrush. I'm going to take a freezing cold shower to help calm me down. Then, maybe, *hopefully*, I'll be able to fall to sleep.

32

TORREN

THE HOUSE LOOKS MORE rundown than it did last time I was here.

The siding is grimier. The roof is more slouched. The small front porch sags toward the middle, and each step groans under my weight as I climb them. The wood is probably rotting, and the next time I visit, I wouldn't be surprised to find cinder blocks where the stairs once were.

Before I knock, I glance over my shoulder at Damon. He's standing next to the SUV with his arms crossed, a stern expression on his face.

The buses are on their way to Miami, but Hammond insisted on Damon accompanying me instead of just letting me have one of the SUVs like usual. I do almost everything with Damon, so him being here shouldn't bother me, but it does. I know that the likelihood of him finding the situation shocking or disturbing is slim, but I still can't get comfortable with the idea of sharing any of this with anyone. It's just another reason to resent Sav's fucking stalker. My annual trip to my mom's house is personal. It's something I'd rather be doing alone. But now? Well, now I've got to do it with a babysitter.

"This won't take long," I call to Damon. He nods, but says nothing, so I turn back to the door and raise my hand to knock.

My knuckles hit the warped wooden screen door and rap three times, disturbing the cracked, faded paint. Once a light blue, it looks more like a dirty gray now. With every knock, the door bounces against the frame, amplifying the sound and adding in a squeak from the rickety hinges.

I wait for a few minutes and listen for any movement inside, but I hear nothing. There's a beat-up truck and an old car in the driveway, and it's too early in the day for her to be at the bar. She's inside. She probably saw me pull up in the SUV and is hoping I'll leave if she doesn't answer.

"I know you're home. Might as well open the door, 'cause I'm not leaving 'til I see you."

I wait another minute before the inside door finally swings open, revealing my mother on the other side. Like the house, she looks rougher. Her long gray hair is hanging limply around her shoulders. Her eyes and cheeks are sunken in, both sporting sickly, haunting shadows. The wrinkles around her scowl are more pronounced, and she's thin. Rail thin. My mother looks like the last year has been hard on her, and the cigarette hanging from her lips is just one piece of evidence as to why. Every time I see her, I tell myself I need to quit smoking, but by the time I leave, my nerves are frayed, and I settle for nicotine instead of something harder.

"Mom," I greet with a nod. "Can I come in?"

She grunts. "If you must."

My mom turns and heads into the house, so I follow. The whole place smells like cigarette smoke, and the old wallpaper has a yellow tinge to it.

"Called you on our birthday," I say as she leads me into the kitchen.

"I know."

"You could have answered."

My mom gestures to the small round kitchen table. "I was busy."

"Right." I nod once, then narrow my eyes at her. "How are you?"

She takes a long drag from the cigarette, blowing the smoke out her nose before finally responding. "Fine. Don't I look fine?"

I don't answer. She doesn't look fine. She looks like she's one more forty-ounce away from the grave.

"That's a real nice car you got outside. Only the best for a superstar like you."

She sneers at me, nothing but resentment and jealousy in her expression. I take a deep breath, readying myself for the inevitable, and speak slowly. Calmly.

"You haven't been cashing my checks."

She arches a thin, gray eyebrow. "We don't need your pity money."

"It's not pity, Mom. I want to help."

"You missed your chance to help, Torren."

It's the same argument we always have, and I should probably just give up at this point, but I can't. Not yet. Just like I can't stop sending the checks even though I know she probably just lights them on fire.

"How's Sean?"

Her sinister laugh is more like a cough as she snaps back at me. "Don't pretend like you care."

"I *do* care, Mom. He's my brother."

She stubs her cigarette out in an overflowing ashtray on the table, then leans toward me.

"He's doin' *great*, no thanks to you. Seein' a real nice new girl down the road. Probably give me some grandbabies soon. Got a good job, too. Sean is better."

I swallow back the urge to ask prying questions like, *how* old *is this girl he's dating*, and *is the job* legal, and instead force myself to smile. I nod, hoping like hell what she says is true.

"That's great. I'm glad he's doing well."

Her eyes narrow in my direction, and she throws me a look of pure hatred that I should be accustomed to by now, but it still fucking hurts. She won't ask how I'm doing because she doesn't care. She wouldn't be happy to hear anything less than massive failures.

I rack my brain for a change of subject when the air in the kitchen changes, feeling heavier and more daunting. I hear the floorboards behind me creak, and I know who it is even before he speaks. I have to work to contain my frown. I didn't want him to be here. Visits with Mom are hard enough without my brother to act as an antagonist.

"Not dating that cunt lead singer anymore," Sean says, his deep voice rumbling as if he just woke up. He must be living here again.

I turn my body so I can see him leaning on the doorframe, and I study him without making it obvious. Like Mom, my older brother is also looking worse for wear. His shirtless torso is covered in faded, cheap tattoos that stretch down his arms and hands. I'm certain he got most of the ink while he was in prison, along with the jagged scar on his bicep. Sean and I have always had the same black, curly hair, but he's shaved his head recently, showing off another set of tattoos on his scalp.

I don't let myself look directly at them, though. I know they'll only disappoint me.

"Savannah and I haven't been together for a few years," I tell my brother, and he snorts a derisive laugh as he heads to the fridge and pulls out a beer. I watch as he cracks open the can and chugs half of it. I attempt to change the subject. "Mom says you have a new job and a nice girlfriend."

Sean snorts again. "Yeah, a real great job, Tor. Love it. Pays great. How many crates of nacho cheese you reckon I gotta deliver 'til I'm makin' what you're makin'? Maybe I should boost a few more cars? Get there faster."

I clench my jaw and bite my tongue on the need to defend myself. Sean laughs.

"Still the cunt bitch's lap dog." He drinks the second half of the beer, dropping the empty can in the sink before grabbing another from the fridge. "So nice of her to give you permission to come here."

The resentment radiating from my mother and brother right now is enough to make my body quake and my eyes sting. I fist my hands and I take a few deep breaths through my nose, working to maintain my composure.

"I'm here because I wanted to see Mom. I wanted to see my family."

Now it's my mother's turn to laugh. "We stopped bein' your family the day you turned on us."

"I didn't turn on you." I flick my eyes from my mom to Sean. "I didn't abandon you."

"Sendin' checks every month isn't the same as stickin' with your blood, brother. You chose that cunt bitch's band over me, and you think our forgiveness can be bought. It can't."

"Sean, your own actions are why you were asked to leave Heartless, and you know it. You agreed."

"I didn't agree to shit." He spits the words through gritted teeth, nostrils flaring, and takes three steps toward me with his finger brandished in my face. "*You* agreed. *You*. Because you give little miss Savvy whatever she fuckin' wants. I should be on that stage with you. Gettin' the same payout as you. I should be fuckin' the women you fuck and snortin' the coke you snort, but you took that away from me."

I push to standing, but I never take my eyes off him.

"That's not how it happened, Sean."

"That's exactly how it happened. You're a shit brother. A shit son. A shit person. You only come back here because you feel fuckin' guilty."

I stare him down, seconds ticking by as I debate whether or not I want to go down this road again. Do I open my mouth? Defend myself? Repeat the fucking truth for the hundredth time?

Is it even worth it?

Because he's right about one thing. I *do* feel guilty. I send the checks, and I subject myself to these miserable fucking visits because I feel guilty, and there is nothing I can say that will change that, even if what I say is the truth.

I sigh and break eye contact with my brother to look at my mom. I nod at her, and then I lie. "Always a pleasure, Mom. I'll let myself out."

The rickety screen door slams behind me, bouncing off the frame once before finally coming to a stop as I stalk back toward the SUV. I half expect Sean to come barreling out after me, but my guess is he's not willing to get into another fistfight. Especially not if he's still on parole.

I don't know why I'm disappointed. I don't know how I could have expected anything different. My brother's revisionist history is what feeds his rage, and he's always had my mom on his side, even when we were kids.

There was a time when I looked up to Sean. He practically raised me after our dad was arrested. He'd protect me from Mom's drunken episodes when she'd get spittin' mad and try to take it all out on me. Me, because I look just like my father. Sean was always her favorite. She always thought I was the poisoned one. But even though I got our father's looks, Sean got his temperament, and by the time the truth was revealed, my mother was too set in her ways to care.

My mom is right. We stopped being family a long time ago. But she's wrong, too. It was long before Sean was kicked out of the band.

I climb into the passenger seat and do my seat belt without saying a word. I put on my sunglasses and rest my head on the seatback, and mercifully, Damon doesn't ask me anything. My blood is boiling, and my chest is aching, but with every mile closer we get to Miami, the more I relax. One mile closer to my band. To my *real* family. And to my Firebird.

One mile closer to the only things that matter.

. . .

The suite I'm sharing with Jonah is quiet when I finally get to the hotel, and I head straight for his room.

When I walk through the door, I'm expecting to see him sleeping, but instead I find him on the bed with a thick book in his hands. He arches a brow when he sees me.

"What if I was fucking someone?"

I smirk. "I didn't hear moaning."

That gets a little half grin out of him before his face grows stern again. "How was it?"

I sigh and sit on the side of his bed. "About how it always is, except this time she had company."

"No shit? Sean?"

"Sean."

"Fuck. He still a bitter asshole?"

"What do you think?"

Jonah grows quiet for a moment before I feel him sit up, the bed dipping from the movement. When I look at him, he's looking right at me.

"You did the right thing. We all did."

I roll my eyes. "I know. I've never doubted that."

"Bullshit. You've felt guilty about it every year since we were signed. But we wouldn't have gotten where we are if we'd kept Sean around, and you know it."

I close my eyes and drag a hand through my hair. He's right. I know he is. About all of it. Kicking Sean out of the band was the right move, but I also feel guilty as hell for it.

"Sometimes I wonder if he'd have ended up in prison if we'd let him stay with us."

Jonah's sardonic grin makes my stomach twist. "You think three directionless druggies and a self-loathing bisexual would have kept him from being a violent creep?"

I mean, when he puts it that way...

I don't respond, and he sighs, his irritation evident. He's tired of having this conversation with me. Truthfully, I'm tired of it too. But it doesn't make me need it any less.

"I fucking mean it, Torren. We were a sinking fucking ship for years. No way we could have been watching after Sean, too. He'd have done something terrible, and he'd have fucked us over while doing it."

I take a deep breath and stare at the wall, running his words through my head. Then I furrow my brow. "Mabel wasn't self-loathing."

"She was, dumbass. For a long time after Crystal cheated on her, Mabes hated herself and all of us, too. You were just too far up Sav's ass to notice anything but your own pathetic obsession."

I snort. "Fuck me, what a mess."

"Yep. But look on the bright side. Mabel doesn't hate herself anymore, and you and Savannah aren't druggies. Woo-hoo for Therapy Thursday. Another win for Savvy."

I don't miss the way he only mentioned me and Sav. Not himself. That heightens my anxiety for a whole different reason. I know he thinks he's a lost cause. I have a feeling if Sav wasn't having everyone watch him so closely, he'd be doing a lot worse than drinking and smoking. He'd be backsliding. It's got me wondering how much longer we have until he stops trying to keep his footing and just gives in to the fall.

"And how is Therapy Thursday going for you?" I ask tentatively.

Jonah groans. He's been against the practice since Sav implemented it a year ago. All four of us meet with a personal therapist via video chat for an hour on the first Thursday of the month. No matter what country we're in, we do it. Sav, Mabel, and me are pretty committed to it. But Jonah? He just does it to keep from being sent back to rehab.

"My shrink is a bitch."

"You're just pissed she won't have video chat sex with you."

He shrugs. "Potato tomato."

"Has it helped, though? At all?"

He sighs and falls back on his pillow. "Yeah. It has."

"Good." I nod decidedly, and then he grows quiet once more.

When Jonah picks up his book, I feel myself slipping back into my thoughts. I replay the visit to my mother's house, focusing on the depressing state in which she lives and the bitter resentment both she and my brother still harbor for me. But then I pull myself out of it and change the subject to the next thing that pops into my head.

"Callie wants us to fuck her."

He doesn't react how I expect. There's no smile. No shock. He just hums.

"That's it? Just *hmmm*?"

He closes the book and shrugs. "I'm not surprised. I could tell she was curious. It was only a matter of time before she gave in."

I arch a brow. "And what makes you think I'm okay with it?"

Jonah smirks. "Because you're a fucking simp, King, and you're obsessed with her. Saw it at that music festival, and I see it now."

My eyes widen in surprise. "You remember that?"

"Sure do. Not all of us are as lucky as you. Doesn't matter how many fucking drugs I take. It all comes back the moment I'm sober."

My eyebrows slant harshly as I consider his comment. I know he's got a lot of demons to contend with. I know there's a lot of shit in his head that he tries to escape from. I never realized how hard it was until now.

"When?"

I blink at Jonah, and he repeats himself.

"*When* are we going to do it? When's she down?"

"I don't know. Whenever she's ready, I guess."

"And you're sure you're good with this? You're not going to sucker punch me in the nose the moment I bottom out?"

Jealousy claws at my throat at the same time as my stomach stirs with arousal. I shake my head once.

"What if I kiss her?"

I shake my head again.

"What if I eat her pussy? What if I make her come all over my fucking face, and then I shove my tongue down her throat and make her taste it?"

I grit my teeth to stave off my anger, my cock hardening as I picture it.

"You can do anything she wants you to do. But it's only happening once. We'll do this once, and then that's it. You're on your own after this."

He smiles. A rare, full smile, stretching slowly across his face until he's flashing just a hint of white teeth.

"Guess I better make it memorable, then."

33

CALLIE

I'M WATCHING the show from the VIP tent on the floor tonight. Levi, Savannah's boyfriend, is here, too, along with a few other celebrities I'm too nervous to interact with.

I've spent every concert since the first either backstage or in a private box simply so I could do anything *except* watch the show. I said I would never watch from the floor again, and while this isn't exactly the same location as the first night, the draw to experience the concert with the audience has been too great to ignore. Especially now that I know the truth about the role the band played in Caveat Lover's downfall. The truth being they played no role at all.

It's made me rethink my past interactions with all of them, but mostly Sav. Of all four band members, Sav was the most furious when she learned about what their label had done. This whole time I was thinking Sav Loveless was this evil villain who had the music industry under her thumb, but I was wrong. I think I was wrong about a lot of things.

"Oh my god, you're Callie James, right?"

The question pulls me from my thoughts, and I spin my body toward the voice over my shoulder. It's a girl about my age standing against the railing that separates the VIP tent from the general admission floor. I give her what I can only assume is an awkward smile before answering.

"Yeah, I am."

"Oh my god, can I get your autograph?"

My eyebrows and nose scrunch, and I have to swallow back a laugh. "Me?"

"Yeah! Please? Here, you can sign my shirt."

How fucking weird. Fake date a celebrity and suddenly their fans start asking you for autographs. I look at Craig and he shrugs, so I shrug.

"Yeah, sure."

Craig pulls a black marker out of his pocket, something I've noticed all the security details carry, and hands it to me before I slowly close the distance between the girl and me. She turns around, giving me her back, so I smooth out the part of her shirt on her shoulder blade.

"I'm absolutely obsessed with your sound. Do you think Caveat Lover will get back together? Maybe tour with Heartless? That would be so fucking cool. I've downloaded all your songs. You're on my constant repeat playlist."

I freeze just as I put the marker to her shirt. "Wait...what?"

"Your music! You guys are so good. I really hope you release some new stuff soon."

I flick my eyes to Craig, and he grins before jutting his chin toward the shirt, reminding me that I need to actually sign the thing. The ink bled into the fabric, making a small black dot, so I move beneath it, so it's positioned just above the *i* in my name. I sign an autograph for the first time in a long time, and then I pose for a picture. By the time the girl goes back to her friends, I'm stunned speechless, and Craig laughs.

"I scrolled your band's social media page. You might want to prepare yourself for that happening more often."

"Really?" I shake my head and look back toward the stage. "It's weird."

He shrugs. "Weird, but real."

I huff out a laugh. I feel like that can be used to describe a lot of shit in my life all the sudden. The thought makes me blush. Torren says it's real between us. He says it's always been real for him. But what about for me?

I know I'm attracted to him. I always have been. He makes my stomach flip and my heart race, and I can't pretend like his touch doesn't conjure dirty thoughts in my imagination. I know the way my body reacts to him is real. I also know I find him to be fascinating and extremely talented. But beyond that? I'm not sure.

Where do I stand with Torren King now that I'm not burning with barely repressed hatred for him? Now that I don't loathe his very existence and blame him for ruining my music career? I can't just go back to the girl I was at ArtFusion. That girl worshipped the ground he walked on and thought of him more as a god than a man. And even if I could, I wouldn't want to. That's not a healthy balance in a relationship. If we're even *in* a relationship...

I groan and drop my head back, tilting my face to the darkened sky and grumbling into the air. "Why can't shit be easy?"

Craig laughs again, but he doesn't answer. I sigh and push any further thoughts out of my head just as the stage lights signal that The Hometown Heartless is about to take the stage. As usual, the crowd starts to lose their damn minds, and the bodies surge forward, and I watch it all from the safety of the tent. It's madness.

"People get wild."

I look up into the face of Sav's boyfriend. He's watching the crowd, too.

"They really do."

"It's like this everywhere, too. Doesn't matter where they play. It's...well, it's kind of amazing."

I laugh at the awe in his voice. "You were on the first leg of the US tour, right?"

"Yeah." He grins slightly. "You looking forward to the Canadian and European legs?"

The question catches me off guard. I thought Levi knew about my contract. I thought for sure Sav would have already filled him in on everything.

"Um..." I purse my lips. "Sure."

"Sure?" He turns glittering eyes on me, his smile growing. "That's not convincing."

I force a laugh and roll my eyes. "Well, I just don't know that I'll be around for the Canadian and European shows. A lot can happen between now and then."

He nods and looks away. "Suppose so. But just so you're prepared, Savannah's got it in her head to make us skydive in every country."

I laugh. "No way."

"Yeah. We did it in Seattle a few months ago, and she's already made plans for England, Italy, Germany, and France." He purses his lips, almost like he's struggling with whether or not to tell me something, before he glances at me again. "She called around and added you to the reservations."

My brows slant as I turn to look at him. I lower my voice and glance around us before stepping a bit closer.

"Levi...you know it's fake, right? Like, this thing with me and Torren? It's PR. I'm only contracted through the rest of the US tour."

Levi nods once. "Savannah told me."

"So why would she be adding me to skydiving reservations in Europe."

"She thinks you'll be there."

The first question that runs through my head is why. Why does Savannah think I'll be with them in Europe? But when I open my mouth, something entirely different falls from my lips.

"How do you do it?"

He arches a brow. "Do what?"

"Handle it," I say bluntly with a nod toward the stage. "Torren and Sav, I mean. Knowing their history."

Despite the invasive and personal nature of my question, Levi doesn't look offended. He purses his lips, and his brow furrows as he glances back at the band. For a brief moment, I wonder if he'll answer me at all, but then he gives me a small shrug.

"I won't lie. It was hard at first, and I was jealous. We got into a few big arguments. But then my daughter and I went on the first leg of the American tour, and it didn't take long for me to realize I was worried about nothing. I trust Savannah. I have faith in our relationship. And honestly, I trust Torren, too." Levi smirks. "Don't tell him I said that."

I laugh. "No worries."

Levi returns my laugh and then sighs, looking toward the stage with an expression that seems almost wistful. It's as if he's filtering through a memory reel. One that elicits just as much love as regret. When he speaks again, his voice is softer and full of longing.

"Savannah and Torren have a complicated past, but so do I, and that's just what it is. *The past.* Savannah is my today and my tomorrow. I'm not going to waste time worrying about what happened yesterday."

Before I can say anything, the crowd erupts with cheers, marking the end of our conversation. The venue is so loud that I couldn't talk to Levi even if I knew how to respond, so I turn my attention to the stage just as The Hometown Heartless appears one by one. Mabel, Jonah, Torren, and then Sav, the audience screaming louder and louder for each bandmember until the sound is nearly deafening.

Sav greets the audience, but all my focus falls on Torren. God, he's sexy, especially when he's in full rock-icon mode. All thoughts regarding skydiving and fake dating and Levi's confession evaporate, until all I can think about is how insanely attractive I find him. How *badly* I want him. It's almost dizzying.

I trust Torren, Levi had said. But can I?

Torren's biceps flex as he picks up his bass and loops the strap over his head, the colorful tattoos covering his skin almost coming alive under the stage lights. His eyes seek out the VIP tent, then scan the bodies inside briefly before landing right on me. The smirk that transforms his full lips is full of suggestive promise, and when he winks, I feel it so viscerally that my toes curl in my heeled booties. My heart kicks up speed in my chest, my teeth sink into my bottom lip, and a flush spreads over my cheeks. I can feel eyes on me. The crowd cheers louder, confirming they all saw Torren's wink, and they all know it was for me. It makes me blush harder, and his wicked smile widens.

I tear my eyes away from him to keep from spontaneously combusting, but because I'm apparently my own worst enemy, I let them drift to Jonah. My reaction to him is different, but no less strong. Less heart and more...well...lower. Jonah's looking down, bleached blond hair curtaining his face, backlit by stage lights and resembling an angry, vengeful god. Then, as if he feels my attention on him, he lifts his head and finds me immediately. I get chills. He doesn't smile, and he doesn't wink, but he doesn't have to. Somehow, his steady eye contact says enough.

It says, *you are so fucking screwed, Calla Lily James, but you will thoroughly enjoy it.*

. . .

I position myself for our post-concert public display of affection, trying and failing to ignore the fact that I've been waiting for it. *Excited* for it.

The moment I see him, skin sweat-slicked and glistening, I have to keep my feet from rushing to him. I stay put and smile, but he covers the distance too slowly for my racing heart, and I find myself reaching for him even before he's close enough to touch.

His hand cups my neck while the other grips my hip, tugging me into him, and he smirks down at me.

"You want your hands on me, Firebird?"

I don't have a response. I refuse to admit it out loud, so instead I do something I've never done. I initiate the kiss. I can tell by the way he freezes that I've stunned him, but it doesn't last. He growls and slides his tongue into my mouth, and I can't tell if he pulls me closer or if I press myself against his body all on my own. I let him kiss me feverishly, and I kiss him back with the same fervor. Then, remembering something he said four years ago, I slip my fingers into his hair.

Pull a little harder next time.

But not too hard, or we might end up giving these people a show they didn't ask for.

As his voice replays in my head, I fist my hands and tug his hair at the root.

"Fuck." He groans into my mouth, and I feel his lips curve upward before he speaks again. "You're playing with fire, baby."

Now it's my turn to smirk. "Who doesn't want to be a fire master?"

He laughs and presses one last kiss to my lips before taking my hand and nodding toward the dressing rooms. With each step, I work to calm my racing heart. The decision has been made even before we're stopping at the girls' door, and when I turn to him, I let the words loose before I can second-guess them.

"I want to come to your suite tonight."

The fire that ignites in his eyes makes my breath hitch.

"You cashin' in on your one time?"

I swallow and nod before forcing myself to answer. "Yes. I am."

His eyes bounce between mine, the air thickening around us the longer we stare at one another. I wet my lips. My inhales and exhales are shaky as I wait for him to speak. Nerves claw up my throat. Irrationally, I start to worry he'll turn me down. That it was a test of loyalty, and I failed. Why would Torren want to be in a relationship with someone who wants to sleep with his best friend? Tattoo or not, song or not, my curiosity might have just reduced his interest in me to rubble.

Finally, his lips curl into a slow, sinful smile, and the tension that had been gathering in my shoulders lessens.

"Whenever you're ready, we'll be waiting."

Torren kisses me once more, heated and sensual, but over too soon, and then he turns and walks to his own dressing room. My whole body is flushed. My heart is still beating rapidly. I don't want to have to interact with Sav and Mabel. My luck, they'll be able to tell that *something* is up. I don't want to have that conversation. I don't want to have *any* conversations. So I turn to Craig and ask him quietly to take me back to the hotel.

He drives me back in silence and lets me into the suite I'm sharing with Mabel, Sav, and Levi. With a nod of thanks, I head straight to my room, strip out of my clothes, and take a long shower. I scrub every inch of my body. I shave. I groom. I scrub again. The whole time, I try like hell to calm myself down. I can't, though.

I'm an anxious, excited, horny mess.

Walking to my closet, which is already full of clothes, I flip through the hangers.

"What does one wear to get spit-roasted by two hot rock stars?"

I bark out a laugh at the utter ridiculousness of that statement and cover my face with my hands.

"Oh my god," I mumble into my palms. "What the hell is happening right now?"

I drop my hands and take a deep breath, then march back into the bathroom and look at myself in the mirror. I furrow my brow and point at my reflection.

"Get it together, James. You're a mature adult. It's just a threesome." I snort out another laugh, then groan. "And now I'm talking to myself." I take another deep breath and meet my own eyes once more. "Get your shit together."

I turn and head back to the closet and think rationally. It doesn't matter what outfit I pick. It won't be on long. I might as well just head over there in lingerie and a bathrobe. I grab a lacy green set—almost everything in this closet is either shades of green or black—and then I take my vibrator out of my duffle.

I make myself come quickly to try to relieve some of the sexual tension, but by the time I'm stepping into the lace panties, it's like the orgasm never happened. My clit is throbbing, and I have to stop myself from rubbing it. My nipples are so hard that when I put on the bra, they're clearly visible through the thin lace. I take one last look at myself in the mirror, then throw on one of the big, fluffy hotel robes and tiptoe out into the suite.

Luckily, Sav and Mabel aren't in the main room, but I run right into Craig the moment I step into the hallway.

"Everything okay, Ms. James?"

I flush bright red, and my eyes widen. I'm so embarrassed that I don't even bother correcting him about not calling me Ms. James. Instead, I clear my throat and force a smile.

"Everything is fine. I, um, I just have to ask Torren a question."

I must look ridiculous creeping out of the hotel suite in a bathrobe like some naked burglar. The man isn't stupid. I'm sure he knows I'm not tiptoeing around after midnight to *ask a question,* but he doesn't call me out. He just nods, then mercifully trains his gaze on the wall at the end of the hallway before I hurry to Torren's door. I throw one last look over my shoulder at my security detail before knocking, and the door swings open immediately, revealing Torren on the other side.

He leans his shoulder on the frame and peers down at me, eyes flickering with heat. He's shirtless, and his hair is wet. He smells clean. Freshly showered. For a moment, I wonder what it would be like to shower with him. He sinks his teeth into the lush curve of his lower lip almost as if he is wondering the same thing. He drops his gaze to my mouth, then to my chest, before bringing his attention back to my face. The way his eyes feel on my skin and the way he's looking at me like he wants to devour every inch of my body both excites me and makes me acutely aware of my security detail at the end of the hall.

I drop my voice low and flare my eyes in warning.

"Stop looking at me like that."

He arches a brow. "Like what?"

"Like you want to eat me."

I realize my mistake as a slow smirk turns up the corners of his full lips. "Isn't that why you're here?"

I force myself to roll my eyes instead of melting into a quivering puddle of lust. Because yes, that is *exactly* why I'm here.

"Can I come in, please?" I ask with false bravado, and he nods before opening the door wider to allow me to enter.

I feel his eyes on me as I walk past him. My heart is pounding so fast that I'm lightheaded, so when Torren gestures to the couch, I take a seat.

"Do want to get comfortable?" Torren crosses the room as he speaks to me, hands tucked into the pockets of low-slung sweats. I keep my eyes locked on his face instead of letting them drift lower. "I could get you something to drink. Wine? Water?"

I open my mouth to ask for a glass of wine, but then snap it shut again. I don't want to suffer through small talk. I don't want to *get comfortable*. I want to get fucked by two capable, gorgeous rock stars until my limbs cease to work and I pass out from exhaustion.

I shake my head and push to standing, then untie my robe, slide it down my arms, and drop it to the floor. The unadulterated need that passes over Torren's face as he scans my body is enough to make my lace panties wet.

"That's my favorite set. You look even sexier than I imagined."

"You know what's in my underwear drawer?"

He smirks. "I know every article of clothing in your wardrobe because I picked them out."

My eyebrows shoot upward at the confession, but I don't have a chance to speak before he's closing the distance between us and running his fingers up the bare skin at my sides. My body erupts with chills, my stomach caving inward with a gasp.

"You have no idea how much I want to keep you to myself, Firebird." Torren traces the outline of my lace bra, then presses his thumb to my swollen bottom lip. "But, fuck, I want to watch you go out of your mind with pleasure while we worship you, too." I swallow roughly, then peek my tongue out to wet my lip, tasting the pad of his thumb. When he speaks again, his voice is a low rasp. "Is that what you want, baby?"

"It is."

He grins. "We won't do anything you don't want to do. This is all about you. Anything you—"

"I want all of it. Anything you did with other women, I want."

A low chuckle sounds from the side of the suite, and I break eye contact with Torren to glance toward the sound. Jonah is standing in front of a bedroom door with his toned arms folded over his sculpted, tattooed chest.

"Anything?" he asks, stalking toward me like a predator on the prowl. "What if I'm into debasement? What if I want to degrade you? You want that, sweets?"

Something about the way he's staring tells me he's fucking with me, but I can't be sure, so I arch a brow and ask, "*Are* you into that?"

He steps up next to Torren, so they're both peering down at me, then pauses for a moment. I tilt my head to the side and study him, waiting for a response.

Slowly, a small smirk forms on his lips. "I'm not."

Jonah drags his knuckles up my arm, then lightly wraps his fingers around my throat. With Torren's hand at my waist and Jonah's at my neck, my pussy throbs, and I have to swallow back a whimper. Jonah's smirk grows before he speaks again.

"I'm not into that. But I am into wrapping my hands around your neck while I fuck you. I *am* into fucking you while your boyfriend fucks you, too."

He squeezes, tightening his hold on me. I swallow again, feeling the way my throat contracts under his palm. I flick my eyes to Torren and find him watching me intently with his pupils blown wide.

"Do you want that?" Torren rasps, and I answer immediately.

"Yes."

Torren and Jonah trade glances, an unspoken question exchanged with a single look, before they both focus their attention back on me.

"Can I fuck your ass, Calla Lily?"

My eyes widen, and my breath hitches at the question that falls from Jonah's mouth. Torren's lips curl into another sinful smirk. The answer is a no-brainer, confirmed by the dampness growing in my panties.

I nod once. "Yes."

Torren chuckles. "What he really wants to know is can he fuck your ass while I fuck your pussy. Is that something you want? Is that something you can handle?"

There's a hint of challenge in his tone that sparks my competitive nature.

"I can handle it, King."

I give him a sweet smile, then reach behind my back to unclasp my bra. When the lacy fabric drops to my feet, I grab Jonah's wrist and guide his hand from my throat to my breast. I don't break eye contact with Torren, and my next statement is half-taunt, half-gasp as Jonah pinches my nipple.

"Can *you*?"

34

CALLIE

Torren's lips are on mine before I finish speaking, his tongue invading my mouth like a man starved.

"Fuck, you're perfect," he growls between kisses.

I'm so focused on Torren that when Jonah's teeth close around my nipple, a surprised moan bursts from low in my throat and I sink my fingers into his long, blond hair.

"Pull it, sweets," Jonah says, breath and teeth grazing the sensitive skin around my nipple with every word, so I do. His groan vibrates over me and goes straight to my clit. These men and their hair pulling. It's quite a thrilling surprise.

Torren bites my lip lightly then moves his mouth to my neck. He nips and sucks in that way that I remember—that way that drove me crazy—and without overthinking, I shove my hand into the front of his sweats and wrap it around his erection. When I squeeze, he grunts, and I grin against his mouth. I pump him twice before I release him then lean back so I can look at both men.

"Take me to a bedroom," I command, and the feeling I get when they obey is a heady one. It's thrilling and empowering, and amps up my excitement for whatever comes next.

Torren sweeps me into his arms and follows Jonah through a door to a bedroom, and the smell tells me it's Torren's. When I see a beat-up acoustic in the corner—the one I've seen him playing on the bus—I know I'm right. I only have a second to scan the rest of the room before he tosses me on the bed, and I bounce once.

Leaning back onto my elbows, I drop my legs wide, flashing them the soaked lace between my thighs. Their jaws tick as they look me over, and I can't help the way my eyes flare when I notice the sizable bulges growing in their sweats. Torren walks slowly to the bedside table, and without taking his eyes off me, pulls a strip of condoms from the drawer, tossing them on the bed beside me. I'm nervous, but I force myself to breathe through it. I shove it down and focus on the thrill of the anticipation instead.

We'd worship you, Torren had said. I believe it. I'm so fucking ready for it. I smirk and glance between them.

"Take off your pants. Both of you."

"You gonna say please?"

I arch a brow at Jonah, his rumbling voice rough with a hint of mirth.

"I think you should be the one saying please," I tease.

He smirks in response, and I watch as he grabs the band of his sweats and pushes them down his tattooed thighs. When his erection springs free, I have to swallow down a gasp.

Fuck.

I feel heat creeping up my neck and chest. My nipples are so hard that they ache, and I want to touch myself, but I don't. When I realize I'm gawking, my eyes jump guiltily to Torren's. I don't know why I expected jealousy or anger, but instead I'm met with blazing lust. His white teeth are sunk into his bottom lip and his hand is already stroking his bare cock. He gives me a wolfish grin.

"You can look, Firebird. You can touch him. You can taste him. You can do anything you want with either of us. Tonight is all about you, baby, because tomorrow, you're all mine."

I open my mouth to speak, but nothing comes out. Thankfully, I don't have to scramble for words because Torren climbs onto the bed and positions his body so his face is between my thighs.

"I have been dying to taste you again."

He runs his knuckle down the middle of the lace covering my wet pussy, pressing lightly on my throbbing clit before replacing his knuckle with his mouth.

"Fuck," I gasp out as he sucks me over my panties.

Torren hums, massaging my clit with his tongue. The rough fabric paired with his warm, soft tongue is enough to make me see stars. My back arches, and just before I drop down onto the bed, a hand threads through my hair and turns my head to the side. I peer up into Jonah's deviously handsome face. With his lips parted, his eyes wild, and his hard cock just inches from my mouth, I know I'm in trouble.

"Open up, sweets. Let's see how far you can take me."

I open my mouth. I don't even hesitate, and Jonah glides the head of his cock along my lower lip before shoving himself in. I close my lips around him just as Torren slides my panties to the side and slips two fingers into my pussy. My eyes fall shut and I moan.

"Fuck," Jonah rumbles. "Do that again, Tor. She likes it."

Torren does, curling his fingers inside me and stroking as he flicks his tongue over my clit. I moan again, pulling a guttural sound from Jonah. He starts to thrust in and out of my mouth, pushing deep into my throat. I do my best to take him, but I'm propped on my elbows while Torren devours my pussy. I massage his dick with my tongue, and I swallow around him when he's in deep, but I can't wrap my hand around him and pump. I can't tease him or touch him. I can't do much of anything, honestly—not with Torren's face between my thighs threatening to turn me into a quivering mess—but Jonah doesn't seem to mind. I squeeze my eyes shut as I gag on him, tears leaking from between my lashes and streaming down my cheeks. I must look a mess, but I think Jonah likes it. The way he tightens his hold on my hair and groans confirms it.

"You look so fucking pretty sucking my cock while your boyfriend eats your pussy. So. Fucking. Pretty."

Jonah's statement brings me even closer to orgasm, and Torren seems to know it. I can hear how wet I am with every thrust and curl of his fingers. Every time I moan, Jonah shoves himself deeper into my throat. My arms ache from holding myself up, but I don't dare move. I don't want anything to interrupt this moment. When Torren sucks on my clit again, the sensation makes me tighten my thighs around his head as my release barrels toward me.

"Look at me. I want to see your eyes when he makes you come."

I force myself to peer up at Jonah through tear-filled eyes, he pulls his dick out of my mouth just as my body explodes. A cry escapes me and my muscles contract, but I don't take my eyes off Jonah until his mouth is on mine and he's kissing me deeply, swallowing every noise I make. Torren doesn't stop finger-fucking me, doesn't take his mouth off my clit until I'm half-crazed. My arms give out and I drop to the bed, clenching my thighs around Torren's head.

"Stop," I say, my voice a strangled gasp. "Stop."

Torren thankfully takes mercy on me and pulls back, pressing wet, warm kisses to my inner thighs and pelvis. He nips at the flesh at my hip, then sucks, and I know immediately that it's another bite mark. Torren King likes to mark me, and I've learned that I like being marked.

I tear my lips off Jonah's and glance down my heaving torso to find Torren grinning up at me from between my legs. I nearly come again just from the sight. His face is glistening with my arousal, his lips red and swollen from his attack on me. He is sex personified, and I almost can't handle it. I don't know how much longer I can wait to feel him inside me. He presses one more kiss to my stomach before crawling up my body and taking my mouth with his.

I kiss him, sucking on his tongue and lips, tasting myself on them. I wrap my legs around his waist and push my soaking wet pussy against his hard cock. I rub myself against him, and he releases a chuckle that tapers into a groan.

"She's so needy," he says playfully, turning to look at Jonah.

"Good," Jonah says. "We've got plenty to give her."

Without a word, Torren wraps his arms around me and rolls over so I'm lying on top of him. A sharp slap to my ass makes me yelp, and I look over my shoulder to find Jonah kneeling on the bed behind me.

"On your knees, Calla Lily."

My eyes widen at the possibilities of what he has planned—of all that he could do from that angle—and his full lips curl slightly into another tiny smirk. Jonah cocks his head to the side, then smacks my ass again.

"It's my turn," he says with a growl. "On your knees."

Quickly, I scoot myself back so I'm off Torren, then prop myself onto my knees. Jonah wastes no time pulling my panties down, then covering my pussy with his mouth. I clamp my eyes shut at the rough way he sucks on my clit, grazing his teeth and making me suck in a harsh breath before shoving two fingers into me.

When a calloused thumb rubs at my jaw, I open my eyes and find Torren sitting in front of me, hard cock jutting straight up and glistening at the tip. I don't even wait for him to speak. I just lower myself to my elbows and take him into my mouth.

"Fuck, Callie," he grinds out, fisting my hair with one hand and cupping my jaw with the other. "Fuck, baby, that feels fucking phenomenal."

I have just enough space to wrap my hand around the base of Torren's erection so I can pump his shaft as I lick around his thick head. I taste his pre-cum, wanting more, sucking at him until his body vibrates with a deep groan that makes his thighs quiver. He thrusts into my throat just as Jonah starts to rub at my clit with his thumb.

"I can feel your throat tightening around my cock," Torren says as he rubs his thumb over the space where my jaw and neck meet. "Swallow again. Swallow me down." He thrusts deep into my throat once more, and I swallow until I gag. "Goddamn it, Calla Lily. I could fuck your throat all day. I bet you'd look sexy with my cum on your lips."

I gag around him again, and then I pull back, taking deep gulps of air into my aching lungs. I choke on an inhale when Jonah's thumb moves from my clit to my asshole. He spits and rubs the saliva around my ass, then sticks two fingers into my pussy before rubbing my arousal there as well. He repeats the moves until I can feel wetness dripping down the crack of my ass.

"Relax, sweets," Jonah says, pressing lightly on my asshole with his thumb. "My dick is a hell of a lot bigger than my finger."

I want to laugh, and I almost do, but I don't get the chance. Jonah's tongue swipes over me, massaging that tight ring of muscle, and I lose myself to the sensation. All I can do is pump Torren's cock as my eyes flutter shut again, and I chant between gasps and whimpers.

"Oh, fuck. Oh, god. Oh, fuck."

Torren's dick twitches in my hand as he laughs and tugs at my hair.

"I wish you could see yourself right now," he says, voice sounding like it's been drug over gravel. "Ass up and fisting my dick as Jo tongues your asshole. Getting you good and ready, Firebird. Fuck me, baby, I want to feel you burn again. I want you in fucking flames for me."

Torren's words echo in my head as something wet covers my asshole and Jonah slips a finger into me. Lube. Lube and the tip of his finger, and I'm about to combust.

Good and ready. Fucking flames.

Burn for me.

I feel more than see Torren's body fold over me, sliding a hand under me before slipping two fingers into my dripping wet, throbbing pussy. He thrusts into my pussy as Jonah works my ass, stretching me and filling me, and while it's overwhelming in the most erotic way, I know it's just the beginning. That thought sends me over the edge, my body seizing with another orgasm. The cry I let out is animalistic, a mixture between a wail and a whine. Tears stream down my cheeks as wetness drips down my thighs.

"Almost there, Firebird," Torren growls into my ear. "Almost ready."

"Please," I beg. "Please. Please."

A hand wraps around my throat from behind and squeezes. Jonah.

"Please what?" The rough tone in Jonah's voice, the commanding warning, makes my pussy clench, wanting more. Needing more. I answer him shamelessly.

"Please, fuck me. Please."

"Two orgasms and you still want more," Torren says into my ear. Jonah squeezes my throat again. "You're so needy, aren't you, Firebird. You need us to fill you up?"

"Yes. Yes. Yes, I do."

"Good. I need it, too."

Torren grabs a condom from the bed beside him, opens the package, and rolls it down his erection. Then he lies back and pulls me on top of him. I'm covered in sweat, my chest is heaving against his with my heavy breathing, and my thighs and pussy are soaked with my arousal as I straddle his waist. Torren kisses me sloppily, sucking and biting at my lips with his hands cupping the sides of my face.

"You're so fucking perfect," he breathes out against my mouth. "I'm obsessed with you. I can't get enough. I can't stop."

"Don't stop," I say, then I reach between us, position his cock at my entrance, and slide myself down it until he's seated deep inside me.

"Fuck."

I don't know who says it. Me or Torren. Maybe both. The feeling of him inside me again is better than I thought it would be. So much better this time than last. Slowly, I begin to move on him, testing out his thickness and length. Adjusting to the overwhelming feeling of being full.

Torren wraps his arms around my torso, holding my body flush against his as he starts to pulse upward. I groan and drop my forehead to his shoulder.

"Oh my god, it's so deep."

My lips drag over his skin as I speak. I can taste his sweat. I can feel his hot, panting breaths in my hair. When he picks up pace, hitting that spot deep inside a little harder, I moan again, then bite his shoulder to keep from screaming.

"I'm never letting you go."

He says it quietly, almost reverently, with his lips pressed to my ear. It's more than a statement. It's a promise. An oath. I want to ask him if he means it—to make him swear it—but two hands grip my hips, and I'm reminded that Torren and I aren't alone. It's not just him and I on this bed, and he's not the only one who's made me come tonight.

Jonah slaps my ass, a loud crack breaking through the sounds of our labored breathing, and I yelp. More lube slides over my asshole, his fingers returning to stretch me out some more, before he replaces them with the tip of his cock.

"You sure you want this?" Jonah asks, pressing against my ass so he just barely breeches the barrier.

In response, I push back onto him, coaxing the head of his cock in a bit farther. Jonah grunts and his hands tighten on my hips.

"Words," Torren says. "Words, Calla Lily."

"I want this." I kiss him to punctuate how much I mean it. "I want it now."

35

TORREN

I FEEL the moment he enters her.

Slowly, pausing only briefly to add more lube, he pushes in, only the thin barrier between her pussy and her ass separating his cock from mine. Jonah's eyes are trained on her ass, watching himself disappear into her. I know how erotic and dizzying that view can be. I'm jealous he gets to experience it before I do, but her pussy is mine. *Only* mine. The low, long moan that escapes Callie vibrates through her whole body, increasing my pleasure. Driving me crazy.

"Fuck me," Jonah says on a groan.

Callie's pussy tightens, adjusting to the fullness, accepting our cocks inside her. She buries her head in my shoulder again. Her panting breaths warm then cool my sweat-slicked skin, and I hold her closer. I kiss her hair and whisper in her ear.

"You're doing so fucking good. You're taking us so fucking well."

She whimpers in response. When Jonah is fully seated, he stills, giving her a moment to relax. I know the pause is just as much for him and me. Callie's tight, warm, soaking wet pussy is almost too much. I want to savor it. I want to ink this moment into my memory, onto my skin. The feeling of her. The absolute perfection that is my Firebird.

"I can feel just how full you are. Stretched so tight, both holes taken care of. So, so good, baby."

I flick my eyes to Jonah after a moment and find him looking at me, eyes hooded and chest heaving. He nods once, then slowly we start to pulse, alternating our rhythm, moving our cocks back and forth. Inside her and against each other.

Jo's mouth falls open and his eyes clamp shut. Callie and I moan, the sounds in perfect harmony. When Jonah speeds up, elongating his strokes and pulling out a little farther just to shove back in, Callie lets out a strangled gasp.

"Oh god."

"*Gods*, baby," I correct. "There's two of us fucking you. Two cocks driving you crazy."

A small smirk turns up Jonah's lips, then I speed up my own thrusts. I jab my hips upward, hitting Callie deeper, and her pussy spasms. The orgasm hits her fast and hard. Her nails dig into my skin, the pain igniting pleasure, shooting straight to my dick. When she sinks her teeth into my shoulder, I almost come with her, and she lets out a muffled scream.

"Don't you dare," Jonah growls. "I want to fucking hear it."

He folds himself over her body, wraps his hand around her throat, and pulls her up. Her back arches, her hands sinking into the bed to support her body. It puts her breasts directly in front of my face, and I take a peaked nipple between my teeth. I bite and suck, tasting our sweat. I feel her pussy fluttering around my cock with every alternating thrust from Jo and me.

Jonah speeds up a little more, and just like he wanted, Callie lets out another strangled cry. I can tell from the sound that he's not choking her, but I know how badly he wants to. He's holding back for her, for me, and it's a testament to how much care he's putting into this moment.

"Jesus fucking Christ, Calla Lily," Jonah grunts out, then he makes eye contact with me. "You should see how sexy her ass looks all stretched around my cock. Her pussy fucking swollen and dripping around yours."

He spits, releasing his hold on her hip to rub the saliva onto his shaft as he fucks her ass. Then he reaches down and circles his fingers around my cock, rubbing her pussy lips and gathering her arousal to rub on his dick as well. He spits again, then slaps Callie's ass. She yelps, her pussy clenching hard around my cock, and Jonah and I both groan.

"Again," I say, and he slaps her ass once more, making her clench harder.

"God. Damn. It." Jonah punctuates each word with another slap. "No wonder you like doing this, Tor. Red fucking handprints on this perfect ass. The way it jiggles. Fuck, I want to come all over it."

The visual of his red handprints painted with glistening white cum makes my stomach tighten. My own release looms just as Callie's pussy starts to spasm once more.

"You gonna give us another one, Firebird?"

"Yes. Yes. Yes."

We fuck her hard. Her body quakes above me as she sinks her teeth into her bottom lip and whimpers with every thrust of our cocks. A gorgeous cadence. The sexiest fucking song.

"Give it," I growl. "Fucking give it to me."

She comes with another scream, clawing up her throat, rasping and breathless, and I come with her. My groan sounds almost pained in my ears, but it's the exact opposite. It's bliss. It's ecstasy. My chest rumbles, and my whole body jerks with each spurt of cum into the condom. Then, just as Callie's muscles start to loosen, Jonah releases his grip on her neck, and she collapses on top of me. It gives me the perfect view as Jonah pulls his cock out of her ass, rips off the condom, and shoots ropes of cum all over her backside with a roar of his own. Red handprints on her ass from his slaps, on her hips and waist from his punishing grip, and painted with white. He jerks himself until there's nothing left, then he falls to the bed beside us.

"Mother fuck," Jonah groans.

I turn my head to face him, but I don't let go of Callie as she pants heavily on top of me. Jonah has one hand sprawled on his chest, the other still stroking his cock, and he's staring wide-eyed at the ceiling.

"You sure we can't do that again? Cause that was—"

"Don't even try it," I growl, cutting him off.

He turns to me with a trouble-making grin, bigger than I've seen in a while, and it almost makes me reconsider. *Almost.*

"Can't blame me for askin'."

I shake my head at him and press a kiss to Callie's head. "How are you feeling?"

"Like my body has been lit on fire. Like my bones and lungs are ash. Completely consumed."

I drag my fingers up and down her side. "That a good or bad thing."

She releases a tired laugh. "The best thing."

I hum and listen as her breathing starts to calm, and Jonah's grows deeper.

"Hey, Jo."

"Hmm?"

"What was my nickname?" Callie tenses at my question, and I can tell she's listening closely. I specify, so she knows for certain what I'm referencing. "For the game. What was the nickname I used?"

Jonah snorts. "Sugar. Fucking lame."

I roll my eyes, but I don't respond. Instead, I put my lips to her ear and repeat the truth. I say it slowly, clearly, and I mean every fucking word.

"You were *always* different, Firebird. You have *always* been more."

Hours later, in the moonlit darkness of my hotel room, I'm coaxed awake by soft lips on my neck and a delicate hand stroking my cock.

It's quiet except for Jonah's deep, heavy breathing, and I tighten my hold on Callie. I kiss her deeply, growling into her mouth as my cock hardens between her slender fingers. Her tongue caresses my tongue, gentle and soft and warm.

Slowly, she hooks her leg over my hip, lining me up with her pussy. The head of my cock nudges her entrance, and I have to swallow back a groan. She's soaked and ready. She must be aching. She wraps her hand around my dick again and swipes it through her pussy lips, teasing her clit with a quiet gasp. I pull back and hold her gaze, the thin ring of green around her pupils almost glowing as my eyes adjust to the dark room.

"I'm not wearing a condom."

She shakes her head once, a soft smile forming on her lips. "I want to feel all of you."

For half a second, panic threatens to seize me. I force a swallow down my tightened throat. I haven't had sex without a condom in years. Sex without a condom moves past fucking, and just the idea of it stokes the pain of vulnerability I've buried deep in my chest, as far away from my heart as possible.

It's another wall reduced to rubble. Another shield pierced.

Then her lips press to mine gently, and her warm, safe touch erases every fear. I nod and let her guide my dick inside her. She kisses me again, muffling our twin moans as she begins to move. Our bodies stay pressed together, making slow, steady, deep strokes, careful not to make too much noise. Not to jostle the mattress and wake up our slumbering bed partner.

"This is all I will ever need," I confess between kisses. "Just you. Only you."

She doesn't respond. She just kisses me again, moving on me languidly. Lazily.

As if we have all the time in the world.

"So, she's not coming back, then?"

Sav arches an eyebrow as we wait backstage. I shrug and flick my gaze to Jonah.

"As long as Jo doesn't run her off, she's staying on our bus."

She purses her lips, eyes narrowed as she runs them over my face. "Is that wise?"

I sigh. "I know what I'm doing."

"She's here on a contract. She's being paid to be here. I like her, too, but I want to make sure—"

"Savannah. Stop. I know you feel like you have to be some sort of guardian over us now, but you gotta fucking trust me."

I whisper the words, but they sound more like a hiss with the anger simmering behind them. It threatens to boil when she rolls her eyes.

"I know how you are, Torren. I know how you get. I just don't want your heart broken again."

I choke out a laugh, humor and pain blending to form a menacing sound.

"Callie's not you, Savannah."

She jerks back as if I hit her. "Torren, I just—"

"You just find it hard to believe anyone could actually love me since you couldn't, right?"

Her jaw drops on a scoff. "You know for a fucking fact that's not what I'm saying." She shakes her head and takes a step back just as we receive our cue to take the stage. "Fuck you, Torren. I'm sorry for fucking *caring*."

She whips around, hair fanning wildly about her shoulders, and folds her arms. I bite my tongue on the impulse to argue. She's right. I do know that's not what she meant, but learned instincts die hard, especially when they're born from trauma.

When Jonah walks on stage, I follow suit, sticking to the order we've used since the beginning. Mabel, Jonah, me, then Sav. Sometimes, like now, it stings, and I wonder if it would hurt less if we didn't have such a turbulent past. Probably not. Sav is the one people want to see. She's the one people idolize. She's the one people put on a pedestal.

It doesn't bother me out of jealousy. It bothers me because I used to be one of those people. I knew all her flaws, all her demons, and I loved her still. I accepted her as she was, I idolized her, and I put her on such an unrealistic pedestal that it shattered me when she fell short.

I regret it. Not because of what it did to my heart, but because of what it did to us. I know I'm lucky we've made it this far, given the aftermath. We could have drowned in our toxicity. Our decisions could have ruined us, but the fact that we're still here gives me hope.

When Sav takes her place behind her mic, I train my eyes on her. I stare hard willing her to turn around so I can apologize. I know she can feel it just like I know she's ignoring me, and that makes me feel worse. Family looks out for each other. That's what she was doing. Instead of being grateful, I spit vitriol in her face.

"How are we doin' tonight, New York?"

Sav's voice echoes through the stadium, and the crowd screams in response, none of them noticing the heaviness in her tone. None of them hear the dejection. But I've known her for ten years, so I hear it. I know, at the very least, Mabel and Ham can hear it, too. Fuck.

It's like two steps forward, one step back. Just when something starts to work in one aspect of my life, I let my insecurities fuck up something else. For all of Sav's flaws, she didn't deserve what I just threw at her. She's the one people idolize, but she's also the one that gets the most hate. Tabloids print vile lies about her. Paps shout disgusting things at her. She has a fucking psychotic stalker, for Christ's sake. She doesn't fucking need it from me, too. Especially when she was just looking out for me.

My stomach roils for the duration of the show. Sav won't even glance my way. She doesn't interact with me. The songs we usually sing together are spent firmly planted in front of our own mics. The only time I feel peace is when I play Callie's song, but when it's over, my anxiety spikes again.

When I start to feel myself spiral, I seek out Callie in the VIP tent. I fix my eyes on her and she becomes my anchor. She quiets the storm in my head, and that's how I know for sure. What's happening between us is something real. Something solid. We're not headed for heartbreak. We're not dissonance. We're harmony, and I have to let myself trust it.

By the end of the show, my head is clear, and I'm determined to make things right with Savannah. At the very least, I need to apologize. We're finally starting to patch up our friendship. I don't want to torpedo it with an unwarranted temper tantrum.

When Sav stalks off the stage, I follow quickly, pulling her to the side just out of view of the stadium full of people.

"*What*, Tor?"

Her voice is tired. There is so much less bite to her words than there was two hours ago, and I hate knowing I'm part of the reason for it.

"We need to talk," I say, wrapping my hand around her wrist and pulling her down one of the hallways full of roadies and stadium workers.

I try two locked doors before I find a bathroom and drag her inside. She sighs and closes her eyes.

"I don't have the energy for this right now."

"I'm sorry, Sav. I know I overreacted. I'm sorry."

She shakes her head, nostrils flaring as she breathes deeply. Her forehead creases and her eyebrows slant, but she keeps those stormy gray eyes clamped shut. When she speaks, her voice shakes with hurt, and all I feel is shame.

"I've turned myself inside out trying to make up for the shit I've done, Torren. I'm doing everything I can to repair the damage. I've got my hands clutched so tightly around this band that sometimes I worry I'll snap us in half, but I can't keep doing it. I'm not going to keep fighting if you're never going to forgive me."

"I know."

My stomach clenches as a single tear slips from her lashes and trickles down her cheek. I fist my hands against the impulse to wipe it away. Her jaw ticks as she clenches her teeth, and when she speaks again, there's anger in her tone.

"At some point, you're going to have to recognize that I'm not the only one to blame for this fucking mess, but I'm the only one making any fucking attempt to pull us out of it."

It's the truth, and it fucking hurts. "I know, Sav."

She opens her eyes and pins me with a scathing glare.

"I like Callie, Torren. She's talented and she's smart. I'm still going to talk to her about Caveat Lover, but Heartless will always be my top priority. I won't just stand by and watch quietly while you—"

"It's not like that, Savvy." I take a step forward and hold her gaze. "This is different. When I said she's not you, I didn't mean it as an insult. I didn't mean to imply that you were the only one to blame for our relationship imploding. Fuck, we were so toxic. Both of us. I know that. You and I were completely wrong for each other, and I was an idiot for not believing you the first time you realized it. For not listening when you said it a hundred more times after that. But Callie...Callie's not *you* because she's perfect for *me*."

Sav's eyes flash with surprise before she scans my face. It's as if she's looking for any sign that I'm being delusional—that I'm imagining connections that aren't there—and I want to laugh. I give her a self-deprecating smile instead.

"Thank you for wanting to protect me—for wanting to protect our family—but I need you to trust me, here. I'm fucking in love with her, Savannah, and I know it's real this time. You know how I know?"

"How?"

"Because it's *nothing* like us."

She holds my gaze as we fall into silence, and I watch as the frown on her face slowly smooths out. From raging defensiveness to placid relief. Then she huffs out a laugh and tilts her head to the ceiling. "Thank fucking god."

A smile spreads across my lips, and this time I let myself laugh, too. In an instant, the hazy gloom that had surrounded us lifts, and we're no longer dueling ex-lovers. We're friends. We're family. We're adults who have learned from our mistakes and come out stronger. In this instance, the ground under my feet solidifies a little more, and so does my faith in myself.

"God, we were such a fucking mess," Sav groans after a moment, swiping a hand through her hair. "How the fuck did we not see it sooner?"

I snort. "Drugs and desperation?"

"Probably." Sav sighs, her face softening as she makes eye contact with me once more. "I'm rooting for us, you know? Me. You. Mabes and Jo. I'm rooting for us."

"I know. Me too."

"I really hope it works out with Callie."

I smile. "I have a good feeling about it."

I gesture to the door and Sav nods, turning to leave. I follow her back into the hallway and we walk side by side to the dressing rooms.

"I'm glad you're still going to talk to her," I say just before we part ways.

"Don't think it was your idea. It was *my* idea. You just cosigned."

"Whatever, Savvy," I tease.

"Whatever, Tor."

She smirks and flips me her middle finger, then backs into the dressing room and shuts the door in my face. Everything about the exchange makes me smile. The playfulness. The ease. The honesty.

We're going to be okay. I know it.

36

CALLIE

"You are radiant."

I smile at the compliment and do a little twirl for him, enjoying every second of having Torren's eyes on me.

"Did you pick this one out, too?" I ask, smoothing my palms down the cream-colored designer dress.

"I picked them all out."

"You have good taste."

He smirks, then closes the distance between us slowly. When he's close enough, he grabs my waist and pulls me against him. He runs his hands up and down my back, mesmerizing me with his emerald eyes before lowering his face to mine.

"I know."

Then he captures my lips in a sensual kiss, one that turns my legs to rubber and threatens to make us late for our reservation. Maybe we can sneak back into the bedroom for just a while longer...

"Fucking *get out*."

Jonah's gruff voice makes me jump backward, breaking the kiss with Torren. When I whip around to face him, he's scowling from the bathroom doorway, chest still wet from a shower and his bottom half wrapped in a low-slung towel.

"I have company coming. You two can't be dry-humping in the suite unless you're gonna make it a group project."

I narrow my eyes at him, but Torren chuckles. "Don't worry. We're leaving now."

He takes my hand in his and leads me toward the door.

"Fucking finally," Jonah shouts, then a door slams, and when I look over my shoulder, he's gone.

"What company does he have coming at nine in the morning?" I ask as Torren ushers me out the door and toward the elevator. Since I've started staying with Torren, Jonah has never been up before noon. "I've never seen him up this early."

Torren presses the elevator button. "Honestly, it's probably a video chat with his therapist."

"It's not Thursday."

"Sometimes we schedule more if we need them."

His brows slant slightly as we step into the elevator, and I watch him through the mirrored walls. When his lips purse, concern tightens my chest.

"Is he not doing well?"

Jonah's back to being distant and standoffish, and I'll admit that it bothered me at first. I thought we'd somehow be closer after that night in Miami, but the next morning, and every morning since, Jonah's proved me wrong. He doesn't talk to me on the bus. He doesn't spend time around Torren when I'm with him. He's back to rarely looking at me. Forget any chance of a smirk or a smile. He's ArtFusion Jonah again, and before this moment, I thought it was just...normal. Torren's silence tells me it's not.

"Tor, I can move back to Sav and Mabel's bus. I don't mind Levi. He's nice."

"No. That's not necessary."

"Obviously *something* is wrong with Jonah. All signs point to me."

He sighs and turns to face me, cupping my face and running his thumb over my jaw. "It's not you, Cal. Trust me. He's just...he's moody. He gets like this. He'll be fine. He just needs space."

I bounce my eyes between his, and the concern I see there makes my heart ache. I'm not always sure what to think of The Hometown Heartless, but one thing I'm learning is that they care about each other fiercely. They've been through a lot together, and when one hurts, they all hurt.

"Maybe we should start getting our own room in the hotels, then? To at least give him the space he needs."

Torren's jaw clenches and he shakes his head. "That won't work. I need to..."

I nod and force a smile. He doesn't have to say it. He needs to *watch* him. The realization fills me with dread instead of hope.

"Anyway, let's stop talking about this." The elevator door opens, and Torren leads me into the lobby. "I've planned a really fun day for us. I want your first experience of New York to be great."

Excitement starts to consume my worry, and I flash him a grin.

"Are you going to give me any hints?"

"Nope."

When he winks at me, my stomach does another backflip, and I have to bite my lip to keep from giggling. They've been consistently growing, but since Miami, it's like my feelings for him have multiplied substantially overnight. It's...*overwhelming*...to say the least.

He keeps surprising me with these thoughtful gestures, small and large alike. Grabbing me coffee in the morning without my asking. Making sure the scones I've started to love are always on the breakfast menu. And now this day-jaunt through New York City all because I mentioned on the drive here that I'd never been. Tonight is the last show at Madison Square Garden before we have to catch a flight to Los Angeles, but Torren insisted on blocking out the entire day for us. It's been a long time since someone has taken care of me, since someone has worried about my happiness, and I'm starting to really enjoy it.

I recognize how reckless that is, but I keep circling back to Levi's confession in Miami.

I trust Torren.

If he can trust him, I think I can too.

In the lobby, we meet up with Craig and Damon and we follow them to the SUV. Aside from a few interested glances, no one pays us any mind, and it makes me that much more excited for the day. Maybe we'll be able to enjoy it without cameras flashing.

The drive to our first destination takes longer than I expected, considering the location of the apartment-style hotel where we're staying. Twenty minutes to drive less than two miles thanks to traffic and pedestrians. Not even LA is this bad, and I hate driving in LA.

"I'll drop you at the back with Craig," Damon says from the driver's seat. "I'll park."

Then he grumbles something to himself about parking the SUV in the city, and I catch Craig smirking. I don't envy that task, either.

An adorable diner comes into view, a line of people already waiting to get in, and I shoot up in my seat and turn a manic smile on Torren.

"I know this place. I've heard about it."

Torren grins. "Next time I'll show you more local favorites, but we're going full tourist mode today."

I unbuckle my seat belt as Damon pulls into an alley beside the diner and as soon as he puts the car in park, I hop out. I don't even wait for Craig to get the door for me. Torren climbs out behind me and I can't tame my smile. It's only 9:30 and this is already one of the best days I can remember in a long time. Not as good as Constance Chen, but fucking close.

I open my mouth to tell Torren, but my words are swallowed by shouting. When I turn around, my excitement plummets to my feet and is replaced by panic.

The sound of cameras clicking blends with the invasive questions hurled in our direction as we're swarmed by people. By *paparazzi*. I don't have time to blink. I don't even have time to shut my gaping mouth; I'm frozen like an animal in a trap, and each question is worse than the last.

Callie, how do you feel about Torren and Sav in the bathroom?

What do you have to say about the PR relationship claims?

What was the five grand for? How much is he paying you?

Is this another of Wade Hammond's schemes?

Is this a sham to distract the public?

Is Sav using again?

Is the band on the verge of break up?

My head spins. My stomach churns, bile rising in my throat, and then Torren wraps his arms around me and all but throws me into the back seat of the car, slamming the door closed behind us.

"Drive, Damon," Torren barks.

"I'm fucking trying." Damon honks the horn and inches the car forward as paparazzi press close to the hood, angling their cameras to try and get a photo through the non-tinted windshield.

"Jesus Christ. They're fucking crazy." Craig cracks the window. "Get out of the way! You're gonna get yourselves killed."

Damon honks again, this time laying on the horn in one continuous blare until we're finally able to turn onto the street. But even then, fucking traffic hinders a swift getaway. By the time the cameras are behind us, I've got my head dropped between my knees, trying to calm my panic, and Torren is yelling into his cellphone.

"We were just fucking swarmed, Ham. Swarmed! You said it would be discreet."

He pauses, and then groans.

"Fucking hell. Why didn't you warn us?"

Another pause.

"Fuck!"

He groans again, and when I sit up, he has his hand fisted in his hair and he's glaring at the ceiling, fuming over whatever Hammond is telling him. He grits his teeth, sharp jaw popping and nostrils flaring as he shakes his head.

"No...I get it. Just...how bad is it? Yeah. Send it. We'll be back in twenty."

Torren hangs up, then opens a text message. I watch his eyes as they scan whatever he's reading, and I can tell from the growing fury that it's bad. Really bad.

"What is it?" I ask, my voice cracking. When he doesn't acknowledge me, I speak again, urgency rising in my tone. "What is it, Torren? Tell me."

He looks at me, ire changing to remorse, and then he hands me the phone.

I hold my breath as I read the article, paragraph after paragraph until my chest burns. When a hot tear trickles down my cheek and my vision starts to fizzle at the corners, my body takes over, and I suck in a lungful of air with a strangled gasp. The first words that I can manage surprise even me.

"Fucking Quinton." I clamp my eyes shut and swallow back a scream. "Mother fucking Quinton!"

Someone took pictures of Savannah and Torren entering and then leaving a bathroom after the show two nights ago. Her eyeliner is smeared, but they're both smiling slightly.

This isn't the worst part, though. Levi's voice echoes in my head, lessening the blow of the photos and outlandish claims printed in the article.

I trust Savannah. I trust Torren.

It stings, but I push through it. I'll deal with it later. The worst part is the second half of the article. The one that has an *"exclusive tell-all"* interview with Quinton. The visit from Torren at the store. The offer of five grand just to meet with him and "hear him out." My absolute disinterest in him followed by me quitting my job the next day. Quinton's even provided a sketchy video that he obviously took on his phone.

"It sounded more like a business proposition than a date," Quinton Teller told The Star. *"Like five grand just for a meeting? No way Callie would date Torren King. She hates The Hometown Heartless. She calls their music uninspired, watered-down, poor excuse for rock and roll. She, like, really hates them, but she's pretty hard up for cash."*

"Jesus."

I clamp my eyes shut and drop my head to the seat, pinching the bridge of my nose. I don't finish the sentence that outs my relationship with Torren as a sham. I can't bring myself to continue, certain there are accusations of another Sav Loveless and Torren King affair, among other heinous things.

"What are we going to do?"

Torren's hand lands on my thigh and squeezes. "Ham says we keep doing what we're doing. We act like it's not true. If it continues after the LA shows, he'll release a statement."

"But what about the stalker?"

Torren doesn't respond, so I open my eyes and turn my head to look at him. He's frowning, and then he shrugs.

"We just wait and see."

I don't like it. I don't like it at all. I feel so fucking guilty, despite knowing it's not my fault. I'm not even surprised. I should have seen it coming. Quin's always bent over backward for any sort of attention. He was an idiot in high school, and he's an idiot now.

"I'm sorry," I whisper into the air.

Torren squeezes my thigh again. "This isn't on you, Cal. I shouldn't have talked to you in front of him. And when I did, I should have made him sign an NDA. This is on me."

This is on me.

The photos of Torren and Sav leaving the bathroom creep back into the forefront of my mind. I try to push them back, try to repeat Levi's statement over and over, but my insecurities swirl with my memories from ArtFusion. Torren with Sav against the bus. His eyes on me as he came inside her.

I force myself to keep my eyes on his face even though all I want to do is close them and swallow myself in darkness. I watch him, hold eye contact, and ask what I want to know.

"What were you and Sav doing in that bathroom?"

"It's not at all what they said it was. I swear, Callie. I said something shitty to her before the show, and I just needed to apologize. There's nothing between us like that at all. Nothing romantic. Nothing sexual. No feelings like that at all. I swear it."

He swears it.

I trust Torren.

Nothing between them.

Nothing.

"Okay," I say with a nod.

"Okay?"

"Okay."

Torren reaches up and twirls a strand of my hair through his fingertips, then rests his forehead on mine. My eyes flutter shut as his breath fans over my lips.

"You're all I want, Firebird. Only you. I swear it."

I nod again, just a little so as not to make him move, and then I whisper the truth against his lips.

"Okay."

37

CALLIE

WE'VE ONLY BEEN BACK at the hotel twenty minutes before I find myself knocking on Sav's door.

If I don't do it now, I'll lose my nerve, and I refuse to put myself in a vulnerable position again. Not without covering all my bases. Not without being almost certain that I'm safe.

When the door opens, Sav's still in pajamas with her hair in a messy bun, her dog wagging her body on the floor beside her. Ziggy attacks my legs with kisses, and when Sav sees it's me, her face falls and her eyes flare as she waves me in.

"How are you doing? Fuck, what a mess, right? I told you those bastards are ruthless."

I huff out a laugh. "Word travels fast."

"Ham just left."

When she goes to sit on the couch, I stop her with a quick glance around the room. Her security detail is by the wall, and I can hear music coming from Mabel's room.

"Actually, Sav, can I talk to you in private?"

She pauses for a second before answering. "Yeah. We can talk in my room. Levi's at the fitness center."

I follow her into her bedroom. She takes a seat on the unmade bed, and I sit in a chair in the corner. It's only a little awkward. I take a deep breath before speaking.

"I want to ask you a question, and I want you to be totally honest with me. And I need you to know that no matter what you say, I won't break my contract. I'll still stay and help however I can with the whole stalker media diversion thing. If you want me to, of course. But I just...I need to know."

Savannah sighs and gives me a grim smile.

"Callie, there is absolutely zero truth to the shit they printed today about me and Torren. There hasn't been truth to it for a long ass time, now. But it's a juicy story and they print what sells."

When I don't speak, she keeps talking.

"I don't know if you noticed, but I'm completely obsessed with Levi," she says with a smile that almost looks shy.

It's the smile that makes me listen closer. It makes me open my heart more to what she's saying.

"I've been in love with him since I was fifteen. It never changed. Torren and I...god, we were terrible for each other. We were terrible *to* each other. I did and said a lot of things I regret, and one of the biggest is dragging things out with him as long as we did. You have nothing to worry about. Trust me."

I bite the inside of my cheek as I consider what she's just told me. The more I think about it, the more I believe her. But...

"And you're sure it's the same for him?"

"Yeah. I'm completely sure." She smiles softly. "You have feelings for him."

She doesn't phrase it as a question, so I don't answer. I don't say anything—I just bite my cheek harder—but she still sees something in my expression that makes her smile widen.

"Calla Lily Sunrise James, listen to me." She leans forward, holding eye contact so fiercely that I feel frozen, held captive by her stormy gray eyes. "You have absolutely nothing to worry about. Not about me and Torren, and not about *you* and Torren. I know it."

It almost seems as if she wants to say more, like she's actively biting her tongue on some secret she's dying to share, but she stays quiet. It makes my respect for her grow, and more importantly, it makes me trust her.

It's a far cry from how I felt about her a few months ago. I was so certain Sav Loveless was a villain. A corrupt, power-hungry woman with no regard for anyone but herself. I couldn't have been more wrong.

"Thank you," I say finally. "I appreciate you being willing to talk to me. I appreciate your honesty."

"You're welcome." Her soft, kind smile morphs to something more mischievous before my eyes, one brow arching almost deviously. "Now, if we're done with this conversation, I'd like to talk to *you* about something."

My brow furrows, my lips mirroring hers without me trying. She's contagious and all-consuming when she's like this.

"Okay..."

"How close are you with Becket, Rocky, Pike, and Ezra? You still talk?"

I tilt my head to the side and try to sus out the reason behind her question, but her face is giving nothing away. Nothing but mischief, and it gives me the feeling she was quite a handful as a child. Wild and fearless and always breaking rules.

"Yeah," I say with a shrug. "Kind of."

"Kind of?"

"Well, I talk to Ez more than anyone else. But yeah, we're on speaking terms."

"They still play?"

"I think so, yeah..."

"Together?"

"Rock, Ezra, and Beck do. They actually were in some talent management thing in Houston a few weeks back. But not Pike. Guess he's got a girlfriend and a real job, now. Ez says he ditched them."

Sav hums and nods, pursing her lips. After another painful pause, I can't fight my curiosity anymore.

"Why? Why do you want to know?"

Her smile returns, and magnetically, so does mine.

"Well, Calla Lily Sunrise James, I'm starting a record label, and I want to sign Caveat Lover."

My jaw drops, and I blink at her as she grins impishly like some crafty cartoon mastermind. She's so fucking proud that she shocked me, and a laugh bubbles out of me before I can stop it, which just entertains her more.

"Well, whatchya say, Cal? Want to call your boys and see if they can meet us in LA?"

I give my head a little shake, then blink a few more times. It seems too fucking good to be true. It seems unbelievable. I'm trying to wrap my head around it when something Torren said creeps up from the recesses of my memory. *I'm going to fix this*, he'd said, and that thought serves as an ice-cold bucket of reality crashing down over my head.

"I don't want a pity contract, Sav. I don't want people to say I slept my way into a record deal. It's bad enough that my manufactured relationship with Torren is what put a spotlight on my band. I won't be some nepotism baby, too."

Sav snorts. "You'd have to be my kid to be a nepo baby."

"You know what I mean." I roll my eyes. "Thank you, but you don't have to do this. It's not necessary. I don't care what Torren said."

"Ugh," Sav groans. "That man does *not* get to take credit for this. Sure, he suggested it after we found out what our label had done, but it was my idea first. You've been on my spreadsheet since that show in Chicago. Torren's late to the fucking game."

I shake my head. "Your spreadsheet?"

"Yeah." She takes her phone off the nightstand and types in her passcode, pulling up the spreadsheet then handing it to me. "Look. It's my spreadsheet of bands I have my eye on."

I recognize a few of these bands as I scroll through the list, stopping when I see Caveat Lover. The column contains all our information, but it's highlighted in red.

"Why are we in red?"

"Because you were already signed when I found you. Which, by the way, was extremely disappointing, but I kept you on there just in case."

I look up from the phone and cock my head to the side. "You said you saw us in Chicago a few years ago?"

"Yeah. This is something Ham's been helping me out with for a while now. Once we're out of our contract—which will be happening sooner than we expected, thank god—I'm launching Rock Loveless Records. Not the cleverest title but Ham says my name is a successful established brand, and I'd be an idiot not to use it. Don't tell him I said this, but he's usually right."

I choke out another unintentional laugh, my head once again spinning around the possibility that's been laid at my feet.

A record deal.

A record deal with a label that Sav is starting.

The fact that it will be a brand-new venture for her doesn't bother me in the slightest. Sav doesn't seem to accept failure, and the way I've watched her mother hen this band over the last few months is proof. I've gone back and read the old tabloid articles. I've paid attention to the side comments and dark-humored jokes. The Hometown Heartless was on the brink of self-destruction, and Sav clawed everyone—herself included—from the foot of the grave by sheer determination.

I know in my gut Sav's label will be a success. I feel it almost as solidly as the chair on which I sit. That's what coaxes my excitement out of hiding. My faith in her—which she earned in spite of my raging grudge—and my desire to be part of this with her. My fingers itch to call Ezra. To grab my keyboard and play Beethoven's "Ode to Joy." I want to jump up and tell Torren right this second. I want to hug Sav Loveless and fall into a fit of hiccupping, sobbing laughter.

Instead, I give her a calm, not at all creepy smile, and keep my voice as normal as possible as I agree.

"I'll call the guys now and ask them to meet us in LA."

Sav claps her hands together once and bounces on the bed. "You won't regret this, Callie. This is going to be something special. I just know it."

My eyes start to sting as they threaten to fill with tears, and I suck in a shuddering breath.

"Me too."

The last show at MSG is brilliant.

The Hometown Heartless are always great live, but this time there's something else. An excitement glittering in Sav's eyes, resonating in her voice, amping up the energy in the stadium until every person in the venue is irreparably changed by her performance.

But while Sav is mesmerizing, I can't keep my eyes off Torren. He's so fucking beautiful up there, stage lights shimmering off his glistening skin and talented fingers plucking the strings of his bass. I know exactly how those fingers feel on my body, how his rough callouses can illicit the most erotic sensations with just a feather-like touch. I haven't gone a single night without those hands on me. In me. Driving me wild. Just thinking about it makes heat surge through my bloodstream, and his unwavering attention tonight only makes it worse.

Torren's eyes have barely left me all evening. He didn't want me in the crowd tonight due to the newest gossip, but Ham insisted, and I agreed. We have to stay the course. We have to go on as if nothing is wrong. One misstep and we'll only fuel the rumors. Reluctantly, Torren conceded, but the result is his eyes on me constantly.

While he sings and smirks and winks, sweaty and sexy, Torren's focus never leaves me. At one point, while Sav works the crowd, he blows me a fucking kiss and mouths *hi baby* in my direction. I can barely register the crowd's shrieking reaction over the sound of my own heart beating frantically in my ears. Sometimes this man leaves me so off-balance that it's all I can do not to faceplant on the cement, and it's becoming a more common occurrence with every passing day. He's a cyclone, and he turns me into a raging fucking wildfire of hormones. It's all I can do to breathe through it and pretend like every ounce of blood in my body isn't rushing to all my erogenous zones.

Fucking Torren King. I'm wet in a crowd of thousands of people, and he hasn't even touched me. By the time the band finishes the last encore song, my restraint has been worn to nothing. I'm needy and aching for him, and when he spots me backstage, I know he can tell.

He smirks, eyes dragging up and down my body as he grabs an offered towel from a roadie. Instead of rushing to me, he stops and runs the towel over his face and chest. His naked, sculpted chest. The same chest I had my palms on as I rode him last night. The memory taunts me, the ghost of his touch making my clit throb. When he finally reaches me, he wraps his arms around my waist and bites his lip before giving my ass a squeeze.

"Firebird, you need to work on your poker face because I can read every naughty thing going on in your head."

I don't bother denying it, and the heated flush that colors my chest, neck and face has nothing to do with embarrassment.

"Do you know what I'm thinking right now?"

God, even my voice sounds horny. Breathy and needy and horny as hell. When he presses himself against me, dick already hard against my stomach, I have to choke back a shameless moan.

"I think I have a guess."

I press my pelvis forward and he grunts. I smile. "Then what are you waiting for?"

His expression goes hooded, lustful, then he lifts me up and throws me over his shoulder. I yelp and then laugh as he rushes to the dressing room. Roadies and stage workers watch us curiously, but I don't have time to say anything. They're all a blur as Torren pushes past them, and within seconds he's barging into the dressing room and pointing at Jonah.

"Get out."

"The fuck?"

"Out. Now."

"For fuck's sake," Jonah grumbles, but he doesn't argue, and he doesn't even look my way as he stalks out, slamming the door behind him.

Torren sets me on my feet, spins me around, and presses my back against the door. He reaches behind my back to turn the lock, then drops to his knees. Within seconds, my shorts are at my ankles and his face is sunk between my thighs. He inhales deeply, humming.

"Fuck, I can't get enough of you. The way you smell. The way you taste."

His mouth covers my pussy, and his tongue laves against the silk fabric of my underwear. I grab his hair and tug, staring down my heaving chest at him. He pulls back, just far enough to crook his finger into the crotch of my panties and pull it aside. I'm hot, wet, and aching for him. When he puts his mouth on me again, that wicked tongue of his wastes no time.

"Jesus, Tor."

My back bows. I press myself against him, grinding on his tongue without inhibition. We're past that now. I have no issue with riding his face in the dressing room after a sold-out show. I don't even care if someone hears me at this point. I'm that gone for him.

Torren slides two fingers into me, thrusting roughly as he sucks my clit, and I come with a strangled cry in a matter of seconds. I barely catch my breath before he's kissing me, driving me crazy with the way he tastes of me. Blood pulses through my lips, my clit, my nipples. I want to rub myself on him to get some relief. I want to feel him.

My hands go straight to his pants, undoing the button and shoving my hand into his underwear so I can wrap my fingers around his hard cock. We both moan as I squeeze, using my other hand to shove his pants down his narrow hips.

He keeps his arms braced on the door, caging my head between sculpted, tattooed forearms. His lips stay parted, breathing heavily and watching with rapt attention as I touch him frantically. As soon as his pants are below his ass, his cock jutting out proudly between us, I notch my leg on his hip and guide him to my pussy. He shoves into me in one stroke, our pelvises kissing as I gasp.

"I dream about this, Firebird. I wake up hard as fuck just needing to be inside you."

He hits me deep with small pumps of his hips, pinning me to the door with his whole body, and I meet his thrusts with matching ones of my own. I can't get enough of the way he looks when I fuck him back, when I move on him like this. His green eyes are thin halos around his enlarged pupils, his full lips flushed and swollen as he pants. When I clench around him, his lashes flutter, his eyes roll back, and he lets out a groan that vibrates in his chest.

"God damn it, you were made for me." He speeds up his movements. "You were fucking made for me, baby."

He snakes his hand between our bodies and rubs my clit, the sensation setting my whole body ablaze. I tingle from my head to my toes. When he thrusts harder, faster, my moans resemble chants, crying out every time he hits that place deep inside me.

"I'm going to come," I manage to force out just before my orgasm crashes over me.

I sound like I'm drowning, unable to make a full sound due to the way the air has been sucked from my lungs. The way my soul is fucking rattled. It takes me several moments before I can feel my limbs again, and my pussy pulsates around his dick. When I finally open my eyes, I can tell from his face that he's holding on for me.

"You want to come?" I ask breathlessly.

"Fuck, I do."

I move my hands to his chest and push, backing him up and breaking our connection, then I drop to my knees.

"Christ." It's barely a whisper, then he stares, lips parted, as I take his cock down my throat. "Fuck, baby. Fuck."

I only have to pump him twice, swallow around him once, before he's filling my mouth with his release with a long, drawn-out groan. I suck him until he pulls out of my mouth and tugs me back to my feet.

"Firebird, you're trying to kill me," he rasps, kissing my lips while he tries to catch his breath. "You're going to fucking kill me."

I smirk. "I didn't think there was anything I could do to surprise you, King."

I mean it. I'm sure there's not a damn thing he hasn't done or had done to him. It doesn't bother me. It's just a fact. Letting him fuck me against the door is likely tame compared to his past antics.

Torren chuckles. "Baby, everything you do surprises me. Everything."

38

CALLIE

My phone rings just as Torren and I are about to leave the suite.

Jonah's gone already, and Damon and Craig are in the lobby. Everyone is just waiting for us, so I don't stop as I answer the phone.

"Hey, Glor."

"Are you here yet?"

"Not yet. Heading to the airfield to board the jet now."

"They own a jet?"

"I don't know, actually." I pull the phone away from my ear and turn to Torren as he steps out of the suite to join me in the hallway. "Do you own the jet?"

He shakes his head. "Nah. We just charter one when we need it."

"Boring," Glory says, overhearing him, and I laugh.

"Did you get the tickets for the shows?"

"Oh my god, yeah, thank you so much. I can't believe it. Bummer we're gonna miss night one, but this is still so amazing. Can I get a picture with the band? Everyone is going to be so fucking jealous that I get to be there two nights in a row."

"We can get a picture, but don't say fucking, Glory." She sighs dramatically, but she doesn't argue, so I change the subject. "What are you doing right now? Walking your dumb dog?"

"Oh, I actually just left Bruno's!"

"The store?" I arch a brow in question even though she can't see me. What's Glory doing at my old job? It's too far from the house for grocery shopping. The only reason I shopped there was because of the employee discount. "Why were you at the store?"

"Oh, you know...*Browsing*..."

There's a pregnant pause, and a whisper of unease skates down my spine. My steps halt, leaving me frozen in the middle of the hallway. Glory's overly casual tone has me in full-blown big sister mode. I don't trust her when she's draped in faux-innocence, and I don't have the patience for her theatrics.

"Glory Bell, what did you do?"

"Nothing. Honest..." Another intentional pause. Another dramatic sigh. I brace myself for what comes next. "I just *accidentally* spilled an entire extra-large blue raspberry slushie on the magazine rack, is all. Then I dropped two dozen eggs and one of those glass half-gallons of the expensive chocolate milk on the floor. Eggs and glass and chocolate milk everywhere. Buncha magazines ruined, too. I'm such a silly, clumsy girl. Poor Quinton had to clean it all up by himself."

My jaw drops at the fake contrition in her voice. At the *very thinly* veiled pride.

"Glory Bell! Tell me you didn't do that on purpose."

"Bet your ass I did! And I'd do it again. That douche nozzle deserves worse for what he said about you in that stupid tabloid. He's lucky I didn't glue his big fat stinking mouth shut."

I gasp. My sister is a tiny devil. That's what she is. A tiny little revenge monster, and I'm flabbergasted.

"Did Quinton think it was an accident?"

She snorts. "No. He's a jerk but he's not an idiot. Dwayne did, though, so that's all that matters. I cried real good. You'd be proud. Really sold it and didn't have to pay for any of the damaged stuff."

"What the hell were you going to do if he *did* try to make you pay for it?"

Her voice is saccharine when she responds. "I'd just tell him I was *hard up for cash* and couldn't pay it. After all, that's what Quinton told *The Star.*"

Oh my god. She's ridiculous. She's an evil mastermind.

I bark out a laugh and shake my head. "You're kind of scary, you know that?"

She giggles. "I know, right?"

My cheeks hurt from smiling and my heart is flooded with warmth. My sister is ruthless and out to defend my honor. Wreaking havoc to avenge my name. She's nuts and unpredictable, but she loves me.

"Thanks, Glor," I say with another laugh. "I know I should probably tell you that was not acceptable behavior, but...well...just thanks."

"No problem. It's the least I could do since you gave me the Coach clutch you found in that thrift store near the pier."

I gasp. "Glory! I didn't say you could have my Coach clutch."

"Oh, well, look at the time. I need to go clean egg yolk off your sneakers. Love you! See you in a few days! Bye!"

The line goes dead. I pull the phone back to stare at the screen in disbelief.

"She's a little devil child," I whisper to myself. "She's completely unhinged."

Torren laughs, and I look up at him with wide eyes.

"Don't let her get around Sav and Mabel. I don't think the world could handle it."

"Did you hear what she did?"

"Every word." He laughs again and shakes his head. "I'm not mad about it, though. I kind of feel like I should thank her too."

"Oh god, no. It will go straight to her head. She's already off her rocker. We don't need her ego inflated, too."

He drops his hand over my shoulder and leads me to the elevator. "Baby, I'm afraid that ship has sailed."

"Thanks for getting them tickets to the shows," I say, leaning into him as the elevator carries us down to the lobby. "She's really excited."

"Yeah, of course. Since your mom only has PT on Tuesday, maybe she and Glory can come up early on Wednesday and hang out."

I squint up at him like he's just offered to lie in a tank of spiders just for funzies. This trip to LA is a quick turnaround, playing shows Tuesday, Wednesday, and Thursday nights to make up for the ones they had to cancel a few months ago when everyone caught the flu. Then they have to get back on the jet and fly to North Carolina so they can resume the regular tour. Torren will be exhausted. The last thing he should want is to spend time with my mom and bonkers little sister.

"Are you high?" I ask, only half joking, and he laughs.

"I'm serious. I know you miss them, and I'd like a second chance

333

with Glory. You know, since last time she more or less threatened my life."

He's got me there. And I'll admit, it will be fun to see how he handles her. Or rather, how she handles him. No one handles Glory. It's something I've come to terms with since I moved back home.

"I'll ask her," I say as the elevator door opens and we step into the lobby. "But I just need to warn you, Glory is a lo—"

"Miss James."

Torren and I turn toward the voice, a hotel bellhop. He's young, maybe early twenties, and I open my mouth to greet him, but nothing comes out as my eyes fall on the object in his arms.

"Someone left these for you. I was about to deliver them, but the front desk said you were checking out."

The boy holds the bouquet of calla lilies out to me, but I don't reach for it. Instead, I take a step back and look at Torren. He's frowning at the bouquet.

"Where did you get those?"

The boy's smile falters at the tone of Torren's voice, and he stammers when he responds.

"Uh...someone...just...just dropped it off. A, uh, delivery person. But we don't allow delivery people past the lobby. Only ho-hotel staff, so it was given to me. Sir. Mr. King, sir."

Craig and Damon step up beside the boy, and the poor thing jumps. I try to give him a reassuring smile, but I'm too busy panic-spiraling about another bouquet. The first one was weird. But this one? This one feels ominous, and I can tell from the looks on Craig and Damon's faces that they think so, too.

Without asking, Craig takes the bouquet from the boy while Damon goes straight to the front desk. Torren turns back to the bellhop.

"Did you happen to see or talk to the delivery person?"

The boy shakes his head. "No. The desk manager just flagged me over and told me to bring them up. She's the one who talked to the delivery guy."

Torren looks to the desk. Damon is speaking with a blonde woman who is wearing a pencil skirt and blouse.

"That the desk manager?" I ask, and the boy nods.

"Okay, thanks." Torren gives the bellhop one flat smile, then stalks to the desk.

"Thank you," I say, trying to make my smile friendlier than Torren's. The boy just frowns at me and nods again, so I follow Torren to the desk where he's already speaking with Damon.

"She's going to get permission to pull security footage for me."

"What did she say he looked like?"

"Male. Thirties, maybe. Had a hat on."

"Not helpful," Torren spits, and Damon shrugs.

"Delivery people come here all the time. She didn't think to pay attention."

"When will you see the security footage?" I ask, and Damon softens his face to look at me.

"She has to go through her boss. Might be five minutes. Might be five hours."

My eyes flare as I look between Damon and Torren. "We're supposed to take off in an hour."

"This is more important," Torren says, and I shake my head.

"You can't miss the flight because of me."

"It's not because of you."

"Don't worry," Damon cuts in. "I'll wait here. Walton will head with you to LA. I'll meet you there when this is done."

Torren is still frowning, and a concerning glance is exchanged between him and his security detail. It makes my frown mirror theirs.

"How worried do I need to be?"

Torren flicks his eyes to me. "Probably not at all, but I'm not taking chances."

"You think it's Sav's stalker?"

When Torren doesn't answer, I look at Damon. His face stays neutral, but he gives it to me straight.

"We haven't heard from them, but with the recent press and considering past behavior, we need to be vigilant."

"Okay." I jerk out a nod and take a deep breath, failing to soothe the swarm of bees that have invaded my stomach. "Awesome. Cool. Totally fine."

Torren wraps his arm around my body and pulls me against his chest, pressing his lips to my hair.

"We're good, Callie. I got you. There's nothing to worry about. I promise."

I relax into him, breathing in the scent of detergent and body wash and *me* on his skin, and the nausea I'd been battling starts to fade.

I trust Torren, Levi had said and sometime in the last few weeks, I've come to trust him, too. I tilt my head up so I can look into his gorgeous green eyes, and I smile.

"Thank you. Let's go catch our flight."

"You can leave your shoes here."

Torren gestures to the floor of his foyer as he kicks his own shoes off, so I follow suit. It's been almost three months since I was in Torren's apartment, but it's just as imposing as ever. I stand awkwardly by the door as he crosses the living room and enters the kitchen. He pulls open the fridge and looks inside.

"You thirsty? I have regular water, mineral water, sparkling water, a few energy drinks, and two protein shakes."

"I'll take a regular water," I say with a laugh.

He grabs two waters and shuts the fridge door. When he turns to look at me, he quirks a dark brow.

"You can come into the apartment, you know. You don't have to stand in the doorway."

I take two steps in, then halt. "I don't want to break anything or get anything dirty."

He smirks and walks toward me. "What if *I* get *you* dirty?"

I roll my eyes. "That was dumb."

He chuckles and hands me a water. Then he takes my free hand, tugging me into the kitchen with him, and starts pulling plates out of the cabinet and food from the fridge.

"Since we get to stay here, I called ahead and had them get me some things."

"Had *who* get you some things?"

"Oh, the building management. It's like a concierge service for residents."

Of course. Rock star perks.

"You like turkey? I'm going to make sandwiches, but I've got ham, too."

"You're gonna make me a sandwich, King?"

He pulls a few slices of organic whole grain wheat bread out of a bag and winks at me as he lays them out on the table.

"Baby, I'll make you anything you want."

Heat stirs low in my belly at his suggestive tone, the way he looks at me with so much need igniting a fire in my veins. I force a cool smirk of my own to my lips and give him a shrug.

"Turkey is fine."

I watch as he gets to work fixing sandwiches and decide there's something very sexy about this larger-than-life rock god carrying out such a domestic task. Stop anyone on the street and ask them to imagine Torren King making a sandwich, and I bet money no one could do it. Those hands are for playing bass guitar, talented fingers meant to create music. Seeing them artfully construct a picture-perfect turkey and cheese sandwich? I'm dumbstruck.

I take a sip of my water, and he slides a plate in front of me.

"Got anything you want to do tonight? We can go out if you want? Club or dinner?"

I pick up the sandwich and move it to my mouth. "Honestly? I'm tired. I'm not used to jet lag."

Torren laughs. "Just wait until Europe."

I blink and take a bite of my sandwich, so I don't say anything stupid. Like, *but I'm not contracted for Europe*. I chew slowly and swallow, then take another sip of my water before speaking again.

"I'm good with staying in tonight, if you are."

"Want to watch a movie and fall asleep on my couch with me, Firebird?" Torren's playful grin makes my stomach flip.

"That sounds nice."

"Wait. Actually..." He puts his half-eaten sandwich on the plate and rounds the kitchen island to do the same with mine before he grabs my hand. "Come with me. I have a surprise for you."

Torren leads me back through the kitchen and down a connecting hallway. We pass a bathroom and a laundry room before he slows just before we round another corner.

"How fucking big is this place?" I ask, arching a brow, and he grins.

"So, around this corner is like a second living room. It's supposed to be for entertaining, and when I bought the place, I thought I'd be throwing parties and jam sessions and shit, but I've never used it for that. Not once."

"You have a second living room that you don't use?"

He shrugs in response.

"Then this isn't a studio apartment," I say flatly, and he laughs.

"Yeah, I guess not."

He grins at me as we stand in the hallway, and prickles of excitement start to tease my arms and legs.

"What did you do?" I ask slowly, and he nods toward the end of the hallway.

"Go see."

I wait only a moment before I brush past him and walk around the corner, and the moment the large room comes into view, I freeze with my mouth gaping.

"Do you like it?"

I can't even look at him. I'm still too busy staring at the grand piano in the middle of the room. It's a Steinway, and it's gorgeous. I fist my hands at my sides. I bet the keys would be a dream under my fingers. Smooth and cool and perfect. My toes flex in my sneakers, imagining pressing those solid brass pedals. The concert piano I played at Barnum Hall was nowhere near this nice. I've never even been in the same room as a piano this nice. I feel like I'm standing feet away from royalty, and I don't know how to act.

Torren steps up next to me. "Are you going to play it?"

My jaw drops. "I can't play that! It's, like, one-hundred-thousand dollars, easy."

He smirks. "I paid one-twenty, actually."

A squeak escapes me, my eyes probably as big as frisbees. "You don't even play!"

"Yeah, but you do."

I blink. My brows slant and my forehead creases as his words sink in, and then I gasp. "What?"

"I got it for you."

"What? Why? When?"

He shrugs. "The day after I heard you play on the roof."

I stare at him, speechless, and suddenly his smile slips. He shifts his weight from foot to foot and runs his hands through his thick, black hair.

"This is too much, isn't it?"

I blink again, I huff a laugh, but I still can't speak. Not yet.

"I've overwhelmed you. I'm sorry."

The remorse in his voice helps me find my own, and I swallow, shaking my head.

"No...it's just...you didn't even like me then. We'd argued hours before that. And then, just because you heard me playing Beethoven *one time*, you decide to drop a hundred grand on a piano? That's bananas."

"One hundred and twenty."

"Torren."

"Calla Lily."

He steps forward, self-assured smile returning to his full lips, and closes the distance between us. He rubs his thumb over my lower lip before notching his finger under my chin and gently closing my gaping mouth.

"Just play it for me, please." He smirks. "Don't make it a waste of a hundred and twenty grand."

I groan, an irritated laugh escaping my throat as I roll my eyes. "You're dumb."

"So, you said. Now play. Please. You know you want to."

He's right. I want to. I *really* want to.

I scowl at him, though there's no heat behind it, then walk to the piano bench and sit down. I rub my sweaty palms on my jeans, then open and close my fists to stretch my fingers. I breathe in and out. Then slowly, I move my hands to the keys, and I have to suppress a shiver as my fingertips barely graze the surface.

I play scales first, and the gorgeous sound that comes from the piano brings tears to my eyes. Even without concert hall acoustics, it sounds amazing. When I tap out "Twinkle Twinkle Little Star," Torren chuckles, and I look over to find him seated on a couch, eyes trained on me. The way he's looking at me sparks something in my chest, something thrilling and fearless.

Slowly, a smile stretches across my face and my heart starts to thrum faster. Then, before I lose my nerve, I look back at the keys and begin the third movement of Beethoven's "Moonlight Sonata." It's the same piece I chickened out of playing on the roof weeks ago, but this time, I don't hesitate. For seven minutes, my fingers glide over the keys playing the notes from memory, my body rocking with the unbridled emotion within the music. I do it almost perfectly. By the time I've played the last note, my hands ache and my heart pounds behind my rib cage, but I'm filled with an overwhelming sense of accomplishment. I feel grounded, centered, in a way only playing classical music has ever done for me. I feel *at peace*.

"That was amazing," Torren says, drawing my attention to him. "That was so fucking good, Callie."

I give him a half-smile. "I'm no Constance Chen, but I do love it."

"Will you play me something else?"

"I could play classical all night," I say honestly.

He settles back into the couch and folds his hands in his lap. "Then that's what we'll do."

For the next few hours, I play a solo piano recital for Torren King while he lounges on the couch, and he's the most enthusiastic audience I've ever played for. Between pieces, we talk and laugh. I tell him a little about each piece and each composer, and he ask questions about my experience learning how to play them. At one point, he sits on the piano bench next to me, and I teach him how to play "Heart and Soul." He's a fast study, and I'm smiling so big my cheeks hurt when we're able to play it together.

"Thank you," I say quietly as I sit on his bed wearing one of his T-shirts. "Not for the piano—I can't accept that—but for tonight. Thank you."

Torren smiles, then sits on the bed beside me. Slowly, he pushes me down onto the plush mattress, so his body is between my thighs and his face is just inches above mine. His green eyes glitter in that magnetic way that makes my heart skip and my knees weaken, and just as I lean up to kiss him, he says words that take the breath from my lungs.

"Move in with me."

39

TORREN

I PULL my car into the spot next to Sav's Porsche and scan the underground lot for Jonah's car.

Normally, I'd be with him. He'd have stayed at my place, or we all would have opted to stay in the hotel. Instead, I wanted to be alone with Callie, so I took her to my apartment, and I left Jo to fend for himself. I didn't want to admit the whisper of worry that it had caused, but the relief I feel when my eyes land on his car makes it undeniable.

It all worked out fine, though. Thankfully.

As Callie and I are climbing out of my car, a pink sport bike rumbles to a stop behind me. I flash Mabel a grin as she hops off the bike and removes her helmet.

"I thought you'd ride with Sav."

"I slept at Kat's last night," she says with a playful waggle of her brows, then she bounces her eyes between our vehicles. "Damn. Everyone rolled up separate. Not a single armored SUV."

I chuckle and move toward the elevator. With the exception of Sav, band security is always a little more relaxed when we're in LA. We don't use drivers unless we want them. We don't take bodyguards unless we think we'll need them. In fact, this is the first tour where Mabel, Jonah, and I have each been assigned our own 24/7 detail, and it was difficult as hell to get used to. Having some slack on the leash again feels fucking delightful.

"Feels almost like old times." I say the words on a dramatic sigh, sounding just as wistful and nostalgic as I intended, and Mabel laughs.

"Don't get used to it."

"Why not?"

Mabel looks toward Callie as she answers her. "Now that we tend to draw more attention, we always travel together for shows. Even in LA, we stay in a hotel. It kind of serves as a home base, I guess. It's safer and easier and more efficient. This whole staying wherever and rollin' up on our own thing before a show is *not* the norm. Ham must be getting an ulcer having so many moving parts to track."

Callie flicks her eyes from Mabel to me. "So why did we do it this way?"

Mabes points her finger at my head, calling me out, and I shrug.

"I wanted to have you to myself for a night." Callie's cheeks pinken, and I pull her under my arm. "And I'm glad I did it."

Callie hasn't given me an answer yet. I surprised us both when I asked her to move in with me, but as soon as I said it, I knew I meant it.

I'll think about it, she'd said, but there was a smile on her perfect lips as they formed the words, so I'm hopeful. If I could spend every night like the one I spent with her last night, I wouldn't want for anything else. I could listen to her play Beethoven every single day and not grow tired of it. When she fell asleep naked and wrapped in my arms, I stayed awake and replayed memories with her over in my mind while listening to her soft breathing.

I'm fucking in love with her.

It's so intense that I want to laugh at myself from five years ago. The version of myself who thought he knew what love felt like. That fucker was clueless. How I feel for Callie pales in comparison to how I've ever felt about anyone else. I ache for her. I wake up and go to bed with her in the forefront of my mind. I even have a running list in my phone's notes app of random ideas that will make her happy. Gifts, trips, gestures. I'm fucking gone for this woman, and there's no coming back from this.

I rest my cheek on the top of her head as we step into the elevator and Mabel hits the button. We head to the lobby, then we cross the lobby to the private elevator for the penthouse suite.

As with all other shows, we have rooms reserved at a hotel while we're in town. Like Mabel said, it serves as a home base. We'll start here before heading to the venue. We'll end here when the show is over. But unlike in other cities, tonight we'll have the option to sleep at the hotel or head back to our own places. I already know what I'm doing, and the thought of getting Callie back in my bed sends a surge of heat straight to my dick. I'm fighting off an erection when the elevator pops open and we step into the private hallway outside the suite we've rented.

Walton stands outside the elevator and focuses on Callie the moment she comes into view, his shoulders loosening slightly. Poor guy. He didn't like when I told him I'd drive her, but the fact that he takes her safety so seriously makes me respect him more.

"Walton," I greet with a nod, which he returns.

"Mr. King."

Callie snorts a laugh at the formality, and I narrow my eyes playfully at her as I lead her into the hotel suite. Jonah is sprawled out on a chair with his headphones on, and Mabel skips off toward one of the bedrooms, probably to get dressed, but I'm stopped by Hammond immediately.

"You're late."

I resist the urge to roll my eyes at him. "I was in the garage early. You track my phone, so you know it's true."

He huffs, and I flick my eyes to Sav snickering behind him. She's dressed for the show already in a pair of ripped black jeans, black fishnet tights, and black combat boots, but when I see the band on her shirt, I bark out a laugh. Callie looks to see what I'm laughing at, then she gasps.

"Oh my god! Where did you find that?"

Sav smirks and gestures to the Caveat Lover tank top she's wearing. "Oh, you mean this super cool vintage band tee? Online."

"Damn, that's years old. Like *pre*-Black Widow old."

"I had to pay like two hundred bucks for it, too, so the buzz is buzzing about your band."

Callie shakes her head. "That's crazy. I could have gotten you one for free. Pretty sure Rock still has stacks of them in his mom's garage."

"Keep 'em," Sav says with a wink. "Maybe we'll use 'em."

I leave Callie with Sav to talk record label things—they have a meeting set up with the rest of Caveat Lover before Thursday's show—and I seek out Damon.

He called me last night and told me there was nothing helpful on the hotel security footage. He even went to the florist, but it was a dead end. I didn't tell Callie, but this second bouquet has my anxiety spiraling. Something is just fucking off, and I don't like it.

"You're still good to stay with her?" I ask the moment I'm in front of him.

"I won't leave her side."

"You and Walton both."

"Yes, sir."

My body relaxes knowing Callie will have them both with her tonight in the VIP tent. I went back and forth over whether to ask her to stay out of the crowd, but I can see her clearly when she's in the VIP tent. When she watches from backstage or in a private club box, I can't. I want her to stay where I can see her.

I know it's probably nothing. I'm probably being overprotective, and the bouquet is likely just from an adoring fan.

But I love Callie James, and I won't take risks with the woman I love.

The rest of the afternoon goes on like usual. We eat together. We ride to the venue together. We go through soundcheck. We fall into routine, and by the time the opening band is finishing their set, my earlier concerns have been dampened by the pre-show adrenaline rush.

I kiss Callie one more time before Walton leads her to the VIP tent, and then I post up with Sav, Mabel and Jonah, readying to play the first of three make-up shows in Los Angeles. The energy before this show is especially heightened because it killed us to cancel the original shows a few months ago, and we pushed hard to reschedule those shows as soon as possible. You can actually feel the excitement humming throughout the arena, not just from the fans, but from us as well.

The lights dim, the crowd starts to cheer, and just as Mabel takes her first step toward the stage, Red throws himself in front of her.

"Stop. We have to get to the cars."

Before any of us can even ask what's happening, the lights in the arena turn on, the whole crowd groaning from the shock of the lights. I can barely make out an announcement asking attendees to calmly find the nearest exit before we're being shoved down a hallway and herded by Sav, Mabel, and Jonah's security details.

"Where's Callie?" I ask, craning my neck to find her. "What's going on? Where's Callie?"

There are a lot of frightened, anxious faces backstage—roadies and venue employees rushing about, directed by police and security guards —but none of them belong to Callie. My throat tightens and my heart starts to race. My feet stop working.

"Where the fuck is Callie?"

"She's okay," Red says. "She'll meet us outside. Walk."

"What the fuck is going on, Red?" Mabel's voice is high-pitched and shaking as we rush down the hallway.

"There's been a threat. That's all I know right now."

I turn immediately, ready to rush to the VIP tent, but Red throws his body in front of mine.

"Callie and Levi are with Damon and Craig. They will meet us back at the hotel. Walk."

I let myself be shoved down the hall toward the exit doors, and the moment I step into the night air, I scan the darkness. The traffic noise is loud, but it's blended with muffled sounds of the announcements being made inside the arena and the buzz of the concertgoers evacuating out into the street. Still no Callie. No Damon and no Craig.

"What the actual fuck is happening?" Sav asks, turning wide eyes on Red. "Was someone hurt? Is Levi okay?"

Red doesn't answer, and my skin crawls.

"Red," I bark. "Was someone hurt?"

"I don't know yet," he says quickly. "We need to get back to the hotel."

In a daze, we're split up and shoved into cars to be shuttled back to the hotel. We're dropped at an entrance off the street and snuck into the elevator, trying to avoid the growing crowd of reporters in the lobby. The moment the elevator doors open on our floor, I run into the suite and find it empty. One by one, my band members and their security details appear, but no Callie. I take deep breaths and try to stay calm, but I'm failing. I can feel myself succumbing to panic.

"Where are they?" I say, flinging myself on Hammond the moment he steps through the door. "What the fuck is going on?"

Sav's hands are clutched together in front of her body, face twisted up with worry. Levi isn't here either, and the expression of fear on her pale face is exactly how I imagine I look. It's certainly how I feel.

"An arena security guard found a backpack with three guns stashed near a trashcan on the club level."

To Hammond's credit, his voice stays steady, but the news is no less shocking. Mabel gasps. Jonah curses under his breath. My stomach clenches.

"Do they know how they got there?" Sav asks, voice trembling. "Do we think it was...I mean...was it meant for our show?"

I know what she's thinking. What we're all thinking. It's her stalker.

"We don't know yet. We're working on it."

The room falls silent seconds before the door to the suite opens, and it's like a tidal wave of relief hits me when I finally set my eyes on Callie. I rush to her and wrap her in my arms. She feels cold and she's trembling slightly.

"Are you okay? Are you hurt?" I rub my hands up and down her back trying to soothe her. "It's okay. You're here. It's okay."

She shakes her head against my neck, and I hear her sniffle as her shoulders start to shake. I hold her closer.

"It's okay," I whisper. "It's okay." I look up and make eye contact with Damon. "What happened?"

"Evacuating from the floor was a bit chaotic," Damon says slowly. "Some pushing and shoving. A lot of yelling. It was...overwhelming."

I nod and tighten my hold on Callie. "Let's go lie down. They'll tell us when they learn something."

She shakes her head and pulls back. "My sister. My mom. I need to check on them."

"We can call them. I'm sure they're fine."

"No. No, Torren." Callie lets go of me so she can pull her phone out of her back pocket. "I got this from Glory. I didn't see it until after we were in the car coming back here."

Callie hands me her phone, a text thread with her sister open on the screen. I scan a few texts between Callie and Glory about the show tomorrow, then there's a message from Glory that says, "okay, fancy." I furrow my brow and scroll to find a photo of a bouquet of calla lilies.

For a moment, it doesn't register what I'm seeing. At first, I think

Callie sent her sister a photo of the bouquet she got in New York, but then I see the background of the photo. It's Callie's kitchen. My eyes widen as the realization takes over, and I whip my eyes back to Callie.

"Were these delivered to them?"

"I don't know," Callie says, voice trembling. "They're not answering their phones now. Mom or Glory. I'm trying not to freak out, but...I just think I need to go to them. I just need to check on them. I can be there in thirty minutes."

"No. No, I'll figure it out, okay? I'm sure they're fine. It's past nine, now, so they're probably in bed. It's okay."

"Glory never goes to bed this early."

I smooth my hands down her hair. "Did you show Damon?"

"Yeah. He said he'd look into it."

"See? It's okay. I know it's hard, but just stay calm." I wrap her in my arms once more. "God, I'm so fucking glad you're safe."

"Me too."

I press a kiss to her head and close my eyes, breathing through the absolute terror I had felt just minutes earlier. If something had happened to her...

"C'mon," I whisper. "Try to rest a little. They'll figure it all out soon."

Callie nods and lets me lead her to one of the attached rooms. It's empty but for some of Mabel's things, and I pull the sheets back and sit Callie on the bed. I kick off my shoes, then kneel to the ground and pull off hers before urging her to scoot over. Just as I move to climb in with her, there's a knock at the door connected to the suite.

"Torren, I need to speak to you."

Hammond's voice is clipped, and I sigh, forcing a tired smile on my lips. Like I'd hoped, Callie returns it.

"I need to go humor Ham," I say, pressing a kiss to her forehead. "You stay here and rest."

"Sure."

"Everything is okay," I repeat, forcing confidence in my tone. "We'll see Glory and your mom tomorrow."

Callie smiles, and I head back into the suite. Mabel is sitting on the couch, but Sav, Levi and Jonah are missing. I make eye contact with Hammond, and he jerks his head to the door heading into the hallway.

Without question, I follow him. Hammond leads me down the hall and into another empty suite, presumably the one Jonah and I would be staying in if we were staying in this hotel. When I find Jonah inside, my assumption is confirmed, but then I see Damon, Craig, and two people I've never seen before. A woman in a pantsuit, and a man in a police uniform. I arch a brow and look right at Hammond.

"What's going on?"

"I've got something I'd like you to watch." Hammond holds his hand out to one of the strangers and is handed a tablet. "This is security footage from the club level of the arena. I want you to tell me if you recognize the person wearing the baseball hat."

I nod, but I can't bring myself to say anything as I train my eyes on the tablet. The woman next to me reaches over and pushes play, then surveillance video covers the screen. My heart is thundering, echoing in my head as I watch the footage.

A man in a baseball hat comes into the frame holding a black backpack. He keeps his head down, but something about the way he moves, about the hunch of his shoulders, makes my skin feel tight and uncomfortable. It's eerily familiar yet wholly foreign, and I find myself holding my breath. I don't breathe as I watch him set the backpack next to a trashcan, and then he paces. The quickness of his gait, the unnatural thinness of his frame. Chills skate down my back.

"No," I whisper. No one responds.

The man peeks his head into the arena a few times, making sure to duck away whenever someone comes close, and then he takes a phone out of his pocket. He seems to send a text, a move that makes his hands visible. I focus on the tattoos covering his fingers, and then on the jagged scar on his forearm, just before he takes off running.

My jaw drops, and I shake my head, but I can't bring myself to speak yet.

"Do you know who that was, Mr. King?"

I look into the eyes of the woman. Instead of answering her, I deflect.

"Who are you?"

It's Hammond who answers.

"Torren, this is Detective Amy Gallagher and Officer Stuart Draft." When I bring my attention to Hammond, he's frowning at me. "I need you to tell me if you recognized who that was in the video."

When I don't speak, Jonah scoffs, and I whip my eyes to him. There's a slight mocking smile curling his lips, anger coming off him in waves. He sneers at me.

"You're a fucking coward."

"That video doesn't mean shit."

"Are you fucking kidding me, right now?" Jonah takes a step toward me. "You saw exactly what I saw, and I know who that was."

I grit my teeth, my jaw popping under the pressure. "He wouldn't do this."

"That backpack—the one your deadbeat felon brother stashed behind the trash can—that backpack had fucking guns in it." He steps so close to me that I can smell alcohol on his breath mixed with spearmint gum. "What the fuck is Sean doing with three guns at our show, Torren?"

"Back up."

"You think it was an accident? Maybe he forgot to take the three fucking Glocks out of his bag, huh?"

"He wouldn't..."

The defense dies on my tongue as my head starts to spin, and Jonah lets out a taunting laugh. I try my best to ignore him and turn my attention to Ham.

"How'd he get the guns in? There are metal detectors everywhere."

"We're still looking into that," the detective says.

I drag a hand through my hair, trying and failing to get control of my errant thoughts. Sean. Fucking *Sean*. He brought a gun to my show? Why? I know he resents how successful the band is now. I know he hates us for kicking him out right before we made it big. But a gun? *Three* fucking guns? What the hell was he going to do? Kill us? Kill our fans?

The realization makes me dizzy.

He brought three guns to an arena filled with nearly twenty thousand people. If someone hadn't found that backpack...

"Do you know where he is now?" I ask, opening my eyes once more and setting them on the grim faces staring at me.

"We're still searching. Now that you've made an ID, we can put out an APB. We've swept the hotel, and we've set up a patrol—"

"You think we're in danger?" I cut the detective off. "You think he'll come after one of us?"

Jonah laughs again, and I scowl in his direction.

"He's been fucking stalking Sav, Torren. He's not just going to go away."

"The fuck are you talking about? He hasn't been stalking Sav."

"God, you're such a fucking moron. Use your fucking head, would you? Who else would hate seeing you and Sav dating? Who else would want to send Sav death threats anytime there's even a hint that you're fucking her?"

My eyes widen as Jonah's image goes fuzzy around the edges. His voice wobbles as he speaks, my ears straining to hear him over my own labored breathing. The letters Sav got from her stalker...they always called her a cunt. Over and over. A cheating cunt. A lying cunt.

A cunt *bitch*.

My brother's voice from my recent visit home blares in my head, and as I remember his words, I can see them written in the same font as Sav's letters. Like it should have been glaringly obvious all along.

Not dating that cunt lead singer anymore.

You chose that cunt bitch's band over me.

Still the cunt bitch's lap dog.

The realization must show on my face, because Jonah claps his hands together. Once, twice, three times, until I'm dragging my eyes back to his sneering face.

"And now that you're done with Savannah, he's moved on to Callie."

"What?" I fist my hands at my sides, resisting the urge to swing. To cut off his taunting voice.

"The fucking flowers, Tor? The calla lilies? Sav's letters stop but then Callie starts getting flowers? You think it's just a fucking coincidence? Or maybe he came to shoot up the place tonight because *sources* now say you're sticking your dick in both of them. Either way you flip it, this is your fucking fau—"

I swing.

My knuckles connect with the bridge of his nose, a sickening crunch vibrating through my wrist and forearm. Jonah stumbles backward, hands moving to cover his face as blood gushes down his lips and chin. He lets out a laugh that tapers into a groan.

"Fuck you, Torren."

I watch him sit onto the couch and drop his head between his knees, then I turn back to the other people in the room. The two strangers look extremely uncomfortable, but Hammond looks irritated.

"Was that really necessary?"

I shake my hand out and nod. "Yeah, it fucking was."

Hammond flicks his eyes over my shoulder and assesses Jonah cooly. He's now slumped back on the couch with his head resting on the cushion, neck and shirt covered in blood. I don't wait to see if the bleeding stops. I don't ask if he's okay. I'll apologize later.

"I'm going back to Callie. Come get me when you find him."

I leave the room without another word. I bypass the door to the other suite and instead walk directly to the room where I left Callie. I knock, but there's no answer. She's probably sleeping, so I pull the keycard from my wallet and open the door as quietly as I can.

I walk on light feet toward the bed. I have every intention of climbing under the blankets and holding her against me for as long as possible, but I find the bed empty, and even before I rush through the door connected to the suite, I know she's gone.

40

TORREN

"Where is she?"

Savannah glances up at me from her spot on the couch. She's got her legs thrown over Levi's lap with her lyric notebook on the coffee table, and her beat-up acoustic is resting on the cushion beside her.

"Where is who?"

She's still wearing the outfit she wore for the show, and the Caveat Lover tank top taunts me as I try not to lose my shit. I have to clench my fists to keep from shaking her. To make her answer me. To make her stop wasting time.

"Callie." I scan the room quickly. "She was just here. Where is she?"

Mabel is sitting on the floor next to Sav, staring at the ceiling with her headphones on, but when she sees me, her brow furrows and she slips them off. Mabes hasn't changed out of her outfit either. Jonah is probably still slumped over where I left him, bleeding all over his vintage Nirvana T-shirt from the jab I landed to his nose.

"She's not in the room?"

Sav's voice is laced with panic as she bolts up from the couch and crosses the floor of the hotel suite. My stomach twists with anxiety as I take out my phone and dial her number. I listen to it ring and ring before it goes to voicemail.

Sav swings the door wide to the connecting room and disappears inside. I know she won't find Callie in there. I already checked. Instead,

I check the bathroom and the other two bedrooms while dialing Callie's number again.

"Fuck," Sav says, and I turn to find her staring into a small, sleek designer handbag. "My keys are gone. I think she took my keys." She drags her eyes to mine and chills race up my spine at the way her face goes ashen. "Why would she leave now? She was out there when—"

I push past Sav without an answer. I don't stick around to hear her finish the sentence. I know what happened out there. I don't want to recount it.

Just before I reach the door, Red steps in front of me and puts his big hand on my shoulder. It doesn't matter that I'm almost thirty—Red makes me feel like a teenager trying to sneak out after curfew. I'd laugh at the thought if I wasn't on the verge of succumbing to my panic.

"Let me go, Red."

He shakes his head. "Can't do that, kid."

"I have to get to Callie. She's alone. She's upset. She's not answering her phone. I need to get to her."

His stern expression doesn't change, but I think I see a flicker of concern in his eyes.

"You don't know where she went."

He speaks slowly and with authority, studying my face as he does. He's going to shut me down again. He'll probably bind me to the chair with my own bootlaces in the name of safety. I've always appreciated that behavior when it was out of concern for Sav, but now, when I'm the focus, I hate it. I narrow my eyes and open my mouth to argue, but Sav steps up behind me and cuts me off.

"She's in my Porsche," Sav says, her hand reaching past in my periphery, holding something toward Red. "The tracker says she's heading toward Santa Monica."

I drop my attention to the phone screen. The security tracker Red put on all of Savannah's vehicles shows a little red dot heading west on the freeway.

"She's going home." My heart sinks, but I steel my resolve. "I'm going, Red. You'll have to beat me bloody to keep me here."

"Go with him if you're worried," Sav says, but Red shakes his head.

"I'm not leaving you."

"For Christ's sake, Red," Sav says, putting her hands on her hips.

"This place is crawling with security. It's been swept twice already. I'm fine. *We're* fine. Go with Torren or you're fired."

A flicker of humor flashes in Red's eyes. He knows she's full of shit. She threatens to fire him at least once a week, and we all know she never would.

Finally, he nods, and I follow as he strides out the door.

In a matter of minutes that feel like hours, we're in the underground garage and he's tossing me a new set of keys. I follow his lead and swing my leg over a black sport bike, taking a moment to shove the helmet on my head. Red starts his bike, so I start mine, and then I follow him out of the garage and toward the freeway.

Behind Red, I weave in and out of cars, moving onto the shoulder when traffic starts to thicken. It's late at night, way past rush hour, so it shouldn't be this congested right now. The coil of anxiety tightens in my stomach, and despite my rational mind screaming at me to stay calm, I can't. I have to get to her. I just have to make sure she's okay.

I speed up, blowing past Red and racing as fast as I can down the shoulder of the freeway. So fast that the cars on the road seem gridlocked and at a standstill. Faster than is safe, but all I can think about is getting to Callie. My heart speeds along with the bike. My need to get to her clouding my logic and taking over my instincts.

I can feel it, though.

In my stomach, in my chest, I know something is wrong.

The scene is revealed all at once, but my mind registers it in slow motion, one devastating detail at a time.

The cars are indeed at a standstill. No one on either side of the freeway is moving.

Flashing lights materialize into vehicles, and I slow the bike just enough so I can drop it to the pavement and take off at a run toward them.

A fire truck blares on its horn in the distance. A cop car parks on the shoulder thirty yards away. It's like scanning a junk yard. It's like a still from an apocalyptic movie, and I know. I *know* Callie is here somewhere.

The smell of burning rubber and gasoline stings my nose. My eyes start to water. More horns blare. Sirens wail. People cry out for help.

Among the wreckage, I hear shouts of first responders arriving, and

I want to scream at them. Hurry. Find her. Run faster. How am I here first? Why aren't they helping? Why aren't they hurrying? A helicopter arrives overhead as my feet crunch over broken glass.

My eyes scan over the wreckage decorating every lane of the freeway. Skid marks and ashes. Car parts and broken glass. Papers blowing about, soaked with water and stuck to the pavement. A shoe. A child's car seat. I take note of four vehicles, all with varying degrees of damage, before I find the one I'm looking for.

And when I finally see it, all the air is sucked from my lungs.

Sav's red Porsche is upside down, crammed between two other vehicles, and I take off at a run toward it. Panic lodges in my throat, my feet moving slower than I want them to as I scan my eyes over the wreckage.

It's like an impressionist sculpture, the way the metals are twisted and skewed. The Porsche is only a two-seater. It's small to begin with, but now...it's accordioned. Like a beer can after you step on it.

It's eerily silent.

There are noises coming from everywhere right now—shouting, crying, sirens–but as I reach Sav's Porsche, I hear nothing. The hairs on my arms, on the back of my neck, stand on end, and chill bumps cover every inch of my skin.

The car next to Sav's Porsche is black, and when I'm close enough, I realize it's a soft-top convertible. A metal rod protrudes from the top, glinting in the red and blue flashing lights, and there is a person in the front seat. They're slumped over the steering wheel, not moving or calling for help. Briefly, I wonder if I should check on them, if there is anything I can do, but my feet don't stop. My body has other plans. I walk until I'm at the front of Sav's car, then I drop myself to the ground.

"Callie. Callie, baby, can you hear me?"

My knees and palms sting from the shards of broken glass littering the pavement. When I can't see into the car, I flatten myself to the ground, slicing my forearms and abdomen, too.

No sound. No movement. But then...

I see her hair. Covering the roof of the car. Shielding her features from me. It's plastered to her face, and I reach out gently and try to brush it away, but it's wet. For a fraction of a breath, I think it's not Callie in this car because this hair is black.

But then it hits me.

Not black. Blood.

"Baby..." I choke on the word and reach through the window, seeking out her hand. "Baby, I'm here. Can you hear me?"

I turn my head and yell out into the night.

"Somebody help! Somebody! I need a paramedic over here!"

I turn back to Callie. I find her right hand. It's warm, but limp, and I rub her knuckles with my thumb. I use my other hand to gently move sticky strands of hair off her beautiful face.

"Firebird, baby, I'm here, okay, but I need you to wake up. I need you to wake up, okay?"

I turn and shout behind me once more, screaming for help. For anyone to come save the love of my life as tears stream down my cheeks.

"Torren." I flinch as Red's voice sounds from above me, cutting off my screaming. "Just hang on. I'll get them." I listen as his boots pound off in search of help.

I lay my face flat on the ground, then tilt so I can see Callie better. So I'm almost suspended upside down like she is. Everything about it is unnatural and wrong, the way her body hangs from the seat belt. The way her hand doesn't so much as twitch in mine.

I move my thumb to her wrist and try to take a pulse, but I feel nothing. I don't even know if I'm doing it right. The last time I tried to take a pulse was when Jonah had overdosed, and I couldn't find one that time, either.

I squeeze my eyes and give my head a shake as an image of Jonah's lifeless body invades my head, blending with the horror taking place right in front of me. No.

I open my eyes and focus back on Callie.

"Baby, please. Please, just hold on, okay? I'm going to get you help, but I need...I need you to hold on. I can't...I can't lose you, okay? Okay, Calla Lily?"

I rub my thumb over her hand and ignore the stickiness of blood. I keep my eyes on the side of her face and stare at her lips, begging for them to move. I ignore the blood there, too. It doesn't matter. If I could reach, I would kiss her.

This can't be how it ends. This can't be happening.

I squeeze my eyes shut, blinking away more tears before I settle my attention back on the side of her lifeless face. I can't look away. I *won't* look away.

"Someone is coming," I whisper, hovering my fingertips over her cheek. Over her lips. "Someone is coming, I promise. Just hold on."

"Torren."

A weak, raspy whisper. At first, it's so quiet, I think I imagined it. If I hadn't been looking at her mouth, I might have missed it entirely.

"Torren."

"I'm here, baby. I'm here." I swallow back the urge to sob and try to keep my voice as steady as possible. I fail, but I try. "You just...you just hang in there, baby. There's been an accident, but someone is coming, and then I can take you home, okay?"

"Torren."

I rub my thumb over her hand some more and do my best to keep her talking. Every instinct in my body says to keep her talking, even if it's just a single word. Even if it's only my name. God, just let her keep saying my name.

"What if you teach me how to play piano, Firebird? Would you do that for me?"

Silence.

"I love hearing you play. Remember last night when we played 'Heart and Soul' together?"

Silence.

"Can I tell you what I imagined last night? I imagined sitting with you at that piano and listening to you play every night. Beethoven and Bach and Chopin."

Silence.

"Can you see it, baby? Can you see it?"

Silence.

"Just hang in there, okay? Just...just don't go. Please, baby. Please, Firebird. Someone is coming. Please don't go."

Silence.

41

CALLIE

I HEAR VOICES.

Faint, whispered conversation in a language I should know, but can't make out. Two people. No three. Voices that fill me with warmth. That sound like music and home. That feel like smooth, rich honey and salty, ocean air. I see flames dancing on the backs of my eyelids. Strong, decorated fingers holding a lit match. Full lips. Secrets.

I listen more closely, deciphering words through the haze.

Weeks. Sleep. Recovery.

Go home, someone says. *We'll stay with her.*

I want to be here when she wakes up.

Weeks. Sleep. Recovery.

I'm not leaving.

Warmth encases my hand. A familiar sensation, both soft and rough. My fingers squeeze, and I tell myself to squeeze back. I try. I try again.

Nothing.

"I'm here, Firebird."

Green eyes. Lit matches. Full lips.

"I'm right here. I miss you, but take all the time you need, baby. I'll be here when you're ready."

Loud music. Silver rings. White teeth.

"I love you, Calla Lily Sunrise James. I'm right here."

Torren.

My throat aches.

I try to swallow to ease the pain. I feel like I'm swallowing sand. My chest burns, and all I want is water. Ice water. Gallons of it.

My eyelids are sticky and heavy as I force them open, but the light in the room burns, so I have to force them shut again.

"Fuck."

It comes out more as a cough than an actual word. My voice sounds strange in my head, and my mouth feels like it was stuffed with cotton balls. I try to open my eyes again, this time more slowly, letting the light in bit by bit. It still stings, but less so, until I'm able to peer through my lashes into an unfamiliar room with cream-colored walls.

"Callie?"

I turn my head toward the sound.

"Glory?"

"Oh my god, Callie."

She rushes to me with her arms outstretched like she's going to hug me, but she stops just before she reaches me and drops her arms back to her sides. The tears streaming down her face fill me with immediate fear.

"Is Mom okay?"

My anxiety is punctuated by a beeping. It grows faster as my panic rises.

"Callie, no. She's...she's..."

Glory's face contorts with pain, tears falling faster, and my only thought is my mother. Something happened to her. She's hurt. She's dead. I open my mouth to ask for answers, but then someone looms over me and everything goes dark and silent.

It's late when I wake up.

I can tell because there's no light filtering through the curtains on the window. I look around slowly, seeking out the beeping, and find it coming from a machine beside my bed. I squint at it. Listen again to the steady beeping...

Vitals.

The machine is monitoring my vitals.

The realization appears as though out of a fog, slowly taking shape around the edges. I'm hooked to a machine that is monitoring my vitals. I don't recognize this room. I don't recognize this bed...

I'm in a hospital.

I look around again. It's dark except for the light seeping in from the hallway, but I can still make out some furniture. A chair. A couch. And...

I reach out and run my fingers lightly through Torren's curls. They're longer than I remember, and they stand out starkly against the shock white of my hospital blanket. I trail my fingers over his sharp cheekbone, to his jaw, then over his lips. They're chapped and rough on my fingertips.

"Callie."

Hot breath ghosts over my hand as his lips move with the whisper of my name. Then slowly, as if scared he'll spook me, he lifts his head. His eyes land on mine, leaving only briefly to scan my face before they grow glassy with tears.

"Is this real?"

The child-like fear in his voice makes my heart break, and I nod as tears of my own fall.

"It's real."

Softly, his hands frame my face, green eyes jumping from feature to feature like he doesn't trust me. Like he needs to make certain himself.

"It's real," I say again. "I promise."

He kisses me, lips tasting like tears, and I kiss him back.

"I missed you. I missed you so fucking much."

I nod, but I don't speak. I don't know if I missed him. I don't know how long I've been in this bed hooked to a machine monitoring my vitals while he slept in my lap. I don't know how much of what I'm remembering is just my imagination. I don't know anything except...

"I love you."

Torren whimpers. I feel his fingers trembling in my hair. He's hovering, barely touching me, but I wish he would. I wish he would kiss me harder. I wish he would hold me.

"I love you," I say again, louder this time, and it hurts. My voice sounds ragged and raw.

Torren releases a choked, breathy sob.

"I love you, Callie. So, so much." He looks at me like he's still waiting to find out this is a dream. Like it's all one big prank. His eyes drag over my face, then up and down my body. "How do you feel? Do you feel okay? Does it hurt?"

I smile softly and shake my head. "What happened?"

He flinches and blinks before answering. "You were in an accident."

I nod slowly. "On the I-10."

His eyes go wide. "You remember?"

"Sort of. I remember driving home. I remember taillights. I remember slamming on my brakes and swerving, and then..."

I trail off as I remember something else...Glory...my mom...the pictures. My eyebrows shoot up with a gasp.

"Glory. Mom. Are they okay? Did something—"

"They're fine. Everything is fine. They're both safe. They were never in any danger."

I shake my head. "But the pictures? The text..."

Torren tilts his head to the side slowly, his eyebrows slanting harshly with concern. "What pictures?"

"I got a text. Pictures of Glory leaving the apartment. I just..." I furrow my eyebrows and sift through my muddled memory before finding what I'm looking for. "Glory always answers her phone, but she wasn't. No one was. I wanted to check on them, but everyone was gone, and I couldn't...I just thought..."

"That's why you left...? Someone sent you pictures of Glory?"

Torren says it slowly, as if he's confused. He's trying to understand, but it makes me defensive. It makes me angry, and all the emotions I'd had when I got the text surge back through my system.

"Yes, Torren. Creepy pictures. Like she didn't know they were being taken, and I didn't know the number. I got them right after I saw the text from Glory of the flowers...oh god..."

I stare down at my bed, eyes frantically searching back and forth as if the answers will appear in my lap. Distantly, I hear the beeping from my monitor speed up, and I breathe. I breathe.

"We'd just had to evacuate the concert," I say, trying not to panic, clawing for clarity. "I saw Glory had gotten flowers. Then I got this creepy text with pictures of her, and they weren't answering their phones. I was worried, but everyone was busy. Sav and Levi and Red were on a video call, and Mabel was on the phone in her room, and you were in a meeting, and everyone was fucking busy, so I thought, you know, it's late, so traffic is probably light. I could be there in thirty minutes. It wouldn't take long. I was just worried. I wanted to make sure it was nothing."

Despite my rising anxiety and the tense set to Torren's shoulders and jaw, he continues to speak slowly. He rubs his thumb over my hand. His voice stays even, and I try to match his calm. I latch on to it and breathe.

"Your mom was asleep, and your sister was out with a boy. They were and are perfectly safe."

"Oh, thank god," I whisper. My body slumps with relief and my eyes sting. "Those pictures," I continue, shaking my head. "The flowers. I just...I just needed to make sure. It's not like I could have known that this would—"

"No. No, I know. This isn't your fault. You didn't know there would be an accident. No one could have known."

My thoughts begin a new spiral, this time focusing on my mistakes. I scold myself for being so impulsive. For overreacting. If I hadn't left. If I'd have just waited. Hell, if I had taken a different route, I wouldn't have been in an accident, and I wouldn't be here. Instead of sitting in this hospital bed, I'd be going to tonight's show with Glory and my mom.

Fuck. *The show.*

"What are you doing about the show tonight? Are you still playing?"

Torren's face falls and his lips part, but he doesn't speak right away. The longer he's silent, the more my skin starts to prickle with anxiety. Then he shakes his head once.

"No. The shows were cancelled and will be rescheduled."

In the silence that follows, I search his face. I note the scruff on his jaw when he's usually clean-shaven. And his hair...it *is* longer. Then it dawns on me.

"How long have I been here?"

He swallows once before he answers. "Twelve days."

"Twelve days?"

My jaw drops as I try to wrap my head around the number. That's almost two weeks. I look back at his hair. Two weeks' worth of growth. Has he not left? Has he been here this whole time?

"How?"

Torren's face goes ashen and tears well in his eyes once more. I brace myself for the worst, but I don't look away. "Tell me. I can handle it. Please."

"The accident was pretty bad." His voice cracks, and I track a tear as it slips down his cheek. He sniffs, uses the hand not clutching mine to wipe his eyes, and continues, slow and steady. "They had to cut you out of the Porsche and airlift you. You had head trauma and internal bleeding in your abdomen. They performed emergency surgery, and then they induced a coma to allow your body to heal. Then they took you out of the coma, and tonight you woke up."

He trails off with a forced smile, but I can tell there's more he's not saying. There's something he doesn't want to talk about.

"You're leaving something out," I say slowly. His face tightens, and my stomach twists. "Just tell me, Torren."

He jerks out a nod. "They were able to stop the internal bleeding, but...the accident... There were six other cars. You swerved, but the car behind you didn't. The Porsche rolled twice and then was T-boned. The driver's side took a significant impact. You're lucky to be alive..."

"But?"

The pause is a physical pain that I can feel swelling inside my chest. I can hear it whooshing in my ears. When he finally speaks, it's how I imagine the accident would have felt if I could remember it.

"Your left forearm and hand were broken pretty badly. They've already done three surgeries, but—"

Torren's voice fades into static as I realize I can't move my left arm. I look down and find it wrapped and pinned into some sort of cage. And then, all at once, it starts to throb. Sharp, consistent pain radiating from my fingertips to my shoulder, to the side of my face. My head pounds.

"Oh my god." I try to move my fingers, then gasp in pain. "Oh my god." I whip terrified eyes to his. "Why am I only now...How come I couldn't..."

"Pain meds," he forces out. "Disorientation from the coma, I guess."

A thought hits me that seizes the air in my lungs. A question so terrifying that I can barely form it on my tongue, but Torren knows. He can see it in my face, and when his tears fall faster, my whole world tilts on its side. I fist my right hand, tucking my trembling fingers into my palm, and force myself to utter the words on a shaky whisper.

"Will I be able to play again?"

His silence tells me everything I need to know.

———

It's mid-morning when I wake again.

The sun is streaming into the room, illuminating cream-colored walls and ugly grayish-beige tile, and I'm alone.

All at once, the news washes back over me. A freight train of heartbreak.

Will I be able to play again?

Deafening silence.

They had to come sedate me. Again.

I clamp my eyes shut and try to focus on something else. I wiggle my toes. I flex the fingers on my right hand. I breathe in and out.

It's fine. I'm alive. My family is safe.

It will be fine.

When my stomach cramps, I find a button next to my bed and push it. A nurse arrives immediately.

"Ms. James." She smiles warmly. "It's good to see you awake. Are you in pain?"

"I, um, I actually have to use the bathroom."

"Okay. Would you like to attempt the restroom, or would you prefer a bedpan?"

I wince, then give her a weak smile. "Bathroom, please."

She gets to work unhooking my arm cage and helping me into some sort of sling. It hurts like hell—my arm, my stomach, my head—and several times I feel dizzy because of it, but I'm determined to make it to the bathroom. The nurse helps transfer me and all my "accessories" to a wheelchair, then slowly, she brings me to the bathroom.

My legs are weak. I'm unstable on my feet, and each movement seems to shoot pain through every inch of my body, so I need a lot of help. The nurse must be able to tell that it frustrates me, because when she speaks, her tone is warm and encouraging. I'm sure she sees this a lot. Hell, I'm sure she sees worse.

"Take it easy, Ms. James. You've had several major surgeries. It's going to take you some time to adjust."

We have to be careful of the incision site on my abdomen. We have to be careful of the wound on my head. We have to be careful of the mess of metal and bone dust that is now my arm. I push through all the pain and make it to the bathroom, determined to succeed in this small, normal task that suddenly feels like climbing Everest, but the unexpected thing sends me over the edge is that I'm wearing adult briefs.

I start to sob.

I sit on the toilet, hooked to an IV bag with my ruined arm in a vise and three separate major surgical sites on my body, and I sob over the fact that I'm wearing an adult diaper.

Even the crying hurts.

When I'm washing my hand, I keep my head down and avoid the mirror. I focus on lathering soap through my fingers and over my palm, then let the nurse help get the back of my hand and wrist. Just before she wheels me back to my bed, I take a deep breath and look up at my reflection.

I blink. I blink again.

A part of my head has been shaved. White gauze and tape cover what I'm assuming are sutures. The hair that's left is greasy and stringy, hanging around my shoulders. There's also a bandage on my left cheek. I could feel it there when I woke up. I could even see the gauze from the corner of my eye, but I was so focused on everything else that hurt...

"Can you take this off?"

I glance at the nurse through the mirror. Her face gives nothing away.

"We can go ahead and change it."

She puts on a new pair of gloves and steps in front of me. I watch her face as she peels my bandage off carefully. She cleans my skin, pressing gently, then steps out of the way, allowing me to finally see my reflection.

"It's healing well. We can leave the bandage off if it's been irritating you."

I don't answer her as I stare at my reflection. There's bruising and swelling on the left side of my face, and a laceration, maybe three inches long, slashes across my cheek. The skin around it is red and inflamed, but I imagine it looked even worse before someone with expert hands sutured it back together.

But still...

I clear my throat and tear my eyes away from the mirror to look back at the nurse.

"How badly will all of this scar?"

I almost want to laugh at the vanity in the statement. I'm lucky to be alive, but here I am worrying about scarring and sobbing over wearing a diaper. I bite my tongue on the urge to apologize, though. It's a valid question. It's an important question. This is my body, the only body I'm going to get, and wanting to know what to expect is normal.

"It will scar, but you had one of the best reconstructive plastic surgeons on it, so it won't be as bad as you think. And as for your head, your hair will grow over it. In a few months, no one will even know."

I nod and look back at the mirror. "Okay."

She places her hand on my shoulder and gives it a squeeze. "I know this is a lot. It's scary and feels overwhelming, but you're going to get through it. Your fiancé brought in the best surgeons in the country to take care of you. No one who touched you after the initial emergency was anything less than top of their field. You're in great hands, Ms. James. I promise."

I stare at her through the mirror, running back over every word. I can't bring myself to speak. I can't bring myself to look back at my reflection, either. I nod instead and let her take me back to my bed.

Just before she leaves, I stop her.

"I'm sorry...I didn't ask your name."

"I'm Kim."

"Thank you, Kim. You can call me Callie."

She smiles again. "You're welcome, Callie. Just hit the button if you need me."

I watch as she leaves, pulling the door shut softly behind her, and then I sink back into my pillow, aching and more exhausted than I've ever been. I close my eyes and feel my body relaxing, surrendering to sleep, but just before I drift off, one word flashes behind my eyelids.

Fiancé.

Torren is here.

I can feel him sitting beside me. I crack my eyes open and see him reading a paperback book. I clamp my eyes back shut and turn away from him. I will him to go away. I'm not ready to see him right now.

"Callie?" His voice is soft at first, but it grows more urgent. "What's wrong? Are you in pain? I'll get Kim."

"No!" I blurt out the word, but I keep my eyes shut and my face turned away. "Can you just...can you just leave?"

I hear him suck in a surprised breath, but he doesn't speak. I can feel his eyes on me, though. I hear his footsteps round the bed, so I turn my head the other way.

"What's going on?" His voice is calm again. Reassuring. Soft, and patient, and so much more than I deserve in this moment. It makes me feel worse. "Why do you want me to leave, Firebird? What's wrong?"

Tears start to leak through my lashes and trickle down my cheeks. I sniff. I attempt to calm my breathing, but all I see when I close my eyes is my own reflection... My half-shaved head of greasy, dirty hair. My dull eyes sunken into my swollen, bruised, lacerated face. My battered, useless arm. I've got an eight-inch-long incision on my stomach. I was wearing a fucking diaper.

And the one thing that made me *me*—my ability to play the piano—is gone.

If I can barely handle the reality of it all, how can I expect him to?

"I don't want you to see me," I whisper finally. "I don't want you to see me like this anymore."

He doesn't speak. Instead, I hear him round the bed again, and he takes my right hand in his. "Why not?"

I don't answer. I can't even bring myself to confess it.

Because I'm ugly. Because I'm horrifying. Because I'm not worthy of him.

Because in the light of day, if he sees what this accident has made me —what my stupid, impulsive decisions have caused—then there's no going back.

I'd rather break my heart before he can. It will hurt less.

When almost a minute passes and I don't answer him, I feel his knuckle notch under my chin.

"Look at me."

I shake my head.

"Firebird, look at me. Please."

Slowly, I open my eyes, blinking to clear them of the tears that were trapped behind my eyelids. I look into his beautiful green eyes to find they're shimmering with tears of his own.

"I am not going anywhere. I am in love with you. I am not leaving your side, and you have never looked more beautiful to me than you do right now. Do you know why?"

"Why?" I whisper as more tears fall.

"Because you're alive."

"But my—"

"Listen to me, Callie. I love you. I loved you before this accident. I love you now. I will love you after you've healed, no matter what that looks like. You, alive and breathing, that's the most beautiful thing in the fucking world to me. Tell me you believe it."

I sniff and laugh lightly, the sound strangled and tired. "Okay. I believe it."

"Never ask me to leave again, okay? Not because of that. Promise?"

His thumb, calloused and familiar, rubs over my jaw. A feather's touch, and I lean into it. I let myself feel it and draw strength from it. I let myself believe him.

"Promise."

42

CALLIE

THE MOMENT TORREN and my mom leave the room, Glory turns to me with wide, apologetic eyes.

"I'm so, so sorry for scaring you before, Cal. I didn't know what to say. I froze and I made it worse and—"

"Glory, no. You didn't do anything wrong. Honestly. I was disoriented and confused. I barely even remember it."

Her face twists into a frown. "But we'd been waiting for days for you to wake up, and then when you did, I freaked you out and then they had to put you back under. I thought for sure Torren would flip."

I furrow my brow. "Did he?"

"No. He said it wasn't my fault. But still. I feel like an asshole."

"You're not an asshole, Glory Bell..." My lips twitch with a small smirk. "Well, not about this, anyway."

Her face goes flat and unamused. "Ha. Ha. Ha."

I smile and suppress a yawn. It's only been two days since I woke up, and I've only spent a matter of hours actually awake, but it feels like I've gone a week straight without sleep.

"Oh, I almost forgot." Glory jumps from her perch at the end of my bed and digs through the large duffle bag my mom brought with her. She pulls out a phone and hands it to me. "The old one was..." She grimaces. I get it. The old one was ruined in the seven-car pile-up. "Well, anyway, this is your new one. We transferred your number and contacts and everything. It's working."

"Thank you, Glor." I tap the screen on, then promptly tap it back off again when I see over three hundred text messages and missed calls. "Jesus."

"Yeah, it's been blowing up. We've already blocked a bunch of reporter numbers, too, but the texts are all legit."

I take a deep breath and drop the phone on my lap. "I'll start going through them later."

Torren and my mom reappear in the doorway with bags of takeout from a local clean-eating restaurant. I have to eat foods that are "gentle" right now, so they are all doing it in solidarity. It's kind of them, but what I really want is a giant cheeseburger or a greasy slice of pizza. Instead, I am handed a leafy salad, light on the dressing, with unseasoned chicken and a dairy-free fruit smoothie. It's delicious despite not being what I want.

"Oh, Sav wants to know if you'll be up for visitors on Monday," Torren says through bites of salad. "I told her probably not, but she threatened my life if I didn't ask."

I furrow my brow realizing I have absolutely no concept of time at the moment. "What day is it?"

"It's Saturday."

Saturday. I don't know if I'll ever wrap my head around just how many days I spent unconscious. I force a smile and nod.

"I'd actually love to see her. Mabel and Jonah, too?"

I don't miss the way Torren doesn't make eye contact when he answers. "Yeah, Mabel will come. Jo probably won't, though. He's got some shit going on."

I wrestle down the questions circling my brain. I think there's a lot I'm still unaware of, and I get the feeling Torren is choosing to reveal all the details slowly. I both hate it and appreciate it. Damn him for already knowing me so well.

"Ezra has started texting me, too," Glory chimes in. "He and the guys want to come see you. I told him to stop texting me and to wait for you to contact him. He's worse than Torren King with the whole need for constant attention thing." She waves her hand in Torren's direction. "The dog, obviously, not you."

Torren snorts out a laugh and shrugs. "I mean, sometimes me."

I don't comment on their exchange as I pick up my phone and send

Sav a text.

> I'd definitely be down for visitors. Fair warning, I look like I've been in a severe car accident.

SAV LOVELESS

Breaking out the dark humor? You must be feeling better.

> Feeling alive, at least. Can you do me a favor when you come?

Anything.

> Can you bring me some hair clippers? Like the kind a barber would use?

Consider it done. See you soon!

"Traveling barbers, at your service."

Mabel comes skipping into the hospital room in a pair of lime green faux-leather shorts, a Van Halen shirt, and black combat boots. She looks like she just walked off the stage. It's a direct contrast to the men's sweats and slouchy tee Sav is sporting behind her.

Sav smirks, then flares her eyes, letting out a low whistle as she scans my face. "You weren't kidding, Cal."

I laugh lightly, tension disappearing from my body the moment she cracks the joke. I didn't realize how worried I was that they'd tiptoe around me. I'm already metaphorically climbing the hospital walls. I want out, and I want things to go back to normal. Or, well, as normal as they possibly can, now.

"Told you," I say with a grimace. "At least seven cars."

"But alive," she adds with a tilt of the head. I mimic the move.

"Alive, indeed." I wince. "Sorry about your car, by the way."

Sav waves me off. "Don't even stress over it. Promise. I won't miss it. I'm just glad you're awake now."

She and I share a smile, one that fixes something small inside me, and then Mabel breaks the silence.

"So, what are we shaving?" She sets a pair of hair clippers on the foot of my bed, then waggles her eyebrows. "Your pussy?"

"Jesus, Mabes." Torren groans just as a choking sound comes from the side of the room. Sav and Mabel turn toward the noise to find my sister sitting wide-eyed on the couch.

"Oh shit. Sorry." Mabel scrunches her nose, flicking her eyes to me before looking back at Glory. "I didn't see you. I didn't actually think we were going to shave her, uh, vulva."

Sav barks out a laugh, then sticks her hand out for my sister to shake.

"You must be Cal's sister, Glory. I'm Sav, and this is Mabel. Thanks for letting us crash your family time."

Glory just nods silently as she shakes Sav's hand. I don't think she even blinks, but Sav is unfazed. She just smiles, then turns back to me.

"Where's your mom?"

"Physical therapy. She got it moved here while I'm in the hospital. She refuses to leave."

Sav grins, then waves her hand around my head. "So... I'm guessing you want us to fix *this*? Are you sure? It's very rock and roll."

I sigh and shake my head. "Please, god, shave it off."

Mabel salutes me. "On it."

Sav and Mabel get to work shaving my head. They're surprisingly gentle. I don't know why I expected something else. They've never been anything but kind to me, but I guess the hard exteriors they portray to the world at large are still difficult to reconcile with their actual personalities sometimes.

When the first chunk of my hair falls to the floor, I make eye contact with Torren. I'm worried I'll see a frown on his face, but he's smiling like he means it. Like he truly isn't bothered that his girlfriend is shaving off all her hair while sporting large, unsightly injuries on her face and head. He smiles like he's just happy to be here with me, and damn if that doesn't do wonders for my confidence.

"Voila." Mabel hands me a compact mirror when they're finished. "What do you think? I like it. Very Sinéad O'Connor."

Sav nods in agreement. "It's pretty badass."

I take a deep breath and open the mirror, then rip off the proverbial Band-Aid. I move the mirror from side to side, surveying my head from different angles. I avoid my face. I don't look directly at the wound on my scalp either. I keep my assessment focused solely on the haircut. It's *just* a haircut. My red tresses will grow back. It's not like it's an important facet of my personality. It's not like it's my ability to play piano... I squeeze my eyes shut and give my head a shake to derail that train of thought. Then, I pretend I'm in a salon and force myself to remain objective.

"I don't hate it, actually."

I snap the compact closed and hand it back to Mabel. It's weird seeing the half of my head that's not sliced open and bruised. It's pale and untouched, and from the right side it almost looks like nothing happened. The buzzed head could easily pass as a fashion choice. To anyone who can't see my left side, anyway. But I mean it. I truly don't hate it.

"Low-key was worried your head would be lumpy or misshapen or something."

I narrow my eyes at my sister, and she throws up her palms.

"What? I was. I'm just saying it looks good. It's totally normal and round. Hooray."

Sav and Mabel crack up laughing, which gets me laughing. It makes my stomach and head and arm ache, but it also feels good. It feels cathartic. It feels like some of the weeks' worth of pain are being purged from my body with each rumble of my chest and gust of air from my lungs.

We spend the next few hours talking and laughing. They don't ask me about my arm, and I'm grateful for that. I don't want to talk about it. I don't want to think about it. And for the time they're here, I almost don't.

After a while, Damon drives Glory back to the hotel where she's been staying with my mom. I didn't even realize Damon was here, but apparently, he's been camping out in the lobby and shuttling my mom and sister to and from the hospital every day. Craig, too. Just another thing Torren didn't disclose right away. He probably knew I'd feel bad. I do.

When Sav and Mabel stand from their chairs, I look at the clock. It's nearly ten. I didn't even realize it was past visiting hours. They kept me entertained and distracted, and without the distraction, I'm left to my own thoughts. My heart sinks. My thoughts always come back to my injuries and my uncertain future with music. The train of thought always starts rolling again.

"Thank you so much for coming and spending today with me," I say honestly. "It was really great to see you guys."

"Of course," Mabel says. "As soon as we knew you were awake, we chartered the jet."

"The jet?" I furrow my brow just as Mabel's eyes go wide. She flicks her eyes to Torren, so I do the same, and I find him frowning at her. Then he looks at me, and his face falls. "Why did you need to charter the jet?" I look between the three members of The Hometown Heartless currently looking guilty in my hospital room, and my anger flares. I'm so sick of tiptoed around. I'm so sick of being remind just how fragile I am. "Would someone just fucking tell me what's going on?"

Sav and Mabel both look to Torren, and he sighs. "It's the last few American shows."

"Oh." My stomach twists, and I have to breathe past the sting of tears that overwhelm me. "Right. Of course. You've got to finish the tour. Yeah." I smile at Torren. "I can't wait to watch you on the live streams."

Torren worries his lower lip. "Baby...*they're* touring. Not me."

"What? Why not?"

When Torren doesn't explain, Sav speaks up. "Well...I think this is a conversation that is best had without us, yeah, Mabes?"

"Yep. Agreed." Mabel and Sav approach my bed, and each give me awkward side hugs to avoid bumping my left arm. "We'll be back soon, okay?"

"Yeah." I nod and take my eyes off Torren long enough to tell them goodbye. "Thanks again. Travel safe."

The second they're out the door, I'm on him. "Explain. How are they touring without you?"

"They have a backup bassist right now."

"Who? Why? How is that possible? You can't skip the tour because of me. That's ridiculous."

"It's Becket Walker. He's doing it because we asked him to, and he said yes. And, Firebird, what's ridiculous is you thinking I would want to be anywhere other than here." He steps forward, holding me with intense eye contact, and crouches by my bed. "The sooner we finish this tour, the sooner we're out of our contract. None of us wanted to postpone, but I wasn't willing to leave you, and honestly, no one wanted me to. We all agreed that getting someone to fill in for me was the best option."

"And you went with *Becket*?" The whole concept is strange to me, but Torren shrugs.

"Yeah. He's been doing a good job, as far as I hear."

I sit with the news for a few breaths, considering everything. It's just...it's just overwhelming, and I start to cry. I've cried so much in the last few days that if it weren't for the IV, I'd probably be dehydrated.

But...

It's also been so fucking long since someone has taken care of me. Since I've been in a position where someone has been able to make me a priority.

I don't resent my mom for her stroke. I don't regret coming home and taking over so I could care for Mom and Glory. But fuck, it was so lonely. It was exhausting. To know that Torren has given up touring so he can sit by my bedside while I heal...it's *everything*.

My guilt is consumed by my gratitude. By the absolute relief I felt when he told me he wasn't leaving me.

"Thank you," I whisper, and he smiles.

"I love you, Calla Lily Sunrise James. Anywhere you are is where I want to be."

"I hear you're being discharged tomorrow."

A tall man with dark curly hair and a white coat stands at the door to my hospital room. He smiles at me with dazzling white teeth, and Torren hops up to shake his hand in one of those low-five type moves.

I smile between them, confused, and the man laughs.

"Apologies. I should introduce myself."

He closes the space between the door and my bed in three strides, his long legs eating up the distance confidently. Something about him makes me relax and brings a smile to my face. If it weren't for the fact that I know without a doubt that I would remember a face like his, I'd swear I knew him from somewhere.

"I'm Jesse." He sticks out his hand to shake mine. "I'm supposed to introduce myself as Dr. Hernandez-Calligaris, but that's a bit of a mouthful, so you can call me Jesse."

I clear my throat as he releases my hand. "Um. Hi. I'm Callie."

He laughs again and gives me another one of his magnetic smiles. "I've been the lead surgeon on your case. You'll be seeing me again in a month for a follow-up, also."

"Oh." I widen my eyes and glance at Torren, then back at Dr. Hernandez-Calligaris. "Did you do this?" I gesture to the wounds on the left side of my face and head where my skin had to be sutured back together.

"No. Actually, that was done by Dr. Vanessa Hernandez. Torren pulled some strings and got her out of semi-retirement. She's got the steadiest hands of anyone I know." He winks at me. "And I'm not just saying that because she's my mom."

I must gape at him because he chuckles. "I know. I don't look a day over twenty-three."

"Wow."

"Wow, indeed. I'm an orthopedic surgeon, but I specialize in hands, specifically."

"He's the best in his field, too," Torren says with a grin. "Don't let him pretend he's humble."

"I get it from my mom." The doctor shrugs with a sly smile that matches Torren's. "I was hoping to take a look at your arm and have a chat with you about your case before they get your cast on tomorrow. Next steps, what to expect, et cetera."

"Yeah, sure. I'd love that, actually."

As the doctor unwraps my arm, he explains each incision and why it's there. The plates in my arm. The bone grafting and pins in my hand. The repair work he conducted on two of my tendons. As he speaks, I have to force myself not to disassociate. I have to remind myself over and over that he's talking about me. This is *my* arm. This is *my* hand. These precise, straight incisions are on *my* skin. Several times, I have to swallow back bile.

"You'll need extensive physical therapy," he tells me as he wraps my arm again. "Torren tells me you play piano."

I nod. "Yeah. I do."

I *did*.

"I kept that in mind during surgery. You had a serious injury here, Callie, and I want to be completely honest with you—"

"I won't play again."

"Now, I didn't say that. In fact, I'm sure you'll be able to play again after physical therapy..."

My heart soars. I bite the inside of my cheek to keep from smiling as the doctor continues to speak.

"...but I can't be certain what level of dexterity and movement you'll recover. We're going to do all that we can, but right now, I can't promise that you'll be able to play anything that requires extensive flexibility or precision."

The hope that had been building collapses as my breath turns to cement. I run through the hundreds of pieces in my head. I focus on the left-hand, on the bass notes, and my heart breaks all over again.

Basically, he's excluding almost everything except beginner-level pieces. Maybe some intermediate. In a way, it almost feels worse than never playing at all. Guilt surges and coils in my chest with the sorrow.

"Right. Of course." I choke out. "I'm sorry. I know I should be grateful that I'll be able to play at all. I should just be grateful to be alive."

"Callie, you're allowed to be upset about this. You're allowed to mourn the life you had before the accident, no matter how much it's changed. It's normal, and completely acceptable. Expected, even."

I look up into the doctor's eyes. Browns and greens swirl together in his irises. They're sincere. He's not just placating me. It makes me feel a little better about thinking my passion has been ripped from my life without mercy.

"Thank you," I say honestly. "I appreciate everything you've done."

"You're welcome." He smiles again, then gestures to Torren. "Your fiancé got me out of bed at midnight and chartered a jet from Chicago so I could be the surgeon that took care of you. I'm honored to help."

When the doctor leaves with a plan to see me in three weeks, I turn my attention to Torren. He's smirking, but he almost looks bashful. I arch a brow, and he talks without me even having to ask.

"I told them I was your fiancé. They wouldn't tell me anything and your mom can't drive, so Damon had to go pick her up, but it was taking forever because of the accident clean up on the freeway, and I was going out of my mind. I'm not sorry for doing it, and I would do it again. It was the only way I knew about your hand, and it's why I was able to make all those calls."

I stare him down for a minute, but I don't bother trying to hide the smile that curves my lips. I also don't fight the tears that, once again, well in my eyes.

"Thank you. Seriously. I just...I don't know what I would have done without you. You didn't have to do it, but I'm so grateful you did."

Something sad flickers in his green eyes, but it disappears quickly, and he smiles.

"I'm in love with you. Don't you know that by now? I'd set myself on fire if I knew you'd rise from the ashes, Firebird. I would do anything for you. I'm in love with you. I'm not going anywhere."

"Good," I whisper, my chest warming with the truth I hear in his words. "Me, too."

43

TORREN

"Yeah, this is Torren King. I'm returning a call."

I take a drag from my cigarette and blow the smoke through my nose while the receptionist puts me on hold. For the tenth time since dialing this number, I look through the glass doors that lead to my bedroom. Callie is still sleeping, and if tonight is anything like every other night since she was discharged, she'll be out for at least a few more hours.

When the hold music clicks off, I don't bother turning back around. I don't care about the view from my terrace. The view of Callie, sleeping soundly in my bed, is much more appealing. More than that, even. It's *necessary*.

Lately, I have to remind myself not to stare at her. It makes her uncomfortable—she's sensitive about the lacerations—but I need frequent reassurance. I need to know, for certain, that she's here and safe. She's alive. I need to know that I'm not going to wake up from this dream only to realize I'm actually living a nightmare.

I blink away the images that try to invade my mind and take another long drag from my cigarette as a familiar voice on the other end of the phone greets me. The same voice I heard in my voicemail inbox yesterday.

"Mr. King, hello. This is Detective Gallagher. We met at the hotel a few weeks ago."

"I remember." I flick the charred end of my cigarette into the ashtray, once again forcing away memories of that night. "I'm assuming this is about my brother."

"It is. I wanted to let you know that we've apprehended your brother. He returned to your mother's house in Florida two nights ago. We had the house under surveillance, so we were able to arrest him before he even made it through the front door."

I wait for the surge of sympathy. Of guilt. The emotions used to be inevitable any time my brother or mother were the topic of conversation. That internal conflict has always been familiar and insistent, so I tense for it. I expect it. I stay silent for several breaths, preparing for even a flicker of pain.

It doesn't come.

"Okay," I say on an exhale. "Thank you for telling me. What happens next?"

"Well, he violated probation by crossing state lines and being in possession of a firearm, so he's going back in for that alone. If you're planning to press charges—"

"I am."

The answer comes without hesitation as I watch the comforter on my bed rise and fall with Callie's steady breathing. Sean is the reason Callie left the hotel that night. He's the reason I almost lost her. She'd never have—

I squeeze my eyes shut again and give my head a shake to clear the images before setting my attention back on Callie's sleeping body.

She's alive. She's here. She's safe.

"Anything else we can use against him, I want to do it," I add calmly. "The threatening letters he sent to Savannah. The flowers he sent to Callie. The pictures he took of her sister. I want them to use it all. I don't want him to ever get released. He deserves a life behind bars."

"I agree with you. I think the prosecutor will, too."

"Good." Before I hang up, a question comes to mind, and I allow myself to ask. After this, I'll be done for good. "How did he get the guns into the arena?"

Detective Gallagher hums, and I hear the clacking of a keyboard before she answers. When she speaks, it sounds like she's reading the information from a file.

"He was working for the food distribution company as a truck driver in Florida. The night of your concert, he posed as an employee. No one even asked questions."

Something Sean had said the day I stopped by my mom's house flashes in my memory. *How many crates of nacho cheese you reckon I gotta deliver 'til I'm makin' what you're makin'?*

"Huh." I shake my head and mumble under my breath. "Nacho cheese."

"What was that?"

"Nothing." I huff out a tired laugh. "I just never thought I'd wish my brother had stuck with boosting cars."

For the briefest of moments, I almost ask the detective if Sean has said why. Why did he bring the guns? Why did he start targeting Callie? Why did he stalk Sav at all? Before the words can even form in my throat, though, they disappear. I don't actually care. I don't want to know why he did any of it. I just want to be done with him. The realization is freeing.

"Well, thank you for calling and letting me know, Detective Gallagher. I appreciate it."

"Of course, Mr. King. And I was wanting to ask..."

She trails off for a breath, hesitating. People are so afraid to ask about Callie, and to an extent, I get it. No one wants to pry. No one wants to seem nosy. No one wants to be told to mind their fucking business by Torren King. I cut the detective some slack and give an answer before she can ask.

"Callie is doing well, Detective. She's been discharged and is home." I smile to myself as a I speak, my eyes never leaving my bed. She's here. She's safe. I take a deep breath. "She's healing," I say finally. "Thank you for asking."

After I hang up with the detective, I pull up my mom's contact. I block her number, then delete it from my phone. I do the same with Sean's, though I doubt he'll be using his cell while in prison. When that's done, I call Hammond. He answers on the third ring despite the late hour.

"Torren. Is everything alright?"

"Everything is fine, Ham. I just got off the phone with Detective Gallagher, actually."

"She told you about Sean?"

"She did." I take one last drag from my cigarette, then stub it out in the ashtray. "I want the checks to stop."

Hammond doesn't respond right away, but I know he knows what I'm talking about. He's been against sending my mom money from the very beginning, but he's done what I asked without fail. Every payout from the label, Ham's sent a portion of my check to Florida. For almost a decade.

"It will be done by morning."

"Thanks."

"Torren."

"Yeah, I know. You told me so."

"No."

"Then, what?"

"I'm proud of you."

My lips turn up at the corners. I think hell might have just frozen over. I almost say as much, but I don't want to ruin the moment.

"Thank you, Hammond," I say sincerely. "That means a lot."

Hours later, I jolt up from the bed with a gasp.

I rub at my eyes, chasing away the picture of Callie, upside down and bleeding. Of Sav's Porsche, a heap of twisted metal. Of a gravestone.

I turn to Callie and stare at her until my eyes adjust to the darkness. I focus on her chest until I'm certain it's moving, then I hover my trembling fingers centimeters from her lips. Each steady exhale from her mouth works to calm my heart rate as I chant over and over in my head.

She's here. She's safe. She's alive. She's here. She's safe. She's alive.

When my hands have stopped shaking and my heart is beating at a normal pace, I ease myself back under the comforter. I'm careful not to bump Callie's arm as I snake my hand around her waist and rest my palm on her stomach so I can feel it rise and fall with her breathing. The incision site from her emergency surgery is right below my hand. If I slipped just a fraction of an inch lower, I'd be touching it, but I don't. I don't want to hurt her. I just need to know she's real. Then, I can get some sleep.

It's barely dawn when I realize I'm alone.

I sweep my hand over the bed finding the sheets cold, and fear seizes my lungs. I kick the blankets from my body and rush to the bathroom, but it's empty. Trying not to panic, I make my way to the living room, but it's empty, too. She's not on the terrace. She's not in the kitchen. I nearly jog down the hallway, then skid to a stop when I find her sitting at the piano.

Slowly, I release the breath I'd been holding, and I walk to her side. She doesn't look at me. She just keeps her eyes on the piano keys with her casted left arm cradled in her lap and her right arm hanging lifeless at her side.

She looks so small right now. So lost.

My T-shirt hangs loosely off her body, and the laceration on her face stands out sharply against her pale skin. Her hair has grown a bit since it was first shaved, but it's still buzzed short, and the pink wound is still clearly visible on her scalp. She blinks, and a single tear slips from her eyelashes. It rolls down her cheek and catches the long, healing wound there, following it to her chin.

"Firebird," I whisper, and she flicks her eyes to me.

"Sorry. I couldn't sleep." She lets out a sad laugh. "Usually when I can't sleep, I..." She blinks again and shakes her head. "Anyway. Sorry. I forgot."

I take a seat beside her on the piano bench. "You don't have to apologize. You can come here anytime. It's yours."

She sniffles and nods. "Right. Mine."

Callie lifts her right hand and hovers it over the keys. For a moment, I think she'll try to play something, but then she drops her arm back to her side, and my heart aches. I can't imagine how painful it would be if playing music was taken from me. It's the one thing I'm good at. It's the one thing that fills me with purpose. I wouldn't know how to even begin moving forward without it.

This must be agonizing for her, and the longer she sits in silence, staring blankly at the piano keys, the more I can feel her grief. It's a living being in this room. In this apartment. No matter how close I get, or how tightly I hold her, her grief is there, taking up space between us.

She's wrapped herself up in it. All I want to do is help, but I can't figure out how to penetrate the grief.

I open my mouth to ask her what she needs—to once again ask her how I can make it better—but then I snap it shut. She won't answer. She doesn't know. And the last thing I should be doing is putting that burden on her, anyway.

Slowly, I wrap my arm around her waist, and my muscles relax when she leans her body into mine. I blow out a slow, relieved breath when she rests her head on my chest.

"I know I'm being ungrateful. I should just be happy to be alive. I know I should stop dwelling on this..."

"No, Callie. It's okay to be sad about this. It's okay to grieve. You're not ungrateful. You've gone through something traumatic, and you need to be gentle with yourself."

She falls silent again, and I wish I knew what was going through her head. I'm sure it's a lot of conflict. I would give anything to help her sort through it.

"Let's go back to bed. I'm fine."

I don't let my shoulders droop with defeat. I'd give anything to just have her talk to me about this.

"Are you sure?" I press a kiss to the top of her head, her short, soft hair tickling my lips.

"I'm sure. I'm just tired."

"Okay," I say, giving her once last kiss. "Let's go back to bed."

I lead us back to the bedroom in silence, and when we climb back into bed, she curls up beside me and lets me hold her. I close my eyes and breathe in the scent of her bodywash, then listen to her breathing until it's deep and even.

She's here and safe and alive. We'll get through this.

Callie's got an e-reader lying in her lap when I step out onto the terrace.

She gives me a small smile, but it doesn't reach her eyes. She's out of bed today, though. She's reading. That's a good sign.

In the five weeks since the accident, I feel like we've each lived ten lives, but hers have been the most turbulent. I still have frequent nightmares, but they vanish the moment I open my eyes. The minute I find Callie, I can breathe again. But for her? Her fears don't disappear in the daytime hours. If anything, daylight is worse. At night, while asleep, she can dream. Awake, she has to contend with reality.

These days, when I'm lucky enough to see her smile, I find myself sneaking longer glances, taking mental pictures so I can frame it in my memory. So I can use the stored joy to uplift us both next time she's awash in sun-drenched darkness. Grief has permeated the walls and seeped into the cracks. I've found myself searching for anyway to soothe it.

"Hey." Her voice is raspy and quiet, like she hasn't used it yet today. Like she'd rather not be using it now. "How was the meeting?"

"Fine." I bend down and kiss her. "We've adjusted the calendar so we can get some studio time once everyone is back from Canada, and we'll play the LA make-up shows before we leave for the UK."

"Oh, good. I'm glad you got that figured out." She purses her lips. "You really should reconsider skipping out on the Canadian shows, though."

I shake my head. "I'm staying with you. Beck's already agreed to continue filling in."

Callie arches a brow. "So, he's *Beck* now?"

"He's a good bassist," I say with a shrug. "He's earned my respect." I give her a smirk. "And I have no reason to be jealous since I'm the one you're in love with."

"I might have liked you better when you were jealous and possessive."

Her lips twitch with the urge to smile. That twitch makes me want to laugh and cry at the same time. She's being playful, and I crave more of it. Moments like this, when I see a spark of life behind her sad eyes, I grow even more desperate. I would do anything, *be* anything, if I can just make this moment last. If I can just get her full smile to break free.

I let my smirk grow, quirk a brow, and lower my voice. "I'm still possessive, Firebird. But I can act jealous if you want me to."

She shivers and her eyes flicker with heat. It's a look I haven't seen in weeks, and lust stirs low in my stomach. I hold her every night, but I miss touching her. Feeling her. I miss knowing she wants me. When she worries her lower lip, my restraint almost snaps, but then her spine straightens, and a curtain closes on her expression.

"If I ask you to act jealous, will you fire Becket and go on tour?"

"Nice try," I say with a forced huff of laughter. I try to act unbothered, but I'm worried I fail. "Anyway. *Becket* has it handled. I'm here with you, and that's final."

Her lips bow into a frown. It's the same look she gave me last time we talked about Becket filling in for me in Canada. I expect I'll get the same look again the next time this conversation pops up. Apparently, *that's final* means nothing to the love of my life.

"You don't need to stay here for me. I'm not even doing anything. I'm just...existing between follow-ups right now. It's boring. You should go tour Canada instead of potatoing with me."

She keeps asking why I would want to put my whole life on hold for her. What she doesn't understand is that she's become the most important aspect of my life.

"Firebird," I say clearly. "There is literally nowhere I would rather be than *potatoing* with you." She rolls her eyes, and I laugh. "I'm serious. *Just existing* here with you is better than anything I could be doing somewhere else."

"Well." She squints at me. "You're full of charm today, aren't you?"

I wink, then gently take the e-reader from her and set it on the small table beside her chair.

"I have something I want to show you," I say, offering her my hand. "It's a surprise."

"Oh. Should I be scared?" She pushes to her feet and follows me as I lead her through the apartment.

"Patience," I tease. "You're lucky I'm not blindfolding you."

She lets out a laugh that almost resembles a giggle, and the sound seizes my chest. I miss her laugh. I'm hoping that laugh means this will work in my favor, but as I turn down the hallway that leads to the second living room, her steps slow. When I look at her, her brow is creased with worry, so I rub my thumb over the back of her hand.

"Just trust me," I say, seeking her gaze. "Just trust me, okay?"

Callie hasn't gone anywhere near her piano since that early morning I found her sitting dazedly on the bench. She even uses the ensuite bathroom so she can steer clear of the hallway that leads to the room housing the piano. She has a few more weeks before she can start physical therapy, but something tells me the sooner she gets her hands on the keys, the better she'll start to feel. If she continues to avoid it, her grief and fear will only fester.

I give her an encouraging smile and squeeze her hand, then she nods. Once in the living room, I take her to the piano bench and gesture for her to sit. Reluctantly, she does, and I take a seat to the left of her.

I glance at her. Her posture is stiff, her face contorted in a frown, and her eyes are focused somewhere just above the piano keys. Her breathing is steady and even, she protectively cradles her casted arm in a way that makes my chest tight with sympathy.

I close my eyes and hope like hell I'm doing the right thing. Then, I find the C-sharp octave, place my left hand on the keys, and begin to play only the left-hand part of Beethoven's "Moonlight Sonata."

As the descending bass note fills the room, I hear Callie's breath hitch. The moment I play the B octave for the second measure, she turns her body to face me. "Torren?"

I take my hand off the keys, look into those pale green eyes that I love, and give her a soft smile. "Let me play your bass notes, Firebird."

She bounces her eyes between mine, fear giving way to uncertainty, and all I want to do is hold her. I want to give her back what she's lost. I wish I could take away that fear and replace it with confidence.

"Play with me." I kiss her once, then whisper against her lips, "Let me play your bass notes."

Her breath tickles my lips as she inhales and exhales slowly. She doesn't speak, but she jerks out a nod, and that's all I need.

I turn back to the keys and find the C-sharp octave once more. When Callie moves over to place her feet on the pedals, I can't fight the hopeful, upward curve of my lips. When I begin to play, so does she, and though our pace is slower than I've heard her play in the past, we're still beautifully in sync.

When I hear her start to cry, it takes everything in me to keep my eyes on the keys in front of me. Before last week, I hadn't played the piano in twelve years. If I look away for even a second, I could ruin this moment by fumbling the keys. I will let nothing ruin this moment.

But god, do I wish I could see her face.

She rocks lightly as we play. It's the same motion I've seen from her when she's losing herself in a piece, and I know the tears streaming down her face are not from sadness. They're from relief.

I bet her eyes are closed. I bet there's a serene smile on her full lips. I bet she looks like she's completely, totally free. Free of heartbreak. Free of pain. Free of dissonance.

Nothing but perfect harmony.

I hope every note chips away at the fear she's collected over the last five weeks. I hope it starts to mend the cracks in her heart and confidence. I think it will.

We stop playing when we finish the first movement, and for several breaths, we sit in silence. I can hear her sniffling as she works to calm her shaky breathing. I watch her wipe tears from her face in my periphery. I keep my eyes on my hands to give her time. To let her settle into her emotions. I know this was probably overwhelming for her. I want to give her space to adjust.

Slowly, I feel her turn her body toward mine, and I allow myself to mirror the movement. When I settle my eyes on her face, I'm overwhelmed by what I see.

She's flushed deep pink. Her eyes are red, and her lashes are matted together. Her cheeks are shiny and wet from the tears still falling down her face.

And she's smiling.

She's pure joy, and my own smile is unbidden in response. She's so fucking beautiful in this moment. In every moment, but especially now. This vision of her is one that I will think of often.

"Torren...I..." Her voice cracks, and her words trail off as she closes her mouth around a whimper. "I..."

"I know." I wrap her in my arms and hold her to my chest. "I know, baby."

Callie's body shakes against me as she cries. Her tears seep through my shirt, warming my skin. Out of nowhere, a vision of her from ArtFusion is pulled from my memory. Dressed in feathers and flames, clever and carefree. It's that memory, that vision of her dressed as a phoenix, that confirms it for me: this moment is a catharsis. A rebirth.

She's here. She's safe. She's alive.

"My firebird," I murmur against her. "Rising from the ashes."

She laughs lightly and shakes her head, but she doesn't pull away. "I love you."

I smile. "I love you, too."

44

CALLIE

THREE MONTHS LATER.

"Hey. How was PT today?"

Sav kicks her shoes off at the door and saunters into Torren's apartment. I guess my apartment now, too, but it's still weird to say.

"Honestly? Fucking killer." I flex my hand as best as I can because it aches just talking about it. "But otherwise, I think it's going well. Dr. Hernandez-Calligaris says he's really pleased with the way I've been progressing."

"That man is hot." She bounces her brows playfully. "Don't tell Levi."

I grin. "His *wife* is hot, too. We went out to dinner with them when we flew to Chicago for my last follow up. A whole family of attractive people."

She heads to the fridge and pulls out a mineral water. She and Mabel have been here so much in the last few months that it almost feels like we're roommates on the bus again. With all the changes lately, it's been nice to have something familiar to focus on.

I want to laugh at myself.

How surreal that hanging out with members of The Hometown Heartless feels *familiar*. It's crazy how much things can change in less than a year. My chest tightens, and I flex my hand again. So many things.

"Callie?"

I blink out of my thoughts and look toward Sav. "Yeah?"

"You kind of tuned out. Got a little misty-eyed. You need anything?"

"Oh." I laugh awkwardly. "No, I'm fine. Sorry. Tired, I guess."

Sav smiles softly. "You sure?"

"Yep." I nod. "Totally sure."

"Okay. Good. Because I have an idea I want to run by you."

She's sporting a sly grin that makes me suspicious. I narrow my eyes and tilt my head to the side as I assess her.

"What have you done, Savannah?"

"Nothing..." She throws up her palms and takes a step backward. "...yet. I just wanted to know how you'd feel about inviting the guys to come to Europe with us when we leave on tour next month."

"What guys?"

"Ezra, Rocky, and Becket." She purses her lips. "Pike, too, I guess. If you can convince him."

"Why would we invite them to come on tour? It's weird enough that I'm going to have my own physical therapist. I don't want an entire entourage of idiots, too."

Sav laughs, which makes me laugh despite the fact that I'm genuinely confused. And genuinely trying my damnedest not to let disappointment overtake me. Touring with Heartless is going to be difficult knowing what was once again ripped from my fingertips. Touring with my old band tagging along as spectators?

No.

I'm preparing to tell Sav as much when she turns that sly grin on me again, throwing out another casual shrug.

"I just thought you could use the time to write, you know? Work on your album. We could get you some studio time in Italy if you're ready by then." She barks out a loud laugh. "Don't look at me like I've got five heads, Cal. This is an honest suggestion...*and*...I might have already made all the necessary plans for it. Well, I had Ham make them, but you know."

Sav's grin widens, and she reaches across the counter, puts two fingers on my chin, and gently closes my gaping mouth. I try three times to say something, but I have no words. I can barely wrap my head around *her* words, let alone form my own.

Finally, all I can manage is, "Why?"

"I'm protecting my investment. What kind of record label would I be if I left my first signed band to fend for themselves?"

My chest aches, and her smile flickers. I can see the sympathy in her eyes. I'm sure she can see the devastation in mine.

"Sav... I don't know if or when I'll ever be able to play again. I... God, I can barely play 'Écossaise in E-Flat Major' right now, and it's considered one of Beethoven's easiest pieces. I learned to play it in my first year and now I..." I close my eyes and sigh, giving Savannah a shrug. "You can't bet on me, Sav. You just can't."

We sit in silence for a moment before Sav speaks up, prompting me to open my eyes and meet hers.

"When you had to leave Caveat and move home after your mom's stroke, how did you feel?"

"Incomplete," I say immediately. "I felt like a part of me was missing."

"And when you sit on your piano bench to practice every day now, how do you feel? Even with the accident putting you back at square one. Even fumbling through 'Écossaise,' how do you feel?"

This answer doesn't come as easily. I have to sift through it. I have to really dig deep to sort it out, and even when I start speaking, I'm not sure what I say fully encompasses it all.

"I feel a lot of things," I say slowly. "I feel anger for having years of practice and mastery stolen from me. I feel mournful, like a defining part of my life has been irreparably altered. I feel stupid for putting myself in a position for all of this to happen in the first place. And then... At the heart of it... Under all of that... I feel whole."

Sav nods, an expression on her face that makes me feel more understood than I have since waking up in that hospital bed. I feel like she gets it, even if she hasn't lived it.

"*That* is why you're still the first band I want signed on Rock Loveless Records. *That* is why I'm betting on you. But more importantly, you need to bet on yourself. You're not a musician just because you play piano. You sing, you write songs, you perform and entertain. I saw you in Chicago. I know the potential you have." Sav spreads her hand on her chest, right across her heart, and pats twice. "You feel it in here, Callie. I know you'll play again. And even if you never get back to the level you were, you'll adapt. You'll adjust, and you'll make fucking great music, because you have to. It's the only way you'll feel whole."

I blow out a long slow breath and blink back the sting of tears. She's right. She's fucking right, and she knows it, but it doesn't make it any less terrifying.

"I still don't know if I feel comfortable letting you put so much faith in me. I don't want to disappoint you."

"So, we'll sign a provisional agreement contingent on you producing an album within two years. If you get to the end of that two years and you still don't think you can do it, we'll part ways amicably."

I arch a brow. "You'd do that? Even knowing everything, you'd do that?"

"Uh, yeah, Cal. I'd give you a formal contract right now if I thought you'd take it." She smirks, and I almost blush.

I consider it again. I try to imagine how it would work, what a scenario like that would look like.

"I don't know if the guys would go for it. They'd basically be in limbo for me."

Sav snorts out a laugh. "Calla Lily, those boys are just happy to be included. And trust me, there is no one they'd rather do this with than you."

The more I think about it, the more excited I get, and it's like a candle has been lit in a room in my mind. The one that went dark after the accident. My fingers itch to feel the keys. My mind starts swirling with potential lyrics. When my lips twitch with the urge to smile, Sav grins in triumph and pulls Hammond's tablet out of her bag.

"Look..." She pulls something up on the tablet and slides it in front of me. "I just happen to have a provisional agreement right here that you could look over, if you want."

"Oh. What luck," I deadpan, my eyes falling to the tablet.

She shrugs in my periphery. "I'm being a proactive businesswoman."

As I scan through the contract, I can't help but draw comparisons between today and the day seven months ago when Torren propositioned me. I'm feeling much less dread this time around.

"I should talk about this with the guys..." I mumble.

"Oh, they already read it. Pike's out, but the other three are ready to sign whenever you are. But I definitely agree you should talk to them."

I look up at her through my lashes and quirk a brow. "You're something else, you know that?"

Her only response is that mischievous grin. The one I can't help but return.

THREE MONTHS LATER.

"Do we think this is smart?"

Ezra's voice carries over the loud noise from the plane. Even through his goggles, I can see the uncertainty.

"There are approximately twenty skydiving related deaths every year. Maybe we should reconsider."

Becket shakes his head, and even over the rumble of the engine, I can hear his sigh. "I told you to stop googling shit. You literally *just* stopped thinking you have a tumor."

"We're already up here, bro," Rocky chimes in. "You signed the waiver. You took the class. Don't punk out now."

Instead of giving my two cents, I turn my attention to Torren. He's watching them with his lips pursed, and I can't tell if he's amused or annoyed. I'm a little of both. I give his shin a nudge, and he turns to me with a smile. He leans in close, so he doesn't have to shout too loud.

"Are you scared?"

I shake my head. "Not at all."

"Are you excited?"

"Absolutely."

I look out at the blue sky filled with fluffy clouds. We're about to jump from a plane at ten-thousand feet somewhere over North London. It's a tradition Sav has started—skydiving in every country—and I'm actually *really* excited.

In fact, really excited seems to be the theme of this tour, so far.

I was really excited when we landed at Heathrow last week. I was really excited when Sav surprised Caveat Lover with studio time to record a few of the songs we've already written. I was really excited when I played one of our new songs flawlessly three nights ago, too.

When we were checking into our hotel yesterday, a fan recognized me and asked for my autograph. I was standing right next to Torren and Mabel, but they wanted an autograph from me and my bandmates. My mom and Glory are flying in for Heartless's shows in Rome and Paris. And, while it might seem like only a small win, I can officially fit my hair into a half-ponytail without it having to poke out the top of my head like a tree. I was really, *really* excited for that.

But the thing I'm most excited about?

Just *being* here. With Caveat Lover. With Heartless. With Torren. With *me.*

I feel more at peace with myself than I have in a long time, and after the accident, I didn't think I would ever feel comfortable in my own skin again. I've never been so happy to be wrong.

My body is irreparably changed. Some ways are immediately visible —like the scars on my face and arm—but more are not, and I'm okay with that. I'm coming to terms with that fact that I may never play piano the way I used to. I'll never give up attempting the "Moonlight Sonata" third movement, but just playing it is enough. Sav was right—I'm adjusting, and adapting, and I will continue to do so in any way necessary, because making music is the only way I'll ever feel whole.

Just before it's time for us to jump, I do a scan of the plane. I'm spending the next three months traveling Europe with these people. Sav and Mabel have become my best friends. Ezra, Rocky, and Becket are and always will be my family. Jonah and I are...well, he and I are about the same as he is with everyone else, to be honest. But it works.

And Torren King...

I lock eyes with him once more, then give his hand a squeeze.

Torren Fucking King made me fall head over feet in love with him. He broke my heart once, but he's mended it ten times over. He quite literally helped put me back together when I was a shattered, lost mess. He gave me strength when mine was faltering. He played my bass notes when I couldn't. He was my harmony when all I heard was dissonance.

He's my love song.

Torren must be able to read my thoughts because he smirks before leaning down and whispering over my lips, "You better watch it,

Firebird. Somebody might think you're in love with me. Your eyes are giving you away."

I smile. "I'm not trying to hide anything."

"Good."

He kisses me slowly, his tongue swiping over my lips in a way that makes me shiver. I open for him, and our tongues glide together, but when I try to deepen the kiss, he pulls away. He smiles at me, eyes hooded and pupils dilated, then presses a soft kiss to my forehead.

"I love you, Calla Lily Sunrise James."

"I love you, Torren Fucking King." I step back and give him a smirk of my own. "Now let's jump out of this goddamn plane."

EPILOGUE

Callie. TWO YEARS LATER.

"Give me twenty minutes."

Torren stops me before my feet land on the pavement, then walks me back into my bus and locks the door behind him. As soon as we're alone, his mouth and hands and body are on me, and mine are on him.

"Mmm." I hum, my voice breathy as he pulls my shirt over my head, followed by my bra. "Isn't that a little risky?"

Their set starts in thirty, and he's supposed to be there at least fifteen minutes early. *Twenty minutes* will mean he's showing up minutes before he's supposed to take the stage. I open my mouth to remind him of this, but he slips his hand into the front of my underwear and my argument transforms into a gasp.

"Already so hot and wet for me," he murmurs against my lips as he rubs at my throbbing clit. "Twenty minutes, Firebird." He circles the tip of his finger over my entrance before easing it in. "Let me make you feel good."

I reach for his cock and squeeze him once before he picks me up and carries me to my bedroom at the back of the bus. He lays me on the bed, then quickly pulls off his shirt and kicks out of his pants. I prop myself onto my elbows and watch with a grin.

"Gonna make me do all the work?" He smirks. "We only have twenty minutes."

I shrug and lift my hips as he tugs my shorts and panties down my legs and tosses them to the side. "Seventeen minutes no—oh, fuck."

Torren sucks hard on my clit and shoves two fingers into my pussy. He hooks his fingers inside me and strokes as his mouth works me over.

"Jesus," I breathe out. "Fuck, Torren."

My back arches as he throws my legs over his shoulders and reaches up my body to palm both of my breasts. The sight is obscenely sexy. His mouth covers my pussy, and he hums as he fucks me with his tongue. His dark curls stand out starkly between my pale, freckled thighs, and his glittering green irises peer up at me through the valley between my breasts. He squeezes, pinching my nipples, and shoves his tongue inside me before moving back to my clit.

I gasp and jerk my hips, grinding myself on his mouth, and he growls. The vibrations skitter over my swollen, wet pussy, and I move faster. I sink my hands into his hair and pull hard at the root in that way I know he loves, and then I fuck his face as he attacks my clit with his lips, tongue, and teeth.

Within seconds, my body is bowing with the force of my orgasm. Torren kisses and nips his way up my body, painting me with his tongue and my arousal on his lips, until his hard cock is resting on my pelvis. He rocks back and forth, rubbing himself against me slowly while I work to catch my breath.

"Let's fuck in the studio."

I pant out a laugh in response, and he nips at my jaw.

"I'm serious. I want to record the sound you make when you come. Then, next time we're on different tours, I can listen to it while I beat off."

I roll my eyes and snake my hand between us, wrapping my fingers around his erection. "That's a ridiculous idea."

He props up on his knees, giving me the leverage I need to position the head of his cock at my entrance. He groans. "Why ridiculous?"

Slowly, I raise my hips, sliding him inside me, humming my pleasure as I stare into his eyes. "Because Sav's got the next two years planned already, and she's made it so we almost never have conflicting schedules."

I thrust my hips, fucking his cock, and his mouth falls open on another groan when I clench around him. "Fuck, you're evil."

I laugh. "We have fourteen minutes."

"Fuck." He drops his face to my neck and starts pumping his hips, taking control. "I love how wet you get."

He kisses me deeply, swallowing my whimpers as he fucks me harder. Deeper. So deep, hitting that spot, my muscles start to spasm.

"Fuck yes. Come for me again, Firebird."

I choke on a moan, tightening my thighs around his hips, digging my nails into his biceps. Then he cocks his hips to the side, and I come with a scream that I bury in his chest. He speeds up, fucking me faster, chasing his own orgasm. When I can tell he's close, I clench, and he spills himself inside me. He fucks me until he's spent, and then he collapses beside me.

"How'd we do," he mumbles into the pillow, and I cast my eyes to the clock on the wall.

"One minute."

He groans, then kisses me, tongue gliding over mine in a way that could make him late. I push on his chest with a laugh. "Go. I'm right behind you."

Reluctantly he pulls out of me and stands, and just before he leaves to throw his clothes back on, I let my legs drop open. His eyes fall on my exposed pussy, still swollen and dripping with his release.

"Jesus fucking Christ."

He starts to stalk back toward the bed, but I slap my legs closed with a laugh and point at the clock. "Get out!"

He narrows his eyes and smirks. "Your panties better be soaked with my cum when we get back here. I want it leaking from you all night. I want you to smell like me. I want it dripping down your fucking thighs."

I arch a brow. "In front of one hundred and twenty-five thousand people."

"More than that, Firebird." The smile that takes over his face is nothing short of indecent. "This show is being live-streamed."

He winks once, then turns and walks out.

I give myself ten minutes to breathe, then I get up, get dressed, and head out behind him. When I get to the main stage, Sav is just stepping up to her mic, and the crowd is already going nuts for her. This show is going to be epic.

"Good evening, Arizona! How you all doing tonight?" Sav's voice booms through the crowd, the echoes being swallowed up by the cheers of Heartless fans. "We are honored to be back here in the desert to celebrate ten amazing fucking years of ArtFusion with all of you. It's going to be a great show, and we have a few surprises planned for you."

She grins as the crowd noise rises once more, and she throws a look over her shoulder at Mabel, Torren, and Rocky.

"I think y'all know my band, right? Torren King over here on bass, Mabel Rossi on drums, and Caveat Lover's own Rocky Hallstrom on lead guitar."

She pauses for a moment, excitement mounting, and even I can't stop smiling.

"Let's all give Rocky another round of applause for filling in for us these past few months. Hasn't he been fucking great?"

Rock plays a guitar riff as the crowd cheers for him, grinning ear to ear, and then Sav starts again.

"Unfortunately, we've got some bad news, though. Rock's not going to be able to play with us any longer."

Sav tries to look sad as Rocky slips his guitar strap over his head, but she fails miserably, and he can't contain his grin either. Then Jonah steps on stage, guitar in hand, and walks up to Rocky, and everyone loses their fucking minds.

"I think they're happy to see you, Jo. What do you have to say about that?"

Jonah smirks, then plays the same guitar riff Rocky played, but he adds his own flare at the end. Show-off. Rocky pretends to bow to Jo, then waves to the crowd before leaving the stage.

"She's such a showman," Rock says with a grin when he reaches me. "She just eats it up."

I laugh and watch Sav work the crowd. "She definitely does what she's good at." I turn my attention to Rocky and take in his wide smile. "How do you feel?"

"Great. It was awesome touring with them. Fucking crazy being part of the headliner in those stadiums, you know? But I'm glad he's back."

I smile. "Me too."

"Plus, I'm exhausted from pulling double duty, and we've got a record to finish."

"That we do."

And it's an important one, too, even though we don't want to admit it. Our first album took off, so this next one is going to have a lot more eyes on it. We're ready, though.

Rocky and I watch the show together backstage. Ezra and Becket show about halfway through, but our last bandmate isn't with them.

"No Crue?"

I'm met with shrugs. It concerns me momentarily, but Torren's voice grabs my attention before I get a chance to dwell on it.

"Did you guys get the chance to see Caveat Lover on the main stage last night?"

The crowd cheers, and it makes me smile wider. When I look at the guys, they are wearing matching expressions.

"Well, we've got another surprise for you." I watch as a roadie brings two stools out and sets them together center stage, and the crowd grows impossibly louder. "Did you all know we played here a while back? About seven years ago. Well, I met a woman, and she made such an impression on me that I wrote a song for her."

"That's my cue."

Ezra pats me on the shoulder. "Knock 'em dead, tiger."

I step out onto the stage and make my way to Torren amid more shouts and cheers.

"You all know my fiancée, Callie James, right?" I wave, and Torren looks my way with a smile. "Hi, baby. You want to sing your song with me?"

I try to wait until the crowd noise lessens before I answer, but when it doesn't, I just lean into the mic.

"I would love to."

I take a seat on the stool beside Torren's, then adjust my mic. The version of this song that we recorded has piano accompaniment, but for tonight, we decided to play an acoustic version with just the guitar.

Torren strums out the opening chords, and I take a deep breath and close my eyes. Then, trading out verses and harmonizing throughout, we begin to sing.

A little magic can go a long way

Whether night comes or bleeds into day
When the morning sun rises, your breath tantalizes my brain
This pain won't go away easy, I'm still here to please you, oh baby

You're the fire-colored flower at the end of the yard
If you're trying to grow you won't get very far
We don't need much, just keep all the touching in vain

Firebird, make it all new
We're just ashes in the end
I don't need you my friend
But I want you

It's light out, you don't have to stay
You made it all better now you can just go on your merry way
When the morning sun rises, your breath tantalizes my brain
This pain won't go away easy, I'm still here to please you, Oh baby
Baby

You're the fire-colored flower at the end of the yard
if you're trying to grow you won't get very far
The pickins here are poor, I promise life has more to give you

Firebird, make it all new
We're just ashes in the end
I don't need you my friend
But I want you

Phones are lit and held in the air, waving back and forth with the melody, and the crowd sings along so beautifully that it gives me chills. But when we come to the last chorus, Torren switches up the lyrics, singing the revised version that he gave to me the night he proposed.

Firebird, you made it all new
We're just ashes in the end
But I need you my friend
Oh, I need you

406

He calls it our love song born of heartbreak and harmony, and even now, months later, it brings tears of happiness to my eyes.

The End

EXTENDED EPILOGUE

Callie. ONE YEAR LATER.

"Don't be nervous."

I laugh. "Sure. Don't be nervous. We're just performing in front of an audience of celebrities and music icons, and we're up for album of the year *against* The Hometown Heartless. But sure, I'll just not be nervous."

Torren smirks at me from his place on the couch.

"You've performed all over the world for hundreds of thousands of people. This show will be cake in comparison." I scowl at him, but he doesn't stop. "*And*, your album is objectively better than ours. It's better than every other one in that category, too. I've listened to them. I've analyzed them. Your album is sonically cohesive. It's daring. It tells a story with poetic, clever lyrics. You've got it in the bag."

"I can't think like that."

He pushes to standing and walks toward me, then pulls me into his arms. "That's okay. I'll believe it enough for both of us."

I take a deep breath and flex my left hand. Sometimes it still aches, and I don't always know if it's real or imagined pain.

All of our old songs have been altered to accommodate my new playing level. We write the new ones with my realistic abilities in mind. But sometimes... Sometimes, I overdo it, and this album is the most challenging we've written so far. Making mistakes in front of thousands of fans isn't nearly as mortifying as doing in front of my much more famous peers.

I pop three ibuprofen and say another whispered prayer that I don't fuck this up for all of us.

I ride to the show with my bandmates. Ezra tries like hell to lighten the mood, but he's just as nervous as the rest of us. When we walk the red carpet, we do it as a band, while Torren remains with Heartless. Thankfully Rocky remains close and will occasionally touch my arm or shoulder to remind me that we're in this together. I'm an anxious mess.

Fifteen minutes before we step on stage, I throw up, then have to drop my head between my knees and breathe slowly.

"You got this, Cal. We got this."

I nod, but I don't answer Becket. I just count my breaths until I don't feel like I'm going to pass out. Which, luckily, is two minutes before we have to be on our marks.

"Ready to rock, Calla Lily?"

I glance over my shoulder at Rocky. "Nope."

Ezra laughs. "Too fucking bad, babe."

His words are followed up by orders in our earpieces, and then robotically, I follow the guys on stage. I step up to my keyboard and adjust my mic, and without greeting the audience, the stage lights turn on and we launch into our most recent single. The one that has been at number one on the charts for two months and makes no sign of dropping. Instead of closing my eyes like I want to, I search the audience and find Torren, Sav, Mabel and Jonah at a table front and center, with my mom and Glory sitting right next to them. They're all on their feet. They're all singing along. They're by far our biggest fans.

I keep my eyes locked with Torren's, and his smile is contagious. I smile through the whole thing, and when I make it to the end without a single fuck up. When the song is over and the lights go down, it's all I can do to make it off stage without collapsing with relief.

"We fuckin' did it," Crue says, his British accent wobbling as he shakes my shoulders excitedly. "We fuckin' crushed it."

All I can do is smile and nod. I don't have words yet.

I stay silent as I change back into my chic awards show dress and zip up my custom knee-high Louboutins. They were a gift from Sav and

Mabel when we released our last album. I reserve them for only the fanciest occasions, which is why this is my first time wearing them.

I'm silent as we're ushered back to our table across the aisle from Heartless and through several great performances and awards acceptance speeches. I'm silent until the album of the year category is announced, and then I hold Rocky and Ezra's hands and chant to myself, *please, please, please, please.*

"And Album of the Year goes too..."

Rocky squeezes my right hand and we all hold our breath

"...Caveat Lover!"

The air is sucked from my lungs, and I don't stand until Rocky physically pulls me up and practically drags me toward the stage behind him. I'm shaking as we pass Heartless's table and Sav and Mabel give us quick celebratory hugs, Jonah hands out shoulder pats, and Torren kisses me.

"Congrats, Firebird."

I smile against his lips, and then Rocky tugs me onto the stage.

"Oh my god," Ezra shouts into the mic. "This is absolutely nuts."

"Absolutely nuts," Rocky leans into add.

Ezra, Rocky, and Becket run through their thank yous. Then Crue, taking time to thank his family in England for believing in him enough to send him to America to audition for our band. He thanks us for welcoming him with open arms. And then it's my turn. It's all I can do to keep my voice from shaking.

"Um. This...to reiterate Rock and Ez, this is nuts. We truly didn't think we'd win. I know our time is limited, but the list of people to thank is a mile long so I'll try to go fast. I want to thank my mom and my sister. I want to thank Sav Loveless and Rock Loveless Records for believing in Caveat Lover when no one else did. I want to thank The Hometown Heartless for being such amazing mentors. Our producer. Crue's family. Dr. Hernandez-Calligaris, I owe a lot of this to you. And I want to thank the Lovers. You guys are why we do this. You're why we're up here tonight. You're the best group of fans in the world. And Torren King for being...well...for being everything I've ever needed and then some. A few years ago, I'd thought I'd lost everything. I thought my dreams were gone. You gave me strength when I had none. You helped me find my way out of that darkness. You're a beautiful, wonderful human, and I'm so grateful you're in my life. Thank you for being you. I love you so much. And to anyone we forgot, I'm sorry, we love you, I'm just...we're just stunned."

We wave and bow and take our awards off stage, and then I finally let the floodgates open as tears flow freely down my face. My guys surround me in a group hug. Some girl wipes my eyeliner and fixes my makeup. We get photos taken and answer some questions from entertainment reporters. And when we finally make it back to our table, I'm grateful the awards show is almost over because I'm exhausted.

"Are we going to any after parties?" Crue leans over to ask, and I shake my head.

"I'm not. I'm going straight to bed."

"You have to come to Taylor's," Ezra says with pleading eyes. "You don't turn down an invite from her."

I laugh. "I'll text her. I know she'll get it."

"We'll have a drink for you," Rocky says with a wink.

I open my mouth to say something, but Becket cuts me off, reading my mind.

"Don't worry. We won't get sloppy and embarrass you."

I share a smile with my band. The guys who have become part of my family. My brothers. I wouldn't have it any other way.

At the end of the night, I head back home with Torren. We shower, eat peanut butter and jelly sandwiches, and then go to bed. I fall asleep with my head on his shoulder and a smile on my face.

I meant what I said tonight. After the accident, I thought my life was over. I thought my future was gone. I was afraid to dream and hope, but Torren stood beside me. He held me up. He believed enough for the both of us. He loved me when I didn't love myself.

I snuggle in closer to him, reveling in the way everything has changed.

"I love you," I whisper, planting a kiss onto his naked chest.

"I love you, too."

And then I fall asleep grateful for today and looking forward to tomorrow.

Keep flipping for a sneak peek of Jonah's book!

Curious about Sav and Levi's love story?
You can read their book, Between Never and Forever, now!

SNEAK PEEK

Jonah

I light my cigarette and take a long drag, deliberately ignoring the four pairs of eyes burning holes in my back.

My head is fucking pounding, and an intervention staged as a band meeting is the last thing I want to deal with right now. They should have stayed in Paris.

I close my eyes and tip my face to the ceiling. Christ, I really fucked it up this time.

When my cigarette is gone and no one has said a word, the silence becomes lethal, and I'm ready to lay my neck on the executioner's block just to put an end to it. Jeer. Pelt me with rotten vegetables. Celebrate as my skull falls into the dirt with an unceremonious thud. It would be better than the silence.

"Okay," I say on a tired exhale. "Can we just get this over with? I've had enough of the funeral atmosphere this weekend."

No one laughs at my joke. I guess that's the real test of the evening. When even the dark humor goes unappreciated.

I turn to face them and raise my eyebrows. "Get on with it."

"Get on with what, exactly, Jonah? I don't think you need me to tell you what a mess you've made. A Class E felony in New York State. Do you need me to remind you what that means?"

I clamp my eyes shut so I don't roll them at Hammond's dry, patronizing tone. "No. That was covered, thanks."

Hammond *humphs*. "Then maybe you'd like me to *get on* with reminding you that we're in the middle of a tour. Should I go over the schedule? Do you need me to tell you where we're all supposed to be right now?"

"No." I sigh. "I'm aware of that, too."

"Then what *exactly* should we *get on* with?"

"I don't know, *Wade*. You're the ones who decided to charter the jet and invade my hotel room at four in the morning. You tell me."

I watch Hammond's jaw tick and his nostrils flare as he tries not to lose his temper.

"Need I remind you where we picked you up from, Jonah?"

His voice quakes with repressed anger as he speaks. It's more emotion than we're used to seeing from him. Well, except Sav. She's been on the other end of some serious verbal ass-beatings from our manager. I don't know how I've managed to avoid one for this long.

I shake my head, but I don't have anything snarky to retort. I really don't need the reminder. It will be plastered all over the tabloids by sunrise.

I finally let myself look at the other three people in the room. When I do, I immediately wish I hadn't. It's been a while since I've seen those expressions on their faces. It bothers me more this time than it did last time.

Fuck.

I *really* fucked up.

I bring my fingers to my temples and rub, trying to lessen even a fraction of the tension in my head. I'm going to sleep for a week after this.

"Look. I appreciate you p—"

A firm rap at the door cuts me off, and my eyebrows slant. I didn't make plans with anyone. I'm not expecting a visitor, but one look at the four other faces in the room tells me that they are.

"What the fuck did you guys do?" I say with a growl, and Sav scoffs, drawing my attention to her as Hammond moves to open the door.

"It wasn't us, dickhead, but it's the best option you've got right now, so I suggest you bite your fucking tongue. The angry, tortured musician act is overplayed and not doing you any favors at the moment."

"Oh, shut the fuck up, Savannah. I'm growing really tired of your high-and-mighty bullshit. You don't get to scold me."

She smiles sweetly and bats her eyelashes. "Stop acting like a petulant child and maybe I won't have to scold you."

I scowl and open my mouth to snap something back at her, but Hammond clears his throat, drawing my attention to him.

To him and the woman standing beside him.

My hackles rise. She doesn't look like another cop, but I can tell right away I'm not going to like why she's here. By showing up unannounced at my hotel room at four in the morning, she already has the upper hand, and I can't let her keep it.

Slowly, I drop my eyes down her body. I don't hide it. I check her out brazenly, but I keep my face blank. Making her uncomfortable is my goal. I linger on her breasts and subtle curves. I track her long legs from the hem of her pencil skirt to the heel on her understated designer pumps. When I leisurely arrive back at her face, I settle my attention on her lips before letting my gaze finally collide with hers.

She doesn't so much as flinch.

She narrows her eyes, lifts her chin slightly, and arches a delicate, perfectly-shaped eyebrow. Not intimidated. Not impressed. In fact, her perfect posture, fit figure, and disapproving expression pisses me off and gets my dick hard.

This woman is going to give me trouble.

"Well," I say smoothly, letting my voice maintain an edge of irritation. "Who do I have the pleasure of welcoming into my room this morning?"

The woman gives me a tight, forced smile before confirming my original assessment.

"Hello, Mr. Hendrix. My name is Claire Davis. I'll be acting as your..." She trails off, allowing a slight sneer to show on her pretty face before it disappears. "*Well*, I'll be acting as your babysitter for the foreseeable future."

When my eyes widen, hers flash with a challenge, and I grit my teeth.

I was right. Trouble. With a capital fucking T.

**Don't miss Jonah and Claire's book
coming soon!**

Join my Facebook reader group and subscribe to my newsletter to stay informed.

ACKNOWLEDGEMENTS

Five months ago, if you'd have told me that Torren King would be my THH problem child, I'd have laughed and said, "no way, that title is reserved for Jonah."

Well. I was wrong.

Torren Fucking King.

Let's just say, it's a miracle y'all are reading him today. We'll leave it at that.

Big big big thanks to my alpha/beta readers with this one. **Haley, Mickey, Shan, Caitlin, Kara,** and **Sarah Beth**, you ladies came in so clutch. Your feedback was invaluable.

My editor, **Becky** at **Fairest Reviews Editing,** who was an absolute life saver. You basically carried my ass over the finish line. I'm so grateful. Hopefully we'll never have to do this again.

My other two editors, **Emily** with **Lawrence Editing** and **Sarah** with **All Encompassing Books**, THANK YOU for polishing this baby so it shines.

Zachary Webber, thank you so much for lending your musical talent to this book. Your song is beautiful and poignant, and it fits perfectly with these characters. I'm forever grateful you agreed to do this with me, and big thanks to **Britt** and **Katie** from **Lyric** for helping facilitate the project! You're all rock stars.

To **Kate** at **Kate Decided to Design**, my cover designer, thank you for working your magic once again. It's GORGEOUS. And thank you to **Katie Cadwallader Photography** for the gorgeous cover image on the model cover.

My ESPs, **Haley** and **Jessie**, thank you for, well, literally everything. All the time, but especially these past six months. I couldn't have made it to August without you. I love you the absolute biggest.

To **Nichole, Carrie,** and **Rosie,** thank you for always fielding my random questions, ideas, and errant thoughts. I'm forever grateful that you put up with my nonsense.

To **Shauna** and **Becca** at **The Author Agency**, thank you SO MUCH for always going above and beyond for me. I appreciate you both so much. **Shauna**, you've been the wind beneath my wings since LYB, and I am so lucky to have you in my corner.

To my **Street Team**, I really, truly, honestly would not be where I am without you. Thank you for for your continued support and enthusiasm. It means more to me than you know.

Jonathan, thank you for being you and for always picking up my slack. I love you.

AND TO THE READERS. If you took the time to read this book, thank you so much. There are so many amazing books out there. Thank you for making time to read one of mine.

I love you all!
Until the next one,

ABOUT THE AUTHOR

Brit Benson writes real, relatable romance. She likes outspoken, independent heroines, dirty talking, love-struck heroes, and plots that get you right in the feels.

Brit would almost always rather be reading or writing. When she's not dreaming up her next swoony book boyfriend and fierce book bestie, she's getting lost in someone else's fictional world. When she's not doing that, she's probably marathoning a Netflix series or wandering aimlessly up and down the aisles in Homegoods, sniffing candles and touching things she'll never buy.

LOVE THAT GROWS

authorbritbenson.com

ALSO BY BRIT BENSON

AVAILABLE NOW

The Hometown Heartless

Between Never and Forever (Sav & Levi)

Of Heartbreak and Harmony (Callie & Torren)

Next Life

The Love of My Next Life (Lennon & Macon, pt. 1)

This Life and All the Rest (Lennon & Macon, pt. 2)

The Love You Fight For (Sam & Chris)

Better Love series

Love You Better (Ivy and Kelley)

Better With You (Bailey and Riggs)

Nothing Feels Better (Jocelyn and Jesse)

Better Than the Beach (Cassie and Nolan)

———

To stay updated on future release dates and plans, follow Brit on Instagram and Facebook, and sign up for her newsletter.

Made in the USA
Las Vegas, NV
12 November 2024

11704273R00243